A slow number cam   **t**
  his other arm ar   **her in.**

"'The Keeper of the Stars,'" he said quietly. "Quite a song."

Her heart hammered as Ty very skillfully swept her along to the music. It was different from any dance she'd ever experienced. Night and day from the one she'd shared with Brawley. He'd been fun. Ty? *Intense* was the only word she could come up with to define the aura surrounding him.

Totally unfamiliar with country songs, she listened to the words over the beating of her heart. "It was no accident me finding you..." Her temperature spiked ten degrees. He was right. The words were captivating. Intense, just like him. And, oh, so romantic.

His hand holding hers was callused and strong, the one at her waist firm. Hot.

Ty did not, in any way, make her think brotherly thoughts. Instead, heat pooled low. Yearnings stirred. Thoughts and desires she'd doubted she'd ever feel.

The man was dangerous. She'd do well to remember that. But for now, she'd simply enjoy the moment. The dance drifted into a second, then a third. Sophie vaguely registered others on the dance floor with them, smiled when Annelise and Cash brushed past.

Ty stood over a foot taller than her five-three, and her head rested on the strapping cowboy's chest. She heard the steady beating of his heart and surprised herself by wishing the song could go on forever.

She was deathly afraid she wouldn't say no if this man wanted to park his cowboy boots beneath her bed. For one night, of course.

"Sophie?" Ty's voice whispered against her ear.

"Hmmm?"

"The music's stopped."

Nearest Thing
to Heaven

Nearest Thing to Heaven

LYNNETTE AUSTIN

FOREVER

NEW YORK   BOSTON

Copyright © 2013 by Lynnette Austin
Excerpt from *Can't Stop Lovin' You* copyright © 2014 by Lynnette Austin
Cover design by Elizabeth Turner
Cover image © Shutterstock, iStock
Cover copyright © 2016 by Hachette Book Group, Inc.

Forever
Hachette Book Group
1290 Avenue of the Americas, New York, NY 10104
forever-romance.com
twitter.com/foreverromance

Originally published as an ebook in October 2013 and as a print on demand in August 2014

First mass-market edition: December 2016

Forever is an imprint of Grand Central Publishing. The Forever name and logo are trademarks of Hachette Book Group, Inc.

The publisher is not responsible for websites (or their content) that are not owned by the publisher.

The Hachette Speakers Bureau provides a wide range of authors for speaking events. To find out more, go to www.hachettespeakersbureau.com or call (866) 376-6591.

ISBN: 978-1-4555-6943-4 (mass-market edition)

Printed in the United States of America

OPM

10 9 8 7 6 5 4 3 2 1

To Joyce Henderson
Thank you for being my friend…

Acknowledgments

Books are seldom written in isolation, and this one was no exception. To Joyce Henderson and Diane O'Key, my long-time critique partners, go many thanks. Their honesty and encouragement have made me a better writer; their friendship has made me a better person.

I'd like to thank Robb and Tracy Goins at the Chunky Gal Stables, located at the base of the Chunky Gal Mountains in western North Carolina, for time spent with the very hand-some Beau, who waited patiently while my wonderful—and equally patient—friend Linda Hiner took photos of us for my website.

Childhood memories are precious and lasting. A nod to my aunt Eileen for the incredibly soft, pale blue sheets loved by both Annelise in *Somebody Like You* and Sophie in *Nearest Thing to Heaven*. My mom always bought plain white sheets—very practical. I loved sleepovers at my aunt Eileen's—for a lot of reasons—but the blue sheets were a huge bonus. So when Annelise went shopping for her new apartment in Maverick Junction, nothing but blue sheets would do! And, yes, I do have my very own soft, blue sheets.

A big shout-out to my editor, Lauren Plude, whose edits always, always improve my books, and to my incredible agent Nicole Resciniti of the Seymour Agency, who has made my dream come true.

Last, but in no way least, all my love to Dave, who feeds me and takes care of me when I get so lost in my characters' world that I forget to do it for myself. He's all the best heroes rolled into one.

Nearest Thing
to Heaven

Chapter One

Not fair!"

Forehead pressed against the icy windowpane, Sophie stared out at the gray Chicago skyline. The mere thought of hopping on a plane made her palms damp.

And now this weather.

Sighing, she sipped from her mug of cocoa and fingered the amethyst in her pocket.

Mother Nature, who'd either gotten up on the wrong side of the bed or suffered from a major case of PMS, was throwing herself one monstrous, rip-roaring tantrum. During the course of a single hour, the sun had disappeared and left behind a low, ominous cloud cover. The temperature had dropped almost twenty degrees.

A mix of snow and rain spit against the glass. Even tucked away in her fourth-story apartment, Sophie swore she could hear the slush on the sidewalks contracting and solidifying to ice. Her taxi ride to O'Hare would be a slip-sliding, horn-honking nightmare.

Only mid-November and already the temperature had dipped below freezing. Dirty snow and boot-soaking slush blanketed the sidewalks. Frigid gusts of wind, intent on seek-and-destroy missions, whipped off Lake Michigan and zeroed in on pedestrians unlucky enough to be out and about.

But by tomorrow, none of this would matter. This afternoon, nerves or not, Sophie fully intended to be on a flight headed to Texas, sipping a glass of wine, and eating the last of her carefully hoarded birthday stash of Godiva.

Breathing deeply, she turned her back on the ugly outdoor scene. Enya's ethereal voice poured from her stereo and relaxed her...until she glanced at the clock. Shoot! Where had the morning gone?

Her suitcase—her still-empty suitcase—lay open, dead-center on her bed.

With this weather, she'd need an extra half-hour to make it to the airport. Checking the time again, she slapped her forehead, upset with herself. She'd procrastinated—again. Now? She had ten minutes. Ten lousy minutes to pack. Adrenaline surged through her. Being on that plane when it took off wasn't optional. She had a wedding to attend. Thank God it wasn't hers.

What should she pack for Maverick Junction, Texas? She'd only been there once before. She'd flown in with her aunt and uncle who'd hoped to talk some sense into her cousin. Turned out they didn't need to. Annelise's cross-country trip on her Harley had already accomplished that. They'd stayed all of one afternoon.

But that was then, and this was now. In a panic, Sophie

studied her closet's contents, an eccentric mix of vintage pieces and quirky thrift store finds. Last time, like an idiot, she'd taken white silk to wear to a Fourth of July barbecue at the Hardeman ranch.

The memory brought to mind a handsome cowboy whose kid had dumped his cherry soda in her lap...and the way said cowboy had tried to wipe it clean. Whew! Maybe she should stick her head out the window and cool off.

Ty Rawlins. So hot she could almost forget he cowboyed for a living. The man was something else. Yeah, and wasn't that the truth? How about starting with the fact he had three-year-old triplets? No, they'd turned four in August, hadn't they? Annelise had mentioned a birthday party.

Three, four. Made no difference. Any way you cut it, it still added up to three little boys. And didn't that cool a gal off faster than any Chicago winter. Yikes. She loved kids. Loved spending time with them. But a mother? She didn't see herself in that role. Didn't know if she had enough to give a child.

Toss in the fact that Ty was a widower, to boot. Talk about baggage. *Three* little ones? And a dad who'd lost the woman he loved? She'd have to be insane to jump into that mess.

Insane? Her? No. Behind on her work deadline? Definitely.

And if she didn't meet it, she'd also find herself behind on her mortgage—and out on her butt on that ice-covered sidewalk.

All that had to wait, though, because this weekend her cousin, her BFF, was tying the knot. Annelise, who'd grown up in the lap of luxury, was marrying a cowboy. An honest to God cowboy. Sophie still couldn't quite wrap her head around that.

And now she had six minutes. Sophie grabbed clothes and stuffed them willy-nilly into her bag. She opened drawers and pawed through them, pulling out everything she might need and dumping it in her suitcase. She added her iPod to her carry-on along with her pouch of crystals.

Her bedroom looked like a hurricane had roared through. Her fingers itched to set it to rights, but there simply wasn't time.

Or was leaving it like this tempting fate? Her fingers found the amethyst in her pocket, stroked its smooth surface. No time. She had to go.

Satisfied she'd done all she could, she slung her carry-on over her shoulder, zipped her large suitcase, and, with one last look around, rolled it out to the living room. She had one hand on the doorknob when her phone rang.

Without thought, she answered—and instantly regretted it. Nathan.

"Hey, beautiful," he said. "What are you up to?"

Her stomach dropped, and she leaned against the jamb. "Actually, you just caught me. I'm heading out the door as we speak. I'll be away for a few days."

"Business?"

"No."

"Want company?"

A low-grade headache instantly took root. Her neck and shoulder muscles tightened, and she wet her lips. "No, I don't."

She hated that he forced her to walk so close to rude.

"Where are you going?"

"Out of town."

Uncomfortable silence fell between them.

"You won't even tell me where you're going?" Petulance seeped into his voice.

She closed her eyes and breathed deeply. "Nathan, we've had this talk before."

"What talk?"

Okay, now he was being deliberately obtuse. "Look, I have a plane to catch."

"What talk, Sophie?" His voice lost the wheedling tone and took on a harder, demanding quality.

"This isn't a good time—"

"It's the perfect time."

"Okay." Resolve squared her shoulders. "We decided this wasn't going to work. That we both needed to move on with our lives. Separately."

"*You* decided."

Her pulse kicked up a notch. She hated confrontation, but she couldn't give in on this.

"Fine." Her carry-on slid off her shoulder, and she hitched it back up. "You're right. *I* decided."

"I figured by now you'd have changed your mind."

Oh, boy. This had been hard the first time—and the second and third times. She didn't want to rehash it. Why couldn't he simply accept they were done?

Actually, they'd never really started. Nathan Richards. Good-looking, successful, and, at first blush, personable. They'd dated a couple times and had fun. Then he became possessive. Very possessive. He started showing up at her door. At the grocer's. At the theater.

Truth? He spooked her.

"I haven't changed my mind. I'm not *going* to change my mind. Good-bye, Nathan." She hung up and stared at the ceiling. She'd been foolish to get involved with him, but smart to end things.

Her plants. In her hurry, she'd nearly forgotten about them. Dropping her bag to the floor, she moved to the window. Scooping up pots of herbs and lavender, she walked across the hall to her neighbor's.

Dee was at work, so Sophie set the plants in the hallway outside her door. Rushing back into her apartment, she scrawled a quick note.

Take care of my babies for me, Dee? Thanks so much! You're a doll!

Love, S.

She propped the card against the pale blue pot of English lavender. Okay. That was taken care of. Her plants wouldn't wither and die while she played bridesmaid.

The heat kicked on, reminding her to adjust the thermostat before she left. This summer had been a scorcher, and she'd practically lived on Lake Michigan in her little sailboat. But winter had come roaring in early, teeth bared. Only a few weeks into colder weather, and she was tired of it already.

This wedding might be exactly what the doctor ordered. Time and space should cool Nathan's heels while sunshine and warm weather cured her sudden lack of creativity.

Speaking of…She slid her laptop into its case in the happy event her muse stirred. Even with all the pre-wedding madness, she should be able to sneak in a few minutes of work time.

If she planned to catch that flight, there was no more time

to fuss. Sophie turned off the lights, locked her door, and headed for the elevator. Unconsciously, her hand slipped into her pocket to touch the amethyst again.

As she let herself out of the building, she glanced cautiously up and down the street. She wouldn't have put it past Nathan to have called from right here on her doorstep.

Not a soul in sight.

Chapter Two

Scrunched between Chatty Cathy and the Hulk, Sophie mentally kicked herself for turning down Annelise's offer of a first-class ticket. This was worse than awful. She couldn't even reach her candy stash.

The chocolate in her bag became an obsession.

She wriggled a hand free and undid her lap belt. Scooting forward in her seat, she dipped into the carry-on between her feet. When her fingers touched the Godiva box, she sighed. Popping a piece in her mouth, she closed her eyes, savoring the rich, dark chocolate. She sent a mental smoke signal to the chatterbox beside her, begging her to take the hint. Amazingly enough, she did.

The taste of chocolate lingering on her tongue, she put in her earbuds and switched on Enya. Nice. Sophie willed herself, body part by body part, to relax. To ignore the bumps as the plane hit little pockets of turbulence.

Her thoughts turned to her cousin's trek from Boston to

Texas. Not only had Annelise located her missing great-aunt, she'd found true love...and saved her grandfather's life.

Never in a million years would Sophie have the guts to do that. But then, Annelise always had been the more adventurous one.

* * *

Sophie stepped from the skyway into the sunny concourse. There stood her cousin. All that gorgeous, long, dark hair and that tall, willowy body. Elegant even in jeans and a cotton T-shirt, Annelise waved at her from behind the roped-off area. Sophie waved back. Would she ever get used to seeing her cousin dressed so casually? Beside her, an arm snug around her waist, stood the reason for that change. The handsome cowboy she was marrying.

The instant Sophie passed the cordoned-off section, Annelise broke free and ran to meet her, wrapping her in a hug. "Oh, my gosh, I'm so happy to see you!"

"And I'm happier than you can imagine to be here." Sophie hugged her back. "Do I still have slush on my shoes?" She picked up one foot and examined the sole.

They laughed and turned as Cash Hardeman joined them. He dropped a kiss on Sophie's cheek, then slid the bag from her shoulder onto his. "How was your flight? Annie said you're a nervous flier."

"Nervous?" Sophie rolled her eyes. "You don't want to know. To top it off, I had the seatmates from hell. After I finished my Godiva cache, I fell asleep in self-defense."

Her cousin's brows rose. "That wouldn't have happened in first class."

When Sophie opened her mouth, Annelise threw up her hands. "Just saying."

Sophie shoulder-bumped her.

Annelise squealed in delight. "I'm getting married, Sophie!"

"This weekend!" Laughing, Sophie turned to Cash. "How are you doing? Holding up okay?"

Her cousin's fiancé shook his head. "Eloping would have been a hell of a lot easier."

"Bite your tongue," Annelise said.

He gave her a peck on the cheek.

Annelise brought her up to speed on the wedding as they walked to baggage. Sophie trailed along beside her, gawking at the men they passed, wondering if she'd dropped into some alternate universe. They sure did grow their guys big here in Texas.

She definitely wasn't in Windy City anymore. Practically everybody in the airport sported Stetsons and boots—men, women, and children. Oversized belt buckles seemed to be requisite.

"Your mom here yet?"

"No, she and Dad arrive Friday, so we'll have some catch-up time before they descend on us. How about a pajama party tomorrow night?"

"Am I invited?" Cash grinned. "I love pajama parties."

"I'll bet you do." Sophie raised a brow.

Annelise jabbed him with her elbow. "Behave yourself."

"Always." Then, without breaking stride, he said, "Guess I'll be forced to get the guys together for a poker game."

"Guess you might."

Once they'd collected her luggage and were safely ensconced in the SUV, Cash asked, "How are things in Chicago?"

"Cold and wet." She shivered. "Have I thanked the two of you for choosing November for your wedding? It made for a perfect escape—from everything."

When Annelise frowned at her, Sophie shrugged. "I needed a break. You provided one."

Annelise's eyes narrowed. "There's something you're not telling me."

"No, I—"

Cash met Sophie's eyes in the rearview mirror. "It's useless. You might as well spill it."

"Nothing to spill." She didn't intend to dampen her cousin's happiness with worries about Nathan. She was making a mountain out of a molehill, anyway. A thousand miles of separation would do the trick just fine.

"So, a question, Annelise. What did you do with all your business suits now that you're about to become a rancher's wife?"

"I donated a ton of them to Dress for Success."

"Way to go." She looked down at herself, at the cargo pants paired with a filmy top layered over a long-sleeve T-shirt. "I seriously doubt they'd want anything I own."

Her cousin grinned. "You have your own sense of style, Sophie. It's you. It's a little...different, that's all."

Sophie snorted. "You're so full of it. I dress like a street person most of the time—as my mother is quick to point out."

"You dress the way you want to."

"Yes, I do."

"You hungry?" Cash asked. "We're gonna meet the gang for dinner tonight, but my guess is you didn't get lunch on the plane."

"Good save, Cash. I think you'll do just fine in this

family," Sophie said. "How long till we're in Maverick Junction?"

"Couple hours."

"In that case I need a cup of tea."

"Got it."

Spotting a Starbucks, he eased the Escalade into the turn lane.

After he parked, he opened his door but stayed behind the wheel as she and Annelise climbed out and started toward the store.

"Aren't you coming?" Sophie called back to him.

He nodded. "I was sitting wondering at my good luck. Here I am with two of the most beautiful women on the planet, and, in a few days, one of them is going to be my wife."

"Oh, cuz, you really hit the jackpot, didn't you?" Annelise winked.

Sophie threaded her arm through her cousin's as they walked into the store. Would she ever be so lucky? Why couldn't Nathan be more like Cash, someone she could spend a lifetime with?

When it came right down to it, she doubted she'd ever find her soul mate. Some people were simply meant to be alone. And she was seriously afraid she was one of those.

She liked things neat and tidy. Liked order. Liked to be in control when it came right down to it.

*   *   *

They talked nonstop from Austin to Maverick Junction, and the trip flew by. Cash pulled into Annelise's drive, and Sophie studied the simple two-story white frame house her cousin called home. Thought of the multi-million-dollar estate she'd lived in back in Boston. Glancing at Annelise's face, she saw the glow there and knew the pundits were right. Money didn't buy happiness.

"Let me reintroduce you to Dottie, then take you upstairs and get you settled," Annelise said.

Cash moved to the back of the vehicle and unloaded the luggage. "I'll take these up to the apartment, Annie."

"Okay. We'll just be a minute." She turned to Sophie. "Do you mind spending tonight alone here?"

Sophie bit back a chuckle. "And where might you be going?"

"I should have said something sooner. I'm sorry, Soph."

She narrowed her eyes. "You'd look a lot sorrier without that cat-ate-the-canary grin."

Annelise's smile grew.

"Don't worry about me. I'm a big girl. I'm actually allowed to stay all by myself in Chicago." She shook her head. "And, truthfully, if I had to make a choice between spending the night with my cousin or a cowboy who looked that good in his jeans . . . Well, not much to think about there."

"I can't get enough of him, Sophie. He's like a drug in my system. I love him."

"Oh, Annelise. I'm so, so happy for you." She caught her cousin's hand in her own and gave it a quick squeeze.

"Brawley will pick you up for dinner tonight. He's in town for the wedding. You met him at the barbecue."

"The easygoing veterinarian who's so gorgeous you just want to lap him up?"

"That would be Brawley."

By this time, Dottie, Annelise's grandmotherly landlady, had spotted them and come out the door wiping her hands on a dish towel. Rhinestoned pink glasses dangled from a chain around her neck.

"Welcome to Maverick Junction, honey." Dottie gave her a quick hug, her charm bracelet jingling. "The Weather Channel said a storm was moving in up north. Hoped you'd make it out of Chicago okay."

Sophie nodded. "Twenty degrees and getting really nasty when I escaped."

"Good for you. And who knows? Maybe you'll follow Annelise's lead and decide to stay put here in Maverick Junction, too."

Sophie barely controlled a shiver. She remembered the cows with those long, pointed horns, the smells around the barn. No. She wouldn't be staying. She didn't belong here. The place gave her the willies. She'd come for Annelise's wedding. Period.

After vows were recited and rings exchanged, she, city girl through and through, would return to Chicago with its delis and boutiques, its museums and theaters. Civilization. Where the only animals she'd risk coming face-to-face with would be dogs on their owners' leashes. Where she could hail a cab to take her where she wanted to go.

Where nothing but the buildings was supersized.

Chapter Three

Ty Rawlins banged around in his kitchen, feeling more than a little frayed along the edges. Things weren't going well. He glanced at the clock, then did a double take. The thing was practically sideways on the wall. Twelve o'clock settled somewhere around the spot where two o'clock should be. One of the triplets must have whacked it with a sword during last night's duel to the death.

Guess he'd have to hang it higher.

He should have let one of the hands finish up the horse feeding so he'd have enough time for the kid feeding. Somehow, time was something he never had enough of.

Okay, so he was a single parent. All across America, single moms managed to take care of the kids, the house, and hold down a job. If they could do it, he sure as hell ought to be able to.

And now he had to go to this damn dinner tonight. He dropped a spoon into the far-from-empty sink. It wasn't that he wasn't happy for Cash and Annie. He was. But it stirred up memories he didn't want to visit. Memories of far happier times now gone. Forever.

A crash sounded from somewhere in the vicinity of the living room.

"Uh-oh. Daddy's going to be mad."

That would be Jonah, Ty thought. The conscience of the trio.

"It was your fault."

Jesse, the finger-pointer.

He set the pan of over-cooked spaghetti on a hot pad and strode off to the front of the house to check out the latest damage. "What happened?"

Josh started to cry.

Books covered the floor. An orange rubber ball sat on the shelf—the former home of the books.

"I didn't mean it, Daddy. Jonah told me to throw the ball to Josh, and I did. But it went up there." Jesse pointed at the shelf.

"What have I said about throwing balls in the house?"

"That we're not asposed to." Jesse's eyes remained glued to the floor now.

"That's right. And why aren't we supposed to?"

"'Cause things get broked," said a sniffling Josh. "But nothing broked, Daddy. Look." He hurried over to the books. "They're okay."

Ty took a deep breath and surveyed the mess. Nobody was hurt. No blood anywhere. And Josh was right. Nothing was broken. In the grand scheme of things, this was a minor bump. A mere blip on the uh-oh meter.

"All right, troops. Time to wash up for dinner. I'll take care of this later. To the bathroom. Now. And use soap."

"Can Trouble come with us?" Jonah asked hopefully.

"No."

Three pairs of solemn eyes met his, wordlessly pleading clemency for the holy terror temporarily kenneled in the downstairs bath.

"Look, guys, Trouble needs to stay right where he is till dinner's done." Even as Ty spoke, the puppy's whimpers grew louder. He grimaced when sharp little nails raked the door. "I don't have time for any more messes tonight. We'll get him trained, then he can have the run of the house."

"'Kay." Jonah started upstairs, and the others trudged behind him.

Feeling like an ogre, Ty bent and scooped up books. He should have made the boys clean up their own clutter. All the parenting books and magazines said so. But it was easier to do it himself. He still had to feed the kids, clean up the kitchen and any messes Trouble made, give the pup yard time, and shower and shave. He'd promised Cash he'd be at Bubba's by seven.

He rolled his eyes skyward. It would take divine intervention for him to make it.

*　*　*

Feeling overwhelmed and more than a little guilty, Ty backed down the drive. Haley, the wife of one of his ranch hands, had offered to babysit tonight. She'd shown up early and saved his bacon. Maybe not divine intervention, but he'd take it.

While he'd gone upstairs to shower and change, she'd settled the boys—and the pup—in front of a movie and set off to clean up the dinner mess.

She had a birthday coming up in a couple of weeks. Maybe he could send her to one of those fancy spas in Austin. He'd have to ask Babs to recommend one.

Babs. His sister-in-law and Cash's sister. What would he do without her? She'd been a steady rock when he'd lost Julia. These past four years she'd stepped in more times than he could count and pulled him out of a tough spot. The woman made motherhood and running a house seem like a walk in the park. She was his hero.

He wondered if she'd be at dinner tonight. Probably. And she'd undoubtedly tell him to find time to hit the barber tomorrow. He glanced in the rearview mirror as he pushed his hair off his brow.

When the hell had it grown so long? Fact was, it simply didn't matter—most days. But now, with the wedding coming up, he'd need to see to it. He couldn't ruin Annie's wedding photos with shaggy hair. And there'd be no hiding it beneath his Stetson. She'd made that more than clear. No hats during the ceremony. They could wear their boots, though.

He smiled. Annie was gonna fit in just fine.

He hadn't gone two miles when the phone rang. His stomach dropped. Had something happened to one of the boys?

"Hello?"

"Hey, pal, it's me, Brawley."

Ty's stomach settled back into place.

"I was wondering if you could do me a huge favor."

"Maybe," Ty said.

Brawley chuckled. "That's what I like about you. Never one to leap off a tall building without looking first."

"Saves a lot of bruises. What do you need?"

"I told Cash I'd pick up Annie's cousin, drive her over to Bubba's. I stopped to see Doc at the animal clinic and got hung up. I really need to shower the smell of wet dogs off me before dinner."

"I think we'd all appreciate that," Ty said.

"Yeah, no kidding. So do you think you could swing by and get her?"

"I can do that, sure. What's her name? Stacy? Stephanie? Can't remember."

"Sophie. Sophie London."

"Yeah, that's right. She staying at Dottie's with Annie?"

"Yep. But Annie's snuggling with Cash at his place, which is why Sophie needs a ride."

"Makes sense. Okay, will do. See you at Bubba's."

Ty hung up. Good thing he'd left on time. It wouldn't take long to buzz by and pick her up. A few extra minutes tops—if Annie's cousin was ready on time. If not—well, not his fault.

Sophie London. He'd met her at the Fourth of July bash Cash had thrown. Yeah, and he and his kids had no doubt made a lasting impression on her. Not a good one, either. Grimacing, he figured he still owed her for the outfit Jonah ruined with his cherry soda.

She'd looked like one of those fairies in the movies the boys watched with their grandmother. Like a sprite. She kind of reminded him of Tinker Bell. Only her hair was lighter, so pale blond it was almost white. And tiny. She couldn't weigh much more than a bag of feed.

And wasn't that a romantic thought.

Why did he care? He had no time for romance. No desire for romance. When Julia died, that part of his life died with her. He'd had his one true love . . . and lost her.

Besides, little rich girls didn't do much for him, Annie being the exception. He doubted this Sophie would give anybody not listed on the Fortune 500 the time of day. Birds of a feather, right?

He pulled into Dottie's driveway, cut the engine, and headed for the flight of outside stairs leading to Annie's apartment. Dottie Willis stepped around the corner from the backyard. She wore gardening gloves, and dirt stains smeared the knees of her pink slacks.

"Hey, Dottie." He stopped, one foot on the bottom stair, a hand on the railing.

"Ty. How are those boys doing?"

"Wearing me out," he drawled.

"And you love it."

He grinned. "I do."

"Annie's not here."

"I know. I came by to pick up her cousin, the maid of honor. The wedding party's getting together at Bubba's. Brawley was supposed to take her, but he got held up at Doc's."

"Well, she's up there getting ready now. She's a sweetheart."

Ty grunted.

Dottie eyed him suspiciously, then asked, "Want some cookies to take home?"

"No, ma'am. Don't really have time right now. I don't mean to be rude, and I sure hate to refuse your cookies, but I gotta go. I'm running late."

"Nonsense. I'll have them ready by the time you're back downstairs."

"Thanks. I'd appreciate that. I mean, the boys will."

"Oh, I'll add plenty for their daddy."

"You're a good woman, Dottie Willis."

"Yes, I am." With that, she headed indoors.

He bounded up the stairs, taking them two at a time. Reaching the landing, he gave a quick knuckle-rap. The door swung open, and he simply stood and stared.

Dressed in skin-tight black pants, a top that bared a hint of smooth, flat stomach, and killer heels, Annie's cousin sent him a shy smile.

He'd thought he remembered what she looked like. His memory had failed. Provided only a shadowy reflection. Lost the essence of her.

Not a fairy. The woman was a sorceress. An incredibly beautiful sorceress. She stole his ability to speak along with his thoughts.

And made him feel like a damn fool.

He swiped off his cowboy hat and held it in front of him. "Sophie." He gave her a quick nod. "Not sure you remember me. Ty Rawlins. We met at—"

"Cash's barbecue," she said. "I remember. How are you?"

She held out a hand, and he took it in his. As soft as a newborn baby's backside, he thought. He cleared his throat. Best not to think of backsides when hers was showcased by those pants.

"Brawley called. Seems he's tied up and running a little late, so he asked if I'd give you a ride to Bubba's tonight."

"Oh. Thanks. I appreciate it."

Ty rubbed his forehead. Was that disappointment in her voice? Why not? Brawley Odell was one good-looking SOB.

Anyway, what difference did it make to him if one of Annie's friends got involved with Brawley? No skin off his nose. Thing was Brawley'd been going through women at a pretty good clip lately. He'd hate to see Sophie hurt.

And none of that was really any of his business, was it?

He slapped his hat back on. "You about ready?"

"Give me a minute." Sophie disappeared into the bedroom.

Ty shook his head. He knew what a minute meant to a woman getting ready to go out. Walking over to the window, he was surprised to hear her behind him.

Hmmm. A minute actually meant a minute.

"Just needed to grab my purse." She held it up, stepped outside behind him, and closed the door. "Annelise forgot to give me a key." She bit her lip. "Do you think it's okay to leave the door unlocked?"

"It'll be fine. This is Maverick Junction, not Chicago."

"You can say that again."

Seeing the expression on her face, he laughed. "You're not impressed?"

She hesitated. "I don't know that I'd say that. It's just— well, very different."

"Yeah, guess it is."

Dottie met them at the bottom of the stairs with a foil-wrapped package. "Here you go, Ty. Fresh chocolate-chip. Enough for you and the boys to make yourselves sick. Don't forget to give them a nice big glass of cold milk to go along with them."

"No, ma'am. I won't."

Walking to the truck, Ty said, "Dottie makes the best cookies this side of the Mississippi. Hell, maybe on both sides of it."

"I know. She gave me some, too. And I have to admit, I scarfed most of them down while I was getting ready for dinner."

He ran his eyes down her length. Model-thin, she didn't

look like a cookie eater. He'd have taken her for a lettuce nibbler, period. Maybe she was exaggerating...or maybe she'd been gifted with one heck of a metabolism.

"Guess I won't have to share with you, then, huh?"

Laying a hand on that incredibly flat stomach, she laughed. "No. Thank you."

He opened the door of his truck, helped her up, then walked around the front and slid in.

Closing his door, he cocooned the two of them inside the truck's cab, very aware of her.

Sophie.

Damn, she smelled every bit as good as she looked. Something stirred in him, kind of like the popping and snapping of the ice on the river after a long, cold winter.

Chapter Four

The proverbial fish out of water, Sophie thought as they passed through the outskirts of town and headed toward Main Street. Country-western music played over the sound system.

Lashes lowered, she sneaked a peek at Ty. Dressed in black jeans and a crisp white shirt, he'd rolled up the sleeves, showing off strong, tanned arms. She loved men's hands, and Ty's, resting easily on the steering wheel, made her think wicked thoughts. Best not go there. This guy had erected a wall around himself that was almost visible with a sign that read *Do Not Touch*. And with good reason, she supposed, considering what Annelise had told her.

The cowboy obviously loved his truck. Jet black with lots of chrome, the thing was massive. She'd spotted a toy truck on the back seat and a lightweight jacket. Other than that, not a speck of dust, no litter, no discarded coffee cups.

He didn't seem to want to make small talk, so she simply

relaxed into the leather seat and watched the alien landscape zip past.

When he pulled into the dirt parking lot of Bubba's Roadhouse, she seriously regretted her clothing choice. The black ankle-length pants paired with a cropped mint-green top and mile-high heels had felt right when she'd pulled them from her suitcase. Now she realized she should have gone with her jeans, but dinner out had seemed to call for something a little dressier. That idea flew out the window as she took a good hard look at the—what? Bar? Restaurant? What exactly was a roadhouse, anyway?

The place looked like one good Texas breeze would reduce it to kindling. Dust swirled around them when they parked in the lot nearly filled with pickups and Jeeps. Didn't anyone here drive an honest-to-goodness car?

She picked her way across the lot, unhappier at her shoe choice with each step. She hadn't realized she'd need to cross the Gobi Desert to earn her dinner. Sheesh!

Neon lights glared from the windows and advertised Lone Star beer, Dos Equis, and good food. A couple of hanging flower baskets added a spot of color to the porch and faded wood siding.

Ty at her side, she hesitated inside the doorway and drank in the atmosphere. She'd never seen anything quite like Bubba's. The floor, the walls, the ceiling, the bar—all made of rough-hewn wood. And the bar stools. Could they be real cowhide? She wrinkled her nose. Those darn cows seemed to be everywhere in Texas. And on the far wall, the Texas flag.

The place was packed and noisy. Voices rose and fell, silverware clinked, and the jukebox belted out a country song about cheating hearts.

Ty leaned close, his breath warm against her ear. "Welcome to Bubba's. Place is a little busier than I thought it'd be. My guess is with Thanksgiving only two days away, everybody's in town buying all those last-minute groceries for the big spread and decided to stop in for a meal rather than go home and cook. Figure they'll be doing enough of that later this week."

She nodded, although, having lived in a city all her life, she couldn't quite relate to that idea. She was used to running down to the corner deli and buying what she wanted, whenever she wanted. When she'd lived in Boston, she and her parents had spent the holidays with Annelise's family. And to her shame she'd never really thought about the work that went into the preparations for the feast. She'd simply enjoyed it, her family, the celebration.

Conversation swelled around them. A harried-looking blonde scooted between tables, dropping off meals and pulling bottles of ketchup and barbecue sauce from her deep apron pockets.

Another waitress, also dressed in jeans and a T-shirt, delivered two pitchers of beer to a large table by the door.

"Hey! Sophie! Ty! We're over here," Annelise called from the far corner of the room.

Several tables had been pulled together to accommodate the large group. Since there were only three empty chairs, she assumed they, along with Brawley, were the last to arrive. The smell of grilled steak and barbecued pork hung in the air.

Ty placed his hand on her lower back. Heat! His touch dredged up too-long-dormant feelings. Feelings totally inappropriate. Feelings she smacked down. The two of them wove their way across the room, his hand remaining at her back. He spoke to a few people as they passed, smiled at others. Sophie politely nodded as she walked by.

She felt Ty's eyes on her. But when she lifted hers to meet his, he looked away, his face closed, his smile gone. Had she done or said something to upset him?

Mentally, she chastised herself. She didn't know Ty Rawlins, so how could she presume to make assumptions about his feelings? Maybe that moody expression was his trademark.

If so, who could blame him? His life sure as heck hadn't turned out the way he'd imagined.

Annelise's gaze flitted from Sophie to Ty, then back to Sophie, a question in her eyes. Sophie answered with a slight shrug.

"I thought Brawley was picking up Sophie, Ty."

"He got hung up at Doc Gibson's, Annie. No big deal. Said to tell you he'd be here."

"Okay. Thanks for playing substitute chauffeur." She gave him a quick kiss on the cheek, then tapped a water glass with her spoon. "Everybody, my cousin, Sophie London. Sophie, I know you met most of these derelicts before—"

Boos and hisses rained down on her.

"Oh, did I say derelicts?" Her forehead creased in a mock frown. "I meant dear *ones*, of course." She grinned.

That was met by a round of cheers and raised glasses.

"They're in their beer, Sophie. What can I say?"

"And we're only getting started, darlin'," Cash assured her.

Annelise laughed and started around the table, reintroducing everyone and giving her a quick one-line bio on each. Sophie's mind reeled. Would she ever get them all straight?

Cash's sister, Babs, and her husband, Matt—who was Ty's brother-in-law. Mel Ryker, the blond Adonis who owned the local newspaper, the *Maverick Junction Daily*. Maggie Sullivan, who'd created Annelise's fantasy gown for the fund-raiser and now her sure-to-be-even-more-incredible wedding gown. Pauline and Quentin Hardeman, Cash's parents.

When Annelise finished, Sophie laughed. "Sure hope there's no quiz on all that."

Ty pulled out a chair for her, then, despite the fact there was an empty seat directly across from her, took one farther down the table. She blinked. Well, that certainly sent a message, didn't it?

Brawley came in just then, gave Annelise a quick kiss directly on the lips, and fell into the chair by Sophie. He picked up her hand and dropped a kiss on the back.

"Sorry about that. Don't usually stand up ladies as pretty as you. Did Ty explain?"

"Yes, he did." Sophie drew her hand away. "No problem. I got to ride in his big black truck."

Brawley laughed as he leaned across Babs and bumped knuckles with Ty. "Thanks."

Their waitress appeared.

"Hey, Mitzy. How's it going?" Ty asked.

"Can't complain. What can I get you tonight?"

Sophie ordered a white zin while Brawley and Ty ordered Lone Star beer. Everyone else asked for a refill, and Cash ordered some appetizers for the group.

Sophie laid her napkin in her lap and studied the people gathered to help Annelise celebrate her upcoming wedding. How was it possible, she wondered, that so much gorgeous had been dumped in one spot? Had the ugly stick broken before it reached Maverick Junction, or were all Texans this good looking?

She glanced at Brawley across from her. At Cash. Her gaze drifted to Maggie. A cloud of fabulous red hair set off the designer's stunning beauty, and Sophie had to admit that it would be easy to hate anyone that beautiful—if given the slightest chance. But Maggie didn't offer one. She laughed loudly and often and was as down-to-earth as they come. Her square-necked gold top had to be one of her own creations. She'd paired it with earrings that dangled to her shoulders, and Sophie felt less out of place in her own outfit.

And Annelise. Sophie studied her cousin. She fit right in here, which defied logic. The heiress to the largest oil company in the country was totally at home in this country hangout, drinking beer and eating peanuts.

Sophie noticed how often she and Cash touched, brushed lips, held each other's gaze.

The conversation rolled around Sophie and sucked her in. Before long, she found herself ribbing and being ribbed right along with all the others.

It didn't take a genius to see what had captivated her cousin. To understand why Annelise was willing to walk away from her Boston family home to live here in the backwater with her cowboy.

Sophie sipped her wine and reminded herself that everyone had a niche. This sure as heck wasn't hers.

They made short work of the onion rings and the jalapeño poppers. Then they polished off a mountain of nachos.

"Annelise said you design greeting cards, Sophie," Babs said. "I think that's fascinating."

"It's fun. I like to draw. To paint." Sophie smiled. "I studied both art and business in college. One thing just kind of flowed into another, and I started playing around with sayings to match my sketches."

"You work for somebody? Kind of on contract?" Matt, Babs's husband, asked.

Sophie shook her head. "No. That doesn't really work for me."

"Our Sophie's a free spirit," Annelise said. "She has her own company. Sets her own hours, her own direction."

"There's nothing wrong with that," she said defensively.

"I didn't say there was. I'm proud of you."

"What's your company's name?" Ty asked.

"Stardust Productions."

"I like that. It would be great for a clothing line," Maggie said. "Fanciful. Dreamy."

"Speaking of dreamy, here's our food." Cash rubbed his hands together in anticipation as Mitzy set their meals in front of them.

"Anything else y'all need?"

"If there is," Cash said, "I can't imagine what it would be."

The table quieted as everyone concentrated on some of the best food Sophie had ever eaten. Amazed, she looked down at her now empty plate.

"I can't believe I ate all that."

"It's the Texas air," Brawley said. "Makes you hungry."

"Right." She chuckled.

A song about honeybees came on the Wurlitzer, and Brawley reached for her hand.

"Come on. Dance with me."

"Now?"

"Sure, why not? Work off some of that grub we just ate."

She tipped her head. "Why not?"

Cash and Annelise joined them on the small dance floor, then his parents and Mel and Maggie. Babs and Matt smiled at each other while they danced, and she ran a hand over her husband's shaved head. Out of the corner of her eye, Sophie glimpsed Ty at the table alone. Chair balanced on its rear legs, he tipped back his bottle and took a long, slow drink. He looked relaxed, yet somehow a tad on edge. Mitzy walked past and leaned down to say something to him. When he grinned, Sophie caught sight of two of the deepest dimples she'd ever seen.

Brawley dipped her in his version of the Texas two-step and she laughed.

The dance ended and everyone started back to their seats. Annelise caught up with her. "Let's take a girls' break."

"Okay."

She followed as her cousin led them back to the little-girls' room...or in Bubba's case, the heifers' room.

"I'm not sure I like being a heifer," Sophie muttered as she caught the door before it closed.

"You're in Texas, darlin'," Annelise mock-drawled.

"Yes, I am."

"So, what do you think of him?" Annelise asked the moment the door shut behind them. "Isn't he to-die-for handsome?"

"Who? Brawley?"

"Yes, Brawley. I watched the two of you on the dance floor. Nice picture. You move well together." She sighed.

"Don't start, Annelise. I'm not in the market."

"I know." But the twinkle in her eyes said otherwise.

"I'm serious," Sophie insisted.

"This is where Cash and I had our first dance. Right here at Bubba's. The second night I was in town. Technically, this is your second night in town—if you count the evening you spent at the ranch for the barbecue."

She groaned. "Actually, we left late in the afternoon—before it turned evening."

"You're nit-picking."

"And you're matchmaking. That's why you asked Brawley to pick me up tonight, isn't it? Did the change of plans upset you?"

"I want you to be happy, Sophie."

"News flash, cousin. I *am* happy." The toe of her black stiletto traced a pattern in the seen-better-days linoleum.

"Look me in the eyes and tell me that."

"Annelise." Sophie put a hand on either side of her cousin's face, met her eyes. "You're getting married in a few days. That's right for you, and I'm thrilled you've found someone to love, someone who loves you."

She hesitated. "Not everyone needs that, though. Not everyone wants that. I'm happy with my life."

"But Brawley—"

"Is certifiably gorgeous. Women must fall at his feet. But there's nothing between us. Dancing with him was like dancing with my brother."

"You don't have a brother."

"And you're splitting hairs, Annelise. I'm sorry, but there wasn't a single volt of electricity when we touched, when he held me. Nothing. Sad, huh?"

"Darn it! I'd really hoped there'd be something there."

"Sorry. Besides, if I'm not mistaken, Maggie's got a thing for Brawley, and I don't poach."

"*Used* to have. In high school they were an item, but that's over and done with a long time ago."

"I wouldn't put my money on that. I think those fires are

still smoldering." Since she was here, she used the facilities, washed up, and tucked her hair behind her ears. "It was nice of Ty to go out of his way to drive me tonight."

Standing side by side, Annelise studied Sophie's reflection in the mirror. "What do you think of him?"

"Ty?" She rolled her eyes. "Where do I begin?" She fanned herself.

"So he didn't make you think of your non-existent brother."

"Are you kidding?"

Annelise smiled.

"Oh, no." Sophie shook her head. "You're forgetting something. He's the father of three little boys. It's enough to make a grown woman cry."

Annelise made a *tsk*ing sound.

"What's that supposed to mean?" Sophie asked.

"Nothing."

"Bull! I thought you wanted to set me up with Brawley."

Annelise cocked her head. "I was wrong. I think you're more Ty's type."

"Cuz, Ty's posted a no trespassing sign. My guess is he's still in love with his dead wife."

"There is that possibility."

"Yes, there is." Sophie swung open the door and marched out, straight into Ty Rawlins.

He put his hands on her arms to steady her.

"Sorry," she mumbled.

"Don't be. My fault. I wasn't watching where I was going."

"Ask the girl to dance, Ty." Annelise stood behind them in the narrow hallway.

"I—" He raised his hands.

"That's okay." Sophie moved to skirt around him.

"No." He reached out, caught her hand. The jolt was instantaneous, and she knew he felt it, too, when he momentarily broke contact.

"It's all right. I don't need to be entertained." She heard the snap of temper in her voice but couldn't control it.

"Understood." Ty nodded toward the jukebox. "But here's the thing. Cash fed the machine enough coins to fill a good-size swimming pool. All those quarters. All that music. Why waste it?"

He looked at Annelise. "Matt and Babs said to tell you good night, Annie. Since it's a school night, they had to head out. Get the sitter home."

"What about you?" The question popped out before Sophie could stop it. "Oh, jeez. Sorry again. That was rude... and it's none of my business."

"No, that's okay. Haley, the wife of one of my hands, is manning the fort." He flashed a quick grin. "She doesn't have school tomorrow, so I can stay out as late as I want. Besides, aren't you supposed to save at least one dance for the guy who brought you?"

He held out a hand; heat flooded her face.

No way to avoid it. If she refused, she'd come off as a prickly snob. He had to think the worst of her anyway. Whatever social graces her mother'd drummed into her seemed to have flown out the window.

She had no idea why he'd want to dance with an idiot, but who was she to deny him that dubious honor?

"In that case, I'd love to." She smiled, took his hand, and they walked together to the small center square reserved for dancing. She refused to so much as look at her cousin. Refused, for that matter, to meet any of the eyes in the restaurant watching them speculatively.

A slow number came on and Ty turned her to him, put his other arm around her waist, and drew her in.

"'The Keeper of the Stars,'" he said quietly. "Quite a song."

Her heart hammered as Ty very skillfully swept her along to the music. It was different from any dance she'd ever experienced. Night and day from the one she'd shared with Brawley. He'd been fun. Ty? Intense was the only word she could come up with to define the aura surrounding him.

Totally unfamiliar with country songs, she listened to the words over the beating of her heart. "It was no accident me finding you..." Her temperature spiked ten degrees. He was right. The words were captivating. Intense, just like him. And, oh, so romantic.

His hand holding hers was callused and strong, the one at her waist firm. Hot.

Ty did not, in any way, make her think brotherly thoughts. Instead, heat pooled low. Yearnings stirred. Thoughts and desires she'd doubted she'd ever feel.

The man was dangerous. She'd do well to remember that. But for now, she'd simply enjoy the moment. The dance drifted into a second, then a third. Sophie vaguely registered others on the dance floor with them, smiled when Annelise and Cash brushed past.

Ty stood over a foot taller than her five-three, and her head rested on the strapping cowboy's chest. She heard the steady beating of his heart and surprised herself by wishing the song could go on forever.

She was deathly afraid she wouldn't say no if this man wanted to park his cowboy boots beneath her bed. For one night, of course.

"Sophie?" Ty's voice whispered against her ear.

"Hmmm?"

"The music's stopped."

She opened her eyes, felt the blush heat her face. "Oh, brother." Quickly, she jerked free. "And once again, I'm sorry. Maybe I should have it tattooed on my forehead."

"Don't be sorry." He shook his head. "I'm not."

His black cowboy hat shadowed his eyes. She wished she could see them, read the expression in them.

Silently, they walked back to the table. She was careful not to touch him, not to brush up against him.

He pulled out her chair, said, "Thank you."

"You're more than welcome." She took her seat across from Brawley, who picked up his beer.

He held it high. "A toast to the future Mr. and Mrs. Cash Hardeman and to friends, both old and new."

Everyone raised their drinks.

"May the most you ever wish for be the least you ever receive," Brawley said.

A loud cheer went up from the group, and Cash leaned toward Annelise and kissed her, long and deep.

When he raised his head, he stared into his soon-to-be bride's eyes. "I have everything I've ever needed, everything I'll ever need, right here."

Annelise blushed and everyone laughed as they scraped back their chairs and stood. Time to go home. Before Sophie had time to collect her things, Brawley's phone rang.

He answered it, frowning. "Sure," he said. "Give me ten." Sliding the phone into his pocket, he said, "Ty? That was Doc. He's got an emergency and needs some help."

Ty nodded. "No problem. I'll drop Sophie off at Dottie's. It's on my way home."

A look passed between the two men. "Thanks, pal."

Brawley stood. "Gotta go, guys. It was a nice evening. See you all for a wedding, if not sooner."

"I'm thinkin' we might get together for a poker game tomorrow night," Cash said.

"Sounds good. Let me know." Brawley stopped beside Sophie. "I'm sorry, sweetheart. Hope you don't mind if this ne'er-do-well takes you home."

"I think we'll manage."

"That's twice now I've stood you up."

"And in one evening. You're a scoundrel." Sophie gave him a quick hug, picked up her purse, then turned to Ty. "You sure you don't mind?"

"It'll be my pleasure."

Brawley gave a quick wave and headed out the door.

"Give me a second," Sophie said to Ty. She made her way to Annelise. "What are the plans for tomorrow?"

"I'll pick you up at ten o'clock sharp. We'll grab breakfast at Sally's Place, then drive over to Lone Tree for your fitting." Annelise took her hand. "Wait till you see Maggie's shop, Sophie. You'll love it!"

"I'm looking forward to it." She shot a look at Maggie. "And my maid of honor's dress better not be matronly."

Maggie, standing at the table's end, laughed. "I don't think you need to worry about that. Your cousin's taste is too good, and my ego's too big. You'll look magnificent—and sexy as hell."

"Great! See you tomorrow then."

She joined Ty, and together they walked out, side by side. Sophie felt the sting of a dozen pair of eyes burning into her back as they passed curious townspeople at the tables.

Because she was the new girl in town or because she was with the widower?

Or maybe because they really were giving off sparks—despite his reluctance. If she touched him again, would Bubba's go up in flames?

Her heart did a little happy dance in her chest.

Too beautiful. Too tall. Too broad-shouldered.

Too everything.

And, lest she forget, the daddy of triplets.

Her heart stopped dancing to collapse on the floor and cry as she mentally crossed the to-die-for cowboy off her list.

It had to be done.

And wasn't that a shame?

The night had cooled off. As Sophie and Ty walked through the parking lot, she shivered.

He unlocked the big truck and reached into the back seat. "Here you go. This should keep you warm."

"Thanks." Slipping into the flannel jacket, she breathed deeply. His scent enveloped her. Warm and masculine. Sexy and hot.

It didn't smell like a daddy's jacket.

And exactly what in the world would a daddy's jacket smell like? she asked herself. *Get a grip.*

"Ty—"

"Sophie—"

They spoke at the same time. Both stopped and laughed.

He started up the truck and pulled out, the headlights cutting a swath through the darkness.

"I'm sorry Annelise forced you to dance with me, Ty. She's got this crazy idea that, in order to be complete, I need a guy in my life."

He cut her a look. "You don't agree?"

"No!"

"Good for you. I figured it was *you* getting the nudge

from her. That Annelise was trying to set *me* up, asking you to fall on the sword, as it were. I don't know how much you know about me, but—" He wet his lips, raked fingers through his hair.

"It's okay, Ty." She laid a hand on his arm. "I know."

His voice deepened, took on a gruff edge. "Okay."

"Let's just leave it at that."

"Good enough."

"Does Haley live on your ranch?"

"Yeah, she and Bob have a small place there. Works well for everybody."

"Do you have a bunkhouse?"

"Yep. A small one."

She grinned. "Hmmm. The whole Western thing."

He laughed. "I don't know about that, but before you ask, no, I don't have a gunslinger on my payroll. The bunkhouse is necessary. Running a ranch is a big job, one I couldn't do alone. It's a whole lot easier if some of the hands live on the Burnt Fork. You really are a city slicker, aren't you?"

"Undeniably and unapologetically, yes, I am. Burnt Fork. That's the name of your ranch?"

He nodded and turned into Dottie's drive. Getting out, he moved around the front of the truck to open her door. A born-and-bred gentleman, Sophie thought. She'd noticed lots of that tonight. Apparently, here in Texas, mothers still taught their boys good manners.

As she got out, she said, "Good night, Ty. Thanks for the ride."

He took hold of her arm. "I'll walk you to your door."

"That's not necessary."

"Yes, ma'am, it is. My mama taught me to always walk my—ah, a woman to the door at night. To see her safely inside."

"You said Maverick Junction was safe."

"It is. It's a handy ploy, though, for a fellow to get to spend a little more time with his girl."

But I'm not your girl, she thought. Nor would she ever be.

The moon shone in the big Texas sky as they walked along the drive, and their shadows merged, blending into one. From the darkness beyond, Sophie heard insects chirping and wondered what else was hiding out there in the night.

Paying attention to everything except where she was walking, she stumbled on a loose stone that had kicked into the drive. Ty reached out, put a hand on her arm, and her heart did a little backflip. At the base of the stairs, she turned to face him. "Thanks so much, Ty. For everything. I had fun tonight."

"I'd feel better if you'd let me walk you up. See you safely inside."

She shook her head. "You need to get home to your boys."

He hesitated. "Guess you're right. They're asleep, but they'll be up with the cows tomorrow." After a heartbeat, he said, "You know, you remind me of Tinker Bell."

Her brows furrowed. "Tinker Bell?"

"Peter Pan's friend."

"Yes, I know who she is."

"You've kind of got that fanciful look about you. Like a fragile, blond fairy."

"Fanciful?"

He blushed. "You know what I mean."

She tipped her head. "Well, that's, ah, the first time anyone's said that to me. But it's good, right?"

"Absolutely."

A smile tugged at the corners of her mouth. "I love fairies, actually." She wiggled her brows. "I keep them close."

"You keep them— No, that's okay." He shook his head. "I don't need to go there."

She slid out of his jacket and handed it to him, suddenly awkward. How did you end a date that wasn't a date? Glancing at him, at his face silvered by the moon, she realized he was probably stuck in the same quandary.

He reached for his jacket, and their fingers brushed. That same shock of electricity zinged through her.

Clearing her throat, she said, "Guess I'll see you at the rehearsal dinner?" She laid a hand on the stair railing.

"If not before."

As she raced up the steps, she was all too aware of him watching her. After she turned on the inside light, she moved to the window, careful to stay out of view.

He hadn't moved a muscle. Still as a sentry, he stared up toward her window. Then, with a grace that would have surprised her before their dance, he walked back to his big black truck and drove away.

It would be a long time, she decided, before sleep would visit tonight. Ty Rawlins might be a good person to avoid while she did her time in Maverick Junction. For the next few days, she'd best stick to Brawley if she needed a partner.

Turning out the light, she curled up in Annelise's cozy armchair and stared into the nighttime sky.

"Star light, star bright, first star I see tonight—"

Chapter Five

Ty grabbed his sunglasses from the dash and slid them over sleep-deprived eyes. He'd tossed and turned half the night, and, as predicted, his boys—the ones he and Julia had created—had been up at the crack of dawn. Sophie's scent lingered in the truck, filled his head, his mind. Julia had always smelled great, too. He tried desperately to bring back the smell of her. Instead, the flowery scent of Sophie pushed in, crowded out memory.

Shit!

He rolled down his windows and let the cool morning air rush into the cab, emptying it of Tinker Bell's sweet, feminine smell.

Yeah, sometimes at night after the boys were tucked in bed sound asleep, he was lonely. Yeah, he missed a woman's touch. Missed a woman to turn to in the middle of the night. But damn it, he and the boys were getting along fine.

Magic and fairy dust had no place in his life. He'd do well to remember that.

Pulling into Dottie's drive, he took a minute to settle himself, then sprinted up the stairs.

He frowned as he rapped on Sophie's kitchen door. How safe could it be to have this flimsy glass window in it? A simple matter to shatter the glass. Anybody could be inside in seconds.

If somebody wanted to break in. Certainly not out of the question, but highly unlikely here in Maverick Junction. He might mention it to Dottie. Ask if she'd consider replacing it with something a little sturdier.

"Come on in. The door's unlocked. I'm almost ready."

Guess the window didn't matter since Sophie didn't even bother to lock up—and then announced it. And hadn't he been the one to tell her it was safe here? That locks weren't necessary? Still—

He turned the knob and stuck his head inside. "Hey, Tink, it's me. Annie asked me to drive you out to the ranch."

"What?"

Sophie's head popped around the bedroom door, big brown eyes framed by that white-blond hair. And bare shoulders. Lord help him, the woman wasn't dressed. He swallowed. Hard.

A frown appeared between those intelligent eyes.

"Sorry. I couldn't hear what you said. Why are you here?"

"A better question is why you didn't ask who was at your door before inviting me in."

Her shrug again drew his eyes to those silky shoulders. Those *bare*, silky shoulders.

"I figured it was Annelise."

"But it wasn't."

"It could have been."

Useless, he realized, and gave up.

"I had to come into town to drop the kids off at day care, so Annie asked me to pick you up and drop you off at the ranch on my way home. It'll save her backtracking. She figured the two of you could go right from Cash's place to Maggie's in Lone Tree. So, looks like I'm your appointed driver this morning."

"Oh, Ty, I'm sorry. This is twice now. Actually, three times. Annelise should have called. There's no reason I can't rent a car."

"Nah. Doesn't make any sense to do that." He leaned against the door, felt the warmth of the sun coming in the window against his back. "I don't mind. And I was already in town, so it's no big. Honestly."

She still looked skeptical. "I need a couple minutes." Her head disappeared around the door frame.

"Pour yourself a cup of coffee," she called from the bedroom. "It's fresh. Only made it maybe ten minutes ago."

"Don't mind if I do." Ty went to the cupboard and dug around till he found a cup, then poured himself some. He carried it to the table and sat in one of the chairs Annie'd refurbished.

He looked around the kitchen and living area, at the blue walls. Tiffany blue, Annie'd told him. He smiled. A woman and Tiffany's. Fitting.

The change made him think of Roger Barry who had rented this apartment from Dottie for years. He'd brought the old guy home a couple times after he'd had a few too many at Bubba's, and this place had been a disaster. Roger had moved out, and the place sat empty until Annie rode into Maverick Junction on that big Harley of hers.

And although she had enough money to buy the state of Texas and still have plenty left over, she'd repainted the walls herself, then furnished the place from the secondhand shop in town and a few yard sales.

The apartment wasn't much, just one main room with a bedroom and bath off to the left. Annie'd divided the big room into kitchen, dining, and living areas. By the far window, he spotted the old brown sofa that had been in Cash's grandfather's living room. Boy, as kids, he, Cash, and Brawley had done some major arm-wrestling on that thing.

Studying the small space, he had to admit she'd done one heck of a job. With a little bit of money and a whole lot of elbow grease, style, and imagination, she'd completely transformed the apartment and made it her own.

Thing was, it fit Sophie, too. The bright colors, the sunlight. The feminine touches. Salvaged crystal mixed with whimsy.

For a split-second, he let himself wonder what Sophie's place in Chicago looked like. Tried to picture her in the cold, windy city. Truth was, he couldn't imagine her looking any more perfect than she did right here in the Texas sunshine.

The sun rose above the tree outside the living room and a rogue beam danced into the apartment, straight through the sun catchers that hadn't been there yesterday. And damned if they weren't fairies.

Right in the center? A stained-glass Tinker Bell.

"Do you think I'm dressed okay?"

Ty turned to look at Sophie, who stood in the doorway between the kitchen and bedroom. And she'd given him permission to stare. *Thank you, Jesus.*

She wore coffee-colored pants with a long-sleeve blouse the color of Texas bluebonnets on a sunny day. It flowed around her like molten glass. Two crosses on silver chains along with a strand of multicolored crystals shimmered at her neck. A bold cuff bracelet encircled her tiny wrist; large silver hoops glinted at her ears. And, again, she wore a pair of killer heels that screamed, *Do me*.

Sweat popped out on his brow.

The woman smelled like a field of wildflowers. The same scent that had filled both his truck's cab and his dreams last night. This morning.

Annie was going to have to get someone else to play chauffeur after this trip. He didn't want the feelings Sophie stirred in him. Never again. He couldn't do it again.

He took a sip of coffee to give himself another second. "You look fine. Maggie's gonna love that top."

"You think? I'm so excited. I'm dying to see her shop after everything Annelise has told me about it."

"Maggie's worked hard and done well. Annie wearing her dress to that big to-do in Dallas gave her a huge nudge. I worry she's gonna leave us. Head to New York City. Be good for her, I guess, but we'd sure as hell miss her."

Sophie nodded. "There are always two sides to the coin, aren't there?"

"Yep." He drank again. "So you girls are going off for the day. I never have understood that. I mean, how long can it take to try on a dress?"

"This isn't just any dress."

He rolled his eyes. "Right."

"Oh, you're such a man."

"Guilty as charged. Seriously, though. Come on. Give. What'll you do today? Really."

"Ohhh. Are you asking me to divulge the secrets of the sisterhood?"

"Yeah, guess you could say that."

"Hmmm." She crossed the room toward him. "Do I have time for a cup of coffee before we go? If I'm going to be divulging deep, dark secrets, I need caffeine."

He grinned. "You bet. I don't think there's any rush." He held up his cup. "Good coffee, by the way."

"Thanks. I brought the beans with me. I buy them at a little deli on the corner. I very rarely drink coffee, but when I do, it has to be the best. I'm spoiled, I guess." She shrugged. "Today felt like a coffee day, and I thought Annelise might like some when she got here."

At the counter, Sophie poured herself a cup, added cream, and walked back to the table. Sitting across from Ty, she thought again what an easy man he was to look at. What an easy man he was to talk to when he relaxed. When he put away the sadness she'd seen at the Fourth of July barbecue and last night when he'd thought no one was watching. When the couples in their group were holding each other close on the dance floor.

She decided to keep things light.

"Well, let's see. What will we do first?" She tapped her chin with pastel pink nails. "Obviously, I'll try on my maid-of-honor gown, but only after I ooh and ahh over Maggie's shop and her creations. Which I'm sure I'll do. We might shed a few tears. Try on a few things."

At his grunt, she took a bracing sip of coffee and closed her eyes. She'd needed that.

"I saw plenty of tabloid pictures of Annelise and Cash at the Dallas fund-raiser. The dress Maggie designed for her was nothing short of spectacular."

"Like I said, our Maggie's good."

"Good?" She laughed. "That's like saying *Pride and*

Prejudice is a nice little story. What a gross understatement. But since we've already established you're a guy, I'll let it go. You just can't understand. It's not in your genes."

"Whoa, are you male-bashing already? It's not even nine o'clock."

"Nope. No bashing. Simply telling it like it is. Anyway, after I slide into my gorgeous gown and we all dry our eyes, Maggie will no doubt decide she needs to take a few nips here, a couple tucks there."

She grimaced. "She might even have to let out the side seams. Northern winters tend to pack on a few pounds."

"Hah, I seriously doubt that's a problem for you," Ty said.

"Thank you, sir. Your mother taught you well." She wrapped her hands around her cup. "Anyway, once Maggie's satisfied the dress fits me and is up to her standards, we'll probably stop by the liquor store and pick up a couple bottles of vodka or, better yet, tequila. Then we'll head to Maggie's to eat pizza, drink margaritas, and smoke cigars."

For just the barest second, his mouth dropped open. Then he rolled his eyes and groaned. "You're putting me on."

"Yes, I am."

Disarming dimples popped out again when he grinned, and she could barely keep her fingers from reaching out to touch.

"The truth? I honestly don't know what we'll do today. I've never been to Lone Tree, and I have no idea what's there."

Now he laughed out loud. "What was your first impression of Maverick Junction?"

Thrown off by his change of subject, she hesitated. "Seriously?"

"Seriously."

She pulled a face. "There's not much here. I mean, it has a certain charm. And everybody's unbelievably friendly."

"But?"

"But, well, the town's small. It's...I don't know."

"Well, Tink, when you see Lone Tree, you're gonna think Maverick Junction's the big time."

"You're kidding." She stared at him. "You have to be. Tell me you are."

"Wish I was. You're probably going to be disappointed in Lone Tree. But not in Maggie's," he added quickly. "She's got herself a first-class operation. It was in the planning stages when my wife was pregnant with our boys. Julia helped her pick the wall colors." A hint of grief shadowed his eyes.

Just as quickly he blinked it away. "Our Maggie fixed the place up cuter than a button and whips up clothes fine enough for a princess."

Sophie nodded.

"But," Ty continued, "the town? Less than impressive. Not a lot to do there. Although, I've got to say, Ollie makes a mean lemon meringue pie at the Cowboy Grill. My guess is you and Annie will stop in there and have a bite of lunch."

He took the last drink of his coffee and set the cup on the scarred table. "Maggie's probably going to— No, on second thought, Maggie *will* close the shop when you gals get there. I was thinking she wouldn't be free to leave, but all things considered, my guess is she'll take the day off to play with you girls."

"I hope she does," Sophie said. "From everything Annelise has told me and from my own first impressions, Maggie seems wonderful. I'd like to get to know her since she's going to be part of Annelise's life now. It's so strange to think of her living here. In Texas. On a ranch."

"Nothing you'd want, huh?" Ty asked.

Sophie shook her head. "No. I'm city through and through. I love having the opera and art museums, the ball park, the shopping at my fingertips. I actually like a throng of people on the sidewalks, in the cafes. I like the diversity, the ever-changing face of the city. The energy and vitality rejuvenate me. I can't imagine living here."

"That's what Annie said a few months ago."

Sophie shrugged. "Yeah, go figure. But it's not for everybody."

"No, don't suppose it is."

"Anyway, back to our girls' day. Maggie will put on some music, and we'll break out a bottle of champagne."

"Undoubtedly," Ty agreed.

"Maybe we'll get good and tipsy. After all, a girl…or a guy, for that matter…only gets married once."

A shadow passed over Ty's face, and Sophie could have ripped out her tongue.

"Oh, Ty." She set her cup down so quickly, coffee sloshed over the rim. "I'm so sorry. I'm an idiot."

"Don't." A look just short of anger passed over his face. "Don't pity me."

"I'm not. I just—"

"Stop." He held up a hand. "What'll you do after you're all good and tipsy?"

"Well, if we do that," she hurried on, rattled by her faux pas, "we might need to call you to rescue us, pick us up in Lone Tree."

"I'm available if you need me. Just give me a call."

"You mean that, don't you?"

"I do."

The simplicity of his answer stopped her. Ty Rawlins intrigued her.

"You don't believe me?"

"Let's just say I'm used to guys who give lip service about being there. When push comes to shove, it's a different story."

"That won't happen here."

She heard the resoluteness in his voice. "You Texans are an interesting breed."

"We like to think so."

And that could be a problem, Sophie realized, because she found this particular Texan very interesting. On so many levels.

Halfway to the sink, coffee cup in hand, her cell rang. "Sorry," she said to Ty. "Must be Annelise."

"That's okay. No hurry."

"Hello?"

"Have a good trip?"

Nathan. Sophie started to groan in frustration, then remembered Ty. "Yes, I did."

"Where are you?"

"We've been through this."

Ty took the cup from her hand and moved to the sink. Water running, he rinsed it, obviously trying not to eavesdrop. In a place this size, that wasn't remotely possible.

"Where are you?" Nathan demanded.

"I have to go." She clicked off her phone, disgusted that her hand shook. Embarrassed that Ty saw it.

"You okay?"

"Sure." She sent him a wobbly smile and picked up her purse. Her tension headache had returned.

"Anything I can do to help?"

And again, she knew this wasn't an empty offer. But she'd be darned if she'd lean on another man to mop up this mess. Nathan was a nuisance. A growing nuisance.

A very demanding nuisance.

But he was in Chicago, and she was in Texas. For a few days, anyway. When Ty cupped her elbow, his touch reassuring, she didn't draw away.

And wasn't that stupid?

She wasn't in any danger.

Chapter Six

An hour and a half later, Sophie and Annelise turned onto the highway, headed to Lone Tree. Although her cousin had ridden into Maverick Junction on her Harley, she'd finally broken down and bought a car, her nod to practicality.

Sophie seriously doubted most people would term the sleek cherry-red Camaro convertible she'd chosen practical, but then, Annelise wasn't most people. With the wind blowing through her hair, though, Sophie found it hard to argue with her cousin's choice.

"I hope Maggie will forgive us for being a little late," Sophie said. "I'll tell her it's all my fault. But I absolutely had to check out Cash's house. *Your* house now. And that lake. Wow. I didn't get to see it last time I was here."

"You didn't see much of anything last time you were here," Annelise reminded her.

"No, I didn't. Your folks were on a mission, and it didn't include sightseeing." She turned to face Annelise. "Cash's place is wonderful. All that wood and stone. I can't believe he built it himself. It's perfect. Warm and inviting. Cozy and comfortable. Texas chic."

"Yes, it's all that."

"And the setting. Oh, my gosh. What a difference for you, huh?"

"It is. And all for the better. I can't tell you how much I enjoy waking up in the morning, sitting on the patio facing the lake for my morning coffee. With Cash."

"You're happy."

"I am."

Anxious, Sophie took a deep breath, a plan forming in her mind. "Has Dottie rented your apartment?"

"Why?" Annelise's head whipped around to stare at her.

"Keep your eyes on the road."

Annelise laughed and fluttered her hand. "Don't worry. Driving here isn't like city driving. Chances of meeting another car are practically nil."

"But there are animals," Sophie muttered. "Animals that don't have any better sense than to stand in the middle of the road. On the way from the airport, we almost ran into those two cows. Jeez."

"When in Texas—"

"Thus, the warning. Keep your eyes on the road."

"Okay, okay." A frown creased her forehead. "But why do you want to know about Dottie's apartment?"

"I might stay awhile."

Annelise's brows shot up. "You? Here? In Maverick Junction? With the cattle and the silence?"

Sophie shrugged. Her idea was either brilliant or the stupidest one she'd ever had. Nathan or big-horned cattle. Hmmm. Quite a choice.

"What's wrong?"

"Nothing. I just thought, you know, a change might be good. A *temporary* change. I'm not talking long-term, believe me. A few weeks."

Annelise's fingers tapped the steering wheel. "Uh-uh. There's more to it than that." She glanced at her again. "I'm not going to be here, you know."

"Right. I understand that. You'll be in Paris with Cash on your honeymoon."

The two looked at each other and squealed.

"I'm good with that." Sophie slid her sunglasses up her nose. "I need some time alone. Time to get my head straight and my spring line pulled together, that's all. I thought, as long as I'm here, as long as you've got this cute apartment, it would be a great fit."

Annelise was silent for a minute. "Okay. I'm still not sure you've given full disclosure—"

"Oh, that is so lawyerish."

"That's not a word, and I am a lawyer."

"I know, and I know. Both duly noted, counselor."

"But," Annelise continued, "as I was about to say, smarty-pants, I'll ask Dottie about it."

"Do you think she'll say yes?"

Sophie hated to admit, even to herself, how much she hoped Dottie'd take her in. Nathan had initially annoyed her. Now? Now he ticked the creepy box. No way, though, would she burden Annelise with this, not so close to her wedding day. Right now, her cousin's priority needed to be flowers, gowns, and honeymoons.

"She hasn't advertised the apartment yet or shown it to anyone. Personally, I think she'll be tickled pink."

"Tickled pink?" Sophie groaned. She'd seen Dottie's pink

downstairs apartment. Her pink wardrobe. "That's bad, Annelise. Really bad."

"Yeah, I know."

They laughed, rocketing closer to Lone Tree and their appointment.

*   *   *

Sophie didn't move, not even after Annelise had turned off the car. "This is Lone Tree?"

"The people here are wonderful," her cousin said, reaching into the back seat for her purse.

"Oh, that's rich. That's like being set up for a blind date with someone who has a great personality. You know he's going to be a minus one out of ten in the looks department. Not that that matters," she added quickly.

Annelise snorted. "You're right. Sorry. But, seriously, the people here really are terrific."

What people? Sophie wondered. Lone Tree could have been a ghost town. The street was devoid of life. No people, no plants, nothing moving.

Beside her, Annelise pointed to the store in front of them.

Cowboy Grill was splashed across the window. "Ollie, the owner and chief bottle-washer, is the one who pointed me in the right direction when I was searching for my great-aunt."

"He helped you save your grandfather's life, then."

"He did. On a lighter note, but still very important..." She held up a finger. "Ollie's wife makes the best lemon meringue pie you've ever tasted."

"Ty said the same thing. I might have to test it myself."

"We will. After your fitting. I can hit the treadmill an extra half-hour to work it off before Saturday." Her expression went all dreamy. "Saturday. Only three more days, and I'll be Mrs. Cash Hardeman."

"Annelise?"

"Hmm?"

"I'd like to thank you."

"For what?"

"Not turning into Bridezilla. Some of the stories I've heard—"

"I couldn't do that. I'm so happy, and I want everyone else happy, too." She took a deep breath, let it out in a rush. "Okay, let's get over to Maggie's before I turn into a waterfall and have to do a full makeup repair."

Walking across the deserted street, Sophie sighed when she spotted Maggie's. The store window's flowing script suited the stylish, gregarious redhead. Very elegant. Very Maggie.

Then they opened the door to the shop and Sophie stood rooted, hugging herself. Ultra-feminine, it smelled of vanilla and lilacs. Sun spilled through lacy white curtains and bathed the boutique in its glow. Soothing, muted pink covered the walls, while chocolate brown carpet and moldings grounded the room and kept it from seeming fussy—and Ty's Julia had a hand in picking these colors. Sophie sighed.

The décor could only be described as eclectic. Antique dressers, overstuffed chairs, and gilded mirrors acted as an underpinning to the clothes on display. If she had the money, she'd go totally crazy in here. But she didn't. With the expense of this trip, she'd have to scrape to cover her mortgage this month.

Well, she wouldn't think about that right now. Today was Annelise's day. And no one deserved this more.

Stepping inside, she whispered, "Incredible."

"Didn't I tell you? Hard to believe, huh?"

"Pinch me." Sophie held out a hand. "I must be dreaming. How can this exist in the middle of this mud-ugly town?"

"Come on in." Maggie moved from behind a glass counter covered with jewelry and accessories. She wore what had to be one of her own designs, a lightweight black and white dress that showcased her curves and made Sophie drool. Phenomenal.

"If I thought for an instant that dress would look half as good on me as it does on you, I'd fight you for it," Annelise said.

Maggie laughed. "Don't tell any of the guys. They'd line up around the block to watch two women go at it."

"Isn't that the truth? I never have figured out what that's all about."

"Me, either," Maggie said.

"I know we're here to fit my dress, but I need a minute." Sophie wandered over to an old dresser and fingered the camisoles tumbling casually from its drawers. One, a soft pink piped in black, caught her eye. "Ooh-la-la. If I had a guy in my life right now, this would go home with me."

"I have matching thongs." Maggie reached into another drawer, flipped through them, and pulled out a tiny scrap of pink and black. "Of course, with the set, you might want to make sure you're handy to an ER, if you know what I mean."

"Annelise, you should get these for your honeymoon." Sophie held them out.

"No, I don't think so. I'll leave them right here, in case you need them."

Sophie snorted. "Fat chance."

"You never know." Maggie's eyes sparkled. "Come on. I

can't wait for you to see your dress. If you don't like it, well, there's simply no hope for you."

Sophie laughed. "You really need to work on that self-esteem problem."

Maggie flipped the sign on the door to read closed. Together, they walked toward her workroom.

"Babs, Kinsey, and both Annie's mom and Cash's have already been in for their fittings. You're the last," Maggie tossed over her shoulder.

"I'm sorry about that. I know this is really pushing it, but I couldn't get down before now. Things have been crazy, and I've been so busy."

"Not a problem. I think the dress will suit you perfectly." She stopped, turned to Sophie, and studied her with a seamstress eye. "We shouldn't need to do more than a couple tiny alterations."

She opened a beautiful old door at the back of the shop and led them into her workroom.

Sophie gaped. "It's like stepping into a secret garden."

"Isn't it?" Annelise grinned ear to ear. "I'm in love with it. It's so girlie, and there's such energy here."

Everywhere she looked, Sophie saw evidence of Maggie's creativity. Swatches, buttons, drawings tacked to bulletin boards and scattered across a well-used table. One wall was weathered brick, and the floor's scarred wood held decades of history.

"Your dress is in here." Maggie stepped to another, smaller doorway.

Sophie followed her along shelf after shelf of fabric. Tweeds, silks, linens, cotton of every color. "This is almost orgasmic."

Maggie laughed. "If the fabric alone will do that for you,

let's see what this does." She reached behind a room divider and held up a floor-length dress.

Sophie gasped. "Oh, my gosh, it's gorgeous. More than gorgeous. It's perfection." She clapped her hands.

The black silk dress was strapless, its skirt a dreamy swirl. One swath of black cut diagonally across the top and fluttered over the red satin band at the waist. Horizontal pleating provided texture to the bodice. Beyond stunning.

She turned from Maggie to Annelise. "You'll really let me wear this for your wedding? Isn't there some rule that says attendants' gowns have to be butt-ugly so the bride looks that much more radiant?"

Annelise laughed. "If there is, it deserves to be broken."

"Don't worry," Maggie said. "Annie is going to shine so brightly, the guests will be grabbing their sunglasses."

"I don't doubt that. Not for a second." Sophie moved to the dress, ran a hand along the sash, trailed a finger over the bodice detail. Sighed. Then she threw herself first into her cousin's arms, then Maggie's.

Maggie tossed Annelise a look. "Told you she'd like it."

"What are the other attendants wearing?"

Handing Sophie her gown, Maggie reached behind the curtain and pulled out a dress bag. She unzipped it and held it up for Sophie.

"The other's identical." The strapless red dress had no draping at the top but was pleated from beneath the bust to the waist where two large, silk roses in the same red nipped it in.

"Gorgeous."

"Cash's niece, Abbie, is our flower girl. Maggie designed a fairy-tale dress for her. A red bodice and miles and miles of white tulle skirt with just the tiniest bit of red trim at the bottom."

"Good job." Sophie high-fived both women. "So where's your wedding gown?" she asked. "Can I see it? You've refused to tell me anything about it, even when I was in Boston for your shower."

"Because it's a secret. And it's going to stay that way."

"I'm your maid of honor."

"Yes, you are."

"Can't I have one little, teensy-weensy peek?"

"Nope. My gown's in hiding."

"Oh, that's so not fair."

Annelise grinned. "I know. But I'm the bride. I get to do what I want. Nobody sees the dress. Sorry."

"You're not at all sorry."

A mischievous grin broke out on Annelise's face. "You're right. I'm not."

"Okay, it's time I take back the Bridezilla comment. Maybe you are turning into the bride from Hell."

"Not even." Annelise patted her check. "Come on, I did let Maggie show you the other dresses."

"Yes, thanks for that." She studied the silk flowers on the red dresses more closely. "Maggie, you're going to explode onto the fashion scene."

"If I do, I'll have Annie here to thank for it." She covered the red dress and put it away.

"Oh, no," Annelise said. "*When*, not *if*, you do, you'll have your own talent, hard work, and persistence to thank for your success."

"Without exposure—" Maggie shrugged. "Okay, enough chitchat. Strip, Sophie. Let's get this on you and see what we need to do."

* * *

Fifteen minutes later, Maggie carefully removed the gown. "Don't put your clothes back on. The alterations won't take long. There's a robe on the hook by the door. Just slip into it."

Hands folded in her lap, Annelise sat on a bench by the door. Sophie slid into the robe and snagged a stool from the corner.

Maggie settled in front of her sewing machine with seam ripper, pincushion, and magic fingers. Sophie watched in awe as she went to work.

Music played softly in the store and drifted back to them. "The Way You Look Tonight." It couldn't be a better choice.

"Maggie, you've known Ty and Cash for a long time, right?"

"Since we were pups."

Sophie grinned, then her face sobered. "And you knew Julia."

Maggie's smile dimmed. "Yeah. She was a special person."

Of course she was, Sophie thought. That's why Ty had fallen in love with her. A little corner of her heart cramped. "What did she look like? What was she like?"

Maggie hesitated.

"Please. I need to know."

"Really?"

"I do."

"Me, too," Annelise said. "Nobody talks about her."

Maggie sighed. "Julia was beautiful, tallish, about five-eight, long dark hair that curled at the ends. In high school, everybody wanted to be like her. She played piano beautifully, captained the debate team, and had Ty, the football team's starting quarterback, on her arm."

Mentally, Sophie winced. Well, she'd wanted to know,

hadn't she? No wonder Ty hadn't married again. How could anyone hope to compete with that? Good thing she didn't intend to.

Before she could stop herself, though, she asked, "Did you make her wedding gown?"

"No, I didn't have my shop then. I was still in the day-dreaming and planning stage. She and her mom drove to Austin to find her dress. Julia and Ty, the first of our group to get hitched. And they were happy—until, well, you know."

Sophie nodded.

"It wasn't totally unexpected. Her dying. But nobody was prepared for it to happen quite so soon." Maggie placed her hands on her cheeks and let out another big sigh. "Enough of the maudlin. Let's get you back into this dress."

"I'm sorry. I didn't mean to make you sad." Sophie raised her hands above her head and eyed Maggie skeptically. "You're sure you removed all the pins?"

"Hopefully. Blood's hell to get out of silk. Although with the black, it might not show."

"Ha, ha."

She slipped the dress over Sophie's head, studying her critically. After she'd walked slowly around her several times, she smiled and gave a fist pump. "And we are done! While you help her out of that, Annie, I'll rescue the champagne from the fridge. I have a special bottle I've been saving for today."

They finished their first glass and started on seconds, dancing to an oldies station Maggie found on XM and making complete fools of themselves.

"I don't know about you two, but I'm famished. Time to eat," Maggie said.

"Amen."

"Count me in," Annelise said.

"Grab your purses, ladies. Let's head to Ollie's and let him feed us."

"What about the dresses?" Sophie asked.

"I'll have those to the church on time, don't you worry. That's my job."

"They're not getting married in a church." Sophie giggled, slightly fuzzy-headed from the champagne.

"No, we're not." Annelise smiled. "And my mom is still near to a coronary over that. The fact that Cash and I decided to marry outdoors and throw our reception in and around a barn is almost more than she can swallow. Dad's doing much better with our plans."

"It's what you want. You and Cash," Sophie said. "It's your wedding."

"Yes, it is. And that's the bottom line."

"Well, I for one think it's going to be amazing. The wedding of the year."

"I don't know about that." Annelise laughed. "Are you free tonight, Maggie?"

"I sure am."

"Why don't we head over to my place after we eat? Have a pajama party and eat and drink some more."

"Sounds like fun."

"You realize, of course, what I'm giving up to do this with my two friends."

Sophie shook her head. "Not a clue. But my guess is you'll tell us."

A slow smile spread over Annelise's face. "I'm giving up a night with Cash. A night of the most unbelievable, toe-curling sex."

"Brag, brag, brag," Maggie said drolly.

Sophie winked at her cousin. "It'll make your wedding night that much hotter."

"I know." Annelise wiggled her brows.

"And you're so doing this on purpose, aren't you?" Sophie asked.

"You bet." With a smug smile, she picked up her purse.

"I wonder if Cash has any idea what he's getting himself into." Maggie herded them out the door and locked up behind her. "I'm playing hooky for the rest of the day and enjoying it. If you can't take some time off once in a while, life's not worth living."

Arm in arm, the three of them crossed the street. When they entered Cowboy Grill, the bell over the door jangled.

"Be with ya in a second," a gravelly voice called from somewhere in the restaurant's back room. "Grab a seat."

A box thumped loudly to the floor, followed by a colorful curse.

"Damn stuff gets stacked so high, it'd take Paul Bunyan to reach it."

"Cough up some of that money you're hoarding, and buy yourself a step stool," an older, unseen female said.

"Right now, you need to come take care of business," Maggie scolded playfully. "You have three starving women waiting for you."

"There's music to any red-blooded man's ears," Ollie muttered as he headed toward them. A heavy stubble shadowing his face and a stained apron around his neck, he looked like a linebacker.

Dropping his hands flat on the counter in front of him, he asked, "What's it gonna take to satisfy you?"

Chapter Seven

You want to do what?" Ty held the phone prisoner between his cheek and his shoulder, his hands full of Kool-Aid-filled sippy cups. "I don't think—"

As he listened, his eyes traveled from the newest puppy puddle in the middle of the kitchen floor to Jonah, flat on his belly, hand-feeding Trouble. The pup was probably a mistake. In a weak moment, Babs had talked him into bringing the pooch home. The half-Lab, half who-knew-what had been the last of her dog's litter. A loose woman, that Lab. Delilah had gotten knocked up by some bad boy traveling through. Ty tipped his head and studied the pup again. Nope. Impossible to say what the other half was.

Didn't matter to his boys, though. And mistake or not, Trouble was part of the family now. For better or worse.

He handed Jesse and Josh their drinks, and they scooted back to the front of the house. Since Jonah was occupied, he set his on the counter.

The TV blared from the living room. One of the boys had switched it to some cartoon show that was probably rotting their brains. When they turned eighteen, one or all of them would likely sue him for letting them watch such drivel. Maybe go on a talk show and tell how it had warped them for life.

Jeez, and wasn't he Mr. Sunny tonight?

"Jesse, turn that down. Right now!"

"Josh turned it up, not me!"

"No, I didn't." Josh started to cry.

"Oh, for— I don't care who turned it up, Josh. Stop crying and turn it down. Now!" Before he could stop himself, he added, "Don't make me come in there."

He groaned. Oh, God. Could he get more pathetic?

"Man, maybe we don't want you coming along tonight." Cash's chuckle rumbled over the phone line. "You sound like my mom."

"So bite me," Ty snapped.

"Wouldn't you rather Annie's little cousin Sophie do that?"

Ty cursed, then turned red-faced when Jonah said, "Daddy, you said a bad word."

"Yeah, yeah, I know. Sorry, son. I won't say it again...and don't you, either."

"I won't, Daddy. And I won't tell Grandma you did."

It just got better and better. Now a pipeline ran straight to his mother to let her know every time he screwed up. He couldn't catch a break.

He rubbed his forehead. Maybe he did need a night out. He looked over at his son, rolling across the kitchen floor with Trouble, the pup slurping wet kisses all over Jonah's giggling face.

Problem was, he'd been gone last night, too. Guilt

swamped him. When he'd lost Julia, he'd pretty much lost any claim to a personal life.

Still...

"What time?"

"There you go," Cash said. "Knew you'd see reason."

"The only reason I see is to try to hang on to the last shreds of my sanity. You have no idea what life is like inside this house."

"Hey, I've been at my sister's when things have been pretty hairy."

"I can't believe anything you've seen there comes even close to what goes on here. Where and when are you meeting? I'll try to make it."

Cash filled him in on the details, then hung up.

Ty rested a hip against the counter and closed his eyes for a couple seconds. Things probably did get wound up at Babs's. She had two kids. But she also had Matt. When the going got tough, they had each other to fall back on. He had nobody.

Stop. That wasn't fair. His mom, his dad, Julia's parents, Haley—they were all there for him and the boys. All he ever had to do was say the word and one or more pitched in. But the day-to-day, the minutia, fell to him.

Sometimes in the middle of the night, he awoke in a full sweat. He'd lie awake listening for the boys, for anything that wasn't right. He'd wonder, if only he listened hard enough, if he'd hear Julia's soft breathing beside him.

But he didn't. He never would again. And that was a fact.

"Look, Daddy, look. See what Trouble can do?"

And he was back, back to fatherhood. With a dishwasher to unload, a new puppy trick to applaud, and two armfuls of love in the form of three wiggly little boys.

While he'd take a break tonight his cell phone would stay on. Just in case.

*   *   *

Ty stood with Cash and Brawley in Dottie's driveway. How many times had the three of them gone out on nights like tonight, bored out of their skulls and looking for some action? Here they were, older and hopefully wiser, yet some things never changed.

He breathed deeply. The night was beyond spectacular. Mid-fifties, a little breeze, and more stars overhead than any man could hope to count in his lifetime.

A window stood open in the upstairs apartment, and feminine chatter and giggles, along with an underlay of music, floated down to them.

Country-western.

"Good girl, Annie," Cash murmured when he heard Luke Bryan. "The girl's really come around. Not too many months ago, she'd have been listening to that long-haired, artsy-fartsy stuff."

"Give me a hand here?" Juggling the pizza and a couple six-packs of Lone Star, Brawley stood by the old Caddy's open door.

Ty reached in for the grocery bag, waited for Cash's dog to jump out, then quietly closed the door. He sure hoped they weren't making a mistake.

Annie'd called Cash to tell him the girls were at her place and intended to have themselves a pajama party. They already had wine and had ordered a pizza delivered.

The minute Cash hung up, he'd called the pizza place and told Arnie to stick a second pie in the oven. He'd pick them both up. That, Ty thought, was when he and Brawley had been pulled into it. They were the buffers.

And why, for the second night in a row, a sitter was putting his kids to bed.

It was a win-win. Unless the girls threw them out on their butts for crashing their party. And knowing the ladies inside, that could very well happen. Well, Maggie and Annie, at least, might toss them out. Ty seriously doubted Tinker Bell would welcome their invasion, either. He didn't know her well enough to say whether or not she'd kick them out.

Nor would he ever. She'd come to Maverick Junction for Annie's wedding. Once it was over, she'd be long gone, and he'd settle back into his routine.

But for tonight, he'd say the hell with it and go along with his pal's harebrained scheme. And that alone sent a twinge of guilt slithering through him. Six of them. Three guys, three gals. Would they pair up?

Cripes, his chest tightened. He hadn't been with anyone since Julia. Hadn't found anyone who even remotely interested him. Yet when he was anywhere near Tink, some part of him, some deeply buried part, started making small noises. Tiny, yearning sounds.

And that wasn't good. That was problematic. Since he realized it, though, he would be on guard.

"Got everything?"

"Yeah, Romeo. We've got you covered." Ty hitched the bag higher on his hip. "Glad to see you're doing your share."

"What can I say?" Cash held a bouquet of daisies. "My bride-to-be's in there. Want to keep her happy."

"Then maybe you should've considered letting her have some girl time." Brawley scowled.

"You're upset 'cause Maggie's in there, and she blew you off last night."

"She didn't blow me off," Brawley groused. "Nothing to blow off. We're friends. Period."

"Right." Cash bounded up the stairs, Staubach beside him. "We won't stay long."

"Famous last words," Ty muttered, his conscience still eating at him.

Dottie was visiting her daughter for the holiday. Otherwise, she'd have shagged all their butts home. A wreath covered in autumn leaves and a goofy-looking turkey hung on her door. Her outside light spilled across the driveway.

Cash waited till all of them, dog included, crowded onto the small landing before he rapped on the door. Nothing. The music continued; the women's voices never stopped.

He knocked again, a little louder this time, and called out, "Pizza delivery!"

It went quiet inside. Through the door's window, Ty spotted Annie spread out on the old brown sofa. Maggie was sprawled in an oversized chair, her feet on the coffee table, while Tink sat cross-legged on the floor, painting her toenails.

One of those foofy girly lights hung over the coffee table, all white and crystals and candlelight. And damned if the women didn't look really good in the soft glow.

A big grin on her face, Annie jumped up from the sofa. When she threw open the door, neither he nor Brawley moved. Cash handed her the flowers, then scooped her up for a big hug and a kiss that was definitely X-rated. Staubach circled them, barking, and jumped up for a kiss, too.

Now, with a clearer view, Ty turned to the other women and about swallowed his tongue. This was how they dressed for an all-woman pajama party? He thanked God then and there he had three little boys tucked into bed at home instead of three little girls.

He'd expected flannel pajamas or baggy sweats and T-shirts. Wrong! Not a scrap of flannel in sight. Tink wore skin-tight black leggings and a short, black lace crop top that showcased her belly button.

His temperature spiked, and desire, unexpected and unwelcome, rushed through him. His nagging unease quadrupled. It had been a long time since he'd felt anything close to this. Almost four years because, carrying triplets, sex had pretty much been off the table from the get-go of Julia's pregnancy. Then—well, then things had gone to Hell in the proverbial handbasket, and their world had been dumped on its ass.

Nothing had ever been the same nor would it.

So why in the hell did his libido, long dormant, choose this moment to stand up and take notice? Frantic, he reminded himself that Tink was Annie's cousin—which meant in a couple days she'd be part of Cash's family. Which meant no fooling around. You didn't mess with family—and he sure as hell wasn't thinking long-term. A night, one night, of hot sex. That's all he needed.

But not with Tink.

Definitely not with Tink.

A bead of perspiration formed on his forehead, despite the cool night temperature.

Then Annie swatted Cash. "Go away. As much as I enjoyed that, you need to scram. This is a girls-only party."

"Come on, sweetheart. Throw a starving man a crumb. One dance. Then we eat and get out of your hair."

"No way."

Brawley gave Cash a nudge. "Step aside, wuss, and let the real men in." He waved the pizzas he carried under Annie's nose. "Look what Uncle Brawley's got."

Maggie pushed out of the chair. "Uncle Brawley, my behind. Leave the pizzas on the counter on your way out."

"You're a hard woman, Maggie Sullivan. No deal. The pizzas are gonna cost you a dance," Brawley said.

She looked him up and down, then crossed her arms. "I guess I'm not as hungry as I thought. I am not dancing with you."

"Give me a break, Mags. Don't hold grudges."

"I danced with you last night."

"Not long enough."

"Oh, please. If you want to dance that badly, go find yourself another Dallas cheerleader. I'm sure one of them will be more than happy to snuggle up with you."

Cash snagged Annie around the waist and led her into a dance in the cramped living room. As close as he held her, they didn't take up much space.

Ty listened to the give-and-take and knew he should offer to dance with Maggie. But that would leave Sophie with Brawley. The idea of them together, of her in his arms—especially in that outfit—didn't sit well. Which, when it came right down to it, was an even better reason to dance with Maggie.

"Come here, Red. Dance with *me*." He took her hand and swung her into a dance.

Brawley tipped his head to Sophie. "Guess that leaves you and me. Can't say this is gonna be a hardship, sugar." With that he pulled her close, and they moved to the music.

When the song ended and another started, Brawley called out, "Switch."

Laughing, everybody shuffled partners, and Ty found himself with Annie. "See, Cash?" He waved a hand between them. "Lots of space here. Not moving in on your woman."

"See you keep it that way." Cash twirled Sophie.

Staubach sniffed the air, looked longingly at the pizza, then entered the mix, knocking against legs and end tables as he circled the dancers.

The song switched again and so did the couples. Ty swallowed and placed his hand at Sophie's waist, touched bare skin above it. He bit back a curse. Soft. So damn soft. And warm.

His heart beat like an adolescent's, touching his first girl. What in hellfire was going on?

Then she looked up at him and smiled. If he'd been raised Catholic, he would have had to head straight to the nearest confessional.

Instead, with a groan, he tucked her into him, held tight, and simply quit fighting it. For the space of the song, he would simply be a man, not a widower. A long-forgotten feeling. Her warm breath teased him, and the rest of the world ceased to exist.

This time when the song ended, Maggie said, "Enough. I'm hungry, and you promised us food."

They sat at the table Annie had sanded and refinished. Ate pizza, drank beer, and told stories on each other while Staubach made the rounds, grinning as each of them tossed him chunks of pizza.

Ty watched Sophie, who sat quietly, taking it all in and smiling at some of the outlandish stunts they'd pulled. He swore a wistful expression settled over her face.

Hadn't she had this kind of closeness growing up? Good friends who could sit around a table and chew the fat? Or had the pampered little rich girl been above that sort of thing?

* * *

A couple hours later, the guys and their dog left. Sophie stood at the window. As the taillights faded into the distance, she wondered if Annelise truly realized how lucky she was.

Cash Hardeman. Her cousin couldn't have done any better. Despite their differences, they'd been made for each other.

And the camaraderie here. These wonderful people who had taken Annelise under their wings made her feel so at home.

Sophie heard Annelise lock the door, was aware of Maggie putting on some new music. Still, the room felt *quiet*. As if all the energy had jumped up and hopped in the old Caddy with the guys.

Staring into the Texas sky, seeking out familiar constellations, Sophie's mind opened to unwanted thoughts and worries. Nathan. She'd have to have another heart-to-heart with him. She shivered.

And her mortgage payment came due next week. Her heart sank. Good luck with that. She still hadn't managed a single new design.

Because Annelise's mother and her mother were sisters, everyone assumed she had money. Wrong. Annelise's mother had married money. Huge money. Her mother hadn't. And it had never really mattered.

Still didn't.

She'd make her payments. Always did, one way or another. She rolled her tense shoulders. Tonight wasn't for this.

Tonight was for celebrating. For dancing with a cowboy who made her all warm and fuzzy.

Determined to put money worries aside till after the wedding, she fixed a smile on her face. Turning to the others, she waved her bottle of midnight-blue polish. "Who'd like her nails done?"

Chapter Eight

Anxiety crawled through Sophie's stomach when she thought of sharing Thanksgiving dinner with what would be, in two more days, Annelise's family. A stranger in a world where everyone else knew each other. Not her forte.

She'd rather stay right here in Annelise's comfortable apartment and eat cold, leftover pizza from last night.

She'd rather have a red-hot poker stuck in her eye.

Well, no. She wouldn't rather that.

She wasn't antisocial. She liked people. Played well with others, actually. But she hated being the odd man out.

"Jeez, Sophie, I don't understand. Yesterday you were fine with dinner at Babs's."

"I know. I changed my mind, that's all."

Annelise came out of the bedroom, buttoning a beautiful soft blue blouse. She sniffed. "You made coffee. I love you."

"I sent Maggie off with a go-cup. She didn't want any breakfast. Said she had too much to do today." Reaching into a cupboard, Sophie grabbed a cup and handed it to Annelise. "Here you go. By the way, your dishes are great."

A slow smile lifted the corners of her cousin's lips. "Yeah. Funky, huh? Totally mismatched, but they work. I felt such a—a sense of freedom, I guess, to break away from all the rigidness I've always known. I can't put it into words."

Sophie shrugged. "Even when the walls are made of Swarovski crystal, a prison's still a prison."

"It wasn't that bad."

Sophie raised her brows.

"Okay, it was pretty limiting. Not my parents, but the demands of society, of being watched all the time. Is that why you moved to Chicago?"

"That and my Cubs." Sophie grinned. "Seriously? Even though I'm only on the periphery of your life, it washed over. There were times the paparazzi really bugged me. I honestly don't know how you stand it."

"The fish-bowl effect is a whole lot more diluted here. Although I understand every room within a hundred miles has been booked this weekend. All the photographers with their invasive, long lenses hoping to get shots of the wedding."

Annelise took a long drink of coffee, her eyes closing. "This is wonderful. And you've managed to avoid answering my question. Why don't you want to go to Babs's?"

Sophie sighed. "These are your friends, Annelise. Your new family. I don't know them. I don't belong at their holiday celebration."

Annelise slipped into a chair across from Sophie and laid a hand over one of hers. "If they're going to be my family, they'll be yours, too."

"I sure hope not," she muttered.

"What?"

Sophie felt the blush flood her checks. "Nothing. It's just, well, I'm not so sure I want them all as family members."

"Sophie London." Annelise's eyes narrowed. "It's Ty Rawlins, isn't it?"

The heat spread to her neck. "No."

"Liar, liar, pants on fire. Cash and I were concerned that if we got too near you on the dance floor at Bubba's, we'd both end up scorched. And again last night."

"Argh!" Sophie swatted at her. "You were not."

"Were, too."

"He's attractive, okay? But at the risk of sounding redundant, I'll remind you again he's a widower and the father of three. He lives in the middle of absolute nowhere with a bunch of long-horned cows and God only knows what else."

"Your point?"

"Finish your coffee, Annelise. I need to dry my hair." Her phone rang. She checked the caller ID and grimaced.

"What's wrong?"

"Nothing. I just—" With a shake of her head, she answered. "Hello, Nathan." She listened as he wished her a good holiday. "Yes, Happy Thanksgiving to you, too."

"Where are you, Sophie?"

"Away."

"Where?"

She said nothing.

After a few seconds, he said, "I've been thinking. Why don't I join you? Spend a little vacation time with you."

Her jaw tightened, and she noticed Annelise's interest in the conversation. Shoot! But she had to hold her ground. "No. That's not a good idea. I'm busy. I have to go now."

"Don't you hang up on me!"

"Excuse me?"

"I thought you liked me." His voice held a querulous whine.

"I did. Past tense. Just like you and me."

"Are you there with some guy?" His tone turned menacing.

She frowned. "No. I'm not. But even if I was, it's really none of your business. Good-bye." Despite his warning, or maybe because of it, she disconnected the call.

"Who's Nathan and why is he upsetting you?"

Sophie blew out her breath. "Nathan Richards. We dated a few times. He's a nice enough guy, but he wants more than I do."

"Block his calls on your cell." She bit her bottom lip. "Is he the reason you're staying awhile longer in Maverick Junction?"

"Annelise, don't worry about this. Concentrate on your wedding. On Cash."

"Is he why you want the apartment?"

"Boy, you must be a bulldog in court."

"I can be." Annelise kept her eyes fixed on her.

"Geez, let's get ready for Thanksgiving dinner."

"Thought you didn't want to go."

Sophie shrugged.

"You want to change the subject that badly."

"I can handle this."

"Oh, Sophie. You're way too nice. One of these days, it's going to get you in hot water."

* * *

Annelise's words rang in her ears as they walked into Cash's sister's house. Maybe she *was* too nice, because despite her earlier reluctance, here she was, about to have Thanksgiving dinner with a house full of near-strangers.

Within minutes, Sophie realized she needn't have worried. She'd never seen so much confusion or so many people gathered for a family get-together.

At both her and Annelise's houses, Thanksgiving and all other dinners were formal, sit-down affairs with a polite mingling beforehand over drinks and hors d'oeuvres.

Here, as she and Annelise made their way to the kitchen, they passed Babs's kids playing a game of tag while the men sat plastered to a mammoth television. Ty wasn't among them. Nor did she see the Triple Threat, as she'd started thinking of his boys. She felt momentary relief, chased by—disappointment?

She gave herself a mental head smack. *Don't be silly.*

The house itself was impressive. Open, spacious rooms. Beautiful hardwood floors. Wooden ceiling beams. And an enormous stone fireplace. This was a home. Despite the size, it welcomed a person. Warm, cozy, and lived-in. Babs had nailed it.

Cash scooped Annelise up for a hug and a drawn-out kiss. "Happy Thanksgiving, sweetheart."

"Happy Thanksgiving right back at you," she said.

Then he hugged Sophie and grinned. "Welcome to our dysfunctional family."

She laughed. "If that's the case, I should fit right in."

"The girls are in the kitchen." Matt tipped his head toward the rear of the house. "Follow your noses."

"Thanks, Matt," Annelise said. "It smells heavenly in here."

She was right, Sophie thought. She breathed deeply, taking in the mouthwatering aromas of homemade bread, roast turkey, and pumpkin pie. She could happily hyperventilate! She loved the holidays!

As they stepped into the kitchen, a mix of cheers and

boos erupted from the living room behind them. Somebody'd made either a touchdown or a boneheaded play.

"Men and their football." Mrs. Hardeman smiled and shook her head. "Sophie, it's so nice to see you again. I'm glad you came." She pecked her on the cheek, then hugged Annelise. "Don't you two look pretty?"

And that easily, Sophie realized, with no fuss or muss, she'd been welcomed into the family.

Annelise twirled, showing off her new skirt and top. "Maggie's work."

"Oh, you two were at her shop yesterday, weren't you?" Babs stepped away from the stove to greet them both with a hug. Taking the wine and flowers they offered, she asked, "What did you think, Sophie? Aren't our dresses beyond gorgeous?"

"Yes, they are. Everything in her place impressed me. Heck, the shop itself." She rolled her eyes. "I have to confess to more than a little apprehension beforehand. Bridesmaids' dresses are usually—"

"Humiliating?"

Sophie nodded.

"Ugly?"

She nodded again.

"To be used as rags the day after the wedding?" Babs laughed.

Sophie joined her. "Right again."

"Not my attendants' dresses," Annelise said. "I want you all to look gorgeous. To be happy—right along with me."

"And we are," Sophie said. "And thankful, to both you and Maggie."

Over the TV noise, she heard the front door open and a loud squeal. High-pitched children's voices.

"That would be Ty." Mrs. Taylor, Matt's mother and Ty's mother-in-law, laid down her dish towel.

Before she started toward the front room, though, Ty stuck his head into the kitchen, casserole in hand. "Sorry we're late. I went by my folks' place for a short visit and had trouble escaping. Mom sent this."

He passed the dish to his sister-in-law.

"Where are my grandbabies?"

"Destroying the front of the house, no doubt. It's been a trying morning."

"Too much going on." Mrs. Taylor went in search of the boys.

Babs lifted the foil and sniffed appreciatively. "Your mother's enchiladas."

"For Thanksgiving?" The question slipped out before Sophie could bite it back.

Ty sent her a bemused look. "Absolutely. Don't forget, you're in Texas now, darlin'." He ran a finger down her nose. "We eat enchiladas three hundred sixty five days of the year." Crossing to the fridge, he asked, "Beer in here, Babs?"

"Yes, sir."

Sophie watched as he helped himself. Obviously he spent a lot of time here and felt right at home.

Another round of cheering erupted from the guys.

"Damn. I'm missing the game." Ty kissed the top of his sister-in-law's head and took off for the TV.

"What would you two like to drink?" Babs held up the coffeepot. "This? Wine?"

Annelise pointed. "I'll have a cup of that."

"Do you have tea?" Sophie asked.

"Sure do." She swung open a cupboard door, displaying a huge selection. "Pick your poison."

The women talked and laughed. Cooked and tasted. Sophie chopped veggies for the salad and loved every minute of it. Thanksgiving in this family truly was more than a meal. Far more. A celebration.

And in a couple days, they'd all get together again to dance at Annelise and Cash's wedding.

A burst of childish laughter erupted from the front of the house, and Sophie smiled. She'd never spent a holiday with children. It was different; it was fun. It brought remembered excitement, the promise of things to come.

And a lot of worry. A lot of work. Yet everyone here seemed to take it in stride. She'd bet within a year, Annelise and Cash would be adding to the clan, starting their own branch of the family tree.

A sense of—what?—longing maybe, of wistfulness washed over her. She was so happy for her cousin, but tucked inside a tiny pocket of her heart? A wish for a family of her own. Yet the rational part of her brain understood she wasn't Annelise.

No, she'd be better off on her own. She'd never suffered from a broken heart, never cried into her pillow because some guy had walked away. Why? Because she'd never cared enough. None had ever touched her heart. Surely if it was in her makeup, she'd have toppled by now.

Ty's teasing jab at Brawley drifted into the kitchen. Ty Rawlins. Now there was a man who could probably make her cry into her pillow—and, if given the chance, very well might. And that scared the pants off her. Her phone vibrated in her pocket.

"Excuse me. Must be my mom and dad wishing me a Happy Thanksgiving." She wiped her hands on a towel and headed for the back deck.

"Hello?"

"What are you doing?"

Her stomach fell. She'd promised herself she'd check caller ID; she hadn't. "I'm busy, Nathan. I can't talk now."

"Can't or won't?"

She exhaled loudly. "Does it matter?"

"Yes."

"Fine, then. I don't want to talk to you."

"You know you don't mean that."

"Oh, but I do."

"You hung up on me earlier."

She rubbed a spot between her eyes. "We're getting ready to sit down to dinner. I have to go."

"We? Who's there with you?"

"Family." She closed her phone and sank down into one of the brightly colored deck chairs. Dropping her head in her hands, she swore. What was she going to do?

Ignore him. If he called back, she would *not* answer the phone.

"Trouble?"

The deep voice startled her. She looked over her shoulder to where Ty stood, all six-four of him looking a whole lot like trouble himself.

She shook her head. "Not really."

"You sure?"

"Yes." She threw him what she hoped was a blinding smile.

His gray eyes stared into hers, making her want to squirm.

"I think they actually are about ready to eat," he said. "Why don't we go back inside?"

Hand on the door, he hesitated. "Is this Nathan dangerous?"

She shook her head. "Just a pain."

"Sounded like more than that to me. If some jerk is bothering you..."

"No. It's okay." Yet something tugged deep inside her at the thought of this cowboy willing to go to bat for her. It had been a long time since anyone other than her family had her back.

Without another word, she stood and moved through the French doors, Ty right behind her.

*   *   *

Sophie wasn't sure how it had happened, but she found herself seated beside Ty. She looked quickly across the table at Annelise, who sent her an innocent smile.

Oh, this one was up to something. Good thing she'd be leaving on her honeymoon Saturday. Until then, Sophie decided she'd have to keep an eye on her. She shook out her napkin and laid it on her lap while chairs scraped and scooted as everyone took his place.

Once the group was seated, grace said, and plates passed, Babs frowned. "We're missing something."

"What?" her husband asked, his eyes darting the length of the food-laden, groaning table. "I can't imagine what else we could want."

"Babies. We need some new babies." She sent her brother a pointed look.

For a fraction of an instant, Cash had the look of a deer in headlights. Then he threw back his head and laughed. "Give us a chance to walk down the aisle first, sis."

"Don't tell me you haven't already been practicing."

From the far end of the table, their mother started singing. "La, la, la, la, la." She covered her ears. "I'm not hearing this."

"Oh, come on, Mom. You don't think your little boy's celibate, do you?" Babs tossed a mischievous grin at Cash.

Annelise flushed ten shades of red, and Cash laughed again.

"Barbara Jean," her dad said, "you're embarrassing Annie."

"Can I plead the fifth?" Cash asked, earning himself an elbow in the side from Annelise.

"There are children here," she whispered.

"It's all going over their heads," Babs said. "They're clueless."

Amazed, Sophie wondered what she'd missed out on by not having siblings. Was this normal? Talking about sex at the Thanksgiving table with the entire family around?

Babs shifted her attention to Ty.

On alert, he dropped a roll onto his plate and held up his hands. "Hey, don't look at me. I exceeded my biological footprint first time out of the gate."

"So, how's that new pasture down by the river working out, Matt?" Cash neatly changed the topic.

Sophie passed the sweet potato casserole to Ty. "Would you want more children? I mean if circumstances were different?"

"I...To be honest, it's not even a blip on my radar, Tink. I've pretty well got my hands full with those guys."

He nodded toward the small table where the kids squabbled and toyed with their food. Abilene, Babs's daughter, was busy playing mom.

"And," he continued, "it's kind of a moot point, considering."

She laid down her fork. "I'm sorry. I shouldn't have brought it up. It's just— You're so good with them. I thought maybe someday..." She trailed off.

"It's okay."

"No, it was stupid."

He placed a fingertip beneath her chin and forced her head up till she met his eyes. "It wasn't. And it's kind of nice to have someone look at me as a man rather than a widower."

"Ty—" She licked her lips.

"Tink?"

"Yes?"

"Eat your dinner before it gets cold. Babs isn't gonna let anybody have dessert till plates are cleaned, and I'm feeling rather partial to that pecan pie I spotted on the windowsill."

* * *

The day passed quickly, and Sophie wondered how she'd ever doubted she'd fit in here. She hadn't, for a single moment, felt like an outsider.

She sat at the small breakfast nook table talking to Cash's mom and Ty's mother-in-law about gardening. She loved flowers, and, when she traveled, she liked to learn about native species.

Annelise came up behind her and laid a hand on her shoulder. "We're ready to go."

"Oh, okay." Sophie jumped up.

"You and Cash go on ahead." Ty spoke from behind her. "I'll take Sophie home. That is, if she doesn't mind riding in the van with car seats and whiny, over-stimulated kids."

Again, she hadn't heard him come up. Didn't realize he was close. The man was stealthy.

Mindful that Cash's mother was right there, she moved away from the table. "Are you staying at Cash's tonight?" Sophie whispered.

"Do you mind?"

"No. Not at all. But what happened to last night's idea that abstinence makes the wedding night fires burn more fiercely?"

Annelise's eyes sparkled. "A couple really hot kisses out back on the deck changed my mind."

"Hmmm. I can see where that might do it."

"Thank you for understanding." She squeezed Sophie's hand. "You came all this way and here I am ignoring you."

Sophie laughed. "You're not ignoring me. We spent all day yesterday together...and last night. Besides, you're the bride. You can do whatever you want. It's the rule."

Her cousin hugged her, then turned to Ty. "Are you sure you don't mind?"

"If I minded driving a beautiful woman home, there'd be something seriously wrong with me." He hesitated. "And believe me, there's not a thing wrong with me."

Sophie flushed. *Beautiful?* The next second she kicked herself. Ty was a gentleman. Still, her hormones spiked like a sixteen-year-old who'd just been smiled at by the class heartthrob. It had to stop...didn't it?

"You know, I appreciate this. I really do. But tomorrow, I'm renting my own car. Since I'm staying longer than I'd planned, it'll be more convenient for everyone. Besides, I don't get to drive much in the city. It'll be fun to have my own wheels."

"I told you Cash will lend you one," Annelise said.

"I know, but I can rent my own." Though where the extra money would come from when the credit card bill rolled in, she had no idea. Something to worry about later.

"That's silly," Annelise argued.

"Probably. Still—"

Cash walked up in time to hear their conversation. He

shook his head. "Oh, yeah, the two of you are related, all right. Stubborn women. Both of you."

"You got that right," Sophie said. "So tell me, where's a good place to go?"

"To rent a car in Maverick Junction? Bear's place. He's got the best selection in town. And he's honest," Cash told her.

Ty shook his head and chuckled. "He's also the only car rental in town."

"True enough." Cash grinned.

After Annelise and Cash left, Sophie tracked down her hostess to thank her for the lovely day. "It's been wonderful, Babs."

"Well, don't be a stranger."

"I won't."

"Ty's taking you home?"

"Yes."

"He looks so much more relaxed, happier than I've seen him in a long time." She leaned over and kissed Sophie's cheek. "Thank you."

"I haven't done anything."

"Oh, I think you have. And you will."

Sophie frowned.

"Just go with it, Sophie. Don't overthink it."

* * *

Five minutes later, weighed down with leftovers, a tired little boy holding her hand, Sophie stepped out into the cool Texas air. She tipped her head and stared up into the star-strewn sky.

"Mommy's up there," came a whisper beside her. "Daddy told me."

Heart clutching, she looked down into eyes the same gray as his daddy's. "Yes, sweetheart, she is. And she's watching you right now, blowing you a kiss good night."

The child held out his hand, then curled it. "Caught it."

When he grinned up at her, tears filled her eyes. She glanced up and met Ty's, staring at her across the top of the van. Her throat clogged. How did he deal with this, day after day after day?

She had a thousand questions, but now wasn't the time to ask them. Maybe she'd never find a good time. After all, what gave her the right to ask questions that would undoubtedly cause hurt?

By the time they reached her house, all three kids were fast asleep. "How do you get them all in the house and back to sleep?"

"Once they're out, nothing wakes them, thank God. I carry them inside one at a time and tuck them into bed."

When she slid out, he did, too, quietly closing his door.

"You don't need to walk me up."

His brows rose. "Didn't we already have this discussion?"

She sighed. "Yes, but there wasn't a trio of little boys sleeping in the vehicle then."

"Nope. Sure wasn't."

He took her hand, and she sucked in her breath. What was there about this man that affected her so quickly, so easily?

As they headed down the drive, Ty said, "They never knew their mother. She—we lost her before they could even be released from the hospital. They were preemies, you know, which is pretty usual with multiple births."

He looked toward the sky. "In Julia's case, with her heart, they came even earlier. Once her system started shutting down, things happened pretty quickly. The doctor had to take the babies to save them."

His thumb rubbed across the back of her hand, sending shivers through her. "I'm only telling you this so you understand. They've seen pictures of her, and their grandma and grandpa have told them lots of stories about her."

"And you told them she's a star in the heavens looking down on them."

He nodded. "Makes her a little more concrete."

"Oh, Ty." A tear slipped down her cheek, and she swiped at it. "I'm sorry. Really. For everything. For your loss. For my stupid tears—"

"Tears aren't stupid, Tink." He thumbed a fresh one off her cheek. "You've got a big heart. I like that about you." For the space of several heartbeats, he leaned close, then took a step back. "Good night, Sophie London."

"Good night, Ty Rawlins."

She sat on the top step outside her apartment for a long time after his taillights disappeared, thinking about the cowboy who'd brought her home. It couldn't be easy to raise three boys alone. Or bury your wife when they were only days old. Yet here he was, not only doing it, but doing one heck of a great job with it.

The wreath on Dottie's kitchen door caught her eye. Thanksgiving. A day to reflect on all that was right and good. She'd have to say that Ty Rawlins came under that heading, like it or not.

But he wasn't hers to be thankful for . . . nor would he ever be. Their lives were about as far apart as it was possible to get. And wasn't that a shame.

Chapter Nine

By the time Sophie opened her eyes, the sun was well up. She yawned and stretched, her toes curling into the soft blue sheets. One thing about Annelise Montjoy. When she did something, she went all the way, no holding back.

And this sweet apartment was proof positive. Everything about it spelled comfort. Joy. Sophie couldn't think of a single thing she'd change.

She plumped her pillow and slid a second one beneath her head. So peaceful. Outside her open window, a bird sang practically nonstop. No car horns, no buses, no sirens. She could lie here for hours.

Speaking of hours—she had them. She grinned and stretched again, arms above her head. She had nowhere she had to be until tonight's rehearsal and dinner. What should she do between now and then? Lie in the sun? Read? Fill that wonderful old claw-foot tub with bubbles and lounge in it until she was a wrinkled prune?

Nope. Work. She needed to work.

Pouting, she closed her eyes and pulled the covers over her head. She didn't want to work. But wasn't that the reason she'd decided to stay in Maverick Junction? To get caught up with her spring line of greeting cards?

No. She sighed. She couldn't even pretend that was the case. Truth was, she'd chosen to hide from Nathan Richards. And wasn't that a sad state of affairs.

Where was her backbone? She didn't generally wimp out. In her defense, she *had* tried. She'd told him time and again they were over, there was nothing there.

Ty's ruggedly handsome face, his heart-stopping dimples, all that thick, gorgeous black hair and gray, gray eyes popped into her mind. The heat when he touched her. She went all tingly and admitted to herself she wouldn't do much running if he was the one doing the chasing.

But then, he wouldn't chase, would he?

If the number of female eyes following their progress through Bubba's and on the dance floor was any indication, he had no trouble finding accommodating women friends.

What was he doing this morning? Besides fixing oatmeal or whatever it was you fed four-year-olds for breakfast. Did he have a housekeeper? He must. Otherwise, how could he ever begin to keep up, to get everything done?

She couldn't imagine. And didn't want to.

Maybe she'd take a walk before she settled down to work. Check out her new, temporary neighborhood. Walking usually started her creative juices flowing. She scampered out of bed and dug in her suitcase for a pair of sweatpants and a long-sleeve T-shirt since there'd been a definite chill in the air last night. She found her old sneakers tucked into one of the side suitcase pockets.

Outside on the landing, she hesitated. She didn't know Maverick Junction. Would she get lost? How could she in such a small town? Even if she did, she could always ask for directions. Everybody in town had to know Dottie Willis.

After she'd covered several streets, she realized that, while the town might not rate high on the best-dressed list, it had character. Most of all, she loved the porch swings. They spoke of lazy summer evenings. Of afternoon iced tea. Of family.

An hour later, the walk no longer seemed like such a good idea. Storm clouds rolled in out of nowhere, and the world turned dark and ominous. She headed her sneakers toward home. Or at least she hoped so. She'd done a little window-shopping and had covered every street in town—some twice—so there was a good possibility she'd gotten turned around.

A fat drop of rain splattered her face. Uh-oh.

Before she'd taken two more steps, someone in Heaven opened the spigot full blast. Inside a New York minute, her hair lay plastered to her head, her T-shirt and pants clung to her like second skin, and her shoes sloshed.

Exasperated, she slogged on. Hadn't she left Chicago thinking she would get away from the cold? Right now she was freezing...and absolutely, totally miserable.

Behind her, an engine rumbled. The big black truck slowed and pulled to the curb. Ty Rawlins leaned across the seat and threw open the door.

"Get in. You look like a skinned rat."

"Gee, thanks. You use that line on all the ladies?"

"Nope. Only the ones foolish enough to get themselves caught outside in a monsoon."

She hesitated. Water dripped from her hair, her hands, ran down her nose and off her chin. "I'll get your truck all wet."

"Been wet before. Imagine it'll be wet again." He dug a towel out from beneath the seat. "Here you go. You can either wrap it around you or throw it on the seat under you."

She wanted the warmth badly but tossed the rumpled towel on the seat before climbing in.

"I'll turn on the heat." He flipped a switch, and blessed warmth circulated through the cab.

"How is it you manage to show up just when I need you?" The rain hammered incessantly against the truck's roof, and she had to raise her voice to be heard.

Hand on the gear knob, his truck thrumming, Ty grinned. "Didn't you know? I'm one of those comic book superheroes." He patted the dashboard. "Me and my trusty steed. I'm known in these parts as..." His voice deepened. "Black Truck Man."

She laughed and punched his arm lightly. "In your dreams."

"You might be surprised at my dreams lately."

She swore all the air had been sucked from the truck.

He cleared his throat. "How 'bout we chalk it up to good luck."

"For me, maybe. Major inconvenience for you."

He studied her. "Oddly enough, not what I'm thinking." With a glance in his rearview mirror, he pulled out onto the street.

"Had to stop at the bank this morning after I dropped the boys off at my mom's. No day care today because of the holiday, so they'll spend some time with her and come home spoiled as all get-out. Then I ran by Doc's place to pick up some medicine."

"Is one of the boys sick?"

"No." He shook his head. "Doc Gibson is the vet here in town, the one Brawley's been helping. He's getting on in years, though. Not sure how much longer he's gonna be able to take care of our animals."

"Is there another nearby?"

"Nope."

And that, she guessed, was the end of that conversation. Which was okay. She liked Ty. He was easy to be with, the silence friendly.

When he pulled into her drive, he again reached beneath the seat, this time pulling out a collapsible umbrella.

"What's with this?" she asked.

Ty frowned in confusion. "An umbrella. It's raining."

"Believe me, I noticed," she said ruefully. "I mean, what's with the seat? It's like Mary Poppins's bag. You reach under it and, voilà, whatever you need appears."

"Ah, wouldn't the boys love the idea of a truck that's totally supercalifragilisticexpialidocious."

"You're up on your Disney movies."

"Who hasn't seen *Mary Poppins*? I think it's a rite of passage."

"True. Your boys have watched it?"

"At least fifty times." He sang a few bars of the catchy tune.

She blinked. Not only did he know the words, he had a darn good baritone voice.

He stopped, laughed. "Sorry about that. It's a rare occasion when I subject anyone to my singing."

"That's too bad. You should sing more often."

Trailing a finger along the back of her wet hand, he said, "For reasons I don't begin to understand, Sophie, you make me want to do exactly that."

She didn't know what to say.

Torrential rain pounded the roof and defied the windshield wipers. Inside the truck felt very intimate. Too intimate. Time to leave. She reached for the door handle.

"Wait a minute." When he hopped out, she gaped at him. "What are you doing?"

Instead of answering, he slammed the door shut, popped the umbrella, and ran around the front of the truck. Coming to her door, he opened it, holding the umbrella over her as she stepped down.

"Let's go."

"You don't need to walk me in. I'm already soaked."

"Don't argue." He hunched his shoulders. "I'm getting wet. And we're not walking anywhere. We're running. Come on." He grabbed her hand.

"Oh for…" But she raced across the drive, then up the steps with him. By the time they reached the landing, they were both sopping wet.

When she stepped inside the apartment, he followed, leaving the umbrella outside on the stoop.

They looked at each other and started laughing.

"The umbrella didn't help much, did it?"

She shook her head.

His gaze dropped to her shirt, and his laughter faded. "You might want to, ah…" He wet his lips.

She looked down. Oh, Jiminy Crickets! The white tee she'd pulled on that morning had turned totally transparent. The barely-there bra left very little to the imagination.

"I'd better be on my way."

"Wait." She reached out, took his hand. She didn't want him to leave. Despite all the reasons Ty was totally wrong for her, she wanted to spend more time with him. With this man who told his children their mother watched over them from the starry night sky. Who worried about her problem with Nathan.

She had a batting average of exactly zero when it came to picking guys. Yet Ty tempted her. Ty with his three boys. A ranch. Cattle. A man who knew who Tinker Bell was. Knew the words to Disney songs and had a magnificent voice.

Dimples you could get lost in. A mouth that looked like sin itself.

She'd be crazy to tempt fate. Still, she heard herself ask, "Why don't you stay for a cup of coffee? Get warmed up. I'll put on a pot right after I change. Before I do that, though, I'll get you a towel. I'd offer to dry your clothes, but..." She shrugged and held out her hands, palms up. "No laundry here."

"You sure? About me staying?"

Her mind screamed *no*. Her mouth said, "Absolutely. Unless you have something else you have to do, somewhere else you need to be."

"Nope. I'm more than happy right here where it's dry. For now, I'll have that coffee and wait for the rain to let up. Don't think it's gonna hang around long."

She hurried into the bath and pulled a couple towels for him. "Here you go. I found this on one of the shelves. My guess is that it's Cash's. I'm sure he won't mind if you borrow it." She tossed Ty a faded green T-shirt.

He snatched it one-handed out of the air. "Thanks. Now go dry off and change before you get sick. Can't have a snuffling, sneezing maid of honor."

While she stripped and toweled off, her mind kept wandering to the fact that only a single wall separated her naked body from Ty's tall, muscular one.

Quit going there, Sophie London! What is wrong with you?

Taking herself firmly in hand, she reminded herself that Ty was Cash's friend. He'd seen her out, caught in a deluge, and stopped to help. He didn't want her sick for the wedding. Nothing more, nothing less. And unless she wanted to make a fool of herself, she'd keep that firmly in mind.

In dry jeans and a blouse, her hair tied back, she walked into the kitchen. Ty, wearing Cash's old shirt, stood with cup in hand, watching the slow drip of the coffeemaker.

"Hope you don't mind. I made myself at home. You gonna have a cup?"

"No. I'll make tea." She busied herself with the task. "I sure hope you're right about this rain. Otherwise, Annelise will be one upset bride. The ceremony and reception are both outside. It can't rain tomorrow." Her eyes widened. "It can't rain tonight. We've got rehearsal."

"See, that's the thing about Mother Nature." Ty hooked a thumb in his front pocket. "She's female."

Sophie raised a brow. "And...?"

He shrugged. "She's gonna do exactly what she wants, when she wants, darlin'. Regardless of anyone's plans."

When she opened her mouth, he held up a hand. "Now, hold on a minute and let me finish. In this case, you don't need to worry. According to The Weather Channel, tomorrow is gonna be the kind of day every bride hopes for. This front blew in fast, and it's gonna blow out the same way. By tonight's rehearsal, we'll never know it was here. Everything'll be dried up."

"I sure hope you're right."

"I am."

She gaped at him.

"Superhero, remember? I know things." He tapped the side of his head, then nodded toward her computer. "You said you design greeting cards. Do you do that on your laptop?"

"Yes, which is convenient. I can work anywhere."

"Got some on there I can look at?"

She sent him a smile. "Sure. Dottie actually has wireless here, which makes my life a lot simpler." She hit power and brought up her website. "I can stay plugged in to everything."

"Yeah, she wants to be able to Facebook with her grandkids."

"Do you Facebook, Ty?"

"You kidding?" He grimaced. "I don't have time. The only books I'm into are the Little Golden Books. *Goldilocks and the Three Bears, Doctor Seuss. The Little Engine That Could.* I use my computer for work. Period."

He picked up a chunk of blue and gold stone and turned it over in his hand. "Pretty. What is it?"

"Lapis lazuli. It promotes creativity. Fires up the imagination."

He shrugged and laid it on the table.

"You don't believe in the power of crystals?" she asked.

"Whatever floats your boat, Tink."

She studied him. Did he realize what a mass of contradictions he was? How could he stand there and call her Tink, yet deny the magic of crystals?

Turning back to her laptop, she scrolled down the page to show him samples of her cards.

"Nice. Your artwork is spectacular."

"Thanks."

"You draw—or paint—them all yourself?"

She nodded.

"Impressive." He moved closer to the screen, squinted, then scrolled to another and then another. "I see lots of fairies, Sophie." He glanced at the sun catchers he'd noticed in her window. "Kind of like those."

"I put at least one on every card. My signature, sort of."

"Interesting."

A ping sounded, signaling a new e-mail message. She frowned.

"Go ahead and check it. I'm gonna freshen up my coffee." He glanced out the window. "Looks like the rain's slowing down, so I'll hit the road here in a minute."

Though a piece of her sighed in disappointment at that, she logged on and pulled up the new message. "Oh, phooey."

"A problem?"

She started. She hadn't heard him move behind her.

"No." She chewed her lip, wishing she could confide in him. It might help to simply talk this over. Independence was great, but at times it would be nice to have someone to lean on. "Maybe," she added. "Nothing I can't handle."

"Okay, then. I'm gonna be going. The sun's trying to peek through the clouds. Gotta get that medicine home to Ray or he'll be madder than a hornet."

He stopped at the sink and rinsed his cup.

Admirable, she thought. A man who cleaned up after himself. But, then, he'd probably had to learn, hadn't he? Maybe he missed someone to lean on, too.

"Thanks for the coffee, Tink."

"Thanks for the ride."

Hand on the doorknob, he hesitated, turned back. Nodding at her laptop, he said, "Guess you'll be next to walk down the aisle."

"Me?" She shook her head. "No way."

"Your boyfriend might think differently."

"He's not my boyfriend."

Ty looked skeptical. "You sure about that?"

"Oh, yes. Very."

"He's the one who called yesterday?"

"Yes."

"Seems the two of you have some wires crossed. I'm guessing he still thinks you're a couple."

"Because he's not listening."

"Hmmm." With that, he closed the door gently behind himself.

Hmmm? What the heck did he mean by that?

If she didn't know better, she'd swear she detected a touch of jealous in there. But that was ridiculous. Since there was nothing between them, there was nothing to be jealous of.

And if Nathan was her boyfriend, she'd never have danced with Ty the way she had the other night. The memory of his strong, work-roughened hand on her bare skin caused an instant heat wave, and she fanned herself.

What if Ty was her boyfriend? But he wasn't and never would be. All things considered, that was probably a good thing. No, not probably. *Was* a good thing.

Wasn't it?

Tempted to run after him, to ask him what he'd meant, she forced herself to walk to the window instead. She watched as he hurried through the still misting rain. His truck rumbled to life, and he backed out of the drive.

Sophie glanced at her laptop, and her mind shifted to Nathan. Would distance and time be enough to turn the trick?

* * *

Who the hell was Nathan? Ty drove toward his ranch, his new Toby Keith CD for company. He could have sworn Annie'd told him Sophie wasn't with anyone. Sophie herself had said she wasn't with anyone. If that was true, why would this jerk keep calling her? Send love notes?

He'd had no business reading her e-mail. He knew that. And he honestly hadn't meant to. But it had been right there when he'd come up behind her.

He couldn't help himself. He'd stood there, coffee in hand, breathing in her scent. She'd pulled that incredible blond hair into a damp, stubby ponytail.

Then he'd looked down at those hands, so delicate, so dainty. She wore a single thin, golden ring, several colored stones winking from it, on her right-hand thumb. Her fingers had stilled on the keyboard, and he simply hadn't thought. Had read the message before he could stop himself. And hated it. Hated that Nathan had a place in Sophie's life.

Thrown into the mix was his own sense of betrayal. Not on Sophie's part. On his own. For the first time since Julia died, he found himself attracted to another woman. He felt disloyal. Felt like a cheating SOB. He'd never quit feeling married.

Yet here he was with all these emotions, and he didn't know what to do with them. It was like someone had rammed a stick down his throat and was stirring everything up.

Part of him said to stand down. Another part wanted to test the water. But if Sophie had a boyfriend, he'd back off, no questions asked. Whoa! Back off? From what? There was nothing, absolutely nothing, between himself and Ms. Sophie London. Nothing to back away from.

Not yet.

So why this storm raging inside him, one almost as vio-

lent as the one that had dumped two inches of rain on them?
What *was* he feeling? Jealousy? Stupid! He pounded the
steering wheel.

He nearly drove off the road as a flash of fear ripped
through him. Fear of loving someone, of losing that someone.

He wouldn't survive it again.

Wouldn't, ever, put himself in a position where he'd have
to. He couldn't.

Tink had to be strictly off-limits from here on out.

* * *

The rehearsal went well. Ty had wanted to cry off but knew
he'd be out of line. His pal was getting married tomorrow,
and he owed it to him to do his part.

The rain, as he'd promised, was only a memory.

Rosie, Cash's housekeeper, rode herd on the boys while
they went through the drill. Annie and Cash had decided to
marry right here on the ranch under the hopefully rainless
blue sky rather than in a church. As they ran through the
practice a second time, relatives and friends milled around,
watching or simply exploring. He guessed for a lot of them,
this was their first experience with a real, honest-to-
goodness, working Texas ranch.

Annie's life before she'd landed in Maverick Junction
had been board meetings, power suits, and elbow-rubbing
with the rich and famous. Her great-grandfather, Digger
Montjoy, had hit pay dirt when he'd discovered the biggest
oil field in the state on his land. About a year later, he'd hightailed it to Boston with his money to avoid a scandal...and
to separate his wife and mistress.

Annie might have been born with a silver spoon in her mouth, but Ty had watched her, day after day, dressed in boots, jeans, and tees shoveling manure with the best of them.

He flat-out admired the woman. Cash was one lucky bastard.

And from the look on his friend's face when the preacher said he could now kiss the bride, no doubt Cash knew it.

Hoots and whistles sounded as the kiss continued.

"Okay, you two," Brawley drawled. "Save something for the wedding. And the wedding night."

The rehearsal dinner, rather than an expensive catered affair or a sit-down in some stuffy, out-of-town black-tie restaurant, was a down-home buffet served in the farmhouse dining room. Guests spilled onto the wraparound porch and outside onto picnic tables scattered across the yard.

Plate in hand, Sophie came up beside him. "I'll never get everyone straight. I know Babs and Matt, Rosie and Hank, Maggie, Brawley, and Mel. I met Kinsey at Christmas a couple years ago."

"Speaking of Kinsey, glad she made it," Ty said. "Annie was more than a little nervous about her flight, with the weather and all."

"I know. And Kinsey had to be here. Without her, it's doubtful any of this would have happened. She and Annelise were sorority sisters in college, and Kinsey took her in and gave her a much-needed rest during that infamous cross-country motorcycle trip."

Ty added a healthy portion of potato salad to his plate. "Want some?"

She nodded. "Not that much, though."

He scooped up a spoonful. "Good?"

"Perfect."

He plopped it onto her plate. "Annie's grandpa seems like a great guy."

"He is." Sophie's eyes misted. "It's a miracle to see him well again. Thanks to Cornelia."

"And Annie," Ty said.

"Yes, and Annelise."

"You don't ever call her Annie?"

Sophie's forehead creased. "No. She's always been Annelise. I never think of her as Annie."

"Hmmm." He scanned the room. "Guess it's situational. In the boardroom, Annelise probably fits. Here on the ranch, Annie's just right."

They were all here, Ty thought. All the people who meant so much to the bride and groom. Cash's mom and dad, his sister and her husband and kids, Annie's parents and grandfather, and her newfound great-aunt along with their best friends.

"Want to sit outside?" he asked.

"Definitely."

A small body slammed into his leg as he stepped out the door, and two arms wrapped around it. Jonah. He hunkered down so they were eye-to-eye.

"What's going on, partner?"

"Josh was crying, so Rosie gave him a cookie. She gave us one, too."

"Is Josh okay?"

"Yeah, he falled down but he didn't bleed."

Sophie laughed. "That's the standard? No blood, no injury?"

Ty shrugged. "For the most part, yeah. What can I say? We're a household of guys."

He ruffled his son's dark hair, freshly trimmed for tomorrow's wedding. That in and of itself was a minor miracle. Taking three little boys—and himself—into the barber. Cliff had been doing hair, though, since forever and handled them well. Ty himself had sat in the man's chair when he was his sons' age.

"Well, then, no harm, no foul," he told Jonah.

"But, Daddy, we already had a cookie. This makes…" He raised two pudgy fingers. "Two."

"That's okay." Ty chuckled. "It's a party."

"So I can eat this?" He held up the sugar cookie, its pink icing coating his fingers.

"Absolutely."

"Want a bite?" he offered.

"No, thanks, bud. I'll get one later."

Jonah's little face broke out into a huge grin. "Thanks, Daddy. It's okay," he yelled to his brothers across the yard. "Daddy says it's okay! We can eat 'em."

He tore off through the grass to join his siblings.

"Must make you feel omnipotent," Sophie murmured.

"What?"

"Having your word observed as law."

He chuckled and, catching a strand of her pale hair between his fingers, gave it a tug. "Oh, if only that was true, Tink. If only. You have no idea how many times they overrule me. One-on-one, or three-on-one. There are days when I truly wonder who's running the zoo."

He took her arm. "Come on. I'm hungry."

Together, plates loaded, they sat at a little table under an oak tree. This was good, he thought. Very good. The temperature was Texas perfect. Nobody could ask for better. The day's rain had dried up and left a clear sky. Stars blinked to life in the heavens, his boys, stuffed with cookies, rolled around in the yard with Staubach, and he was sharing dinner with a beautiful, if off-limits, woman.

He was suddenly very glad he'd changed his mind and come tonight.

Chapter Ten

Stumbling into the kitchen, Sophie raised the window over the sink. The trill of a bird caught her attention. Must be that early bird. The one that caught the worm. Well, he could have it. For herself, she'd rather do brunch. Mornings weren't her favorite thing.

Nights sure could be, though, when they included dreams like the one she'd had last night! Starring in it with her? Ty Rawlins. The supersexy cowboy. Whew! Sophie fanned herself. Now there was an interesting man.

And today, Annelise would marry *her* cowboy. As maid of honor, Sophie had a thousand and ten things to do.

But before she started on any of them, she intended to indulge herself in a much-needed cup of tea. Last night's rehearsal dinner had been...well, like a dream, too. Who'd have thought a late evening picnic could be so romantic? Even with all those people milling about, enjoying themselves, it had seemed so intimate.

Through her open window, Sophie heard a neighbor mowing his lawn. From the sounds of it, he'd just run the machine through a mound of gravel.

Settled at the kitchen table, she dunked her tea bag and let her mind wander over the evening.

Ty stoked her hormones into an intense storm. She'd like to blame part of that on the foreignness of her situation. Being here in Texas. Living in this strange apartment. All the new people she'd met. In all honesty, she didn't know that she could.

Still, they'd eaten under the huge oak tree and talked about nothing, about everything. They'd laughed.

His boys, dirty and thoroughly worn out, had joined them one by one. Josh had been first. Tired and more than a bit cranky, he'd crawled onto Ty's lap.

Intrigued, she'd watched as he'd cajoled the boy out of his foul mood by feeding him birdlike bites of Rosie's coconut cake. Then he'd leaned across the table and hand-fed her a piece. When a flake of coconut stuck to her lip, he'd thumbed it off, then eaten it himself, his eyes holding hers.

Every nerve ending in her body short-circuited. The cowboy was lethal without even breaking a sweat. What would it be like if he turned his charisma to full power?

The cool night air became supercharged.

As she fought to get her feet under her, to find her bearings, another of the boys stumbled across the grass to join them.

"Hi, Daddy." He propped his elbow on Ty's knee and stared up at him.

"Hi, Jonah."

"Is Josh okay?"

He ruffled his son's hair. "Oh, my little sentry. You have to make sure everything and everybody is okay, don't you?"

Big-eyed, Jonah nodded.

"I'm tired," Josh said.

Jonah dropped to the grass and patted a spot beside him. "Lay down here. With me."

Josh looked up at Ty. "Is that okay, Daddy?"

"Absolutely."

Josh slid off his knee and, with the abandonment of young children, wrapped himself around his brother.

"You, too, Daddy." Jonah ran his hand over the grass. "Right here."

Ty glanced at Sophie. "You game?"

She hesitated only a fraction of a second. "Sure. Why not?" After one last sip of her lemonade, she stood, then stretched out on her side on the cool, green grass beneath the tree, facing Jonah and Josh.

Ty sprawled on the other side of the boys. He plucked a blade of grass and grinned at her. "Watch. Within two minutes, Jesse will be here."

He was right. The words had barely left his mouth when Sophie heard the war whoop, and Jesse took a flying leap onto his dad. Ty grunted, then grabbed his son, rolled onto his back and lifted him in the air like a weighted barbell.

Sophie found herself captivated. He was so easy, so natural with them.

After a couple minutes of roughhousing, they all settled in and lay on their backs, watching the stars come to life in the vast Texas sky. Ty pointed out constellations to her and the boys.

She'd had a little taste of Heaven and had been sorry when the evening ended.

And now, by the time the sun set tonight, Annelise Montjoy would be Annelise Hardeman, a married woman. Destined to be one of the wealthiest women in the country, she'd call the Whispering Pines Ranch home.

Annelise was in love. The big L. A love that started with Cash and extended to his family, friends, and life. The ranch was a huge part of that.

Her cousin looked forward to living here in Maverick Junction, Texas. To calling it home.

Sophie sipped her tea and smiled. When she'd hopped aboard that plane in Chicago, she'd seriously worried Annelise might be headed into a gigantic mistake.

She couldn't have been more wrong.

Her cousin truly had struck gold. It had nothing to do with money or fame, and everything to do with living well. Living happily.

No doubt Annelise would. Cash Hardeman was handing her the world.

Sophie didn't want to envy her. She really didn't. But, oh, it was hard not to. When she left here, she'd return to Chicago. To an empty apartment.

She shook her head. No. She'd return to the apartment she'd chosen, would pay for with her own labor, and had decorated beautifully. To a life of friends, her Cubs, and nights spent at Wrigley Field eating hot dogs and drinking cold sodas.

That was her life, a life that fit her, and it was a good one.

Unbidden came the memory of last night. Of lying in the cool grass with Ty and the boys. Of studying the stars in the endless sky.

Her breath hitched, and she stood.

Not her life. Not her world.

And enough of this. No pity parties today. Today was all about smiles, good thoughts, and happy-ever-afters.

The crystal sun catcher in the window sent an arch of rainbow-hued light across the hardwood floor. Moving to the window she looked out at a cloudless blue sky. *Happy is the bride the sun shines on.* Well, Annelise should be one giddy gal, then. What a gorgeous day.

A door opened and shut downstairs. Dottie. She'd come home last evening. Throwing on a pair of jeans and a beautiful silk short-sleeve top she'd found in Come Again, her favorite vintage shop in Chicago, Sophie dashed outside and down the stairs.

She rapped on the door, and the turkey on the Thanksgiving wreath bobbed its head. "Dottie?"

"On my way." A moment later the door flew open. Clad in a pink nightdress and robe and wearing furry pink bunny slippers, Dottie wrapped Sophie up in a huge hug. "Come on in, sweetie. I was inhaling my first cup of coffee when you knocked. Figured I'd better rev up my system before the day gets in full swing. Want one?"

"No, I already had some tea."

"How about a toffee-oatmeal cookie?" She slid a plate in front of Sophie. "Oatmeal's breakfast food, you know."

Sophie laughed. There was some sort of bent truth to that. Cookies for breakfast? What the heck. Why not? She gave in to temptation.

Taking her first bite, she closed her eyes. "Seriously, Dottie, you could make a fortune on these."

"That would turn baking into a business instead of a joy, wouldn't it?" She brushed the idea aside. "Besides, who, in his right mind, would pay good money for these?"

Sophie raised her hand.

Dottie swatted at her. "Go on."

Sophie relaxed at Dottie's homey pink island, surrounded by pink walls, counters, and flooring. "How was your trip? Your daughter and her family all well?"

Dottie clasped her hands in front of her. "Oh, we had such a good time. My grandchildren...well, they're brilliant. Absolutely brilliant. Every single one of them." Her eyes sparkled.

Somehow, while they talked, a cold glass of milk appeared in front of Sophie. Not skim or fat-free. Oh, no. The real stuff. She luxuriated in the nearly-forgotten taste and texture.

"The wedding's not till two, but I have to be at the ranch early. Makeup, hair, mani, pedi, the whole nine yards."

"Isn't it wonderful?" Dottie's expression grew wistful. "Cash and Annie. The minute they pulled into my drive, I knew they were made for each other. Annie on that fancy new Harley, and Cash in his grandpa's old blue Caddie." She clapped her hands together. "I'm so happy for them."

"Me, too." Serious now, Sophie said, "The family owes you a huge debt of gratitude for giving Annelise a home and taking such good care of her. When she rode into town, she didn't know anyone, and no questions asked, you took her under your wing."

Dottie clucked. "Bosh! The girl's a gem. I absolutely loved having a young thing here at the house again. And now you. Does my old heart good."

"Oh, but—"

"Now, I need to get a move on, too," Dottie said. "I promised Rosie I'd help with some of the last-minute details."

"Haven't they hired people to take care of everything?"

Dottie nodded. "Sure they did. Caterers, decorators, photographers, florists. You name it. Annie's mother insisted. She even brought in some people from back East. Doesn't mean Rosie's not gonna be fussing, though. The woman's like a second mama to Cash, and her little boy's getting married today."

Exactly that, Sophie thought. Exactly what she'd been thinking about before she came downstairs. All-encompassing love. They had it here in Maverick Junction. In spades.

Not that she didn't. Her mother and father loved her. She'd never doubted that. But it had been different. She had no brothers or sisters. Her only cousin was Annelise, another only child.

Their subdued and refined family get-togethers couldn't hold a candle to last night's rehearsal dinner. The family Thanksgiving.

Until now, though, they'd always been enough. What was it about this town that left her feeling unsettled? Unsatisfied.

Jittery with nerves, she laid a hand over her stomach.

Well, she'd get over all of this fast enough once she returned to Chicago. To her Starbucks, her delis, her life.

Dottie had to know she wasn't here long-term. Unlike Annelise, she wouldn't be staying. But, like so many other things, that wasn't a discussion for today. It would wait.

"The limo's coming for me in..." Sophie checked the bubblegum-colored wall clock with pink flamingos at the end of each hand. "Forty minutes. Can you be ready? We'll ride together."

"In a limo?"

"Sure."

Dottie did a little happy dance. "Oooh, I'll be ready." Her eyes rounded. "I rode in a limo in Dallas, you know, to

Annie's big fancy fund-raiser. Cash and Annie treated me like royalty. Annie bought me the most gorgeous dress I've ever seen. And the jewelry." She put a hand to her heart. "Oh, my."

Sophie grinned. "I saw pictures of you that night, and all I can say is, wow! You knocked them all dead."

"What a magical night, and they shared it with me. Oh, and now I'm going to cry." She swiped at her tears. "Happy, happy tears."

Sophie's eyes misted as she hugged this woman who had been so kind to her cousin and now to her. "Okay." Hands on Dottie's shoulders, she pulled back. "The wedding. Are you planning to dress at the ranch?"

"Yep. I've got everything all ready." She nodded to a garment bag and a little tote. "Came home last night, unpacked, and repacked." She shook her head. "I've never been so busy in my life. And I love it."

* * *

When they pulled up at the ranch, Sophie and Dottie both plastered their faces to the limo's window. Everywhere they turned, the place was a veritable beehive of activity.

All the horses had been moved to outer paddocks and the entire area groomed. White paper lanterns hung from the trees. Sparkly white lights covered the barn stem to stern. A crew busily set up chairs, ran streamers, and arranged flowers. It looked incredible. Like a Cinderella fairy tale.

Two of the ranch hands strung still more white lights over the split-rail fencing. White bows hung from each post, and tall white buckets sat at the end of each row of chairs, waiting, Sophie knew, for the daisies that would fill them.

Annelise had decided on simple elegance with a touch of country. Hanging by satin ribbons from the branches of a beautiful old shade tree, pretty little nosegays swayed in the gentle breeze. She and Cash would say their vows beneath that tree.

Sophie hit a button, and the car's window slid down silently, giving them a clearer view.

Tables and benches had been arranged in the reception area. White runners, white candles, and crystal vases decorated each table. Hydrangeas, roses, Queen Anne's lace, amaranthus, and dahlias spilled in profusion from the vases.

At first blush, it all looked simple, almost effortless. But hours and hours and hours had gone into the preparations, and no expense had been spared. The ranch had been transformed.

A window on the second floor opened. "Sophie! Up here!" Annelise leaned out and waved at them. "Hi, Dottie. Come up and have a glass of champagne with us."

And so it began.

Already, the day was a blur of satin and lace, chiffon and ribbons. Flowers and magic.

A knock at the door had all the women stopping mid-sentence to stare at it. A sure sign of nerves...on everyone's part.

"Yes?" Annelise asked.

"It's only me." Rosie peeked her head inside the door. "Wanted to let you know the men are in the house. Wetter than ducks when I saw them. The whole lot of them went swimming in Cash's lake and came in laughing their fool heads off. A person would think they were all ten years old again."

Annelise flashed a smile. "They're having fun."

"Yep. Cash is celebrating his wedding day. And a damn

fine thing that is." Rosie lifted the hem of her apron to swipe at her eyes. "But I threatened the bunch of them with my wooden spoon if I so much as saw any of them near the stairs."

"Thanks, Rosie."

"You all need to eat something." Not a question.

Annelise put her hand on her stomach. "I'm too nervous. I swear every butterfly in the state of Texas has taken up residence in here."

"Understood. A bride's got a right to a few nerves. But a groom has a right to a bride who doesn't faint at the altar. Dottie and I will bring you something." She tipped her chin at her old friend, who nodded back. "We'll toss in extra. I'm guessing your mom will be here any second. Cash's mama is downstairs pacing. I'm gonna send her up to see you. Might calm her down some."

Rosie and Dottie left in a rush.

"And I guess that's that," Sophie said.

"General Rosie," Annelise agreed.

They looked at each other and burst out laughing.

The door opened again and Annelise's mother, followed by Sophie's, slipped in.

"Oh, baby!" Georgia Montjoy practically smothered her daughter in a hug. "You look so beautiful. My little girl." She stepped back and held her at arm's length. "You're a woman."

"Yes, Mom, I am."

"An almost married woman."

A huge smile split Annelise's face. "I know," she whispered.

"I like your Cash, honey."

Cash's mother, standing just inside the door, cleared her throat.

"Sorry." Georgia blushed. "I just..." She gestured toward her daughter.

Pauline Hardeman nodded. "Our children all grown up, ready to start their lives with the person they love."

Marilyn London hugged her own daughter. "How are you, honey?"

"I'm good, Mom." Sophie hugged her back. "You smell so good. You always do. I'm so glad you came."

"I wouldn't have missed Annelise's wedding for the world."

"Look at me, Grandma." Abbie kicked up her feet to show off her new shoes, then twirled across the room to where her dress hung. "Isn't it beautiful?"

"You'll look good enough to eat, sweetie." Pauline scooped up her granddaughter for a hug and a kiss, and turned to Annelise.

"Mrs. Hardeman—"

"Annie, in less than an hour, *you're* going to be Mrs. Hardeman, too. I'd love it if you'd call me Pauline."

"I'd like that."

Sophie couldn't help envying the tears of joy welling in Annelise's eyes. Reminded herself each person had her own destiny.

Pauline blinked away tears of her own. "Okay, that's out of the way. And so you know, I just left the men. They've dried up nicely after their morning escapade and are looking very handsome."

"Is someone taking pictures?"

"You bet."

Another knock sounded. Pauline opened the door and helped Rosie and Dottie into the room. The two toted picnic baskets loaded down with everything they'd need for a prewedding brunch.

"Are the guys eating?"

"Yep, dads included," Rosie said. "Hank took them platters of cold cuts and cheeses for sandwiches, along with potato salad. And beer. Told that man of mine to keep an eye on their consumption. Don't need any of them staggering around. Not yet, anyway."

"Oh, God." Annelise paled. "Do you think that might happen?"

Rosie patted her hand. "Not a chance. Hank knows his life wouldn't be worth spit if he lets them get to that point. Besides, none of them boys is gonna want to do that and ruin your wedding day. They all love you."

The wedding planner, who'd been outside overseeing the final decorations while they ate, bustled into the room. "Time's not our friend right now. Bridesmaids, maid of honor, and flower girl, into your dresses."

Maggie rushed in carrying the bridal veil. "It's ready. I'm done fussing."

Sophie took Annelise's hand. In a teasing tone, she asked, "You're sure about this? You're really going to marry the cowboy?"

"Oh, yes." Annelise's face split in a huge grin. "I've never been more certain of anything in my life."

"Then let's do it, cuz."

The planner dropped the maid-of-honor dress over Sophie's head. The material flowed over her like liquid, and she turned to the mirror. "Maggie, you're a genius."

"Of course." She laughed, looking sophisticated in a tea-length, blush-colored dress that highlighted her curves.

Then all attention turned to the bride.

They held their collective breath as Maggie stepped to the wedding gown, still hidden in its garment bag. She grasped the zipper, then, with a mischievous expression on her face, paused and looked at Annelise.

Annelise shook her head. "Not yet. Everybody, turn around and close your eyes."

"Annie," Babs groaned. "You're killing us."

"I hope so." The bride circled her finger. "Go on. Turn. And no peeking."

Muttering and mumbling about the unfairness, they did. The room went silent but for the rasp of the zipper, followed by rustling and shushing of fabric over fabric.

"Okay, ladies, feast your eyes," Maggie said.

They turned as one.

Sophie's heart caught in her throat. "Oh, Annelise!"

From the corner of her eye, she saw her aunt fumbling a tissue out of a small jeweled purse. Sighing happily, Sophie leaned into her own mom.

"Do you think Cash will like it?" Annelise wondered.

"Like it?" Babs asked. "The poor boy might not recover the power of speech in time for his wedding vows."

"It's perfect, isn't it?" Kinsey whispered.

"And then some," Sophie agreed.

Annelise lifted the hem of her gown. "What do you think girls?" Tiffany blue stilettos encased her feet. "I know they should be white, but...I wanted something fun. They're my something blue."

"They're incredible," Babs said. "Oh, Cash is gonna have his hands full with you, girl. I can't wait to see his face when he catches his first glimpse. He's gonna swallow his tongue for sure."

"I hope not. I've got plans for that tongue."

Sophie chuckled along with everyone else and noticed her aunt's blink at her daughter's naughty comment.

From a small drawer in the dressing table, Annelise drew out a jeweler's box. "Cash gave these to me last night." She opened the lid and took out a pair of dangly diamond earrings. "For today."

She slid the French hooks in her ears, turned her head to admire them in the mirror.

"They're exactly right," Kinsey said. "Your almost-husband has great taste."

"He does, doesn't he? In both jewelry *and* women." She rolled her glacier-blue eyes.

"I want to see." Abbie tugged at her skirt, and Annelise knelt down to give her a better view. The little girl touched them, making them sway. "Oooh, they're pretty."

"So are you." Annelise hugged the girl. "Thank you for being in my wedding today."

"You're welcome." Abbie grinned, showing off a gap where she'd lost a baby tooth.

"I have something for you, from your uncle Cash and me." She took out another box. A single small diamond winked from a silver chain.

The girl's eyes grew big. "For me?"

"It is." Annelise lifted Abbie's blond curls and hooked the necklace, then handed her a small mirror. "What do you think?"

"It's beautiful." She ran over to Babs. "Mommy, look what Annie gave me."

"I see." Babs hugged her. Looking past her daughter, she mouthed, "Thank you."

"Our pleasure." Then she dipped her head, examining her dress. "See these crystals? They're from my grandmother's gown."

"I have my something old, something new, something blue."

"And I have your something borrowed." Sophie lifted the edge of her gown, revealing a thin, golden ankle bracelet, a tiny fairy dangling from it. She secured the chain around her cousin's ankle. "There. A little extra magic. As if it's needed today."

"Thanks." Annelise examined it in the mirror. "You may have trouble getting this back."

Her mother, Georgia, and Pauline took turns giving the bride another quick hug, then left to take their places outside.

Overhead, Sophie heard the instantly recognizable sound of helicopters. They'd buzzed the place all day, hoping for a shot of the bride and groom. The event of the year, and it was being held on an isolated ranch.

Nothing to do about the choppers, but they'd kept the invasion of privacy to a minimum. A few of the guests had run into news crews on the road from town, but security at the end of the drive admitted only those with invitations. Rufus and Silas, Annelise's personal bodyguards, stood post outside the house itself.

"Here you go." Sophie handed the bride her bouquet. "You look stunning."

Sophie smiled. All her cousin's decisions had been the right ones. The groom, her new home, her dress. Annelise's happiness all but blinded Sophie.

Five minutes later, the music started.

"Oh, God." For the first time that day, nerves, undoubtedly present all along, showed on Annelise's face. "I'm really doing this."

"You are. And Cash Hardeman is one lucky man."

Annelise grinned. "You bet he is."

Chapter Eleven

As she stood at the altar beside her best friend, Sophie looked over to see Ty watching not the bride, but her. Their eyes locked, and the butterflies in her own stomach swarmed.

When the minister pronounced Cash and Annelise man and wife, the kiss that followed had every woman practically swooning. Sophie was no exception. Oh, to be loved like that.

She took Brawley's arm, and they followed the bride and groom down the flower-strewn, grassy aisle.

Even the barn was resplendent today. Chandeliers hung from the rafters and antique mirrors covered the walls. Flowers draped over stall doors, sat in buckets and planters, and filled the building with their scent.

Outside, mile-long linen-covered trestle tables staggered beneath the weight of the wedding feast...and more lavish floral bouquets. Sophie estimated the food would feed an army—with leftovers. The cake, square layers decorated with black-frosting ribbons, was flanked by the groom's cake, a tiered banquet of cupcakes, each topped with Whispering Pine's brand.

What tickled Sophie, though, was the cake topper. The bride, decked out in her wedding gown, straddled a Harley. Behind her, the dark-haired groom, dressed in his tux, had one arm wrapped around his bride's waist, the other raised overhead, waving his Stetson. Both had Cheshire-cat grins on their ceramic faces.

Kinsey moved to the table. "Says a lot about the two of them, doesn't it?"

"Yes, it does. That Cash would be willing to take a back seat to Annelise—" Sophie shrugged. "Impressive."

"He did, you know. Let her take him for a ride on the Harley one night. She told me."

"Cash has enough self-confidence, enough self-esteem to be good with that."

"He put up a fuss about it first," Kinsey said.

"That would be mandatory."

Snagging two flutes of champagne from a passing waiter, Sophie handed one to Kinsey. Raising hers, she said, "Here's to men who aren't intimidated by strong women."

"I can drink to that." Kinsey took a sip, then stopped and stared when a man, notepad in hand, scribbling madly, bumped into her.

"Oh, sorry," he said.

Kinsey simply nodded at him.

"Hi, Mel," Sophie said. "You're not working today, are you?"

He grinned. "The news never sleeps. If there's anybody within a hundred miles of here who wasn't invited or couldn't make it, they'll want to read all the details. And everybody who is here?" He winked. "They'll buy a paper to see if their name's mentioned. Won't be able to help themselves. It's human nature. We'll sell a lot of copies when this story runs, and in the newspaper business, it's all about numbers."

"Well, take some time to enjoy."

"You bet." He wandered off.

"Close your mouth, Kinsey. You don't want to swallow a fly."

"You're right about that. Who is he?"

"Mel Ryker. He's the owner and chief reporter of the *Maverick Junction Daily*, the local newspaper."

"Single?"

"Oh, yeah."

"Straight?"

"Very." Sophie picked up Kinsey's left hand and turned it so the sun glinted off her wedding band. "Aren't you forgetting something?"

"Nope. I'm still madly in love with my Ron. Doesn't mean I can't appreciate the scenery, though. And I've got a sister who could really use a good guy in her life right now." Kinsey's eyes wandered over the crowd until she found Mel again. "He should be walking the beach somewhere. All that blond hair. Those blue, blue eyes. And that tan. The man's gorgeous."

"All the men around here are. Seems to be a curse."

Grinning, Kinsey's gaze snapped to hers. "What a shame, huh?" She glanced past Sophie. "Speaking of impressive."

Startled, she spun around. Ty stood behind her, hand out. "Dance with me."

Kinsey took her glass. "Go."

Because she wanted to, she stepped into his arms and rested her head on Ty's chest. The music soothed her, and she sank into the dance.

Someone tapped her shoulder, and Ty turned them so she faced Annelise.

"Thanks for everything, cuz."

"I didn't do anything."

"You ran interference with my parents through that whole miserable search for my aunt." Her gaze traveled across the room, and Sophie followed it to where her now healthy grandfather danced with his newly found half sister.

"And if all that wasn't enough, here you are. At my wedding." Tears shimmered in her eyes. "You're always there for me."

"Hey, so am I," Cash said.

"Yes, you are." Annelise kissed him. "Dance with me, husband."

"Don't mind if I do. Wife." He swept her into the center of the makeshift dance floor.

When the music ended, Ty escorted Sophie back to her table and left. She watched him walk away. He wore a pair of jeans better than any man she knew, yet today in his tailored tux he was to-die-for handsome and James Bond sexy. Comfortable in his own skin, the clothes didn't matter.

The man was an enigma. He made her crazy. He made her want all sorts of things she didn't *want* to want. She brought her hand to her nose. She swore she could smell him on her skin, that rough maleness.

And this wouldn't do. Refusing to think about him anymore, she moved from group to group, speaking to everyone. She took another glass of champagne from a waiter.

She'd long ago passed her limit, but what the heck. She wasn't driving and today was for celebrating.

Her mom and dad whirled by on the dance floor, and, smiling, her mother waved at her. Not far from them, laughing out loud, her usually oh-so-proper aunt and uncle jitterbugged. All the people she loved—right here.

She hadn't enjoyed herself so much in...she had no idea.

* * *

Shaded by the barn, Ty sprawled on an old wooden bench decorated with white ribbon and flowers. Idly he wondered how many flowers had given their lives for today's shindig. Had to be enough to fill a cattle carrier.

The temperature, in the low seventies, was about as close to perfection as it got. He loosened his bow tie and took another drink of Lone Star.

Glancing up, he saw Brawley headed his way. Shoot. He wanted to be left alone.

Right now, his flat-ass wasn't good company for anybody. Even Cash's dog had the good sense to recognize that. Staubach had wandered over a bit ago, sniffed at him, and hightailed it to greener pastures.

"Hey, pal, why the long face? You're not brooding over this wedding, are you? Thought you liked Annie."

"I do. She's a special woman, and Cash is one hell of a lucky man."

Brawley dropped onto the bench beside him and set down his beer. "Something's eating you. What's wrong, Ty?"

"Nothing." He shrugged. "Aw, hell. I think it's past time for me to go home. I'm a wet blanket." He raked his fingers through his hair. "I tried, though."

Brawley frowned. "Tried?"

"All this." He gestured at the people, the food, the festivities, and sighed. "Reminds me of the day Julia and I got hitched. The plans we made. The future we thought would be ours."

Brawley nodded, and the two sat in companionable silence for several minutes. Finally, he said, "I don't honestly know what to say, Ty. Maybe someday— Screw it. That doesn't work. Empty platitudes. You've probably heard a gut full of them."

"Yeah, I have." Ty took another pull of his beer.

"Julia was a beautiful woman, pal. The best. Life dealt the two of you one hell of a rotten hand."

"Yeah, it did. I don't figure it can do me much worse." He looked across the courtyard at Sophie, her head tipped back, laughing. And something inside him twisted.

Finishing his beer, he set the bottle down by his feet. "Problem is, if I leave now, I'll upset Annie, and I can't do that. Besides, I won't fare any better at home. Only upside is that nobody else would have to put up with me."

He hunched over, staring down at his clasped hands. "Speaking of problems, you really need to fix this thing between you and Red."

"Maggie?"

"Yeah." Ty glanced up.

Brawley's lips set in a straight, hard line. "Forget it. She's never going to forgive me. Just the way it is. I'm fine with that."

Ty shot him a sharp look. "No, you're not."

"Sure I am. Besides, I have no choice. It is what it is."

"Bullshit. Life's too short, Brawley. You need to work things out with her."

Both men cut their eyes to the dance floor, where Maggie and Annie's grandfather were dancing a waltz. He spun her, and the wispy skirt of her dress flared around legs set off by mile-high heels. How women balanced, let alone danced, on those stilts was a mystery. Maggie's long red hair curled around silky white shoulders.

Brawley looked away first but not before Ty saw raw pain in his friend's eyes.

"Ain't gonna happen. Not in this lifetime or the next. Maggie Sullivan is surly—and stubborn."

"You two were friends long before you were lovers."

Brawley snorted. "*Were* being the operative word. Major operative word. So past tense the relationship defies memory."

The band started another number, and both men watched Kinsey and Sophie race onto the dance floor. The tempo was fast, the women's movements pure sexual allure. Heat swept through Ty.

"What is it about two women dancing?" Brawley asked.

"Couldn't tell you, but it's hot."

Brawley stood. "Want another beer?"

Ty took a needed breath. "Oh, yeah. An ice-cold one."

As they walked to the bar, he finally admitted the time had come to face the truth. Time to be honest, even if only to himself.

His problem today, this past week, wasn't Julia. It was Sophie. The woman had resurrected deeply buried feelings. Needs. And he didn't know what to do with them.

The men had just grabbed two beers and started toward a table when the announcement came over the sound system that the bride and groom were leaving. All the guests were asked to gather on the drive to see them off.

"Best go wish them a good trip." Ty headed in their direction, Brawley right behind him.

Ty hugged Annie, gave Cash a slap on the back, while Brawley dipped Annie low and planted a doozy of a kiss on her. Setting her back on her feet, he ordered the bride and groom to enjoy their honeymoon.

* * *

"Have fun in Paris," Sophie whispered as she hugged Annelise.

Her cousin's eyes glittered. "It'll be the best trip I've ever made to that city."

Sophie stepped away so the parents could have their moment. She nearly stepped on Brawley and Ty, who stood right behind her.

"They look so right together," she said.

"Yeah, they do." Brawley held up a hand. "Give me a minute. Be right back."

He took off toward one of the outbuildings.

"What's he doing?"

"You'll see," Ty said.

A minute later, they heard the roar of a motorcycle. Brawley cruised up to the newlyweds on Annelise's Harley.

"Here you go, pal." He turned it over to Cash.

"No way." Sophie turned to Ty. "They're not leaving on that."

"Only as far as Cash's place. They'll change there—clothes and vehicles—before they head to the airport."

Sure enough, Cash, in his tux, and Annelise, wearing that beautiful gown, hopped on the bike. The obligatory tin cans and newlywed sign trailed from the back.

Annelise tucked her dress around her and cuddled against Cash's back. "He gets to drive today." She smiled and raised her bouquet.

"Get ready, ladies." Cash revved the bike. "Let's see who's next to walk down the aisle. Ready, Mrs. Hardeman?"

"You bet I am, Mr. Hardeman." Annelise held the flowers higher. The crowd cheered, and females, young and old alike, raised their arms, hoping to catch the bouquet.

Ty watched in amusement as Sophie stepped away, trying to escape the flower toss. She actually turned her back.

Someone laughed loudly, and Sophie swiveled on her heel. *Thwack!* The bouquet hit her, and she instinctively put her hands up. And caught it.

Brawley grinned as she stood, openmouthed, staring at it. "Don't look so panicked, Soph. It's tradition, not a death sentence."

But when she looked up, it was straight into Ty's intense gray eyes. Oh, fairy tales and fireflies. She was in trouble.

Her mother laid a hand on her shoulder. "Promise me, Sophie, you won't get sucked up in all this and stay here." Pale blond hair cut severely short and wearing a cocktail dress in the same shade of blue as her eyes, her mom waved a hand at the barns and paddocks. "God only knows what's on the bottom of my new Louboutins."

"Mom."

"Just saying, honey. I don't think I could stand it if you decided to call this home."

"It's what Annelise wants. She's happy here. Me?" She shook her head. "I'm a city girl all the way. I love a Sunday on the Navy Wharf, love taking my little skiff out on Lake Michigan, the wind in my hair. I love the shopping, the restaurants. Maverick Junction isn't my idea of Heaven."

"Thank God." Her mother pinched her cheek.

Again, Sophie glanced up to see Ty studying her. No smile now. She opened her mouth to say something, but he turned and walked away.

Her throat tightened. He looked—hurt. But why? She'd never made a secret of her love for the city. Besides, why did it matter to him where she lived?

It wasn't as if she'd insulted Maverick Junction. She'd simply stated her preference for Chicago.

* * *

The reception wound down. One by one and two by two, the guests said their good-byes and left.

Finally, only the family and wedding party remained.

Exhausted, Sophie dropped onto an old wooden swing hung from the branches of a tall oak. She slipped her shoes off aching feet.

Kinsey sat down beside her. "As much as I hate to, I have to leave. I've got an important meeting Monday and have to prep for it tomorrow. If the limo takes me to the airport, can you and Dottie get a ride home?"

"I'll take her." Ty's deep voice startled Sophie.

"Are you sure?" Kinsey asked.

"Yep."

"Okay." She turned to hug Sophie. "It's been so good to see you again. Wasn't Annelise the most beautiful bride ever?"

"Yes, she was. Have a safe trip home."

"Will do." Kinsey stood, gave Ty a quick hug. "Thanks, Ty, for everything."

"You bet."

"You might stop by the newspaper, Sophie, and casually mention my sister." She winked.

Sophie laughed. "Will do."

Ty frowned. "What am I missing?"

"My lips are sealed."

Kinsey laughed and crossed the yard to say the rest of her good-byes.

"You don't have to take us home, Ty. I'm sure somebody's going into town and can—"

"I said I'd do it."

"You're mad at me. Why?"

"Don't be stupid. Why would I be mad at you?"

"Exactly what I've been wondering."

He ignored the comment. "Rosie sent me to round you up. She's decided nobody really ate like they should have— her words, not mine—so she's setting out some of the leftovers and wants us all to have dinner together."

"I'm not really hungry."

"Uh-uh. You're not getting me into trouble with Rosie." He held out his hand. "My folks are picking up the boys and taking them home with them, so I've got plenty of time to eat and get you home in one piece."

"Fine. I'll eat."

Once she had food in front of her, she ate ravenously, hungrier than she'd realized. Rosie had been right. While she'd picked at some food, she'd never actually sat down with a plate.

Brawley opened a couple bottles of leftover champagne and they toasted the absentee bridal couple, then themselves for a job well done.

Sophie looked around the table. What a mismatched, delightful group, brought together out of love for Annelise and Cash. Annelise's parents and grandfather, all richer than Croesus, laughed and talked to Rosie and Hank as if they'd been friends forever. Dottie, Maggie, and her grandpa chatted with Cornelia and her lifelong friend Thelma. Her own parents chatted a mile a minute to anyone within shouting distance.

Finally too full to eat another bite, Sophie pushed away her plate.

"Ready to go?" Ty asked.

"I am. Dottie, how about you?"

"Honey, I'm so tired I don't know if I can walk to the pickup."

Ty grinned. "Want me to carry you?"

"Don't tempt me. I might take you up on it." She stood. "Rosie, let me help with the dishes first."

"No way. No dishes for me tonight. That crew Annie hired is cleaning up." Rosie's eyes twinkled. "How about that? I feel like a queen." She primped at her hair.

"You are a queen." Brawley dropped a kiss on the top of her head. "I'm gonna take off, too. I promised Doc I'd give him a hand tomorrow."

Hank asked, "On Sunday?"

"Yeah, he's got a dog that's losing ground. I said I'd take a look, see if I can figure out what's going on."

Rosie patted his arm. "You're a good boy, Brawley Odell."

"Thank you, ma'am." He shifted his glance to Maggie at the far end of the table. "Not everyone thinks so."

Maggie's gaze dropped to her plate.

Nope, Sophie thought. These two weren't nearly finished. The fire between them hadn't gone out. Not by a long shot.

They left, loaded down with plates of leftovers and wedding cake. Her parents promised to stop by in the morning before they flew home.

Totally unaware of the tension between Ty and herself, Dottie chattered the entire way. Sophie couldn't wait to shut herself in her apartment. No doubt about it, Ty had definitely gotten his back up about something.

Well, too bad.

He pulled into the drive and walked around to the passenger side. Holding Dottie's leftovers, Ty helped her climb out of the truck.

Several plates balanced in one big hand, he opened Sophie's door. "Hold on, would you?" he asked. "Let me see Dottie in, then I'd like to talk to you."

Oh, boy. She watched the two walk off, feeling like a kid summoned to the principal's office. But she stayed put.

When he came back, he took her food from her, then offered her a hand. She almost swore at the jolt when they touched, saw the same awareness in his eyes. Whatever this was, she wasn't alone in it.

"I'll see you in."

"You don't—"

"Sophie, we've covered this ground before. Besides, like I said, I want to talk for a minute, and I'd rather do it inside."

Stiffly, she stalked up the stairs in front of him. At the top, she reached for her plates, but he moved them away.

"Unlock your door."

"Jeez, who put you in charge of the world?"

A hint of a smile played over his lips. "Just do it."

Once inside, he reached around her, set the plates on the kitchen counter. Then, catching her totally off guard, he caught her around the waist and pulled her to him.

"I might regret this, but so help me God, I can't resist."

He leaned into her, his eyes storm-gray now. The heat in them started a fire deep in her belly.

Not a single coherent thought remained in her head as his lips touched hers, moved over them. As his tongue slipped between them and mated with hers.

He pulled away as abruptly as he'd begun. His curse rent the night air, and his forehead dropped to hers.

"I'm sorry, Sophie." He stepped back. "I probably shouldn't have done that. I had no right."

"Why not?"

"I've got more baggage than you could begin to imagine."

"Don't we all?" Ignoring her own warning bell, she grabbed his bow tie and, catching him off guard, tugged him to her. When her lips found his, he readjusted, changed the angle. She melted into him. This cowboy's kiss left every other she'd ever known in the dust.

This time, she pulled away. Took a deep breath. Saw that he looked totally shell-shocked. Good. Only fair, since he'd started it.

Now they both needed a time-out.

"Good night, Ty." She laid a hand on his chest and backed him out, then closed the door.

Chapter Twelve

Sophie didn't have high hopes for Sunday. The day was bound to be that deep breath after a job well done. Rewarding, but a bit of a letdown.

Her parents stopped by as promised, and she took them to Sally's Place for an early breakfast. Her mom badgered her till she promised not to fall under whatever spell had gotten its hooks into Annelise. Sophie assured her there was no danger of that happening. Her stay in Texas was very temporary.

A huge sigh of relief escaped Sophie as she stood in Dottie's driveway, waving good-bye to her mom and dad as they drove off in their rental, headed for the airport and Boston. As great as it had been to see them and as much as she'd miss them, she desperately needed some time alone. For the first time in days, she could do exactly as she pleased. She had no demands and no one to answer to. She had nowhere she had to be. Not even Dee expected her back in Chicago by any specific date. Her parents knew where she was and had no reason to worry about her.

Her only deadline? That darn overdue spring line. Since she didn't believe in creative blocks, it was simply a matter of clearing her mind. Once Sophie did that, everything would fall into place.

She'd had no e-mails from Nathan yesterday. Maybe he'd finally gotten the message. A girl could hope.

And this apartment? All hers! Dottie'd been delighted to have her, however short-term. After all the activity here, the place needed a quick going over. Scrounging under the sink, she unearthed a dusting cloth and, with Maroon Five belting out their latest hit, went to work.

A knock sounded on the door, and her heart did a quick pirouette. *Ty?*

Tucking a stray strand of hair behind her ear, she rushed into the kitchen and saw Hank outside the door.

Her heart lurched, nearly bursting out of her chest. She ran to the door and threw it open. "Annelise and Cash? Are they okay?"

"Whoa. Don't get yourself all worked up. They're fine." He laid a hand on her shoulder. "Girl, you've gone whiter than a sack of flour."

She wet her lips. "I thought— When I saw you, I thought there'd been an accident."

"Guess Rosie was right. Damned woman always is. She said I should call first." He swiped the toe of one scuffed boot across the wooden landing. "Afraid if I did, though, you'd refuse the car. Then I'd have Cash to answer to."

She frowned at him. "What are you talking about?"

In answer, he reached into his faded jeans pocket and came out with a set of keys. "Here. These fit the Chevy in the drive. And before you start telling me all the reasons why you can't take it, you need to know it's one of the ranch cars. Anybody in need of transportation uses it. It's not a bad car, and one of the hands cleaned it up for you. I filled it up, so you're good to go."

"But I don't need it." She put her hands behind her back. "I can rent one."

His jaw set. "You want to get an old man in trouble?"

"Well...No."

"Then take the damn car. Otherwise Cash is gonna be pissed at me when he and Annie get back." He fastened his gaze on her. "And then there's Rosie. Woman probably won't talk to me for a week if you don't take these keys."

"You're hitting below the belt, Hank."

He grinned. "Man's gotta do what a man's gotta do. Come on. The car's a beater. Everybody and his brother drives it, so why not you?"

Resigned, she held out her hands for the keys. "Why not me?"

He tipped his hat to her. "Thank you, ma'am."

"Thank *you*, Hank. Do you need a ride back to the ranch?"

"No, ma'am. Liam's waiting downstairs in his truck. If I know him, he's already sweet-talked Dottie out of a batch of cookies, so we'll have ourselves a little Sunday treat on the ride home."

"Thanks again."

He tipped his hat and trudged down the stairs.

Sophie watched him make his way to the drive and across to Liam's pickup. Bowlegged from so many years on horseback, Hank was the stereotypical Texas cowhand. He had an easy way about him and was a good person. He and Rosie made a great pair. Annelise had told her their story, romantic in its own sad way.

Since she had wheels now, she might as well run down to Mabel's Suds and throw in a load of laundry, then stop at Sadler's Store for a few groceries. If she intended to make Maverick Junction and this apartment home for a while, it was past time she settled in.

* * *

By the time Sophie'd finished and had her groceries put away, her head was near to bursting with design ideas. Sitting at the kitchen table, bent over her laptop and sketch pad, she worked furiously, laboring to get them down on paper.

Finally, though, her back screamed that it was time for a break. Looking at the wall clock, she was shocked to see it read a quarter past three. How could that be? She needed coffee.

Her stomach rumbled. Okay, she hadn't eaten since breakfast, either.

First things first. A rare fix of caffeine. She moved to the counter and scooped coffee into Annelise's fancy little machine. While it grumbled, she headed in to draw a bath.

Inside of ten minutes, she slid into the warm, luxuriously scented water. Her aching muscles thanked her. A steaming cup of coffee within arm's reach, she leaned her head against the bath pillow and closed her eyes. Ahhh. The old claw-foot tub should be deemed a national treasure. What a shame they didn't make them like this anymore.

She'd programmed her iPod to a mix of Enya and

Loreena McKennitt, and the music wove its magic, relaxing her. Sophie grinned and reached for her coffee. She'd done some great work today—and had a dust-free house and clean clothes.

Right now, she'd take a few minutes to pamper herself and enjoy the feeling of relief and accomplishment. Afterward she'd take a much-needed walk to Main Street and see if she could find a place that sold art supplies. They wouldn't be open today, but she'd stop in tomorrow to pick up a few things.

Forty minutes later, caffeine flowing through her system, a peanut butter sandwich fortifying her, she opened her e-mail.

Ten new messages. All from Nathan. Her stomach sank.

She read the first.

I miss you. Come home. Nathan.

Shaking her head, she read the rest, one after another, appalled as they escalated from cajoling to whining to explosive anger.

This was nonsense.

She hadn't led him on. Hadn't made any promises. Had, in fact, told him very honestly there was nothing there, nothing between them.

He refused to accept that.

Well, she'd call him. Tonight.

Today, though, she'd put him out of her mind. Refused to let him ruin her Sunday. He was in Illinois; she was in Texas. Her pulse skittered and her breathing quickened. He scared her. More than a little.

And that was stupid.

Still, she was glad there was a thousand plus miles separating them. And she wished Ty was here to tell her everything would be okay. To hold her. Just for a minute. And that was probably even stupider.

Heading out for her walk, she concentrated instead on the robin-egg blue sky, the scent of the bread baking next door, and the clean, fresh smell of newly mowed grass. The kids across the street were playing Red Rover and their shouts and laughter filled the late afternoon.

What a beautiful day. December already. The sun, low in the sky, shone through overhead leaves, creating a lace pattern on the sidewalk and warming her.

If she was in Chicago, she'd be fighting her way through slush and snowdrifts. She'd flicked on the TV while she dressed and listened as the reporter talked about the storm that had dumped almost a foot on the entire northern section of the country.

She didn't miss it.

Hadn't even missed Black Friday.

She turned her head right, then left, taking in the quiet residential neighborhood. No pushing, shoving hordes here. No camping out to buy the latest tech toy. And wasn't that nice. A slow smile curved her lips.

Halfway down the block, a weak mewling sounded from behind a bush in an empty lot. Sophie stopped, tipped her head toward the sound, and heard it again. A cat…maybe a kitten.

Walking to the shrubbery, she stooped and peered beneath it. Her heart nearly stopped. The cat, its hair matted and dirty, hunkered on the ground, big amber eyes staring out at her. One ear was missing a chunk. Dried blood covered one leg.

"Oh, you poor baby," Sophie crooned. "What happened to you, sweetheart?"

Ignoring the dirt, she knelt and laid her hand, palm up, as close to the cat as she dared. Still, it backed up slightly.

"I won't hurt you, honey. Come here. Let me help."

Unblinking, owlish yellow eyes followed her every movement.

Sophie stayed by the bush, as still as possible. Finally, curiosity got the better of the cat. That or hunger. Inch by inch, crawling on its belly, it drew closer.

"Come on. That's it," Sophie encouraged.

With a soft cry, it closed the last bit of distance. Its raspy tongue licked at Sophie's outstretched palm. "That's right, baby." Slowly, she turned her hand to stroke the cat's head.

She sat on the ground, and the cat, still cautious, lay down beside her. "What happened? You're a mess, sweetie."

The cat's ribs showed, and its paws were cut and bleeding. A ragged gash ran down the length of one leg. Hesitant to pick up the animal, Sophie stood. So did the cat. She turned and took a step toward home. The cat did, too. Since she'd only walked about half a block, she hoped the cat would follow her. Limping slowly, it did, right up the stairs and into the apartment.

Hopefully, it didn't come accessorized with fleas.

Sophie rooted around and found an old saucer, poured some milk in it, and set it on the floor. The cat looked up at her as if asking permission.

"Go ahead. It's for you."

The cat lapped it up while Sophie found Doc Gibson's number. Even though it was Sunday, she remembered Brawley had mentioned plans to help out with a dog before he headed back to Dallas. Fingers crossed, she dialed. Doc Gibson answered on the second ring. He was at the office and told her to bring the cat in. He'd take a look at her.

Almost as if she understood, the cat allowed herself to be carried to the car. Following the directions the vet had given her, Sophie found the animal clinic. She pulled into a parking space and turned to the cat curled up on her front seat. It eyed her warily.

"You probably won't like this." She rubbed the cat's head. She wasn't a young thing nor would she win any beauty contests. Still . . . she was sweet-tempered.

She needed a home.

If Sophie intended to stay in Maverick Junction, she'd keep her. But she couldn't take her back to Chicago. Her apartment was too small.

She certainly didn't intend to turn her back out onto the streets, though. No way. And she definitely didn't plan to take her to the animal shelter, if Maverick Junction even had one. They tried to find homes for all their animals, but, face it, it wasn't always possible. And she knew in her heart that this lady wouldn't have a chance at adoption.

Maybe she could keep her for the little while she'd be here and talk Dottie into taking the animal when she headed back to Chicago. Or Annelise and Cash could take her. Staubach would get along with Lilybelle.

Lilybelle. One of the fairies. A perfect name for this beautiful cat. Okay, so maybe she wasn't beautiful right now, but she would be.

Sophie was certain of it.

She scooped up the cat and carried her into the clinic.

"What do we have here?" Brawley came out from behind the counter.

"Brawley? I figured you'd already left for Dallas."

He shrugged. "I decided to stay a couple more days. I like working here. It reminds me why I went to veterinarian school."

"There's something about the town, isn't there?" Sophie asked. "Even when you don't want there to be."

"Yeah, there is."

Sophie nodded at the cat. "This is Lilybelle. I found her hiding in a bush."

"Pleased to meet you, Lilybelle." Brawley reached out and gently took the cat from her. "Looks like you've seen some hard times."

"Do you think someone abandoned her?"

He studied the cat. "Yep, I do. Looks like she's a fairly new mama. My guess is somebody didn't want any more kittens. Rather than spay her, they simply dumped her out."

"That's despicable." The last piece of her heart went out to the poor animal.

"Hard telling what they did with her babies."

She gasped. "You don't think they—"

"Yes, Sophie, I do." He scratched the cat's head, and her eyes closed. "So, what do you want to do with her?"

"Pardon?"

"What are your plans? We have several options. We can patch her up, get some food in her, and try to find her a home. At her age, I can't make any promises."

"What are our other options?"

"You could keep her."

She shook her head. "My lifestyle really doesn't—"

"All right. Fair enough. The third option? Euthana—"

"No." Sophie clapped her hands over the cat's ears—or what remained of them. "Don't even say it. Don't listen, Lilybelle."

"How do you know that's her name? If you heard someone call her that, maybe we can track down the owners."

"No." She shrugged. "She just looks like a Lilybelle."

"Humph." He studied the cat. "Okay. Well, to be honest, Lilybelle needs a lot of work. She's pretty beat up."

Sophie bit her lip. Lots of work meant lots of money. Money she really didn't have. The cat licked her hand again, and Sophie glanced down into those warm, amber eyes.

Oh, heck.

"Do what you need to do. And spay her. When can I take her home?"

He grinned. "Tomorrow."

"I'm going to hate myself."

"No, you won't. You've gained a friend for life. This cat will be devoted to you for the rest of hers."

Sophie groaned. "I must be crazy. I swear it's the air here."

"You won't regret this."

"Easy for you to say." When Brawley carried the cat into one of the smaller rooms, she followed.

"Your folks live in Boston, Sophie?"

"Yes."

"And you live in Chicago." He tugged on a pair of gloves and ran a gentle hand over the animal's injured leg.

"Right."

As the two of them leaned over the cat, talking, their heads touching, the door opened and Ty stepped in.

He stopped dead when he saw them. "Sorry. I took a

chance Doc might be here. I had a question about one of my fillies. Didn't realize I'd be interrupting anything." His voice took on a hard edge.

"You're not," Brawley growled.

Two alpha dogs and one bone, Sophie thought. And she was the bone.

Ty turned, hand on the doorknob. "I'll come back tomorrow." He stormed out, Brawley right behind him.

The door stood open.

"What the hell's wrong with you?" Brawley asked.

"Nothing."

"Bullshit. I know you too well to buy that crap!"

The two friends stood nose to nose, and Sophie held her breath.

Ty waved his hand toward the clinic. "I didn't realize you and Sophie—"

"Me and Sophie nothing," Brawley barked back. "She found a ratty-assed cat hiding under a bush. The thing was half-dead, so she dragged it in for Doc to look at. Since I was here, I'm checking it out. Period."

Ty swiped a boot over the grout line between two of the tiles and swore. "I feel like an idiot."

"You *are* an idiot." Brawley draped an arm over his friend. "Doc's around back. Go ask your question."

Sophie breathed a sigh of relief.

As Ty started around the building, Brawley said, "You might consider asking the girl out."

"Kiss my butt." Ty walked away.

Brawley laughed as he moved toward Sophie and Lilybelle. "Sorry about that."

"Ty's a moody one," she said. "I never know what to expect from him."

"Seems to be even moodier since you've landed in town."

"You think?" She gave the cat one last pat. "You'll call me when I can pick her up?"

"Either Doc or I will. Don't worry. We'll take good care of her."

"I'll need to ask Dottie if I can keep the cat. I don't know if she wants animals in her apartment."

"She'll be fine with it."

* * *

Twilight had fallen by the time Sophie left the clinic. Halfway out the door, she stopped dead. Ty leaned against the front of his van, long legs crossed, Stetson tipped back.

"Did you find Doc?"

"Yep. Where's your cat?"

"Brawley's fixing her up for me. I can take her home tomorrow."

"Good." He turned to go, then stopped. Facing her, he hooked a thumb in his pocket. "I owe you an apology."

"No, you don't."

"I do. I was a jerk in there."

She wasn't sure what to say. *Yes, you were*? or *Why was that*? So she said nothing at all.

"Not gonna help me out?"

"What would you like me to say?"

"Oh, something along the lines of, 'No, you weren't, Ty.' Or maybe just 'It's okay.'"

She smiled. "It's okay, Ty."

"But you don't mean that."

Exasperated, she blurted, "Then why did you want me to say it?"

"So I'd feel better." He kicked at a loose pebble. "Look, you can tell me it's none of my business, but I have to ask. Is there anything going on between you and Brawley?"

"No."

"You sure?"

"Positive."

"Want to go for a ride? I realize the van falls more than a little short of my Cowboy Cadillac, but..." He shrugged. "The boys are at their gram's. I'm a free man for another hour or so."

"Cowboy Cadillac?"

"Yeah. My pickup."

"Oh." She hesitated. "You know, yes, I'd like to go for a ride." The air had a definite nip to it, so Sophie reached into her car for her faded Cubs sweatshirt and tugged it over her T-shirt.

"Hey, Tink." His voice sounded husky.

"Ty?"

He pointed at her shirt. "You know, you might want to put that away, not wear it while you're here."

"Really? And why would that be?"

"We're not big Cub fans down here, sugar."

"What a shame. I feel so sorry for you."

He chuckled. "Yeah, well, consider yourself warned."

Ty pulled onto the street, then reached for the radio and turned the volume up a notch. "You warm enough?"

She nodded, bit her tongue before admitting her temperature had risen a good ten degrees the minute she'd slid into his van. He seemed to have that effect on her.

"You been looking for a cat?"

"No. Absolutely not. But she's not a good candidate for adoption, and I can't bear to think of—you know."

He nodded. "I do. The kids have a puppy—because I couldn't say no to Babs—and I'm seriously thinking of committing myself. Our house is crazy enough without those sharp little teeth chewing up everything in sight, puppy puddles on the floor, and one more mouth to feed."

"But the kids love him," she said.

"Yeah, they do." He adjusted his hat, settled it farther back on his head, giving her a better view of those startling gray eyes.

"And, so, Dad, you'll put up with the inconvenience."

"You got that right."

He drove along Maverick Junction's few side streets, pointing out the school, the small volunteer fire station, a few friends' homes. Lights came on in houses as dusk deepened, everyone winding down from the weekend, preparing for Monday morning.

It was peaceful and so different from Chicago.

Sophie rolled down her window and stuck her head out. "I can't get over the sky here. It's incredible. It goes on forever and ever."

She pulled her head back in and turned to face him. "Do you ever get tired of this?"

"The town?"

"All of it. The small town, the quiet. The isolation."

"Nope. I've lived here all my life. It's home. I'm happy here." He glanced at her. "What about you? You happy in Chicago?"

"I am. It's where I belong."

An uneasy silence settled between them. No matter how she cut it, no matter how attractive she found Ty Rawlins, the chasm between their worlds was too wide, too gaping to ever be bridged.

And wasn't that a darn shame?

Ty swung back onto Main Street and pulled up beside her car. The clinic was dark. Sophie swore a danger warning signal blasted in her head.

Without looking at Ty, she opened her door. "Thanks for the tour."

"Hey." He reached across the seat and caught her hand. "You okay?"

Electricity buzzed through her, and she had to force herself not to jerk her hand away. "I am."

"We're good then?"

She beamed at him. "We're good."

* * *

Ty waited till Sophie started her car and drove away, watched as she turned and disappeared from view. Guilt threatened to eat a hole clear through his stomach.

Checking his rearview mirror, he backed onto the street. Time to pick up the boys. He headed toward his parents', his mind a quagmire.

He and Julia had met in first grade. By the time they'd hit third, he knew she'd be his wife. It had been just that simple. And that certain.

Julia and Ty. Ty and Julia.

They'd been paired forever.

Should have been together forever.

Would have been if she'd— He sucked in a lungful of air and let it out slowly. Again and again.

Still, his heart refused to settle into its normal rhythm. Sophie stirred something in him that had been missing for a long, long time.

Something he'd never felt, actually, because with him and Julia, there'd never been that uncertainty. But there'd also never been that thrill of the unknown. Of the new.

He and Julia grew up knowing each other, knowing everything about each other.

With Sophie he was out of his comfort zone. He snorted. Comfort zone? How about universe?

He'd never even dated anybody except Julia. Never kissed another woman—until Sophie. Damn, his heart raced faster than the van's engine.

What was he going to do?

Reaching above the visor, he pulled out an old, worn CD. Julia's favorite. But when he slid it in and hit play, instead of bringing her closer as it usually did, it confused him even more.

Chapter Thirteen

Ty groaned. What the heck? Groggy, he rolled onto his side and pulled a plastic action figure out from under his back. Apparently, he'd fallen asleep on the sofa.

The laundry he'd been folding had spilled onto the floor. The TV, volume low, cast flickering shadows around the room. Coming to a full sitting position, he flopped against the sofa's back. *Sleepless in Seattle*. He shook his head. That movie must be making somebody a boatload of money. Every time he turned on the TV, it was playing, and every time he switched channels. The film romanticized widow-hood when it was, in reality, nothing but pain and heartache. And a lot of damn hard work.

Still, tonight, he'd found himself watching it as he folded the small T-shirts and searched out mates for tiny socks— socks he noticed needed replacing soon. Tom Hanks and Meg Ryan drew him into the possibility of a second chance at love and happiness.

Was it possible? On-screen, with Annie's help, Sam discovered new love. His son found a new mother. But, then, that was the movies.

An image of Sophie floated through his mind. Their short, impromptu ride had been over a week ago and had left him restless. He'd driven past Dottie's more than once, sorely tempted to stop each time, but he'd forced himself to keep going.

By now, Sophie had no doubt headed back to Chicago and her life. His was here with his kids—three mini-tornadoes who'd be up early. Time he got some sleep himself. Upstairs.

Digging the remote from beneath the cushions where Josh liked to hide it, he flicked off the television set. He'd do one last check on the boys, then collapse into bed.

Alone.

Again.

* * *

Ty's door flew open on a screeching war whoop and all three boys made a flying leap onto his bed. He grunted, then groaned when one sharp elbow landed in his midsection.

"We're hungry, Daddy."

He opened one eye and saw the sun—along with his sons—had risen. And so it begins. Another day in the life of the Rawlins family, he thought.

Jesse lifted Ty's arm and crawled beneath it, snuggling close. "Miss Marcy said it's De—" He scrunched his nose in thought.

"Dexcember," Jonah helped.

"No," Josh said. "It's Chrisember."

Ty laughed. "It's December." Then he sobered. Where had the year gone?

"Yeah," Jesse said. "It's time for Santa to come."

Ty rubbed his eyes with his free hand. "In a few weeks."

"Not tonight?" Josh asked from where he sprawled across Ty's legs.

"No. Definitely not tonight."

"But I want him to come tonight." Josh's lower lip trembled.

"He can't come tonight," Jonah explained patiently. "He's gotta make the toys first. Right, Daddy?" Jonah, flopped on his stomach, hung headfirst over the side of the bed.

"Right, tiger." He rubbed the closest head. "Why don't you guys run on downstairs. I'll be right behind you."

As they tumbled off the bed, he added, "Open the back door and let Trouble out before he makes any puddles."

"He already did, Daddy. In our bathroom."

And they were gone. Ty wondered if anybody else's life could possibly be this chaotic. He hit the head, then tossed on a pair of jeans and a flannel shirt. After a quick stop in the boys' bathroom with some paper towels to clean up after the pup, he traipsed downstairs.

The dog was outside, but so were the boys.

"Hey, guys, get in here. You don't have any shoes on—or jackets. Come in and close the door. You born in a barn?"

"I don't know," Josh said.

"You weren't. Take my word for it." He grabbed bowls straight out of the dishwasher since he hadn't unloaded it last night.

Forty-five minutes later, cereal dishes once again stacked in the machine, kids dressed, puppy fed and redrained, he herded the whole bunch out the door. Buckling the kids into child seats, he thought maybe he'd run by Dottie's again.

If Sophie was still there he might ask her out. But not on a date. He broke into a sweat. Just some kind of friendly outing. After all, with Annie on her honeymoon, Sophie really didn't know anybody in town. She might be lonesome.

It would be the right thing to do.

The more he thought about it, though, it might actually be safer to do something that included the boys. That was probably a rotten thing to do to her, but, as cowardly as it made him, he needed the buffer.

He wouldn't really be playing fair with Sophie, and he'd be using the triplets. He thought about the alternative. He and Sophie alone. His pulse took off at a gallop.

Using them worked. He could live with that.

He unloaded the kids at day care, then went inside to sign the permission slip he'd forgotten at home on the kitchen counter. The class was walking to the library today for story time.

On impulse, he stopped into Sally's Place. "Morning, Sally. How 'bout a plain coffee to go and one of those fancy cappuccinos."

"That cappuccino wouldn't be for a certain young lady from Chicago, would it?" Sally raised her brows.

"Might be. Why?"

"She drinks coffee once in a while, but she really prefers tea."

"I knew that."

"I know you did." She grinned and cracked her gum. "Your brain's on overload this morning, right?"

He threw her a lopsided smile. "Actually, it is."

"You're wondering how you're gonna finagle her into a date without making it an actual date."

His mouth dropped open. "How the hell did you—" He stopped. "Oh, no. I'm not playing this game."

"You already did."

He jammed his hands into his jeans pockets. "So give me a coffee and a tea, bag out." He jerked his chin toward the pastry counter. "And a piece of your apple pie."

"One?"

"Yeah. If Sophie's nice, I'll share with her."

"Oh, you're a bad one." With a shake of her head, Sally moved off to get the order together.

While he waited, Ty sat on one of the stools and chewed the fat with Old Henry Foster and Walt Johnson, there for their daily gabfest. Inside a couple minutes, Sally placed his bag in front of him. "Here you go. Good luck."

He flashed a grin, showing off his dimples. "Think I'm gonna need luck with a mug like this?"

"Maybe I'd better wish *her* luck."

"From your lips to God's ears." Ty dropped a ten on the counter, grabbed his order, and left, wishing he felt even half as confident as he'd pretended.

* * *

He found her at the kitchen table, hunched over her computer. When he rapped on the window, she jerked around.

Recognizing him, hand on her heart, she walked to the door and opened it. "Well, I think I just lost ten years or so."

"Working?"

She clapped her hands, her eyes sparkling. "I am. It's going so well." She tipped her head at the cup. "For me?"

"Yep."

"Thanks." She took the offered tea, then peered in his bag. "What's that?"

"Apple pie. Thought you might want to share."

"You bet. I'm more than ready for a break. Got started early this morning." She rubbed her lower back, then opened a cupboard door for saucers.

Ty shook his head. "Grab a couple forks. More fun to eat it right out of this." He held up the Styrofoam container.

"Okay."

Together, they attacked the pie.

"Mmm," she said around a mouthful of the sweet fruit. "This is incredible."

"Yeah, it is. One bite left." He scooped it onto his fork and held it toward her. Watched as her mouth closed over it. Held his breath as she closed her eyes to savor it.

He chuckled. "Hope that was as good for you as it was for me."

"Oh, believe me, it was." She licked her lips.

She played dirty, he thought. That look on her face could drive a man insane—and she had to know it. Was that why Nathan sent e-mails like the one he'd seen? Why he couldn't give her up?

"So now that we've devoured a day's worth of calories," Sophie said, "why'd you come by?"

"Other than to feed you?"

"Other than that." She smiled.

"Do I need a reason?"

She tipped her head and studied him. "Strangely enough,

I'm going to say yes. You don't strike me as a spur-of-the-moment kind of guy."

He narrowed his eyes. "I'm not sure if that's a compliment or an insult."

"Neither," she said. "Simply an observation."

"Okay. As much as it pains me to admit it, you're right. Here's the deal. It occurs to me you never did let me pay for the outfit Jonah ruined at Cash's Fourth of July barbecue. Thought maybe I could at least treat you to lunch."

She eyed the now empty container.

He laughed. "No. As good as the pie was, it's not a meal."

"It should be." She rubbed her stomach, drawing his eyes to her midsection, her narrow waist, the way the Cubs T-shirt stopped just short of the top of her jeans.

His pulse rate doubled. The woman was downright dangerous to his health.

"I'm not sure it's a good idea for you and me to—you know."

He swallowed and went with instinct. "We wouldn't be alone. Sometimes I spring the kids. Give them a day away from day care. Thought I'd do that tomorrow. We've been talking about throwing together a picnic."

Shrugging, he said, "But it's okay. I should have realized a day with three little boys wouldn't be your idea of a good time. Forget I even mentioned it."

"No. Wait." She laid a hand on his arm.

His eyes lifted to hers, searching them. Did she feel that kick in the ass when they touched, or was it just him?

"I'd love to join you and the boys." She paused. "Why don't I meet you out at your place? That'll be easier than you coming into town to pick me up."

"Sounds good. Elevenish?"

"I'll be there."

He gave her quick directions. "And Tink?"

"Yes?"

"You might want to lose that T-shirt right along with the sweatshirt. You've got piss-poor taste in baseball teams."

Her mouth dropped open. "You do understand I bought my apartment in Chicago's Lakeview district based solely on the fact it's only a couple of blocks from Wrigley Field?"

Slowly he shook his head. "It just gets worse."

She punched him in the arm. "You've got a lot of room to talk. You live surrounded by horses and cows."

"Yes, ma'am." He smiled. "I do. But remember, I did warn you. The shirt's got to go."

He tipped his hat and left, taking the stairs at a fast clip. Tomorrow Sophie'd spend the day with him. Backing out of the drive, he made a mental list of the things he'd need from Sadler's Store.

He was as nervous—and as horny—as a sixteen-year-old. The horny would have to go on the back burner for now. With the triplets around, well, not a chance in Hell he'd get lucky.

Instantly his conscience pricked him.

His gaze drifted to his left hand, the fingers draped over the steering wheel. No wedding ring. In a fit of anger, he'd taken it off over a year ago. Julia should still be here with him. Would be if—

Nope. He drew a deep breath. Best leave those thoughts for the middle of the night when sleep refused to come. No place for them today.

He signaled and pulled into Sadler's parking lot. Turning off the van, he unbuckled his seat belt, then leaned back.

His stomach hurt. Things were changing. Lately, it wasn't

Julia on his mind when he couldn't sleep. It was Sophie. Damn it. He scrubbed a hand over his face.

It should have been over and done with. He'd been sure she'd have gone back to Chicago by now. When he'd turned into Dottie's drive and seen the Chevy that everybody and his brother on Cash's ranch used, a rush of emotions had flooded him.

If he was honest with himself, though, the foremost had been sheer happiness. Happiness he'd see her again. That he could share his dessert. That he could talk to her again, see her smile, hear her laugh.

What the hell was he supposed to do?

Chapter Fourteen

Sophie could not believe she'd accepted Ty's invitation. A picnic with the Triple Threat? Oh, boy. Was there a psychiatrist in Maverick Junction? If so, she needed an appointment. ASAP.

She checked herself in the mirror, unsure of her outfit. What did you wear for a picnic in Texas? On a ranch. With not one, but three little kids. And Ty. The man made her think the most delicious thoughts. That deep voice of his settled low in her stomach and caused feelings she didn't know what to do with.

She laid a hand on her midsection as nerves fluttered like no tomorrow.

She'd been so tempted to wear her Cubs shirt. But she hadn't. Instead, she'd chosen a red plaid that on first blush looked like flannel. It wasn't. The blouse itself was lined, but not the sleeves. So while it was G-rated, the sheer, see-through sleeves gave it just a hint of sex appeal. Her jeans fit well thanks to all those lunges she suffered through.

The temperature today reminded her that, even here in Texas, it was December. Not at all the extremes she'd expect in Chicago, but it had definitely cooled.

With a grin, she pulled her Cubs sweatshirt out of the closet. She'd take it along—just in case.

Hurrying down the stairs, she called to Dottie through the open kitchen window. "Are the cookies done?"

"They sure are." She swung open the door. "Want a cup of tea?"

"Not this morning, thanks. I'm running late."

"Well, then, here you go." Dottie picked up a foil-wrapped package from the counter. "Some chocolate-chip, some M&M's-filled ones, and a few of my date cookies."

"Mmmm, sounds great." Sophie gave her a hug. "Thank you so much. You're an angel."

"No problem." She winked. "Good luck today."

"It's only a picnic."

"Tell yourself that if it helps."

"But it is."

"Uh-huh. Whatever. Go now." She made a shushing motion. "Have a good time."

Sophie slid into the car and laid the directions to the Burnt Fork Ranch on the seat beside her. "Please, God, don't let me get lost in the middle of nowhere with the cows."

Somebody who'd driven the car recently had left a Kellie Pickler CD in the player, and Sophie turned it up as she drove, heater on low, windows down, and the breeze blowing her hair.

What a glorious day.

And she was going on a picnic. She racked her brain

trying to think when she'd last done that...and couldn't remember. Unless you counted Cash's barbecue—and she didn't. That was definitely not a picnic. That was an extravaganza, Texas style.

Up ahead, a road turned off to the left. She glanced at her directions and prayed again this was the road that would take her to Ty's. She'd filled up before she left town, in case she made a few mistakes on the way.

Half a mile later, she slowed, then simply stopped. Wow. This was Ty's home? So not what she'd expected. And so utterly perfect.

Nothing like the white farmhouse on Cash's ranch or the log home he'd built by the lake. Both of those fit their owner. Fit their purpose.

Ty's home did, too. The barn-red, wood-sided house had two dormers on the second story. Trimmed in white, the windows gleamed in the day's sunlight. A split rail fence guarded the front, ran around the side. A tall pine speared into the air on the left side, and small evergreens snuggled against the stone foundation.

On the other side of the drive, a couple horses grazed beyond yet another split rail fence and a small stream ran through the pasture. Several trees provided shade.

A Norman Rockwell scene.

Oh, Ty. You've created a little slice of Heaven here. This wasn't a house. This truly was a home. For him and his boys.

She took her foot off the brake and started down the lane again. The instant she pulled up to the house, the front door flew open and three boys boiled out. Behind them, Ty appeared and leaned on the door frame. His hair was mussed, and he looked casual and relaxed.

He looked so incredibly good.

A golden-haired puppy shot out the door around him. He made a grab for it and missed.

She slid from the car and braced herself for the onslaught. The pup reached her first, pawing at her leg, jumping up in a thwarted attempt to lick her face. Since he was so short, he only managed to hit her waist-high. She held the cookies in the air.

The boys arrived at her side en masse. They all started talking at once. She laughed at the unbridled enthusiasm, then caught her breath as Ty came to her and gave her a quick hug.

"Welcome to Burnt Fork, Sophie."

"Thanks for inviting me. And your home, Ty. I love it."

He grabbed the pup's collar and held him at bay.

"You gonna go with us?" one of the boys asked.

"What's in there?" Another pointed to the package of cookies she held.

"That's a surprise. For later," she said.

"I like 'prises," the third one said, bobbing up and down.

"Have any trouble finding the place?" Ty released the puppy and took her hand as they moved toward the house.

Her breath hitched at the simple gesture. At the jolt the easy touch generated. She'd been right to be wary. She felt too much with Ty, and she knew he didn't feel it back. Couldn't reciprocate.

Because he still loved his dead wife.

"That's Trouble." He pointed at the back of the dog as he raced away.

Oh, you're so right, she thought. Out loud, she said, "Well, he's beautiful, isn't he?" When Trouble shot back to them, Ty let go of her hand, and she leaned down to rub the pup's head.

"He's perfect for us." One of the boys hopped rather than walked his way to the house. "That's what Auntie Babs said."

Sophie glanced up and grinned at Ty. "I'll bet she did."

Ty shook his head. "Babs has no compunction when it comes to using whatever tricks she's got up her sleeve. Trouble was the last of the litter."

"And she needed a home for him."

"Yep."

"Oh, she's good."

"Wanna see our horsies?"

"No, I wanna show her the calf."

"Huh-uh. She needs to see the barn kitties."

"Boys." Ty held up a hand. "Cool your jets. Sophie just got here. Let's give her a minute, okay? Otherwise, she's gonna get right back in her car and run away."

"You're gonna run away from us?" Josh, devastation written all over his little face, stared at her through tear-glistened eyes.

"Oh, for Pete's sake," Ty muttered.

Stricken, Sophie knelt, putting herself at eye-level with the little boy. "No. I'm not going to run away." She sent Ty a look of reprimand.

"He cries at everything," Ty said in his own defense.

"He does." Jesse nodded.

"*I* don't," Jonah said. "'Cause I'm a big boy."

"No bigger than me." Josh sniffed. "We're all the same, aren't we, Daddy?"

"Yes, you're all four years old."

"But I was born firsted," Jonah argued. "Grandma told me."

"That's true," Ty said. "You were."

"So I'm the oldest."

Ty winced and muttered something about mothers and big mouths.

"I'm the oldest," Jonah insisted, his volume escalating.

"Technically, yes, you are."

Josh started sobbing. "Nuh-uh."

"Uh-huh."

Without thinking, Sophie pulled the little boy to her and hugged him. "It doesn't matter," she whispered in his ear. "You look like a big boy to me."

"I am." His chin trembled.

"You want to know what I have in my package?"

He nodded.

"Can you keep a secret?"

He nodded again.

She leaned close. "Some of Dottie's cookies for our picnic."

He let out a scream of joy. "Sophie's got cookies!"

Ty threw back his head and laughed. "So much for secrets."

Then his gaze ran over Sophie, and the amusement in his eyes made her weak-kneed. She realized she had one secret she needed to guard closely. This man, this strong cowboy with the wounded heart, was beginning to matter to her.

And that was a huge problem.

She couldn't afford to leave her own heart behind in Maverick Junction when she returned to Chicago.

Chapter Fifteen

Come on, guys. What do you say we head back inside and put the rest of our lunch together?"

With a mad rush, boys and pup did exactly that. It was like a mini-stampede. Sophie stepped aside and watched them go.

"Sorry about that," Ty said. "We can be a little overwhelming at times."

"Don't apologize. My guess is that life here on the ranch is far from boring."

"You got that right." A hand on her back, he guided her through the front door. "So here we are. Home, sweet home."

She didn't know what she'd expected, but after the charming exterior, the inside both surprised and disappointed her. Utilitarian and practical. No fuss. No frills.

The living room walls were off-white. The blinds were white with no drapes to soften the look. A navy blue sectional, a couple metal bookshelves, and a TV mounted on the wall comprised the entirety of the furniture. Recessed overhead lights and a floor lamp in one corner, its shade lopsided, provided the only lighting. A few toys lay scattered across the dark hardwood floor.

No piano. After Maggie had told her what an incredible pianist Julia was, she'd expected to find one in the room.

There was, though, an incredible stone fireplace.

"You can either come on back to the kitchen while I finish up or plop yourself down on the couch and wait."

"I'll help."

The kitchen was, without a doubt, the hub of this house, but, even at that, it looked pretty much the same as the front room. Off-white and, again, no curtains. What she could see of the granite countertops was gorgeous, but they were littered with a toaster, go containers, and cereal boxes. A heap of action figures tangled together, piled high in one corner. A bag of puppy food leaned against the wall. Everything was very clean—and very cluttered.

Off to the left, she saw the mudroom. Cowboy boots and rubber boots lined up haphazardly on a floor-to-ceiling set of shelves. Ty's and the boys'. Big ones and little ones. A couple wicker baskets filled the middle shelf. Hats, baseball mitts, and footballs tumbled out of them.

Turning back to the kitchen and the task at hand, she noticed a loaf of bread, a jar of peanut butter, and one of grape jelly on the kitchen table.

"Making sandwiches for the picnic?" Sophie asked.

He nodded.

"Why don't I tackle this while you finish whatever else you need to do?"

"Sounds good."

The two of them worked companionably side-by-side.

Sophie squinted at the cock-eyed wall clock.

Ty turned to see what she was looking at. "Whoops. Meant to hang that a little higher."

"That'll help?"

"Yep. It won't get whacked by swords during nightly duels to the death."

She smacked her forehead. "Of course. I should have known."

"So, the house. I'd ask what you thought of it, but your expression when you walked in pretty much said it all. FYI? You should never play poker."

She started to deny it but shrugged instead. "The outside is, well, fantastic. I actually stopped the car partway down the lane just to sit and look at it."

"But—"

"The inside?" She scrunched up her face. "Not quite what I expected."

"Not much, is it?" He didn't seem in the least offended.

"It's not that, really. It's very...serviceable." She shrugged. "No muss, no fuss, no nonsense."

"In other words, ugly as sin." He chuckled. "It's okay. Babs is after me all the time to do something with the place. It works for us, though. There's nothing the kids can really mess up."

"I suppose. The décor is, well, very masculine."

He spread his hands. "Guilty as charged. We're four guys living alone. That's about as masculine as you get."

"But your wife must have—"

"No." He shook his head. "Julia never lived here. In fact, I didn't build this house till a couple years ago. The boys were a little over two when we moved in."

There'd never been a woman's touch. That explained a lot.

As she bagged the sandwiches, the boys thundered down the stairs and scrambled into the kitchen, Trouble at their heels. She watched as they surrounded their dad where he stood at the kitchen sink, all six-four of him with three little boys climbing on his legs. He dwarfed them, yet there wasn't a trace of hesitation on their faces. Love. Nothing but love.

For the first time, the full magnitude of what he dealt with on a daily basis hit her. He held the total responsibility for these little lives in his hands, and that was one gigantic job.

Picking up a wicker basket he'd already partially filled, he opened it and scooped the PB and J sandwiches she'd bagged inside. "Ready, guys?"

Three heads bobbed.

"Anybody need to hit the head before we take off?"

"No," they all said.

"Okay then." He led them outside. "I thought we might take a ride, Tink. The boys and I found a great picnic spot."

"Close?"

"Not too far. A mile, maybe."

"Sounds great." She headed toward his pickup.

He stopped, watching her. "Where are you going?"

"You said we were driving there."

"I said *ride*."

Slowly she turned toward the stables. "On horseback?"

"Yep."

She felt herself blanch. "You know, Annelise? A great horsewoman. Me? I only rode when I couldn't escape it. I'm not especially fond of horses and haven't been on one since camp a thousand years ago."

"Why?" asked one of the triplets.

"Because they're—" She glanced down into baby-innocent eyes and bit back her words.

Backtracking, she said, "I mean, you kids don't ride, do you? Wouldn't it be easier to take Daddy's big black truck?"

"Huh-uh." A second one spoke up, and the others showed solidarity by shaking their heads, too.

She stared at them. For the life of her, she couldn't tell the boys apart. She'd have to ask Ty if there was a trick to it, some little thing that differentiated them. A cowlick or a mole, maybe.

And speaking of Ty. He stood, picnic basket in one hand, the other in his jeans pocket, grinning.

"You're enjoying all this, aren't you?"

"Yep."

"Come on, Sophie. It'll be fun." The third one tugged at her hand.

"Yeah, Sophie, you'll like it."

"Wait'll you see all the poo," said the third. "You have to be careful where you step, 'cause the cows go there some-times."

The other two nodded solemnly in agreement.

"My mother did warn me," she muttered.

"Yeah, I heard." The laughter left Ty's voice.

"You did?" Shocked, she turned to face him.

He nodded.

"Ty—"

"Not now."

She sighed. The sun disappeared momentarily behind a cloud. Wonderful, she thought. The sudden shadow fit her mood to a T. Well, she couldn't disappoint the kids, but she would, she promised, get even with Ty for springing the horse ride on her.

And they'd also have a chat about the conversation he'd overheard at the wedding reception. Darn her mother anyway.

Crossing the yard, Ty said, "It's a short ride, Sophie. Promise. On horseback, the two of us could be there in ten, fifteen minutes easy. But with these boys?" He grimaced. "I'll need to ride herd on them to keep them moving. Otherwise, they dawdle and mess around enough to drive you crazy."

Hands in his pockets, he watched as the trio raced into the barn. "They're gonna make good horsemen. All of them have the basics down, but, well, they're four." He sighed. "And that about says it all."

Walking beside him, Sophie nodded. When she stepped into the stable, she breathed deeply, surprised at how strangely pleasant the scent of hay and horse was. She was amazed, too, to find she hadn't forgotten how to saddle her own mount.

As she tightened her cinch, she glanced across the barn and saw Ty and one of the boys in deep conversation, the two dark heads practically touching. She wished she had a camera to capture the moment. Tucking away the details, she decided she'd sketch the scene when she returned to Dottie's.

When they finished, Ty walked to the far wall and took down some fishing poles.

"Wait a minute." She held up a hand. "What're those?"

"Fishing rods."

She blew out a huff. "I know that. I meant, what are you doing with them?"

"We're going fishing!" One of the kids did a little twist and shout across the straw.

"Yeah." The other two chimed in, dancing in a circle with their brother.

"Ty?"

"Sophie?"

"I don't fish."

He fastened the poles onto his saddle, then put a hand on her butt and boosted her onto her horse. "You said you didn't ride, either."

"I said I didn't *like* riding." She shook her head. "I've never fished in my life."

"Then it's high time you did, right boys?"

"Uh-huh." One dark little head bobbed. "We'll help you, won't we?"

He looked at his brothers who both agreed. The boys chatted a mile a minute about how much fun they'd have as their dad lifted them one by one onto their ponies.

As they rode out of the stable, Ty said, "You don't have a problem with fishing on some philosophical level, do you? I mean, you're not a vegan or anything. I watched you devour too much Texas beef at the wedding to believe that."

"You're right. I'm not. I don't believe, however, a gentleman comments on the amount a lady eats."

His horse ambling beside hers, Ty adjusted his cowboy hat. "No, ma'am, guess not." His dimples twinkled. "So do I apologize for my comment or simply admit I'm not a gentleman?"

"You're bad, that's what you are." She clucked at her horse and realized she was actually having a good time. Who'd have thought?

* * *

Ty was right about the spot. They brought their horses to a stop at the top of a knoll graced by several beautiful old oaks. At the base of the hillock, a small stream flowed, willows draping their branches gracefully over the slow-moving water.

They spread a blanket in the shade of one of the oaks and dug in. While the boys devoured their peanut butter sandwiches and chips as if they might never get another meal, she and Ty enjoyed rare roast beef sandwiches and potato salad from Sadler's.

The sun warmed her back and hair, and she totally relaxed. It was as if the world had shrunk to this one spot, this one moment. The boys, flopped on their backs talking about day care and Miss Marcy, wolfed down Dottie's cookies. Ty reached out and linked his fingers with hers, and she knew she'd remember this moment forever.

Trouble frolicked in the tall grass. He'd ridden in a basket on Jesse's pony and was having a great time just being a puppy. He licked and kissed each of the boys in turn, sending them into hysterical giggles.

The horses, tethered to the trees, grazed peacefully. A butterfly landed on the picnic basket beside her.

The day couldn't have been more right.

Then one of the boys hopped up and pulled on Ty's arm, reminding him he'd promised they could fish. It was Jesse. Sophie knew without asking. As she'd watched them play, listened to them, she picked up small nuances and tiny differences. She grinned, feeling as though she'd clawed her way over some invisible hurdle.

The boys were becoming individuals.

Patiently Ty sauntered to the tree where he'd propped the rods and opened his fishing basket.

A few minutes later, all the warm feelings gone, Sophie was totally sorry she'd come along. "What do you mean I stick the hook through him?" She stared at the worm in her hand. It wriggled, and she shrieked, flinging it to the ground.

"I can't do this."

Jesse scooped it up and let the worm slither over his pudgy little hand.

"Like this." Jonah held up his pole. Another fat worm dangled from the hook, and he stepped closer to her. "Look how all the stuff comes out, Sophie. It's his guts."

She gagged. "Ty, I can't."

"Jonah, get that out of Sophie's face. Go drown it in the water."

Her mouth dropped open.

"What?"

"Is that what you teach them?"

"Sophie." He spread his hands. "It's a saying."

"But that is what you're doing. You're drowning them. After you've impaled them."

He handed the pole he'd baited to Josh. "How else do you think we're going to catch a fish?"

"I don't know. In Sam's deli at the end of my street? At a restaurant? At Sadler's maybe?"

The boys stared at her.

"It's a girl thing," Ty told them.

"'Kay, Daddy," Josh said.

But the little boy's big, dark eyes said she'd let him down. Guilt ate at her, but there was no way she'd skewer that worm.

"Go ahead and get started. Sophie and I will be with you in a minute. And try to stay out of the water."

The three took off for the little stream, the puppy right behind them.

"I'll bait your pole with a salmon egg," Ty conceded.

She nodded, relieved when the orange glob slid over her hook. That she could live with.

They walked down the gentle slope together. Trouble, all feet and ears, splashed in the water, then raced out to shake himself, drenching them all.

When he headed into the stream again, Ty scolded him. "Get out of there, Trouble. You're scaring away the fish."

Sophie was secretly glad. She absolutely did not want to see any fish flopping around in the grass, gasping for breath.

* * *

Ty sat on an outcropping of rock, his long legs stretched in front of him, ankles crossed, pole loose in his hand. The boys had given up even the pretense of fishing, their attention spans that of microscopic gnats. Squeals and laughter filled the grassy area as they chased each other and Trouble through the grass.

No doubt about it. Today had been one of the best days in way too long. And the woman beside him, sitting in the grass, her line bobbing in the water, was a big part of the reason why. To be really honest, it surprised the hell out of him. He'd figured the kids would scare her off. They hadn't. They'd taken to each other like fleas on a dog.

Oh, she wasn't totally at ease with three squirming, noisy boys, but she wasn't put off by them, either. The breeze picked up, and the late-afternoon air turned chilly. Overhead, the willow branches swayed and the leaves rustled.

Ty laid down his pole. "Be right back."

He pulled jackets from his saddlebag and tossed one to each of the boys. "Put these on, guys."

Impressed, Sophie said, "Well, aren't you the prepared one."

"Always. With these three it pays to think ahead. I noticed you already crawled into your nasty sweatshirt."

"Oh!" She slapped a hand over the big red C logo.

"Any port in a storm, I guess," he drawled. "But, hey, if you need it, you need it."

"I do." She tossed a look at the kids, their faces flushed from their exercise. "I'm not running around like them. I got cold sooner."

"Should have told me. I'd have warmed you up." He draped an arm over her shoulder, shooting for playful. The softness of her, though, did things to him. Warned him he really should keep his distance.

She laughed and patted his hand. Jerking a thumb at the kids, she said, "Right, Daddy." She sent him a slow smile. "Maybe later."

The words shot straight south in his body. *Maybe later.* The breath left him as his mind conjured up images far from fatherly.

Space. He needed some space.

Picking up his pole, he reeled in his line and cast another glance toward the sky. "Think it's time to head home. Front's moving in fast."

Inside of ten minutes, they were saddled up and headed toward the house. The boys, tuckered out from all the fresh air, grew quieter and quieter.

About halfway home, Josh started whining. "I want to ride with you, Daddy."

"What about your pony? How's he gonna get home if you don't ride him?" Part of Ty wanted to scoop the tired little boy up onto his lap. The other part feared the consequences of giving in to Josh too often. Still, his son was dragging butt.

"You can tie his pony to mine, Daddy, if he wants to ride with you." Jonah, as ever, made it his duty to find a compromise.

Jesse piped up. "Why does he get to ride with you and not me?"

"Because he's tireder," Jonah said.

"Uh-uh. I am," Jesse insisted.

Sophie, Ty noted, said nothing. She sent him a pitying look.

"Want to step in here? Help out?"

She grinned. "Wouldn't think of it. I don't want to interfere. Don't want to risk stepping on any toes—Daddy."

He shook his head. "You're a sassy one."

"I can be."

Again, heat rocketed through him. This woman was seriously hard on his system. He wanted to do things to her he hadn't even thought of for far too long.

"Daddy!"

Josh's cry interrupted his sexual fantasies and dragged him back to his immediate problem.

"Josh, we're almost home."

When he started to cry, Sophie lifted a brow.

"Hold on a second, guys." Ty held up his hand and everyone plodded to a stop. "Josh, toss me your reins, then crawl on over here with me." He patted the saddle in front of him.

Tears streaming down his cheeks, the boy did as he was told. Ty wrapped the pony's reins around his saddle horn, then lifted Josh onto his lap. "And Jesse, I don't want to hear a word from you. If I'm not mistaken, I've given you a ride home a time or two."

"But I want—"

"Jesse."

His son's lower lip stuck out in a pout, but he held his tongue.

The minute they rode up to the stables, all tiredness was forgotten. Jesse and Jonah dismounted with whoops, and Ty lowered Josh to the ground. Jonah lifted Trouble out of the basket and set him down. The pup flopped to the ground, exhausted from the day's antics.

"The boys and I will take care of your horse, Sophie. No doubt we've worn you out."

"Oh, no. Taking care of the horse afterward was the only part of riding I excelled at. Toss me a brush."

Ty sent the boys outside to play. Working together, he and Sophie had the horses unsaddled and curried in a much shorter time than if his boys had helped. Ty gave each a scoop of oats and some fresh water. Side by side, he and Sophie walked from the stable into the chilled air.

"Gonna see a big change in the weather," he said, eyeing the sky. "The temperature's dropping fast."

She shook her head. "You're talking to a Northerner, Ty. I could be in Chicago right now. Probably should be. It's fourteen below there today—without the wind chill. So I'm figuring the weather's great."

"Guess it's all relative, huh?"

"Yes, it is."

"Want to stay for a bit?" He hoped she'd say yes. Found himself holding his breath.

"I'd love to, but I really should get home. I need to work a bit. I had a great time, though." She rose on her toes, kissed his cheek. "I can't thank you enough."

Raising her voice, she called out, "Boys, thanks for a

wonderful day. Jesse, thanks for the tip about keeping the end of my pole up. That made a big difference. Jonah, the lemonade you helped your dad make was the best I've ever tasted. And, Josh? The flowers you picked for me are beautiful. I'll take them home and put them on my kitchen table." She held up the drooping wildflowers.

If she'd thought a verbal good-bye would do it for the Rawlins boys, she found herself sorely mistaken. As they rushed her, she gave them each a hug and added a peck on the cheek.

And that caused another shift in Ty's chest.

"Can't you stay?" Jesse asked.

"Yeah, just a little bit longer." Jonah tugged at her hand.

"Who's gonna make us hot chocolate?" Josh pouted.

Even though he himself wanted to beg her to stay, Ty stepped in. "Guys, give Sophie a break. She has work to do at her house."

"Why can't she do it here?"

She sat down on a bale of hay left there to prop open the stable door. "Tell you what. I really do have to go, not only because of my work, but because I have a new cat at home. I found her this week, and I'm afraid to leave her alone too much longer. I don't want her to be scared. If it's okay with your dad, though, I'll come back again."

She looked at him as if asking permission.

He nodded.

"You have a kitty?" Jonah played with Trouble's ear when he wandered over to them.

"A cat, actually," Sophie said. "She's bigger than a kitty."

"Can you bring her, too?"

"What's her name?"

Ty listened as she patiently answered all their questions,

smoothed their hair, and zipped up Jesse's jacket. His heart shifted a little more in his chest.

"I'll walk you to your car. Boys, why don't you go inside. It's getting cold. I'll be right in." As they hurried away, he called, "And hang up those jackets. Don't drop them in the middle of the floor."

Sophie stood, one hand on the car door handle. He leaned toward her and tucked a stray strand of hair behind her ear.

"You're a brave woman. You took on the lot of us—and you survived."

"I meant what I said before, Ty. I had a great time. One of the best days ever."

His heart hammered in his chest, and he wondered if she could hear it. He needed to see her again.

He couldn't.

He needed to kiss her again.

He shouldn't.

But his mouth refused to listen to his brain. Before he could stop himself, he ducked his head and tasted her lips. *Oh, yeah. Ambrosia.* He groaned and pulled her to him.

Damned if she didn't turn him inside out.

His lips a whisper from hers, he asked, "Want to go out Saturday night? No kids. Just you and me."

"I'd like that."

"Thank God," he growled. He kissed her again but forced himself to keep it light. "I'll pick you up at seven."

He opened the car door and helped her in.

Then he stood in the drive and watched her drive away. What the hell was he doing?

Chapter Sixteen

Sophie took a long, hot bath and fell into bed exhausted. How did Ty do this every day? Handle the ranch, a house, three kids, and a puppy? And then get up the next day and do it all over again?

By the end of the picnic, she'd been able to tell the boys apart—most of the time. Their personalities were totally different. And physically there were differences, too. Josh had a cowlick. Jonah was left-handed. Jesse's eyes were a slightly deeper gray.

But being with the triplets was a little like being inside a pinball machine. Kids ricocheting off everything...and they'd been outside where they had the run of the place. She couldn't imagine being cooped up inside with them.

The boys were rambunctious now, but she tried to imagine them as tiny babies. How had Ty coped with the bottles, the night feedings, the diapers—times three? She pictured those tiny preemies cradled in his large, capable hands.

She'd never really given much thought to parenthood. Oh, a vague, someday-maybe notion rattled around in the back of her mind once in a while. But she hadn't ever spent any real time with babies or young children. Hadn't ever been given a peanut butter and jelly kiss before today.

Unaware she was crying, the tear that trickled down her cheek and dripped off her chin caught her unaware. She swiped at it, then rolled over in bed and simply gave in to her roiling emotions.

She cried for Ty. For what he'd been through. Was still dealing with. Mourning the loss of his wife, caring for three young boys, struggling to keep all the balls in the air. His love for his sons was beyond amazing.

She cried for the boys, for Jonah and Jesse and Josh. They'd never know their mother. Never know her love. Never be tucked into bed and kissed good night by her.

And she cried for Julia, a woman she'd never met. The woman Ty loved. The woman who'd never had a chance to know the miracle of these wonderful boys to whom she'd given life.

Fate could be cruel.

Lilybelle jumped onto the bed and curled up beside her. Sophie buried her face in the cat's fur and cried till she ran out of tears.

She'd worked herself into a state. Sleep? Not likely. Not till she got herself settled down. Was Ty asleep, or was he restless, too? If she called him...No, absolutely, definitely not.

She threw back the bedcovers. "What do you say to some ice cream, Lilybelle? I have some Cherry Garcia left and a whole new carton of cake batter ice cream."

She tossed on her robe and walked into the kitchen, the

cat at her heels. Flicking on the lights, she decided a little music was in order. The radio was still set to Annelise's new favorite station, a country-western one. Well, that would do. She might as well listen to songs about lost love and cheating hearts while she anesthetized herself with ice cream.

Sitting at the table, Lilybelle at her feet, the two gorged themselves on Cherry Garcia. Sophie ate hers right out of the container. Her butt and legs hurt from the horseback ride. Muscles she hadn't used in a long time were crying foul.

One elbow on the table, her chin resting on her hand, she grinned from ear to ear. It really had been a first-rate picnic. A first-rate day. She couldn't remember ever being this tired or this happy. And yet her eyes were bloodshot from a crying jag. Boy, she was on one heck of an emotional roller coaster.

The peak? Ty had asked her out. And she'd said yes. That's when she'd tumbled downhill. Oh, boy. What had she been thinking?

She flicked on the TV and ran through the channels, settling on an old black-and-white movie, *An Affair to Remember*. Sighing, she settled on the couch, cat tucked close, an afghan over both of them.

*   *   *

Eight hours later, she woke up exactly as she'd fallen asleep. She doubted either she or the cat had moved an inch all night. Turning off the TV, she inched her way off the couch, careful not to disturb Lilybelle.

Filling the teakettle, she took stock of her situation and made a decision. Today, she'd drive over to Lone Tree. Time to pay Maggie a visit. She needed some girl time.

Right now, though, she'd better feed her animal. The instant the cat heard the can opener, she leaped off the sofa gingerly, still favoring her hurt leg. As Sophie emptied the stinky food into the bowl, Lilybelle wound herself around Sophie's legs.

"See, who says you can't buy love?" She knelt and stroked the cat beneath her chin. "A can of food is pretty cheap."

Dunking a tea bag, she headed for the bathroom, ready to prep for the day. Her phone rang and she snatched it off the nightstand? *Ty?*

It wasn't. It was Madison, the owner of a little shop in Chicago that carried her note cards.

"Hey, Madison, how are you?"

"Great. And you? Good trip?"

"The best. I even went fishing yesterday. Just me and four handsome guys."

"Oh, yeah? Maybe I should hop a plane and join you."

Sophie laughed. "Umm, maybe I forgot to mention that three of the guys were only four years old."

"The fourth guy?"

She sighed. "That one checks all the boxes. A tall, dark, and extremely handsome cowboy. And the father of the other three."

"Seriously?"

"Yep."

"I know you wouldn't be messing around with a married man."

"Nope. This cowboy is a widower."

Silence.

"You still there, Madison?"

"I'm visualizing this great big old can of worms springing open."

Sophie laughed. "Yeah, I'm with you on that. But he's staying here, and I'm leaving. Soon. So those worms aren't going to get very tangled." She glanced at the clock. "So what's up? A problem with one of my cards? An obscenely huge order for more because some celebrity discovered my work and has made me an overnight success?"

When Madison remained silent, unease rippled through Sophie.

"Nathan was here a few days ago."

The unease turned to queasiness, and Sophie dropped onto the side of the unmade bed.

"I didn't call sooner because I didn't want to bother you. But it's been nagging at me, and I decided you should at least be aware. He wanted to know where you are," Madison said.

Her throat tightened. "What did you tell him?"

"When you stopped by a couple weeks ago, you mentioned taking a trip to Texas for your cousin's wedding."

Sophie couldn't hide the involuntary groan.

"I didn't tell him that," Madison said quickly.

"No?"

"No. Something about him, Sophie—I don't know. He bothered me, so I said I had absolutely no idea."

"Thank you."

"Is he a problem?"

How did she answer that? She pushed stray strands of hair off her face. "Honestly, I don't know."

"There are stalker laws."

Was Nathan a stalker? Had it progressed to that? She didn't think so. "I'll be fine, Madison, but I really appreciate the heads-up."

"You be careful."

"I will."

"How's the new line coming?" Madison asked. "I've got customers chomping at the bit for some new Sophie London designs."

They chatted a bit longer, but when Sophie hung up she felt more than a little rattled. Before she slipped into the bathroom, she checked the door, made sure she'd flipped the lock.

* * *

Half an hour later, dressed in her go-to black jeans and a loose, flowing red silk top, she headed out the door. Determined to shove Nathan from her mind, she focused on the day ahead. On her visit with Maggie.

The drive relaxed her. There was virtually no traffic to deal with and she found a radio station that played a nice blend of music. She put her window partway down, wanting to feel the wind in her hair. But even here in Texas, it was December, and a slight nip tinged the air. Reaching over, she flipped the heater on low, instantly surrounded by warmth. She had to give it to Hank. The car might not be much to look at, but mechanically? It was in excellent condition.

Growing up in Boston, then moving to Chicago, she'd never known the thrill of the open road. One where you could drive forever, stop whenever, do whatever. She felt almost heady with the freedom. No doubt about it. This trip wouldn't mark the end of her time in Texas. She planned to make good use of Cash and Annelise's guest room. When she needed a breath of fresh air, she knew exactly where to find it.

She and Katy Perry were singing a duet as she drove

into Lone Tree. She smiled. Main Street looked a whole lot better than it had the last time she'd seen it. Storefronts were garbed in Christmas greenery and decorations. Even the ugly, black, utilitarian streetlights, now festooned with pine boughs and red ribbons, had taken on a cheerful holiday spirit.

A snowy forest scene depicting animals and birds celebrating the season had been painted on the Cowboy Grill's front window.

Grabbing her purse, she removed her sunglasses. She'd done the right thing coming here today—especially after Madison's call. But she wouldn't think about that now. Today was all about R and R.

The bell over Maggie's door jingled, adding to the holiday feel. She stepped inside and breathed deeply. Ah, yes. Good decision. Closing her eyes, the scent of evergreens and Christmas washed over her.

"Hey, girlfriend. What are you doing way over here in my neck of the woods?" Maggie stepped out of the back room looking for all the world like a model straight off the runway.

They hugged and Maggie stepped back, eyeing her critically. "Somebody didn't get much sleep last night."

"Really?" Sophie asked, all innocence. "And who might that be?"

"What's wrong, honey?"

Her mind a certifiable disaster area, she tamped down her unease about Nathan and went with her bigger, more immediate concern. "Oh, Maggie. I'm so confused."

"Well, then, you've come to the right place. I'll get out my tea leaves, and we'll see what's going on."

Sophie laughed. "I like you."

"I'm glad, because I like you, too. Annie's got damn good taste in relatives." She walked to one of the overstuffed chairs, dropped into it, and put her stiletto-shoed feet on the coffee table. "Any excuse to sit."

She waved at the chair beside her. "Have a seat, and tell Mama Sullivan your troubles."

Sophie dropped her purse to the floor and collapsed into the chair. "Ty asked me out Saturday night. Just the two of us. No kids."

"Really?" Maggie dragged out the word. Satisfaction shone in her green eyes. "What do you know. Finally."

"Finally?"

"He hasn't been on a date since Julia died."

"No way."

"Yes, way."

"Oh, my gosh." Sophie raised a hand to her forehead. "That makes all this—I don't know—so much more." She toyed with the little gold band on her thumb. "Do you think I should go?"

Maggie laughed. "Hell, yes. Why wouldn't you?"

"Ty has a very complicated life."

"Yes, he certainly does. And he, more than anyone I know, deserves a little happiness. He wants to spend some time with you, Sophie. He wants normal. He's tired of everybody looking at him and seeing the widower. The man with the fragile shell."

Sophie twisted a strand of hair around her finger but said nothing.

"If you're truly not interested, you need to let him know, because him asking you out? That was huge. A really big step. One I wondered if he'd ever get around to taking."

Maggie rested an elbow on the arm of her chair and

cradled her chin in her hand. "Here's the thing, though. I wouldn't dangle him on the line too long. You might not want to take on the boys and all the rest of Ty's baggage, but other females in both Maverick Junction and Lone Tree don't have the same reservations. He could have his pick of them. And believe me when I say they haven't been bashful. Quite a few have offered. But he hasn't taken interest in any of them."

She met Sophie's gaze. "He's got his eye on you. As far as I'm concerned, that's a very good thing."

Sophie nodded. "First, I want to make it clear that I don't see the triplets as part of any baggage he might have. Jesse, Josh, and Jonah are wonderful. Ty's doing a phenomenal job with them."

"Good for you."

"But, that said," Sophie continued, "they are a handful. And they're part of a package deal. A woman would have to be crazy not to take that into consideration. It's a lot to think about."

"It is."

Sophie rolled her eyes. "Then again, Ty's only asked me on a date, not to take a walk down the aisle. I'm blowing this all out of proportion, aren't I?"

"You might be." Maggie kept a straight face.

"I tend to do that. Worry about possibilities. Invent impossible scenarios." She paused. "Okay, let's jump backward a little. You mentioned dangling things on a line. We went fishing yesterday."

"Fishing?"

"Yes, and thank God nobody caught anything."

Maggie smiled. "Not into that sort of thing, huh?"

"No. But, boy, did we have fun. We took a picnic along.

Ty and the boys and me. And Trouble. And we went on horseback."

"Really?"

"I was terrified at first, at the idea of it. I've not spent much time around kids, and I haven't ridden a horse in years." Grinning, she rubbed her aching backside. "Still, I had a ball."

"I can see that." Maggie tipped her head to the side. "You didn't answer my question, though."

"You didn't ask a question. You just filled me in on the lay of the land, so to speak."

"Guess you're right. So I'll ask it now. Are you interested? In Ty?"

Sophie let out a big breath and steepled her hands in front of her mouth. "I'm not going to lie. My survival instincts tell me to run. Fast and far. But I won't, because, yes, I'm interested." She turned and met her friend's gaze. "What am I getting myself into, Maggie?"

"Maybe nothing. The two of you might go out Saturday night and find there's absolutely nothing there. That you have nothing in common. That there's no spark between you." Those fantastic green eyes narrowed.

Sophie fidgeted under Maggie's scrutiny.

"But that's not going to happen, is it? Because you already know. You've tested it, and there's plenty of spark to rev both your engines." Maggie pointed a finger at her. "What aren't you telling me?"

"Nothing." Sophie's grin grew. "Okay. He kissed me and, oh, my God, Maggie. He's so hot. I thought I might ignite and burn to a cinder right there and then."

She fanned herself, thinking about it. Remembering the touch of his lips on hers, the heat, the excitement.

Maggie chuckled. "Well, well. Ty Rawlins, you sexy devil, you." She jumped to her feet. "Want something to drink? A cup of tea, maybe? I'd offer you wine, but it's probably a little early in the day for that."

"Tea would be great. Do you have time, though? I mean, I've crashed in here while you're working."

"Honey, I have all the time in the world. And we'll need it. After all, it'll take a while to decide on your new outfit."

"My new outfit? For what?"

Maggie's mouth dropped open. "Sophie London, don't you dare tell me you haven't been thinking about something new to wear on your date."

"I don't even know where he's taking me."

"Doesn't matter."

Sophie took a few seconds to fight with herself. Oh, she'd love to walk out of here with one of Maggie's creations, but she couldn't. Time to be honest and fess up.

Sophie clasped her fingers tightly together and looked around the incredible shop. "The truth? I can't afford to buy anything new."

Maggie, to her credit, did a good job masking her surprise. But it was there, and Sophie saw it.

"Here's the deal. Annelise's family has mega-bucks. I doubt anyone can count high enough to total their worth. My family?" She laughed without a hint of remorse or bitterness. "We're the poor relations—by anyone's standards. We've always had everything we've wanted or needed, but..." She shrugged.

"I assumed—"

"I know. Believe me, my entire life people have assumed. The Montjoys have been more than generous. They always sent me to summer camp with Annelise, took me on trips, and never, ever made me feel less. But I live on what I earn from my greeting cards. My clothes come from consignment stores and secondhand shops." She fluttered a hand. "My mortgage payment is due. So as much as it pains me, I simply can't afford to buy here."

"Yes, you can," Maggie insisted. "Annie paid way, way too much for her Dallas dress. I argued with her about it, but you know your cousin."

"I do. She can be pretty bullheaded."

"That's an understatement. And the publicity that's come my way because she's wearing my designs? It's like a dream come true. The way I figure it, I owe her, so whatever we choose will help ease my conscience. I'm running a mental tab, and the way I see it, you'll barely make a dent."

When Sophie opened her mouth to object, Maggie said, "No arguing. I want to do this for Ty, too." Brooking no further discussion, she headed to the back room to start a pot of tea.

Sophie was torn. Part of her wanted to sneak out the front door. Wanted to leave before Maggie came back into the display area. Despite herself, though, she fell under the shop's spell. Caving to the allure, she promised herself she'd keep a tally, and someday she'd repay Maggie. She wouldn't be a charity case.

She needn't have worried. Maggie, with her incredible enthusiasm, made it fun. The two talked, drank tea, and mulled over their options, putting together possible outfits. One by one, Sophie tried each on, modeling them for Maggie.

"You know, I told Annie she had the perfect figure to design for, but you're a dream, too." She straightened the shoulders on Sophie's top. "You're not tall enough to model, but everything's in perfect proportion. I'd give anything to have that waist."

"My boobs are too small."

"No, they're not. They're a designer's ideal."

"Guys want big ones."

"Apparently Ty hasn't been turned off by yours."

"He hasn't seen them yet."

"Yet?"

Heat rushed over her face. "You know what I mean."

Before Maggie could dig deeper, the bell over the door tinkled, and Sophie's heart jumped into her throat. She raised a hand to it, then chastised herself. Nathan would not be showing up in Maverick Junction. She was playing the fool.

As several customers drifted into the store, chatting a mile a minute, Maggie's shrewd gaze caught hers. "You okay?"

"Absolutely. A little jumpy. Leftover nerves from yesterday."

"Nothing else we need to talk about?"

Sophie shook her head. She would not entangle Maggie in this whole Nathan fiasco. Besides, she was making too much of it.

Although Maggie didn't look totally convinced, she turned to welcome her new customers, showing them pieces that worked perfectly for each. Sophie watched in awe. Maggie was as good a salesperson as she was a designer.

At one point, she wandered close to Sophie and whispered, "You're not off the hook. I intend to hear more about your boobs and Ty."

Sophie laughed.

None of the women who'd come in left empty-handed.

When the shop was theirs alone again, they decided on a pair of winter white slacks with a long-sleeve, lacy sweater in a rose-pink.

Sophie studied her reflection in the mirror. The color combination was perfect with her hair. The pink brightened her skin. "I have just the jewelry to wear with this. A necklace and earrings made of rose quartz and green tourmaline."

Maggie nodded. "Good choice. Rose quartz, the love stone, heals the heart, and green tourmaline stimulates happiness. Exactly right on all counts."

Surprised, Sophie met Maggie's eyes in the mirror.

"You didn't expect me to know that?"

Sophie shrugged. "Most people don't. I should have known you would. There's a lot of fanciful mixed with the practicality in your designs."

"Nicely said. I like that. I also like jewelry. Even more when there's some significance to it." Her face sobered. "I believe in fate, too. You're right where you need to be at this moment, Sophie. After spending what little time I have with you, I can see why Ty finds you fascinating."

"Oh, I don't think he—"

"Tell you what." Maggie leaped up from the chair where she lounged again. "I'm ready for food. Let's put up the closed sign and grab lunch at Ollie's."

* * *

Driving home to Maverick Junction after having stuffed herself with the special of the day, the most delicious taco salad she'd ever eaten, Sophie let out a happy squeal. If she hadn't needed to keep both hands on the wheel, she'd have hugged herself. Today had been fun. More and more she was coming to realize the pull of this area, of these people, on Annelise.

That certainly didn't mean she'd ever give up her Chicago lifestyle to live here. No way.

For Annelise, the place was perfect.

For herself? She couldn't see it. She needed more.

Her phone rang, startling her.

A silly grin still on her face, she pulled her cell from her purse. "Hello."

"When are you coming home?"

She bit back the groan. Fought the urge to toss her phone out the window. Talk about putting a damper on a great day.

"Sophie?" Nathan sounded angry. "I'll come get you if I need to. You've been gone way too long."

"Nathan—"

"It's time you came home, Sophie. To me."

Threads of fear slithered through her.

Chapter Seventeen

Sophie pulled into the drive. Dead-tired, feet leaden, she moved to the other side of the car to retrieve her new outfit. Draping the plastic-wrapped bundle over her arm, she closed the door.

Saturday night with Ty would be fun. She needed to concentrate on that and put Nathan out of her mind. A thousand or so frozen miles separated them. There was no way he'd fly to Texas, his threat to come get her an empty one. Besides, he didn't know where to find her.

She'd hung up on him without a word. Maybe that would serve to finally get her message across. All the placating, the trying to let him down easily, then the more direct conversations—none had worked.

Well, she wouldn't talk to him again. She'd check that damnable caller ID every time. If it was him, she would not answer.

Halfway up the stairs, she noticed the UPS package on the landing. Her art supplies. Woo-hoo!

Because she hadn't intended to stay more than a few days, she'd only brought the bare minimum. Now that she'd decided to stay longer, had broken through her block and was actually working again, she needed a few more of her things along with some paper files she'd left at home.

Thank God for Dee. One phone call and she'd boxed up what Sophie needed and dropped them in the mail.

Stepping over the box, Sophie opened the apartment door, dumped her purse on the counter, and walked into the bedroom to hang up her new clothes. Back in the kitchen, she stopped at the fridge, grabbed an ice cold Coke, and popped the top. Without even closing the refrigerator door, she took a long refreshing drink.

Fortified, she slipped back outside and picked up the package. She spotted her landlady in the small yard, clipping her few remaining roses. "Hey, Dottie."

"You were up early."

"I was." Leaning on the railing, Sophie told her about her trip to Maggie's.

"Something special going on that you need a new outfit? Can an old lady hope it has something to do with Ty?"

She felt the blush, cursed her fair skin. Deciding to skirt the issue, she said, "I got the most beautiful pair of slacks, Dottie, and a top in your favorite color."

"Pink?" The woman clapped her hands.

"Is there any other?" Sophie laughed. "I'll bring them down later to show you. Maggie's things are so absolutely incredible. I don't know how she does it."

"It's a gift. And speaking of gifts, I see you got a package today."

She shook her head. "Unfortunately, it's not a gift. It's a few art supplies I forgot to bring with me."

"Really?" Dottie looked skeptical. "With all those hearts drawn on the bottom of the package?"

"What?"

"I wasn't snooping," Dottie insisted. "The UPS guy tried to drop it off at my door. I told him he could just carry it right on up to your place. Why should you have to? That's his job. That's when I saw the hearts."

Sophie's brow furrowed as she knelt down and picked up the box. "That doesn't make sense. Dee's return address is on here. It has to be—" She turned the box over and saw the initials NR in the corner along with several bloodred hearts.

Dee wouldn't have done that. It had to be Nathan's work. When? How?

She should have talked to Dee about him. About her concerns. But she hadn't. She'd kept it to herself. Bile rose in her throat.

Seeing the concern on her landlady's face, Sophie pasted on a smile. "It's okay. Another friend did it, fooling around."

"You sure? You look awfully pale."

"I'm sure."

"Fine. Then you can answer my earlier question."

"What was that?"

"Is the boy taking you out?"

"The boy?"

"Ty. Did you buy the new outfit for him? Are the two of you stepping out?"

She had to laugh. "Stepping out? I don't know about that, but he is taking me to dinner. I think."

"You think?"

"He's picking me up Saturday evening. He didn't say where we were going or what we'd be doing, but I'm assuming dinner will be included."

"Well, now, praise the Lord. I was afraid he'd never leap that hurdle."

"It's only an evening out," Sophie warned.

"Understood." Clippers in hand, Dottie stood up, hands on her hips. "Gotta take that first step before you can walk, though, don't you?"

"I suppose so." Sophie looked out over the area. "Think I'll draw a few more scenes this afternoon. The garden looks different every day."

Dottie's eyes twinkled. "You're very good at changing the subject."

Sophie laughed. "Speaking of changing the subject, I'm going to do it again. What's the vine climbing on your rock wall?"

"A trumpet vine. If you're here this coming summer, you'll want to paint its flowers." Catching her expression, Dottie said, "I know, I know. You plan to return to Chicago. But, well, you never can tell what might happen."

Deciding to ignore the woman's blatant matchmaking attempts, Sophie said, "It's possible I'll be down next summer to visit Annelise and Cash."

"You might."

"You spend a lot of time out here, don't you?"

"I do. My husband helped me lay it out. Since I lost him, it's my way of staying connected. There are times I swear he's here with me." Dottie sighed and ruthlessly pulled a few weeds that had dared poke up their heads in her garden. "Gardening in Texas hill country can be difficult. The raised beds help, and I've put in mostly drought-resistant plants. Still…"

She looked around her. "This garden is a task of love. Both joy and heartbreak. But, then, isn't all of life?"

That caught Sophie up short. Joy and heartbreak. Did they balance each other?

"How long were you married, Dottie?"

"Forty wonderful years. Although, in truth, I still think of myself as married. Harry and I raised two incredible kids in this house. A lot of loving went on here." She sighed. "It was good to watch Annie and Cash discover each other while she lived upstairs."

Sophie murmured her assent.

"I'm enjoying watching you and Ty dance around each other, too."

"Dottie—"

"Fine." The older woman held up a hand. "I won't say another word about it."

They chatted another couple minutes, then Sophie went inside, package in hand. She was almost afraid to open it. She needed to give Dee a call. If Nathan had indeed seen the package, she'd been wrong. He knew exactly where she was. He had her address.

Taco salad churning in her stomach, she raced to the bathroom.

* * *

Later, a cup of chamomile tea in hand, Sophie curled up in the overstuffed chair and dialed Dee. When her Chicago across-the-hall neighbor answered, her voice was sleep-heavy.

"Did I wake you?"

"Just catching a catnap. No biggie. It's so cold here, the only place I can keep warm is under the covers."

Sophie blew out a deep breath.

"Is something wrong?" Dee asked.

"My package came today. Thanks so much for putting it together and sending it. I really appreciate it."

"No problem. And I do mean that. I didn't even have to battle the elements to mail it. Nathan came by as I was heading downstairs, package in hand. He said he was checking your apartment for you." She hesitated. "I told him I'd already done that. Didn't you ask me to?"

Sophie's stomach plummeted. "Yes. I did."

"Then why was Nathan—"

"I don't know. Did he have a key?"

"You gave him one."

"Huh-uh. I didn't."

Silence hung heavy, and Sophie's stomach threatened to rebel again. Had he been inside? Going through drawers? Touching her things? Oh, God.

"He said he was headed to the post office and would be glad to drop off your package. I shouldn't have given it to him, should I?"

"I'd like to say it's no big deal, but he's really starting to worry me." Sophie rubbed at her eyes.

"What's he doing?"

Quickly, Sophie filled her in on the e-mails. The phone calls. The increasingly menacing tone.

"I mean, he's no Jack the Ripper," she said. Still, her heart raced, and she fought to steady her voice. "Thing is, besides everything else, Nathan is a tightwad. No way will he spend the money to fly here. I'm overreacting."

"No, you're not," Dee said. "I'm really sorry, and you can bet I'll be a whole lot more cautious from here on out."

"My fault. I should have said something to you sooner. But, listen, if he comes by again, would you call me?"

"You bet I will."

Dee's promise ringing in her ear, Sophie hung up. Nathan sure as heck wasn't going to hop a plane to Texas, and he would never hurt her.

The reassurances fell flat. She wished Ty was here. Wished they were curled up together on the big brown sofa, his strong arms cradling her. Wished she could confide in him. But she couldn't add to his worries. He already had so much to deal with.

Still, with him, she felt safe. Believed all would be right. The urge to call him escalated.

No.

Sticking her phone in her pocket, she hurried over to the door and threw the lock. The sun had gone down. A tree limb brushed against the kitchen window; the old house creaked, its weary bones settling. Turning off the overhead kitchen light, she stared out into the night. Dark in small-town Texas was so much darker than in Chicago.

Chapter Eighteen

It was dinner for God's sake. They'd grab a bite to eat, talk a little bit, then he'd take her home. Period. Nothing fancy. Nothing that even vaguely hinted at more. It wasn't like they'd set up a tryst in some flea-bitten motel for a quick roll in the hay...or some magical, romantic night on the town.

So why was he as nervous as a pig at barbecue time?

Because he'd kissed her.

Why in the hell had he kissed her?

He tossed the last bale of hay from the back of his work pickup and stripped off his leather gloves, slapped them on the leg of his worn denims.

He had to get himself under control. He wasn't some horny teenager.

Nope. What he was, was a horny thirty-two-year-old.

And if there was any difference between the two, it escaped him at the moment.

A cloud of dust warned him of incoming. The kids were

home. Haley'd driven into town to pick up supplies for the bunkhouse and had offered to take the boys with her. He owed her for that. It had given him time to finish up here.

As the car pulled up in front of the bunkhouse, he strolled out to meet them. "Need some help?"

"Boy, do I. The back of this SUV is packed tight." She opened the doors and started unloading boys. "Human cargo first."

Like a swarm of locusts, they descended on him, full of hugs and stories of their trip to town. He hugged back, tousled hair, and listened. Then, moving to the rear of the vehicle, he grabbed small loads for each of the boys.

"There you go. Take those inside and put them on the table." He and Haley together made short work of the rest of it while the boys, bags delivered, tore off for the bunkhouse.

"Did you pick up dinner for you and the kids tonight?" he asked.

"Sure did. You're treating us to pizza and ice cream from Sadler's." She held up two more bags.

"Good for me. Here, why don't you give me those?" Ty asked. "I'll stick them in the fridge for you."

"Sounds good. I'm going to grab a quick shower before I come over."

"Yeah." Ty looked down at himself. "I figure I'd best do the same thing." He whistled, and the boys came tearing out of the bunkhouse, each with a cookie in hand.

"Look what Cook gave us," Jesse said.

"He give you one for me?"

"No, Daddy. But you can have some of mine." Jonah held his out.

"That's okay, bud." Ty slung an arm around him. "I already had one," he lied. "Enjoy yours."

"'Kay, Daddy."

Together the four of them walked across the yard, and Ty herded his brood into the house.

Forty minutes later, the kids had taken over the living room. Action figures scattered the length of it, and a full intergalactic battle was under way.

Upstairs, a towel wrapped around his waist, Ty finished shaving. That task complete, he walked into the bedroom to study the sparse contents of his closet. A suit was out. Period. He supposed, though, he owed Sophie something other than a pair of worn-out jeans. Being a city girl from Chicago, she'd expect a tad more than that.

Heck, he should probably expect more than that from himself.

That in mind, he started to reach for his chinos, then stopped. Hell with it. He was who he was. He'd wear his Sunday jeans and a gray button-down shirt Babs had bought for his last birthday. That would have to do.

Downstairs, he heard Haley come in, heard the boys scramble to greet her. He took a deep breath. Tonight would either be fun or the biggest disaster ever.

* * *

When Sophie answered the door, Ty stood dumbfounded. He couldn't find words. But he didn't have any doubt why he'd asked her out. Or why he'd kissed her.

Tink was breathtaking.

Finding his tongue, he said, "Darlin', you look good enough to be dinner."

She dipped in a mock curtsy. "Why, thank you, sir." Then her eyes traveled the length of him. "You look pretty darn good yourself. That gray shirt with those smoky eyes of yours? Mmmm."

Heat rushed up his neck, and she laughed, a tinkling little sound. She cocked her head. "Do you want to come in?"

"No." He shook his head. "If you're ready, we should probably go. I made reservations. I hope you don't mind. We hadn't actually talked about where you wanted to go tonight."

"Anywhere is fine. Bubba's, Sally's and Oliver's are the sum total of my dining experiences since I've been in Texas."

"Well, that pretty much makes up the triumvirate of restaurants in the area." He swallowed. "Let me just say again that you look great, Sophie. That pink...Wow. Every man who sees you is gonna envy me."

A smile brightened her face. "Thank you, Ty." She rubbed a hand over the sweater's sleeve. "Maggie picked this for me."

"Remind me to thank her. It's perfect."

"That's what she said." She grabbed a purse the size of a small elephant from the counter. "So where are we going?"

"We're heading toward Austin. There's a great little Italian restaurant about halfway there. *Cucina de Luigi*." He stopped on the stairs. "I thought you might be tired of steaks and barbecue. You like Italian, don't you?"

"Are you kidding? I can't think of anything better. How's Luigi's lasagna?"

"The best. And their meatball calzones." He kissed his fingertips.

Sophie dropped a hand to her stomach. "Glad I went light on lunch because I fully intend to pig out tonight."

"Overindulgence can be a very good thing."

"I think so, and I'm looking forward to it. Hope you are, too."

The double entendre hit home. Reminding himself to

breathe, he sucked in a lungful of air. He sure hoped he survived the evening.

The porch light reflected off his gleaming pickup. Randy, one of his ranch hands, had given the truck a good wash and cleanup today. One look at those white slacks and Ty thanked God he'd thought to do it. No cookie crumbs or spilled anything to spoil them.

Dottie peeked out the kitchen window, and he waved to her. Unabashed, she waved back, a wide grin on her grandmotherly face.

Before Ty opened Sophie's door, he noticed her scoping out the yard, her eyes moving slowly over it. "Everything okay?"

"Yes. Of course."

He watched that tiny pink tongue trace her bottom lip. She was nervous. Because of him or something else?

"You'd tell me if it wasn't, wouldn't you?"

She smiled. "Sure."

Studying her, he helped her in, then closed her door. When he walked around the hood and slid behind the wheel, the same feeling he'd had the last time they'd been shut up alone together in the truck hit him. The feeling they were the only two people in the world.

He liked it.

He wouldn't call it comfortable. No. Her scent filled the cab, wrapped around him and tied his stomach into knots. But they were good knots.

Knots he knew how to loosen—if she was willing.

* * *

The drive to Luigi's didn't take nearly long enough. Whatever nerves he'd had flew out the window as the miles passed. He'd forgotten how good it felt to be on a grown-ups-only outing with a beautiful woman.

When they drove into Twin Springs, Sophie lowered her window and leaned out. "Oh, Ty. This is like a little Christmas fairy land."

"Yeah, I thought you might like it. They go all out for the holidays."

The town looked like Santa's Toyland and *Midsummer Night's Dream* rolled into one. White lights twinkled and shone from every tree, outlined the quaint-looking little shops, and encircled the elaborate streetlights.

She turned to him. "Do you think we'll have any time to shop?"

"Absolutely. They stay open till midnight through the month of December."

"Oh, I'm sorry for them, but happy for me."

Ty laughed. "I wouldn't feel too sorry for them. This month puts them in the black, believe me. It's a destination for lots of Austinites."

Christmas carols played over outdoor speakers, and Sophie sang along with them.

When he parked and walked around to open the door for her, he found himself with an armful of delicious woman as she threw her arms around him.

"Thank you."

"The evening's just started," he reminded her.

"I know. But already it's wonderful. Exactly right."

"Then, you're welcome." Taking her hand, so tiny and soft in his, he led her down the street to Luigi's.

They stepped inside to the smell of warm bread, garlic, and tomato sauce. Here, too, white lights sparked magic. A Christmas tree stood tall and proud in the foyer. Gold brocade ribbon trailed over doorways and in centerpieces, giving the restaurant a slightly formal air.

Once they'd been shown to their table, Ty ordered a bottle of wine. After the waiter uncorked it and left, he raised his glass. "To a memorable night with an even more memorable lady."

Sophie smiled. "I'll see you and raise you." She held up her own glass. "To a special night with an unforgettable gentleman."

He winced. "I'm a cowboy, Sophie. Nothing more, nothing less."

"There's a lot to be said for cowboys, Ty. Personally, I find them fascinating." She sipped her drink.

"Oh, yeah?"

"Yeah. But don't let it go to your head."

He chuckled and opened his menu.

When the waiter returned, Sophie said, "I'd love to try that calzone you've been raving about, but I have to go with the lasagna."

"That's okay. I'll share."

And he did. Leaning across the table, he fed her a forkful of his meatball calzone, watched as those luscious lips closed around it. Instantly, he became uncomfortably aroused. The woman played havoc with his system.

As they ate and talked and laughed, he realized a big part of her draw was that she was so unaware of herself. There was no coyness, no sense of self-importance. For the first time, he recognized the resemblance between her and Annie. Not physically, no. They looked nothing alike. But their ethics. Their attitude toward life. Both had a solid foundation.

Annie. Tall, dark, and willowy with those ice-blue eyes.

So self-confident and hardworking. So practical despite all her money.

And Sophie? He could barely keep his fingers out of her pale blond hair and found himself falling into those big brown eyes of hers. She was a devoted believer in fairies and their magic. Yet despite that, she, too, could be practical and hardworking.

Both cousins loved life.

Annie had decided to make hers in Maverick Junction, while Sophie would head back to Chicago soon. He'd originally thought that a good thing. Now, he wondered.

Talk turned to his ranch, then to her greeting card business.

"Why did you decide to start Stardust Productions, Sophie? Seems like a big job to take on."

"Money," she said.

"Excuse me?"

"Money. I needed a way to earn a living. I love to paint, so it seemed a good fit."

"It can be hard to get start-up money for a risky business venture like that, can't it? But then you probably didn't need outside money, did you?"

"I sure did. I really hunted around before I finally found a bank willing to take a chance on me." She tilted her head and looked across at him. "Ty, I don't have any money."

Confused, he said, "That's okay. I asked you out. I've got it covered."

She smiled and shook her head. "No. I mean, I'm not wealthy. I have a couple thousand dollars in savings and run my checkbook week to week."

Surprised, he sat back in his chair. "Seriously?"

That enticing tongue of hers flicked out to wet her lips. "Most people think, you know, that because I'm Annelise's cousin, well…"

So, Ms. Sophie London wasn't an heiress. He reached across the table and caught the hands she was clasping and unclasping. "You think that matters to me?"

"It might. It does to some people."

"It doesn't to me." His eyes met hers unwaveringly. "It doesn't," he said more quietly, but this time he instilled steely determination into the words.

At the same time, his conscience taunted him. *Jerk. The money itself doesn't matter a fig. But you've been judging her, and you know it. Thinking of her as a little rich girl, blah, blah, blah. You've made some bad calls, bud.*

He'd noted an almost haunted look at times. What bothered her? Kept her awake at night? Had her searching the yard tonight for the boogeyman.

He and his demons were on a first-name basis. She'd denied having any. She wasn't being honest, and that bothered him. A whole bunch. How could he protect her if he didn't know what to fight?

Ty wished his inner voice would shut up and go to sleep. Maybe she'd watched a scary movie just before he picked her up.

He didn't believe that, either. Nor did he believe he'd get his answer tonight.

"Do you want dessert now, or would you rather wait and get something at one of the little shops?"

Sophie patted her tummy. "I think some tea and dessert later would be best."

By the time he'd paid and they stepped outside, the night air had turned downright cool. He wrapped an arm around her as they wandered from shop to shop, glad for the excuse to pull her close, to feel her body against his.

It had been years since he'd been out with a beautiful woman. Babs had been hounding him that it was time. Right now, with Sophie tucked close, he had to agree. It felt damn good.

He even enjoyed nosing around in a few of the stores.

"Boy, I might have forgotten the start of the holidays with all the wedding excitement, but the retail world sure hasn't," Sophie said.

"Look at this!" She held up a wreath, its decorations red hot peppers. "I love it!"

"That's Christmas Texas-style, Tink."

After meandering through the displays, she chose some ornaments—a black Harley for Annie, a gaudy pink flamingo wearing a boa for Dottie, and three fishing ones for the boys. She'd even found an ornament that looked a lot like Trouble.

"Nothing for you?" he asked.

She shook her head. "No, but I need you to go next door."

"Why?"

"Because I have one more to buy, and I want it to be a surprise."

He gave her a peck on the tip of her nose. "I'll be in the coffee shop. Take your time."

*   *   *

Nearly back to Maverick Junction, Ty spotted the sign for Blackwater Road. Acting on impulse, without giving himself time to second-guess his decision, he pulled off onto the side road.

As they bumped along the narrow dirt lane, Sophie looked at him, brows quirked. "This isn't the road home."

"Nope. A little side trip. You mind?"

"I guess that depends on where we're going and what we're going to do when we get there."

Oh, boy. Heat flared in his belly. He had plenty he'd like to do, but he didn't figure full disclosure was required or expected.

"It's a beautiful night. Look at that moon." He peered up at it through the windshield. "A perfect crescent. And those stars. Beside me, I've got a pretty lady." He reached across, ran a hand along the top of her leg. "I thought it might be nice to stretch the evening out a little longer."

"The sky is magnificent. Chicago never truly gets dark. Because of the city lights, we never see all these stars. You forget, you know?"

"Can't say as I do, Tink. I've lived here in this open land all my life. But a sky like tonight's? That's a vista I never tire of."

As he arrowed the truck into a turnabout and threw it in park, Sophie sat, hands in her lap, looking around them. "This looks an awful lot like, um, a place you'd take a, um, date to go parking."

"Got it in one." He stretched an arm along the back of the seat and ran a strand of that silky, moon-kissed hair between his fingers.

She laughed. "You've got to be kidding."

"Nope. It occurred to me I'd like to spend a little more time with you, and it's damned hard to find any privacy. My place, we've got the boys. 'Nough said about that. Your place isn't much better. Ms. Dottie's downstairs, and I'd really like to have you all to myself for a bit longer. That okay?"

"More than." Her voice had taken on a breathy tone that curled the toes inside his Tony Lamas.

He played with the pink and green crystals dangling from her ear. The other, he noticed, sported the same earring plus a small silver dangle. It didn't surprise him. Tink didn't seem to like coloring inside the lines. She did everything her own way.

"You want to play a little kissy-face?" he whispered.

"I thought you'd never ask," she whispered back.

Leaning toward her, he dropped a kiss just beneath her ear, then another, and another. "We can pretend we're teenagers," he murmured. "How's that sound?"

"Lovely. Teenagers without all the teen angst."

"There you go. And no parents to chew us out for not making curfew."

He set his hat on the dashboard, turned on the radio, and slid his seat back. Then he turned to her and undid her seat belt. As he pulled her toward him, he gave thanks he'd ordered the truck with a bench rather than bucket seats.

"Oh, Sophie. I've been wanting to do this all night." His lips met hers with a hunger so intense, it blew his mind. She melted into him, her tongue flicking out, teasing, taking.

His hands moved up under that pretty little sweater she was wearing, ran over her soft, heated skin. He trailed kisses along her neck, her quiet sounds igniting further fires in his belly. He'd been right. The woman was a sorceress.

Her hands found their way under his shirt, traced along the edge of his belt, and he groaned. Then she trailed them along his back.

He couldn't get close enough. His hands wandered higher still, played along the edge of her bra. Reaching around her, he unsnapped the scrap of lace that stood in the way of total ecstasy. He had to touch her, taste more of her. Her hair smelled of flowers, of nighttime secrets.

Moonlight filtered softly through the now thoroughly fogged up windows. Ty could no longer tell which sounds were his, which were hers.

He ached for her.

But when his fingers moved to the button of her slacks, she laid a hand over his.

"Ty, we need to stop." Her voice sounded husky and sexy as hell. "This isn't a good idea."

"What's wrong, Sophie? I know I'm rusty at this, but unless I've made a major mistake in reading you, you want this as badly as I do."

"You haven't misread me. I do want you."

Heat shot through him.

"But I can't do this."

"Can't or won't?"

"Both, actually."

Breath ragged, he struggled for air. "Why?"

"Because you and I both know this isn't going anywhere, and I'm really not into one-night stands."

"A one-night stand?" He pulled away. Sophie leaned against the window, all mussed and sexy looking, her lips swollen from his kisses.

"Okay. Maybe a four- or five-night stand." She smiled sadly. "This, well, it's not exactly the best time for me. And you? You're not ready for more."

Reluctantly, he drew her sweater down to cover her and kissed her cheek. "I won't take more than you want to give, Sophie."

"I think maybe you already have."

He spread his hands. "I don't know what to tell you. You

know the way things are with me. I've been right up-front from day one. The boys—"

"I know. The boys come first. And they should. But I don't want to do this and then walk away feeling less."

"Less? I make you feel less?" Hurt? Anger? He couldn't identify the feelings that rushed through him.

"I...That's probably not the right word choice. My emotions, my feelings, are all over the place. I think it's time to take me home." She tossed him a heartbreaking smile. "I'll let you walk me to the door without any fuss, and we can say our good-byes tonight."

Not good nights, but good-byes? That hurt. More than he'd imagined. "What are you saying?"

"I—"

"Sophie." He raked his fingers through his hair. "Why are you doing this? We had a wonderful night. At least I did."

"I did, too."

"There's no need for us to end. Not tonight. Not like this." Panic rushed through Ty. Panic he didn't understand. "I enjoy being with you. We don't have to do this." He waved a hand between them. "We don't have to have sex. I enjoy spending time with you. The boys enjoy spending time with you."

"I know. And I enjoy being with all of you, but...I have to watch out for myself, Ty. I'm sorry."

In the moonlight he could have sworn he saw tears in those incredible brown eyes. Shit!

"Look, Tink, I'm going to step outside. Take a minute to get myself together. You can do the same. Then, if that's what you want, I'll drive you home."

When they reached her apartment, he didn't walk her to her door. The instant he parked the truck in the driveway, she flew out and rushed up the stairs without a word.

In the moonlight, he stood at the bottom of them, waiting till a light came on in her kitchen. He waited there a full five minutes praying he'd hear her door open again, that she'd come back down to him.

She didn't.

Sliding behind the wheel, he wondered how things had gone so wrong. Blackwater Road. He shouldn't have pulled off there, should have taken her straight home. Sent her off to her bed with a hot kiss to dream about.

Instead, he'd screwed things up royally. Wasn't that a kick in the ass? He hadn't touched a woman since Julia. Now, he'd met someone who'd brought him back to life, and he'd driven her away. Had he said his skills were rusty? Corroded was more like it.

Neon lights glowed in the window of Bubba's Roadhouse as he drew close, and the open sign was still lit. Nowhere near ready to go home yet, he swung into the parking lot.

From the number of vehicles, the Saturday night crowd was lingering over drinks and music. Too bad. Spotting a couple cars he recognized, he swore ripely. He definitely wasn't in the mood for company and had hoped he could just go in and brood over a beer or two.

The engine still running, he fought with himself. He really ought to go home and let Haley escape. He didn't want to, though. He loved his boys. He really did. But every once in a while, the weight of it all got to be almost more than he could handle.

And then there was Sophie.

He turned off his black monster and, heading inside, pocketed the key. A few people spoke when he entered. He nodded at them but said nothing as he headed for the bar.

"Hey, Ty. You're out late." Bubba shouted to be heard

over the other patrons' chatter and laughter. The jukebox belted out an upbeat song, adding another layer to the din.

"Yeah, I am. Draw me a draft, would you, pal?"

"Sure thing. Everything okay?"

"Never better." The words sounded bitter to his ears. "Add a basket of chips and salsa to that, would you?"

"You got it."

Ty propped his feet on the bar's boot rail. That had been one heck of a make-out session. That tight little body of Sophie's could make a grown man cry. And her kisses? Hot as jalapeño poppers. But just like when he'd actually been a teen, the girl had put on the brakes and left him aching.

The damnedest thing about it was that she'd been right. Neither of them was ready to commit. A rueful smile curled his lips. He couldn't even offer her his class ring. Nothing was that simple anymore. Bottom line? He could wish things had turned out differently, but he couldn't blame her in the least.

Bubba slid his beer down the bar, and Ty took a healthy drink.

"Here you go." The bartender plopped chips and salsa in front of him. "Anything else?"

"Nope."

"Holler if you need another." He tipped his head at the beer.

"Thanks, but one's good."

Munching chips, Ty pulled a small bag out of his shirt pocket and removed the small trinket. A tiny ornament. The fairy from Peter Pan. Tinker Bell. He'd spotted it at one of the shops they'd gone into. He flicked it with his finger and watched it twirl at the end of the green satin ribbon.

His chest ached. If nothing else, Tink had uncovered a part of him that had been missing for years now.

He supposed he should be happy about that.

Yeah. And maybe he would be. Someday. But not tonight.

Tonight it hurt.

Crossing the dance floor where a couple Texas two-stepped, he dug some quarters from his pocket. Plugging them into the shiny chrome Wurlitzer, he punched in the buttons—twice—for "The Keeper of the Stars." When it played, he remembered dancing across this very floor with Sophie snuggled up close.

"Sure you don't want another beer?" Bubba called. "You're empty."

"Yeah, hit me again." He might as well, because he sure wasn't going to get any sleep tonight. He hadn't felt like this since—never. He'd never felt quite like this before.

But after this drink, he was done. Two was his limit. The boys would be up early tomorrow whether he'd been to bed or not.

Chapter Nineteen

Everybody Ty ran into at Sadler's was in a chatty mood, from Mrs. Sandburg, his second-grade teacher, to the shelf-stocker. They asked about his boys and commented on the weather. Then, invariably, the conversation turned to Sophie, as if he and Sophie were an item or something. They weren't. Damn meddlers. How was he supposed to get her out of his system if they kept throwing her in his face?

Gritting his teeth against the saccharine-sweet "Holly Jolly Christmas" that played over the store's speakers, he focused on his list.

"Hey, Ty."

His head jerked up, and he silently groaned.

Bubba stood in front of the meat counter, one foot perched on a cart's rung. "Decided I'd better pick up some more ground beef before the lunch crowd hits after church. Almost sold out last night, and my delivery won't be in till tomorrow."

Ty grunted in response.

"How you doing today?"

"I've got a headache if you really want to know," Ty snarled.

Bubba made a disgusted sound. "You used to be able to handle more than a couple beers."

"Yeah, and I used to smack people around when they pissed me off."

"No, you didn't. That's one of the things I've always admired about you."

Ty, who'd already pushed away, whipped back to look at Bubba. He swore when the quick movement sent another shot of pain through his already abused head. "What the hell are you talking about?"

"You. You weren't like some of the other kids. You never bullied the ones who didn't quite fit in. You took time for them. Helped them out."

"Now you're seriously pissing me off, Bubba. You're making me sound like a damn pansy."

Bubba's brow quirked, and he pulled thoughtfully at his bottom lip. "Nope. Definitely not a pansy. You could whip anybody's ass when they had it coming. But you didn't go looking for it, and you didn't dump it on someone who already had their plate full."

Bubba met his gaze. "We go way back, Ty. You're a hell of a nice guy. Your own plate's been pretty damn full lately, and you're handling it with class. But—" He scratched his head. "I gotta say I think you're blowing it when it comes to a certain pretty little blonde from up north."

"Screw yourself, Bubba. Nothing's going on between Sophie and me."

"Now ain't that a damn shame."

"Here you go, Bubba." The butcher handed him his package of meat. He dropped it into his cart and walked away, leaving Ty mad as a hornet and with no one to take it out on.

His parents had stopped by on the way to church while he was wrestling the boys into clean but un-ironed outfits for Sunday school. His mom had helped, right after she'd slid a casserole of beef stew into his fridge. Since nobody made beef stew like his mom, he was grateful. They'd have it for dinner tonight.

At the deli he grabbed a loaf of French bread to go with it. In the produce section, he tossed a bag of salad in his cart. And there you go. A well-balanced meal.

"Thanks, Mom," he muttered.

"Talking to yourself?"

Ty turned and saw Mel behind him. "What's up? Is the entire population of Maverick Junction shopping today?"

"Don't know about everybody else, but I have to get it done on my day off."

"Yeah, well, consider yourself lucky to have one. In the ranching business, there is no such thing."

"True enough. Heard you hit Bubba's last night. Why didn't you give me a call? I'd have met you there."

"Oh, for— Does the town set off some warning signal when I step out of the house without my kids?"

Mel shook his head. "Not that I'm aware of."

"Then how the hell did you know where I was last night?"

"Ran into Bubba in the candy section while I was debating between Peppermint Patties and Three Musketeers. He told me to watch out, that you were on the loose and baited for bear."

Frustrated, Ty sighed and tossed two gallons of milk in

his buggy. "I'm fine." Seeing the look of concern on his friend's face, he added, "Really."

"Okay. But if this is about Sophie—"

"It's not about Sophie."

Mel's brows shot up.

"Okay. It is. But I don't need any help."

"Talk to her. Whatever went wrong, just talk to her. And take her flowers. Tell her you're sorry."

"For what?"

"For whatever you did."

"I didn't do anything."

"Sure you did."

"I've got to go, Mel." He headed to the checkout.

Why did everyone assume *he* did something? Why couldn't Sophie be in the wrong? Hell, Sophie *was* in the wrong. She was the one who'd called things off. Not that they'd had a thing.

As he carried his groceries to the truck, he thought about what Mel had said. Maybe he and Sophie should talk. They weren't right for each other. Not long-term. That was a given. But he hated like heck to have her go back to Chicago with this thing hanging in the air between them. Upset with each other.

He turned the key in the ignition, and the radio blared "Joy to the World." Rather than put the truck in drive, he simply sat there, truck running, in the middle of the parking lot.

He needed to sort this out in his mind before he descended on her.

Bottom line? She'd rained on his parade, and he was having a heck of a time forgiving her. He'd looked forward to their night out more than he probably should have. He'd had a better time than he probably should have. He'd liked kissing her. Way more than he should have.

And today? He really ought to be on top of the world. He wasn't. Because she'd been honest with him. Told him she needed to end it.

The upshot of it all, though? He'd broken through some kind of barrier, one he hadn't realized existed. A huge chunk of him had died and been buried with Julia.

Now, life stirred again in him.

It felt wonderful.

It hurt.

Guilt, heavy as a full-grown steer, settled over him.

Throwing his truck in reverse, he backed out of his space. This thing, whatever it was, could wait until tomorrow. He'd give both of them some breathing room. Today, he and Sonny and a couple of the other guys planned to shore up the south pasture fencing. He'd take the boys along, and they could play while the men worked.

The fresh air would do them all good. Then they'd head back to a home-cooked meal.

What could be better?

He and his boys were doing just fine.

Chapter Twenty

Sophie's bed looked like a couple of rhinos had spent the night in it. Covers tumbled to the floor, a pillow lay halfway across the room, and the sheets had been pulled out.

She sighed. Monday morning. The beginning of a new week, and she was still miserable. She'd dragged through yesterday as though waiting for the executioner's ax and prayed she'd wake today feeling lighter. Feeling okay.

She didn't.

Grabbing the sheet, she set about trying to restore order to the bed, since she wasn't having much luck doing the same to her life. She ran a hand over Lilybelle's back. The cat had decided to help by standing smack-dab in the middle of everything, making progress nearly impossible. Sophie solved the problem by carrying the cat to the window seat. Happy in the warm sunshine, Lilybelle curled up in a tight ball and purred contentedly, her tail twitching occasionally.

Once she'd put the bed to rights, Sophie fixed a cup of

tea. Standing at the door, soothed by the tea, the cat winding around her legs, she spotted Dottie in her garden.

In her robe and slippers, Sophie stepped out onto the landing. "Need help?"

"I wouldn't say no. We've got a cold snap coming, so I need to get these roses mulched."

"Give me a minute." Hurrying inside, she threw on a faded pair of jeans and her Cubs sweatshirt. Then she dragged a brush through her tousled hair and ran down the steps, Lilybelle close behind.

It felt good to be outside. To be physically busy. She and Dottie chatted as they worked. A pale sun shone on the roses and the other late-blooming flowers.

Dottie straightened suddenly. "Goldie. Hello."

Sophie's hands stilled on the upended bag of mulch. *Oh, boy.*

"Sophie, you remember Goldie Taylor, don't you? I believe you met at the wedding. She's Matt's mother."

And Julia's mom.

"Yes. We shared Thanksgiving at Babs's," Sophie managed.

"Oh, of course. I forgot you were all going there," Dottie said.

Dread settled in Sophie's stomach. At Thanksgiving, she hadn't yet spent the better part of Saturday night with this woman's dead daughter's husband. Hadn't kissed him. Hadn't wished for more. Oh, boy in triplicate!

Mrs. Taylor couldn't possibly know, though. There was no way. Still, Goldie's warm smile, rather than the reprimanding glare her guilt expected, surprised Sophie.

"It's good to see you again, Sophie. Have you heard from Cash and Annie?"

Safe territory. She grabbed on to it. "I talked to Annie on

Friday. They're having a wonderful time and expect to be home later this week." Her mind raced, searching for more conversation that didn't involve Ty.

Before she could come up with anything, Goldie said, "I was on my way to the post office. When I saw you and Dottie working out here, I wondered if we might talk."

Sophie's mouth went dry as she forced a nod. Had Goldie heard about her date with Ty? But she was smiling, wasn't she? A real smile or fake? Times like this, Sophie cursed her overactive imagination.

Well, if Goldie asked, Sophie'd confess that she and Ty had gone out, but she'd make it perfectly clear it had been a fluke. The two of them weren't seeing each other anymore. They'd ended it Saturday night. Whatever *it* was. Pain sliced through her heart.

Oh, she wanted Ty's kisses, his warm body next to hers, inside her. She wanted so much. Too much. Because of that, she'd said good-bye.

How long until one of those other women Maggie'd mentioned warmed his bed? Won his heart? The pain in her own intensified till she could barely breathe. *Suck it up. You'll get over it. Over him.*

Ty was country and liked living on the prairie surrounded by cows with long, pointed horns. His arms filled with three beautiful sons.

Dottie brushed mulch off her knees and tossed her gardening gloves onto an upturned pot. "Why don't I give you two a little privacy? I tried out a new cookie recipe this morning. I'll go plate some for us, along with a fresh pot of coffee."

"That would be wonderful, Dottie. Thank you." Goldie sat on a wooden bench and motioned for Sophie to join her.

Watching Dottie's retreating back, Sophie understood

what a passenger who'd fallen from a cruise ship must feel like as he watched the vessel sail away. Slowly, she removed her borrowed gloves and walked to the bench. Sitting down, she stared at the toes of her worn sneakers.

"You're good for him."

Sophie's head snapped up at the quietly spoken words. "I am?"

"Yes."

She tilted her head. "We are talking about Ty, aren't we?"

Goldie smiled. "We are." She took Sophie's cold hands in her own warm ones. "There's life in Ty's eyes again, a life that left when Julia died. It's come back."

The older woman raised one hand and placed it on the side of Sophie's face. "My husband and I want that. We really do. We love Ty. Through everything, despite everything, he loved our little girl and was devoted to her. When... when her condition deteriorated, he took such good care of her. He never left her side." Tears swam in her eyes. "Bill and I watched them both die that day at the hospital, helpless to do anything."

Sophie's brows pulled together, questioningly. Her throat burned.

A single tear trailed down Goldie's cheek. "We buried one, and for over four years now, we've watched Ty wander through life with a hole in him that's so huge, it's left him crippled. In those first months, that first year, his pain was nearly unbearable to see."

Goldie swiped at the tear.

"Oh, he loves those boys. Don't get me wrong. But a big part of him seemed to have disappeared. We were afraid it was gone forever." She squeezed Sophie's hand. "You've given it back to him, and we're happy."

"I was afraid—"

"We'd see you as an interloper?" She shook her head. "I'd be lying if I didn't admit my heart was heavy for just a moment when I first saw that spark rekindle in Ty's eyes. But, it's time we all moved on. Especially Ty. Our grandbabies need that. They've never known Ty as he was before. Those boys need to see him happy. They deserve it."

Sophie bit her lip and nodded.

"We don't begrudge his interest in you, Sophie. We welcome it. I wanted to be sure you understand that."

"Ty's the one who can't accept it," Sophie murmured.

"What do you mean?"

"We broke up." She grimaced. She hadn't meant to say that. But her conscience couldn't let this woman hold false hope. "Well, we didn't actually break up," she stammered. "I mean, how can you break up with someone you're not really—" She circled her hand. "I don't know how to describe what we had."

"Is there anything I can do?"

"No." She shook her head. "I'm the one who actually ended it." She met Goldie's eyes. "I can't be with him. I'm afraid if I let myself, I'd...I'm sorry. He loved your daughter very much. He still does, and he's closed himself off. I have to protect myself."

"I guess that explains why he was at Bubba's late Saturday night."

Sophie's mouth dropped open. "He was?"

"Our neighbor saw him there."

"Small towns," Sophie muttered.

"Yes." Goldie smiled sadly. "We knew, too, beforehand, he was taking you out to dinner."

Sophie's eyes widened, and Goldie laughed. "Not much

goes on in Maverick Junction that's a secret. Which can be good or bad. Depending. But when Ray told us Ty'd been at the bar putting down the drafts and listening to 'The Keeper of the Stars,' I wondered."

"'The Keeper of the Stars'?"

Goldie nodded.

"That's the first song we danced to. At Bubba's."

"I'm going to take that as a very good sign, sweetheart. Please do this old woman a favor and don't pack your bags yet."

"I don't plan to. I'm actually working here right now."

Goldie looked past Sophie. "Ah, here's Dottie with refreshments." She gave Sophie's hand another little squeeze. "If you need me, all you have to do is call. Bill and I will do whatever we can."

Leaning closer, she said, "And that includes watching those precious little boys if the two of you need a night alone."

Heat flared in Sophie's cheeks. "I'll remember that."

"Dottie, these look wonderful." Goldie rose and took the tray from her friend, placing it on the flat top of the little rock wall. "What a pleasant way to start the day. Friends, sunshine, and cookies."

* * *

Sophie liked Ty's mother-in-law. The woman had a heart the size of Texas. She'd lost her child. There could be nothing more devastating. Yet here she was playing matchmaker for her daughter's widower.

It tore Sophie apart. But as badly as she felt for Julia's parents, self-preservation was stronger and demanded she stay far, far away from Ty Rawlins. With one touch, one smile, she'd be running straight into his arms...and heartache.

On her drawing pad, she added a few more bluebonnets to the card design. Even as her fingers created with clear, quick strokes, her mind wandered to all the wonderful people she'd met in Maverick Junction and how much they'd come to mean to her.

Glancing up, she caught a glimpse through the window of Dottie moving around in her peony pink kitchen. Strange how reassuring that was.

The garden, so peaceful, felt like home. But it wasn't. Chicago was home.

Go, Cubs!

When she left, Dottie would run an ad in the *Maverick Junction Daily*, and someone else would move into Annelise's Tiffany blue apartment. They'd probably repaint it no-color white. They might even get rid of Cash's grandpa's old, comfy couch and replace it with some modern piece of chrome and leather.

That was reality. Things changed.

She had to remember that for all she loved this town and its people, she wasn't a part of it, of them. Her apartment, her beautiful apartment, so close to Wrigley Field, would feel empty after her time here, though.

After Ty and his three boys. After surprise visits from people like Goldie. Mornings with Dottie. Chats with Maggie. They'd all come to mean so much to her. They'd slid into her life so easily. Or had she slid into theirs?

When she'd agreed to come for Annelise's wedding, she'd intended a hit-and-run. Fly to Texas, put up with the cows and the lack of shopping and delis for the few days necessary, then turn tail and head back to Chicago.

How quickly she, big-city-girl Sophie London, had fallen in love with this small Texas town in the middle of nowhere.

The thought of leaving, of saying good-bye to it and getting on that plane, made her sad.

Thank God she hadn't actually allowed herself to fall in love with the cowboy. That wouldn't have done at all.

"Hey, Sophie. Got some mail for you." Wearing a jacket and long pants today, the mailman came up the walk.

Laying her drawing pad on the chaise, she hopped up to meet him partway. "Thanks, Dave."

"You bet." He handed her the letter, dropped Dottie's mail in her box, and took off.

Sophie stood in the middle of the drive, staring at the letter as if it had grown a head. The return address? Nathan's.

She didn't want to open it. She had to, though, didn't she? Or did she? She supposed she could dump it unread in Dottie's trash can.

Hands shaking, she dropped back onto the chaise and slid a nail under the envelope flap. The rumble of a truck engine had her pausing. When Ty's pickup pulled into the drive, her heart kicked into fifth gear. What was he doing here?

Rattled, Sophie tucked the half-opened letter under her leg. Nathan could wait. One crisis at a time.

Funny. As she watched Ty's tall, lean figure moving toward her, the man didn't feel like a crisis. More like a gift from the gods. One she'd forfeited Saturday night.

Even though her decision had been right, she strongly regretted it.

He smiled at her, a slow, lazy smile that had those dimples peeking out. She all but melted.

"Hey, Tink. Thought maybe I'd find you out here catching some sun." He nodded at her pad. "Working?"

"Off and on." She smiled back at him, unable to resist. "I find my concentration isn't what it should be."

"Something on your mind?"

She took a deep breath. "Ty, I'm sorry about the other night. I—" She spread her hands, unsure what she wanted to say.

Nudging the drawing pad aside, he sat on the edge of her chair, his warmth seeping through her jeans where their hips touched. She scooted over a little to give him room. His black Stetson shaded his eyes, and she wished he'd take it off. Were they stormy gray today or warm and inviting?

"I moved too fast the other night, Sophie. My fault." He thumbed back his hat and met her eyes.

His were smiling today. Friendly.

Hot, though. Still hot.

And precisely why she'd behaved as she had Saturday night. Rational thought fled when she got within ten feet of him.

"No, Ty, you didn't. I wanted you to kiss me. I wanted more. Much, much more." As she watched, those fascinating eyes of his darkened. "And that's why I ran scared. I was afraid of myself, not you."

"A dangerous thing to tell a man, darlin'."

A half laugh escaped her. "I suppose so. But it's the truth."

"Have dinner with me and the boys tonight."

"What?"

"Dinner. Nothing more." He held out a hand to shake on it.

Grinning, she did just that.

"Unless," he added, "you find you can't do without my body. Then, I'll be all too happy to oblige."

Her mouth dropped open. "Men!"

"Yeah, I know." He shrugged. "We're an egotistical bunch. You'll set the rules, though, Sophie. I won't take anything you don't want to give. You have my word on that."

He nodded at the envelope peeking out from beneath her leg. "Letter from home?"

She made a face. "I guess you could say that."

Leaning across her, he read the return address. "Nathan? Isn't he the guy who's been stalking you?"

"I wouldn't say stalking. That's overstating my problem with him. He's a guy who can't seem to take no for an answer."

"Okay," Ty said slowly, edging slightly away from Sophie. "So, I find myself wondering. Is that how you see me? Coming here today after you told me to get lost?"

"I never told you to get lost."

"Different words maybe, same meaning."

"No. You and Nathan are worlds apart. Nathan is... creepy. You're... tempting."

A grin flashed. "Really?"

She punched his arm. "And so full of yourself."

His smile faded. "You need help with him?"

"No. He's in Chicago. I, on the other hand, am in Maverick Junction. I've been ignoring him. I'm not answering his calls or e-mails. He'll get the picture."

"You're sure? You'd tell me if you needed help?"

"Absolutely."

He studied her till she felt twitchy.

"Okay." He nodded. "Six tonight? I know it's early, but the boys hit the sack by eight, so I like to feed them by six thirty."

"Sounds great. Why don't you let me bring dessert?"

Ty's gaze moved toward Dottie's kitchen.

"No," Sophie said. "I'll make something myself."

"All right. We'll be looking forward to it. Do you remember the way?"

"You bet."

Sophie lay back on the lounge chair, the drawing pad on her chest, and watched him walk away. Oh, he sure did fill out his jeans, coming and going. With a big sigh, she went back to work. The sun was shining a whole lot brighter than it had ten minutes ago.

When she shifted, the envelope crackled. She really wanted to throw it away without reading it. Did she dare?

Probably not.

Dropping her legs to the side of the chaise, she sat up and took a drink from her water bottle. Only then did she pull out the letter and unfold it.

I'm still waiting, but my patience is running out.

Enough. She didn't need to read more. She crumbled the note and threw it in the trash.

Nathan Richards was a self-centered, arrogant pain in the butt. Turning on her heel, she went upstairs to shower.

* * *

Juggling her dessert, Sophie closed the car door and stood looking at Ty's house. So much for her resolution.

Problem was she liked Ty—a lot. And she could name a thousand reasons why that was a bad thing.

Lights welcomed her from every room of the house. A pair of tricycles littered the front yard, and she wondered where the third was parked.

Trouble raced around the corner of the house, and she let out a little squeal. Holding her plate high, she pointed a finger at him. "Stop. Sit."

He did.

When the shock wore off enough she could speak, she said, "Good boy."

The front door flew open, and three little bodies crowded into the opening. Trouble sprang up and tore toward them. Laughing, they all leaned down, giggling even harder as the pup gave them all kisses.

"Daddy's busy," Jesse said.

Jonah nodded. "Yeah, something's burning in the kitchen."

"I see." She fought to keep a straight face. "Does that happen often?"

Three heads nodded solemnly.

"Then Daddy swears," Josh said.

"Yeah." The other two nodded and grinned.

Sophie listened to the running dialogue, each boy slipping in one sentence after the other without missing a beat. It was like one mind, three bodies.

"But we can't tell Grandma," Jonah said, shaking his head.

"Uh-uh. 'Cause we promised we wouldn't."

"Yeah. Grandma gives him heck when he does."

"Boys," Ty hollered from the kitchen. "Close the door. I can feel the draft clear back here."

The smoke alarm chose that instant to go off, and the boys covered their ears. Josh's lower lip trembled.

"Shit. On second thought, leave the door open, guys. We need to get this cleared out before Sophie comes. And remember, this'll be our little secret."

Jesse opened his mouth, but Sophie shook her head.

"Shhh, let's surprise him." She set the plate on one of the highest bookshelves, sent Trouble a warning look, then scooped up the still-distressed looking Josh.

She heard the back door open, then a window slid up. A

finger over her lips, she tiptoed to the kitchen, the other two forming a giggling line behind her.

She stopped in the doorway. Ty, looking more handsome than any man had a right to, stood flapping a dish towel toward the open door. A pot sat on the stove, water boiling over. The oven door hung open and tendrils of smoke escaped.

"So, what's for dinner?"

Ty dropped the towel and turned, looking for all the world like a five-year-old caught snooping under the Christmas tree. He looked from her to the boys.

"Traitors."

"What's that mean, Daddy?" Josh asked as Sophie lowered him to the floor.

"It means you're supposed to sound the warning when the enemy shows up."

"But Sophie's not the enemy." Josh wrapped an arm around her leg.

"And," Jonah said, "the alarm was already sounding. It hurt my ears."

"Yeah, I guess you're right." Ty threw a disgusted look toward the stove, an apologetic one toward Sophie. "Afraid dinner's going to be a little well-done tonight."

"You should have come last night." Jesse took her hand.

"Really?"

Josh nodded. "Grandma made beef stew. It was scumptus."

"Uh-uh," Jesse said. "It was good, wasn't it, Daddy?"

"That's what scrumptious means, Jess."

"Oh."

"Well, a day late and a dollar short as always." Sophie tousled Josh's hair. "That's okay. We'll make do." Turning to Ty, she said, "How can I help?"

"You could mash the potatoes."

As she drained them, he withdrew a pan of meat loaf from the still smoldering oven and studied it unhappily. "Afraid it's too late to do anything about this, but I think we can eat the middle."

He shot Sophie a glance. "Have you had all your shots?"

"Believe me, after my mom's cooking, nothing fazes me."

"Oh, yeah? She looked like the perfect June Cleaver mom."

Ty passed her a bowl for the potatoes; she added a little milk and butter.

"You couldn't be more wrong." She turned on the hand mixer she'd found half-hiding behind a cereal box. "There are times I worry myself, afraid I'm verging on OCD. Back in Chicago? If you walked into my studio, you'd probably die of shock. All my supplies are boxed and ruthlessly labeled, each tidily lined up on a shelf that's also labeled."

His brows creased. "Really?"

"And it's all because of my mom."

"So she *is* a June Cleaver clone?"

"No. She's definitely *not*. As a kid, I hated the chaos that reigned in our house. My mom was careless—when it came to housekeeping, meals, laundry, schedules. Never about her family, though."

"You love her."

"I do. But I swore when I grew up, I wouldn't live like that. In public, no one would guess. No one ever sees her as less than perfectly pulled together. She wasn't careless with Dad and me, nor her looks or her clothes. But the master bedroom? Wow. It always looks as if it's been struck by a cyclone—as does the rest of the place. When she steps out of the house, though..."

"So you need control and order to make up for that."

"I guess I do, yes."

"Good luck here at the Rawlins house, then. You'll likely go crazy with three kids this close to the holidays."

"Strangely enough, I don't think so." She moved to the fridge and traced the Christmas drawings stuck to the front of it with magnets.

"Day Care. Miss Marcy is big on arts and crafts," Ty said.

"It's nice." She fingered the cotton balls that formed Santa's beard. "I miss that about the holidays. The excitement on the faces of the little ones."

"We've got plenty of that here."

"No tree yet?"

"We'll get around to it. Soon." He sighed. "Never enough hours in the day. Do you want to get glasses out for their milk?" He tipped his head at one of the cabinets. "Maybe dig out some plates?"

"Sure." She opened the door and saw plastic glasses, kids' divided plates. Looking further, she saw no good china. No fancy casserole dishes.

"You know, I don't mean to be nosy, and I sure don't need it, but where is all your good stuff?"

"Good stuff?" He looked over his shoulder at her.

"Maggie told me you and Julia had a big wedding. I don't see anything here that so much as hints at that. Everybody gets fancy stuff for wedding gifts they'll never use."

"I gave it all away. We didn't have room in our little house for it, so Julia packed it all up. Said she'd wait to put it out in our new house. That didn't happen, so I had one of the hands run it into Austin to Goodwill."

"You didn't keep anything?"

"Nope. Didn't want or need it. The boys and I cope fine without it. End of story."

"Okay." She pointed at the nearest drawer. "Silverware in here?"

"Yep."

While she set the table, raised voices, giggles, and a pup's happy barking filled the house.

"Boys," Ty called. "Run upstairs and wash up. Dinner's ready."

Such fun, Sophie thought, as they finished the chaotic meal with her dessert—cupcakes baked in ice-cream cones and decorated with icing and sprinkles. She'd loved them as a kid and enjoyed watching Ty's boys devour them.

Later, she sat in front of a crackling fire, enjoying a cup of tea. From overhead, the sounds of three very buzzed little boys getting ready for bed drifted down to her.

Trouble had scrambled up the stairs behind them, eager to take part in the routine. A spirited argument erupted over whose turn it was to have the pup in bed with him. Apparently, they took turns, and Ty was smart enough to have a chart. Jesse won.

"Can we say good night to Sophie?"

"Yes, but make it quick."

Freshly bathed and dressed in superhero pajamas, they raced downstairs, launching themselves at her. She knelt down and doled out hugs and kisses.

Jonah wrapped his arms around her neck, then drew back to brush his fingers over her cheek. "You feel soft."

"Thank you." She reached up for his hand and kissed the back of it.

"You're pretty, too." He smiled and melted her heart. "Are you a mommy?"

She shook her head.

"We don't have a mommy." Josh wiggled beneath her arm to cuddle against her. "Do you want to be ours?"

She closed her eyes and pulled him closer, kissing the top of his sweet-smelling head.

A stair creaked, and she looked up to see Ty, hand on the rail, watching. "I'm sorry," she mouthed.

"It's okay," he said. "Boys, come on up to bed."

"But, Daddy," Jesse wailed. "Sophie didn't answer our question."

Our question, she thought. They were such a solid unit. Her thoughts scrambled, and she had no idea what to say.

Ty answered for her. "Sophie's here as a guest, son. She doesn't live in Maverick Junction. Her house is a long, long way from here."

"But she could move, Daddy," Jonah said. "We could help her. We could carry boxes and stuff."

The other two nodded, their little faces serious.

"I have a job in Chicago, honey. I need to go back to it."

"Get a new job here," Josh wheedled.

"Mommies don't need jobs," Jesse said. "They stay home and bake cookies and food that isn't burned. Right, Daddy?"

Brows raised, a half smile on her lips, Sophie looked at Ty. "What do you say to that, Daddy? Do mommies stay home to cook for their men?"

He met her gaze. "Not always, boys. Some mommies like to work. They do important jobs."

"That's okay, Sophie. We'll let you work." Jonah wrapped his arms around her neck again.

"How about, for tonight, I carry you up to bed and help tuck all of you in?"

"'Kay."

Crisis averted. Within five minutes she stood in the bedroom doorway beside Ty as he turned out the boys' light and wished them happy dreams.

"Sorry, Sophie. They don't talk about their mom much. I don't know where all that came from."

"It's okay." She patted his shoulder.

He took her hand in his as they walked down the stairs. "How about coffee? Or some more tea." He grinned. "Wine, maybe."

"I'd better not. It's getting late, and I'm still new to these roads. Time I headed home."

"You afraid to be alone with me?" His eyes twinkled mischievously.

"Not on your life, Mr. Rawlins."

"Good." He pulled her close, and his lips dropped to hers.

She let herself go. Gave in to the moment. He tasted so good. So right. His tongue teased her lower lip, and she met it with her own, nearly cried out when he deepened the kiss and took still more.

Breathing heavily, he lifted his head. "Want to come back tomorrow night? I'll do better than burned meat loaf. Promise."

Oh, she wanted to. Very much. Too much. And so she said, "No. Not tomorrow. How about the day after, and I'll bring dinner. My place is too small for all of you, or I'd have you there."

"Sounds even better." He walked her to the car and gave her another bone-dissolving kiss.

As she pulled out of his drive, she glanced in her rearview mirror and saw him standing there, hands in his pockets, watching her. Not just alone, she thought. Lonely.

Chapter Twenty-One

Sophie was a bundle of nerves.

"Settle down," Dottie said. "Believe me, there isn't a kid alive who doesn't inhale macaroni and cheese and love every second of it."

"But what if Ty's kids are the exception?"

"They're not. Trust me."

"Okay." She wrapped the loaf of barely cooled bread she'd baked herself from her grandmother's recipe. It smelled heavenly.

Adding the creamed peas to her basket, she said, "These will satisfy the rule some fool made up about needing a veggie with every meal. Personally, I think it's the stupidest rule ever ... and therefore meant to be broken."

Dottie laughed. "I'd bet the Rawlins kids have more than a few meals without veggies. Still, it doesn't hurt to train them young."

"As far as I'm concerned, the kids can have a food fight with them if they want. It wouldn't hurt my feelings."

"I'm leaving now." Dottie gave her a quick hug and headed out the door. "You have a great time."

"I will. Thanks for your help."

Dottie stuck her head back inside. "I didn't do a thing."

"You gave me moral support."

Sophie studied the contents of the basket again to make sure she hadn't forgotten anything. All in all, not too bad, she decided. The mac and cheese hadn't come from a box. She'd actually made it from scratch and had even grated her own cheese. How much that would mean to four-year-olds? Absolutely nothing, she guessed.

For some unknown reason, though, it was important her meal not only be edible, but delicious. She wanted to look competent to Ty, so for good measure, she'd added home-made brownies for dessert.

She checked her hair one last time. The difference in water was playing serious havoc with it.

* * *

She needn't have worried. Ty and the Triple Threat devoured the meal with all the gusto of hound dogs. After they'd cleaned up, the boys begged to be allowed to stay up long enough to play one game of Candy Land, and Ty finally relented.

"I'm sure you're used to a little more mature evening's entertainment up there in the Windy City. We must be boring you silly," he said as the boys shot upstairs to find the game.

She sent him a questioning look. "Do you really believe that?"

"What?"

"That I'm bored."

When he shrugged, she punched him in the arm. "Cut it out, Ty. I'm here because I want to be."

He shot out a hand and snagged her around the waist. "You here for the kids or for their daddy?"

Laughing, she tried to push him away.

He held tightly.

"Ty, what if they come down and see you hugging me?"

"I'll tell them it's my turn. They all got a hug. Now I want one."

"You're so bad."

Trouble shot down the stairs first, followed by Jesse and Jonah.

"Hey, wait for me." Josh took the corner too fast and hit the wall. His feet slipped out from under him, and he crashed headlong down the flight of stairs. Jonah turned and tried to catch him.

The impact knocked him off his feet, too, and he slid down the last two on his back with his brother.

"Josh! Jonah! Are you okay?"

Ty bounded to the bottom of the stairs. Josh made not a sound, just lay where he was. Jonah started to cry.

"Blood, Daddy." He held up a hand smeared in red. It covered his shirt.

But when Ty yanked him up, he wasn't the one bleeding. It was Josh, the crier of the group, who was now strangely quiet.

Sophie took Jonah from Ty, and he knelt beside Josh. Blood covered his face, his clothes. "Son, can you talk to me?"

"Uh-huh. I falled."

"Yes, you did." Ty picked him up and rushed him into the downstairs bath, blood dripping in their wake.

Sophie took Jonah to the kitchen sink and started wiping him off. Thank God, he had only a bruise on his arm.

"Sophie?" Ty called. "How's Jonah?"

"I'm okay, Daddy."

"Good. Can you come here, Tink?"

"Sure." She set Jonah down on his feet and walked into the bath. Ty held a washcloth to the side of Josh's head, putting pressure on it. "I think he's gonna need some s-t-i-t-c-h-e-s."

"Oh." Her stomach went queasy, the mac and cheese roiling.

"Can you call Haley? See if she can come watch the other two? I don't want to take them to the ER."

"You don't have to do that. I can handle things here."

He narrowed his eyes. "You're sure?"

"Absolutely." She threw him a phony smile, one that trembled a little on the edges. "We'll do fine."

"I'd argue with you about this, but—" He gestured at the little boy sitting on the sink, sobbing now.

"It hurts." His lips quivered. Big fat tears rolled down his cheeks, mixing with the blood there.

"I know it does, champ, but we'll get you all fixed up in no time."

"How? When Humpty Dumpty fell and broke his head, nobody could fix *him*."

"You're different. You're one of the Rawlins triplets. You have magic powers." Ty picked him up. "You're sure?" he asked Sophie again.

"Positive."

"We'll be good, Daddy," Jesse said.

Behind him, Jonah, still a little shaken, nodded.

Ty grabbed his keys and wallet, then turned to Sophie. "Your last shot at escape."

"We're fine," she said. "Go."

"Okay." He and Josh were out the door.

She and the two boys stood at the window and watched Ty speed away with their brother. Sophie wrestled with a bout of panic. She'd never babysat in her life. Had never been alone with *one* child, let alone two.

She peeked at the faces glued to the window. They wouldn't cry, would they? On a scale of one to ten, right now her fear level ran around a fifteen. She was more frightened than when she'd been stuck on an elevator—alone—afraid no one would ever find her. Or that she'd use up all the oxygen in the car and die before they did.

"Daddy's gonna get Josh fixed." Jesse hugged his brother.

"He'll make him all better," Jonah agreed.

Such absolute trust, she thought. How hard it must be to live up to that, day after day after day.

"Want to play Candy Land, Sophie?" Jesse ran to the game he'd carried downstairs, the one that had started it all.

Relief rushed over her. No tears.

"You bet."

An hour and a half later, exhausted, the boys in their pajamas, the three settled on the sofa, the TV on low, a Spider-Man DVD playing. Jesse curled up beside her, and she put her arm around him. He leaned into her, then looked up at her and smiled tiredly. Jonah sprawled, his head in her lap, and sent her a shy smile. Inside five minutes, both were fast asleep.

She brushed dark strands of hair off their faces. In sleep, they looked angelic. All that massive energy on idle. A feeling she couldn't identify, didn't want to probe too deeply, crept inside her, filled her. Scared her.

Leaning her head back, she let sleep come.

* * *

Ty gently lifted Josh from his car seat. Poor little guy had been brave and even thanked the doctor after he'd finished the last of the stitches.

What a night.

What a frigging disaster.

He kept striking out with Sophie. Red soda on white silk. Burned meat loaf. Blood and stitches. He couldn't win.

With Josh asleep on his shoulder, he quietly turned the doorknob and stepped inside. The lights were dimmed; all was quiet. And there on his couch was Sophie, his two boys curled into her. All three fast asleep.

And he knew.

In that moment, he lost his heart.

Shit!

Very carefully, he climbed the stairs and tucked Josh into bed. Moonlight came in through the window, highlighting the stark white bandage on the pale little face. They'd given him some Tylenol at the hospital, and Ty figured he'd sleep through the night, the worst of the trauma over. By tomorrow he'd be showing off his bandaged head and telling his hospital story to anyone standing still.

He headed back downstairs and carefully slid his hands beneath Jonah. The boy turned into him when Ty lifted him to his shoulder.

"It's okay, bud. I've got you. Go back to sleep."

"'Kay."

Once he had Jonah safely in bed, he returned to the living room. Sophie hadn't stirred. Ty smiled and wished he had the right to kiss her, to carry her to bed. But he didn't.

And he never would. It wasn't in the cards. And, all in all, that was probably a good thing. Wasn't it?

Extracting Jesse turned out to be a little more difficult, but Ty managed it without waking him. One more trip upstairs, one more tucking in, one more kiss good night.

He stood in the boys' bedroom studying his sons. Julia should be here with him. But she wasn't and never would be.

She hadn't played fair with him.

That was in the past. Couldn't be changed.

Still, he took another minute before going downstairs to Sophie.

In the living room, he switched on a small table lamp and turned off the overhead light. Ferreting out the remote, he clicked off the TV and DVD player. The house was absolutely still. No refrigerator hum, no furnace. The fire in the fireplace had burned to embers.

Hands in the pockets of his jeans, he moved closer to the sofa to stand over Sophie. He knew he shouldn't, but his body refused to listen to his brain, and he sat down beside her. One look at those red lips, parted in sleep, and he captured them with his own.

She made a sleepy little noise and brought her hand to his neck, drawing him closer still. Finally drawing back into the couch cushion, she said, "Nice wake-up."

Then her expression became one of panic. "The boys."

"Are in bed, Sleeping Beauty."

"All of them?"

He nodded. "I found you all asleep here, cuddled up nice and cozy in front of the fireplace."

"Your boys are wonderful, Ty." She yawned and combed her fingers through her hair. "How's Josh?"

"He'll probably have a whopper of a headache in the

morning, and, no doubt, will have a fit when the stitches have to come out, but he's sound asleep, too. He did well at the hospital. I was proud of him."

He moved in for another kiss, but she put a hand on his chest.

"I need to go home." Her voice was sleep-husky.

"Why?"

"It's late."

"Stay with me tonight. Sleep with me." He ached for her.

"The boys—"

"Are fine. I told you before, once they go to sleep, a semi driving through the house wouldn't wake them."

She didn't look convinced.

"Sophie, they're sound asleep. My door has a lock on it."

"Still…"

"How do you think kids end up with brothers and sisters?" Sophie blushed.

"Their parents sleep together, darlin'. While they're in the house."

"But that's just it. I'm not their parent."

"No, you're not."

"So…"

He rubbed his hands over his face. "Here's the thing. Most parents fall into all this naturally, without really thinking about it. The kids are always there. No big deal."

Then he broke off, rubbing the back of his neck. "Actually, I've never made love with them in the house, either."

"But you *have* had sex since they were born."

He shook his head. "Pathetic, huh?"

"Maggie said you hadn't dated, but I thought maybe she was mistaken. Or you'd dated but kept it quiet." She ran a finger down his arm. "Really? Four years?"

He swiped at the stubble on his jaw. "It's been longer, actually. Pregnant with triplets, well, we had to be careful. The doctor issued a no-fly zone early on."

"Oh, my gosh."

He shrugged, conflicting emotions battering him. "It really hasn't been a big deal. At first, it was grief. Then, well, I was flat-out too busy. Guilt and apathy played in it, too, I suppose."

"I'm sorry." She laid a hand on his cheek.

"How sorry?" He nuzzled her neck.

She lifted a brow. "Not that sorry."

He dropped his forehead to hers. "You sure?"

"I can't, Ty."

"Can't or don't want to? There's a huge difference, Sophie, and I don't want to pressure you if this...if I'm not what you want." He stared into her big brown eyes.

On a half laugh, she said, "Oh, you're making this difficult. No wonder the boys are so good at wheedling." She ran a hand through his hair. "The thing is I do want you, Ty. Too much. That's part of the problem."

"It doesn't have to be."

"That works for tonight, but what about tomorrow?"

He groaned. "I don't remember this being so hard."

Laughing, she dropped a kiss on his cheek. "Night, Ty."

"Seriously?"

"Seriously."

After she left, he turned off all the lights. Staring into the darkness, he told himself it was for the best. Hadn't he promised himself no more heartache?

As he rubbed his chest, though, he wondered if it wasn't already too late.

Chapter Twenty-Two

Sophie woke the next morning to a winter wonderland. Inside, the temperature in her apartment had plummeted, and she pulled the covers up over her head. Maybe she'd stay in bed. Dottie had warned her a change was coming, but darn, it was cold!

A quick check of the bedside alarm assured her she'd officially turned into a sloth. It was a little after nine. She guessed she could forgive herself since she'd rattled around till almost dawn, unable to sleep.

Why hadn't she stayed with Ty? The kids were there, yes, but he'd been right. They could have handled it.

Cold feet?

Yes. Literally and figuratively!

She hopped out of bed, jammed her feet into a pair of fluffy slippers, then hurried into her robe. If it got any colder, she'd have to do something about warmer pajamas. Or snuggle up with Ty.

That thought had heat racing through her.

Still, she stumbled into the living room and turned up the thermostat. While she waited for the room to warm up, she grabbed an afghan tossed over the back of the sofa and wrapped up in it.

The phone rang, and she answered it after checking caller ID. "Good morning, Ty. How's Josh?"

"He's good and telling everybody who'll listen about his ER trip."

"I'm glad."

"Did you bring any mittens?"

She frowned. "Sure. I wore a pair to the airport in Chicago."

"A heavy coat? Hat?"

"Yes to both."

"Great. How about the boys and I pick you up in, say, fifteen minutes? We're finishing breakfast here at Sally's. I thought with the snow and all, it might be a great day to find our Christmas tree."

She hugged herself. Oh, my gosh! Christmas trees and Ty all rolled up in one! "I'd love that."

The minute she ended the call, she flew off the couch and into the bathroom. Brushing her teeth, she decided a good combing was the best she could do with her hair. A flick of mascara, a touch of lip gloss, and she hurried into the bedroom.

Plowing through the closet, she pulled out her old sweatshirt and jeans, her long-sleeve shirt and heavy jacket. In her suitcase she found a pair of warm socks along with her mittens, cap, and scarf. She hadn't expected to need these till her return flight.

Although, all this might be overkill. How long could it take to choose a tree?

A long time, she discovered. For the Rawlins crew, it

wasn't simply a matter of walking down to the little shop on the corner.

Once she was settled in the truck, Jonah said, "Daddy brought the truck 'cause it's snowing."

"I see that."

Jesse asked, "Are you gonna ride Molly again?"

"When?"

"Today," Jonah said.

"To help us get our tree," Josh added. Then he patted his head. "Did you see my boo-boo?"

"I did. Your daddy said you were really brave."

"I was. The doctor said I was a big boy."

"Good for you." She blew him a kiss in the back seat.

Sophie turned to Ty, who was easy behind the wheel of the big truck even though the roads were snowy. The wipers ran, clearing the big flakes as they began to fall again. He'd cranked the heater to high.

"Where exactly are we getting your tree?" she asked.

"At the edge of the north pasture. There's a nice stand of pines there, and I think we should be able to find what we want."

"You're cutting your own?"

"Sure. What did you think?"

Feeling like an idiot, she shrugged.

He laughed. "You thought we'd planned to buy one, city girl?"

She settled farther down in her coat. "That is what most people do."

"Not us," Jonah said.

The other two boys shook their heads.

"We have our own, don't we, Daddy?" Josh asked.

"Yes, we do." He raised his eyes to the rearview mirror

"For the boys. I've got a pot of coffee ready to go. If you want tea—"

She shook her head. "Coffee's fine."

He watched her walk away. That blond hair with the white coat. The spitting image of one of those angels she'd made with the boys.

Except maybe her butt. He doubted angels had butts as fine as hers.

*   *   *

Lunch with Ty and the boys... the whole day... had been a gift. An early, unexpected Christmas gift. Did he know how blessed he was?

Yes, he did. She saw it when he studied their little faces, when he knelt to put himself on their level, when he hugged one close after he'd been hurt or disappointed.

Ty might have been left alone to daddy three brand-new infants, but he was doing one hell of a job. How many men could have coped with what he had? The loss of his wife. The loss of life as he knew it. And three new little lives dependent on him for everything.

And despite the meat loaf fiasco, the man could cook. That chili ranked in the top ten she'd ever tasted. By the time they'd dived into it, she was famished. The cold weather, the horse ride, chopping the tree, making snow angels...

Now, home in her apartment, Sophie soaked in the big old claw-foot tub. Filled to the rim with heavenly scented bubbles, it made her feel decadent. Pampered.

The Bing Crosby Christmas CD she'd picked up at Sadler's played quietly in the background. "White Christmas" seemed apropos after today's snow.

Sinking deeper into the bubbles, she worried—because everything was almost too perfect.

Jesse, Jonah, and Josh were all becoming very important to her. A bad thing. Because she and their daddy had to say good-bye. Really soon. It would break her heart to kiss those little guys farewell.

And what about kissing their daddy good-bye?

Despite her best intentions, Ty had burrowed under her skin. As far as she could see, she had two choices. The first? End it now. Tell him the next time he came by that she wouldn't see him again. She put a soapy hand to her heart and rubbed at the hurt. She'd already tried that, hadn't she?

Her second option? Enjoy it while she could. Spend as much time as possible with him and the boys. Make memories to take home with her.

Disgusted, she shook her head. Stupid her, thinking she actually had a choice. Time to stop worrying about tomorrow and enjoy today.

She raised her leg and lathered. Sang along with Bing and dreamed. All too soon, though, the tiny vanity clock had her scurrying out of the tub.

Wrapping herself in a towel, she scooted into the bedroom to find something to wear tonight. Annelise and Cash were home. They'd flown in from Paris this afternoon, and everybody was meeting at Bubba's for dinner.

Even though Sophie'd insisted she could drive herself, Ty was picking her up. As if she didn't drive through snow in Chicago. However, she had to admit that the road crews up north were much better prepared to cope than the ones here. They got a lot more practice.

She decided on jeans and a fuzzy maroon sweater. Last time, she'd totally overdressed for the roadhouse. Tonight, she'd blend in a little better. Not that it mattered all that much. She'd already met most of the people she'd see there. She loved that.

It wasn't that she didn't know the name of the deli owner on her Chicago street or the name of the man who sold hot dogs from the street kiosk or the people who ran the small mom-and-pop stores. She did.

Still, there was a real sense of belonging here.

But she didn't belong here, she reminded herself as she slipped in her hoop earrings. She'd already stayed far longer than she'd originally planned.

The phone rang. The number looked familiar, but she couldn't place it.

"Hello?"

"What the hell's going on?"

"Excuse me? I think you have the wrong number."

"Don't pull that on me, Sophie."

"Kyle?"

"Your new boyfriend slashed my tires!"

"My new— Where are you?"

"Where the hell do you think I am? I'm standing in the middle of my driveway, looking at four shredded tires."

"Are you talking about Nathan?"

"Who else? The guy's crazy."

Sophie wished she could argue the point. She and Kyle had dated on and off for a couple months but had ended it before Nathan had asked her out.

"How do you know it was him?"

"A neighbor saw the jerk."

She sighed. "He's not my boyfriend, Kyle. He never was."

"Well, I think he sees things differently. Tell him to lay off. I catch him anywhere near my car, I'm calling the cops."

Her earlier joy drained from her. "Actually, you probably should call them now. Report him."

"The guy's psycho, Sophie." His voice quieted. "You need to watch your back."

"Thanks. I will. And Kyle? I'm so sorry."

"Yeah, me, too." He hung up.

The knock at her door startled her, and she nearly squealed. Nathan was to blame for that.

She peeked around the corner into the kitchen. When she saw Ty's face through the glass windowpane, she relaxed and opened the door...and was well and thoroughly kissed.

When he pulled away, his forehead creased in concern. "What's wrong, Sophie? You're pale as all get-out."

"Nothing."

"Don't tell me that." He lifted the hand he held, his finger at her wrist. "Your heart's beating a mile a minute. What's upset you?"

"I had a phone call. It's not important."

"When will you trust me?"

"I do."

"Not enough."

* * *

The warmth hit her the second she and Ty stepped inside Bubba's. The temperature had continued to drop, and her nose felt like an icicle after the short walk across the parking lot.

Ty had been very quiet on the ride here. She ached to share Kyle's call with him. Couldn't do it.

"Ty?"

"It's okay, Sophie. You've got your life, I've got mine."

"But—"

"Don't worry about it."

She'd upset him and that gnawed at her. They needed to talk. Later. Tonight, though, belonged to Annelise and Cash.

She'd thought nobody would be out, that they'd hole up in this weather. Not so. The rough wood walls of the roadhouse practically bulged with half the town squeezed inside.

The noise level was through the roof! Laughter, conversation, and the clink of silverware on dishes. The jukebox belted out a George Strait song.

Ty's hand at her back felt warm and strong. Right. Even through her jacket. She sighed. Oh, yeah. Despite her best intentions, she was in trouble.

He leaned down to whisper in her ear, and heat rushed to her core. She unsnapped her coat.

"They're in the corner."

Sure enough, there was Annelise, looking more gorgeous than ever, waving at them. A huge smile wreathed her face. Cash looked like a cat who'd dined on thick, rich cream.

In seconds, Sophie and Annelise were hugging and talking over and around each other. It was good to have her home.

As they sat around the table, Brawley said, "You know, guys, take a good look around you. A drop-dead gorgeous blonde, an unbelievably beautiful—and married—brunette, and a hell-on-wheels redhead. Damn, we're lucky."

"You've got that right," Maggie said.

"I'll drink to lucky us," Cash said.

The men raised their glasses.

Annelise dug out a photo album, and the guys talked

sports while the women *ooh*ed and *ahh*ed over honeymoon pictures. Two hours passed quickly. Good friends, good food, good times.

When they stepped back into the cold, more snow covered the ground. Light, fluffy flakes continued to drift from the sky.

Maggie put her hands on her hips. "Well, shoot. It's really nasty out here." She looked at Ty. "Hope you didn't have big plans for tonight, pal."

"Why?"

"I don't intend to drive to Lone Tree in this." She turned to Sophie. "Can I bunk with you tonight?"

"Sure."

One look at Ty, and Maggie laughed. "Doesn't fit your scenario for the evening, does it?"

"It's fine."

"Bull. You were hoping to get lucky."

"Maggie!" Glad the darkness hid her blush, Sophie swatted at her. "Stop it."

"What? Are you going to tell me you two aren't—"

Brawley wrapped an arm around Maggie's waist. "You could come stay with me, sweetheart. My bed's big enough for two."

"Oh, really? You're living with your parents, Brawley. They'd be thrilled to wake up and find me there."

"Actually, they probably would," he drawled.

"Not going to happen." She stepped out of his reach. "And Ty, you're just going to have to suck it up for tonight."

"I suck it up every night, Red."

Her face fell. "I'm sorry. That was careless of me."

"Oh, for—" Ty bit off the curse. "I wish to hell you'd quit walking on eggshells around me." He kicked at the small mound of snow that had built up at the corner of the building. "You're gonna piss me off."

"Fine. In that case, I'll be blunt. I'm stealing your girl for tonight."

"I'm not—"

"She's not—"

Ty and Sophie looked at each other.

"Me thinks they doth both protest too much." Annelise laughed.

"You might as well ride with me, Sophie," Maggie said. "That'll save Ty a few miles."

"Sure."

She'd taken two steps when Ty snagged her arm. "Give us a minute, Mags," he said.

"With your non-girl? You bet." She threw them a saucy wink before walking to her car. Annelise and Cash headed to theirs.

"You sure you don't want to change your mind?" Brawley called to Maggie.

"I'm so positive."

"You're gonna regret it," he said. "When you're tucked in on that cold, lonely couch at Sophie's, think of the fun we could be having."

Sophie noticed Maggie didn't even answer. Then, her brain simply stopped working as Ty turned her into him and covered her mouth with his in a kiss that was so hungry, so demanding, she lost herself in it.

When he lifted his head, his mouth a breath from hers, he whispered, "We're gonna have to do something about this, Sophie. I'm dying from wanting you."

His breath formed a white cloud in the cold air. "You know, the first time I kissed you, I figured it was one of the biggest mistakes of my life. I kicked myself upside down and backward over it and promised I'd never do it again. But we both know I broke that promise." He swore. "To hell with it."

He swooped down and kissed her again. Hot, hot, hot. "There. If that first time was a mistake, then I'm a slow learner, and right now, I don't give a damn."

Resting his forehead on hers, he said, "I have to know. Is this *thing* one-sided, or do you want me as badly as I need you? Give me that, at least."

She could only blink, unable to come up with any of the smart-ass replies she probably ought to make. She felt light-headed. Dizzy. Nothing, absolutely nothing, had prepared her for the power of his kisses. They rocked her...raced to the tips of her toes so fast, they left her breathless. Left her reeling. Wanting more. For the briefest of moments, she saw herself dragging him off somewhere, tearing off his clothes, and having hot, sweaty sex. She'd never wanted it more in her life. Never wanted it quite like she did right now with this man.

The talk she'd planned flew out the window.

How did he make her forget all the reasons she shouldn't and think only of the reasons she should?

Who cared? She grabbed him by the collar of his jacket and pulled him in for another kiss. On tiptoe, she poured all her desire into it.

"This *thing*? It's not one-sided, Ty," she whispered. "I can barely think for wanting you."

He buried his face in her hair. "Damn Maggie Sullivan to hell and back. I swear she did this on purpose."

Sophie laughed. "She made it snow?"

"I wouldn't put it past her."

"She's right, though. The roads are too bad for her to drive back to Lone Tree tonight."

Ty grunted.

She gave him a gentle jab. "You know darn well you wouldn't let her do that."

"So let her find somewhere else to stay."

"Where? Certainly not with the newlyweds."

"Why not? Cash has had Annie all to himself for a couple weeks now. Only fair he shares a little of my frustration."

She gave a quick laugh.

"Her parents live in town."

"It's late. She doesn't want to disturb them. Good night, Ty." She moved to kiss his cheek, but he turned his head, put a hand at the back of her neck and changed the kiss from friendly to passionate.

"Night, Sophie. Sleep tight."

As she walked toward Maggie's car, its engine running and promising warmth, Ty called out, "I'll pick you up at one, okay?"

She stopped. "Why?"

"We've got a tree to trim."

Oh, the man was making her hungry—for all kinds of forbidden things. He destroyed the best of her intentions.

In the pale light that filtered through Bubba's windows, the silent fall of snow turned into whimsical, magical fairy dust.

Chapter Twenty-Three

The boys chased around the house, Trouble at their heels, yipping and trembling with excitement. The scent of warm gingerbread wafted through the rooms.

Christmas music played low, and a wood fire crackled in the fireplace. Boxes of decorations covered every surface in the living room. Ty stood in the middle of it all and grinned. He couldn't remember the last time he'd felt so happy. So content.

And the difference was Sophie. He stuffed his hands into his jean pockets.

She'd insisted that if they were doing the Christmas decorating thing, they had to go all the way. So while he'd been outside wrestling the tree into a stand and shaking out dead needles, she'd herded the kids into the kitchen. Amazed, he'd let the mix of her soft voice blended with the excited ones of his boys wash over him. Somehow, despite their *help*, she'd managed to make a huge batch of gingerbread and salvaged enough from licked fingers to spread over the cookie sheets. It was now safely in the oven baking. While she cleaned up the kitchen, the boys went wild in the living room.

After they finished the tree, she and the boys planned to construct a gingerbread house. He wished her luck with that. When she'd arrived today, she'd come loaded with everything they needed to decorate the gingerbread. Red, white, and green frosting. Bags of gumdrops, jelly beans, and M&M's. Necco Wafers. Licorice ropes. The kids had hopped around her, cheering and clapping like she was the Piped Piper as she'd unloaded her bag of goodies.

From what little she'd told him, her mom would no doubt be labeled ADD in today's world. The one thing that never varied, though, it seemed, was the fantastic houses she and her mom created every Christmas. Gifts might have been bought last minute, wrapped at the twelfth hour, and holiday dinner two hours late, but they'd never missed making the fairy-tale house.

Tradition. One she was sharing with his boys. His heart played leapfrog in his chest.

She'd even brought them a poinsettia for the mantel and had, with great care, placed a dendritic agate in the pot—to keep it healthy. Totally Tinker Bell. Totally outside his realm.

"Hey, guys," she called from the kitchen. "Come help me get the popcorn ready to string."

With a few whoops and more than a little pushing, they descended on the kitchen.

Ty followed them to the doorway. Sophie had insisted, over and over, she wasn't good with kids. He didn't believe her for a second. Instinctively, she gave each one encouragement and said exactly the right things. His boys adored her.

He hoped to hell he hadn't made a huge mistake bringing her into their lives like this. When she left—and she would—would all four of them crash and burn?

Gingerbread houses and popcorn strings. Things Julia had never had a chance to do with her boys. Things the boys had never experienced. Everyone had missed out.

Wouldn't it be wrong to deny them this little bit of happiness? Next year they'd have Christmas again, in their own way, without Sophie. It was nobody's fault.

She'd return to Chicago soon. Back to the city where Nathan waited for her. No doubt in his mind that phone call last night had something to do with the creep. It frustrated him to no end she wouldn't let him in. Wouldn't share.

Would she be safe? Ty leaned his head against the jamb and closed his eyes. It worried him. He hadn't kept Julia safe, and he'd lost her.

How had he let his heart get tangled up like this again?

He'd broken his promise to himself.

* * *

When a car pulled into the drive, Sophie's pulse quickened, and she glanced at her watch. Whew, the afternoon had zipped by. Babs was already here to pick up the boys.

The front door opened, and cold outdoor air pushed in around Ty's sister-in-law. Sophie shivered.

"Wow. What happened here?"

"Christmas came," Jesse cried out.

Josh grabbed his aunt's hand. "Come look what we made."

Tossing a smile over her shoulder at Sophie, Babs followed him into the kitchen. "You guys made this?"

"Uh-huh."

"Sophie helped," Jonah admitted.

"Yeah, 'cause the cookie sheet got real hot."

"I put the pretzels in for the fence."

"I helped with the roof."

"I squirted the frosting for the snow."

Listening to the boys, Sophie smiled.

"I think the house was a success," Ty said quietly, resting his chin on her shoulder.

"I think so, too."

"Thanks for today, Tink. The boys had a great time."

"And their daddy?"

"He had a great time, too." Ty wrapped an arm around her.

Babs returned, the boys trailing in her wake, eating left-over licorice ropes.

"So, you guys ready for a sleepover?" Babs asked.

"Yep. Daddy packed us this morning."

"I'll bet he did." Babs sent Ty a mischievous grin.

"Babs," Ty growled.

"Just saying." She put on her innocent face.

"Run upstairs and get your things, guys. And be careful."

The trio tore up the steps leaving three adults in the middle of the Christmas clutter. Boxes of unused ornaments, stray icicles, and half-eaten candy canes were strewn around the living room.

In front of the window, though, the pine tree stood in all its glory, decorated top to bottom.

"Seriously, you sure you want them?" Ty asked. "They're pretty wired."

"Which means they're worn out and will drop off to sleep in front of a movie, right along with my two. Besides, you and Sophie need an evening without them. And I need an evening *with* them. I love your boys, Ty."

"I know you do. You're a great aunt."

"You got that right. I'm the best."

"You're their only."

"Yeah. Lucky them."

He shook his head sorrowfully. "I never have understood what went wrong, Barbara Jean. Why you have such low self-esteem."

She snorted and punched his arm.

When the boys trooped back downstairs, bags in hand, the adults bundled them into hats and coats. Sophie stood in the doorway with Ty, waving them off.

"Thanks for today, Tink. The boys won't ever forget it."

She hesitated, then said quietly, "I won't, either, but we have to remember I'm temporary, Ty."

"What?"

"This. It's all temporary."

His long lashes fluttered, and his gaze met hers, held. "I know that."

"I don't want to hurt them. The boys."

"Then don't."

"It's not that simple."

"Sure it is. You can work from anywhere."

"My home is in Chicago."

"That's simply a matter of logistics."

"Easy for you to say," Sophie answered. "The thing is, I'm afraid they're getting too attached to me."

"And you to them?"

She nodded.

"Sophie, they have other women in their lives. Babs, my mom, Julia's mom."

"But I'm not their aunt. Their grandmother."

"No, you're not. And I can only say thank God, for that."

The look he sent her had her heart racing. "The more I'm with them, the harder it will be when I leave. For all of us."

Ty laced his fingers through hers. "The boys never knew their mother." A muscle worked in his jaw. "She's a collection of memories, of stories they've been told. Of pictures they've seen. To them, she's that star in the sky. You? You're real."

"Which is exactly why we probably shouldn't be doing this. Shouldn't get more involved. Why I can't spend even more time with them, then leave. It's not fair."

"Maybe you're right." He rubbed his earlobe.

"I am, and we both know it."

"Tell you what." He drew her to him. "Why don't we worry about that later?"

"You're not taking this seriously, Ty."

"Oh, believe me, I am."

He kissed her and sent rational thought flying.

When he drew away, she realized how quiet the house was. "Do you miss them when they're not here?"

"Normally, I'd say yeah. However, in this case, my mind's on other things."

"Oh, yeah?"

"Yeah."

He caught her lower lip in a light nip, and nerves she didn't know she had sang a hallelujah choir.

"You okay to go out in what you're wearing, or do you want to stop by your place so you can change?"

Sophie thought of the soft pink camisole piped in black, the matching panties she had on beneath her jeans and sweater. The set she'd spotted at Maggie's when she and Annelise had first visited. The ones she'd called Maggie about yesterday that she'd brought with her from Lone Tree last night.

"I think I'm good to go. Unless we're eating somewhere fancy."

"In Maverick Junction?" He met her gaze. "Oh, God, Tink." He caught her close. "I want you."

"White Christmas" played on the stereo. Dusk had fallen. He glanced out the window and saw the Christmas tree lights reflected in the light snow cover.

"Dance with me, darlin'," he said.

"Here?"

"Good a place as any." He laid one hand at her waist and caught her hand in his other, tucking her close.

Sophie heard his strong, steady heartbeat, the crackling fire, the Christmas carol. In the soft light from the tree, they danced.

She'd never before experienced the romance this cowboy showed her.

As the music changed, they continued to dance. They kissed. One led to another and another.

He nibbled at her ear. "Hungry?"

"Starving." She twined her arms around his neck. "But not for food."

They practically fell over each other in their hurry to the bedroom. Giggling like a couple of school kids, they stumbled through the door.

"I'll apologize right up front," Ty murmured, his voice unsteady. "I didn't expect company."

The bed was made, but haphazardly. A pair of jeans draped over the back of a chair, a towel heaped on the floor beside it.

None of that fazed Sophie. She could handle a little mess, a little disorganization—especially right now.

What stopped her cold was the photo on the nightstand.

The smiling face of a knock-'em-dead beautiful woman with long dark hair.

"Julia?"

"Oh, shit. Son of a— Sophie, I'm sorry."

"It's okay," she said quietly. But it wasn't.

It wasn't okay to run head-on into the woman Ty loved. Her breath caught.

Ty dropped her hand, opened the nightstand drawer, and closed the picture inside. "I— The boys wander in sometimes at night to sleep with me. One of them, two of them, sometimes all three. Nightmares. Monsters under the bed or in the closet. A sound outside their window."

He raked fingers through his hair. "The thing is I keep her picture here for them. It seems to help calm them." He cupped her chin. "Oh, God, Sophie, I've hurt you."

"No. I understand. Really, I do." She waved a hand. "But—"

"Jesus, Mary, and Joseph." He scrubbed his hands over his face. "I couldn't possibly have screwed up any worse if I'd been trying, could I?"

She tried for a laugh, but it came out sounding more like a strangled sob. "You know what? I am hungry after all. Let's go raid the fridge. You can throw some more wood on the fire. Maybe open some wine."

He picked up her hand and turned it over, kissing the palm. "I'm so sorry, Sophie."

"Don't worry about it." She kissed him, but the heat was missing.

* * *

Working side by side, they put together a hodgepodge meal and carried it into the living room to eat in front of the fire.

Although she'd insisted she was hungry, Sophie only picked at her food.

Ty kicked himself every way but Sunday. What in the hell had he been thinking?

He hadn't been. That's what.

Talk about a wet blanket. He'd dragged her up the stairs into his room, wanting, needing, to tear off her clothes and sink into her. And there, right beside the bed where he'd planned to seduce her, sat a picture of his wife.

What a boneheaded move.

Watching her tear apart her turkey sandwich, he had the sinking feeling he'd destroyed something innocent. Something miraculous. Something he wasn't at all sure he deserved and doubted very much he'd be able to revive.

She'd been willing to give of herself freely, asking for no promises in return. And what had he done? Crushed her beneath his boot heel.

He was an ass.

An ass who owed her an explanation.

Sidling closer, he removed the sandwich she was busy mutilating and laid it on the plate. When he wrapped an arm around her, she rested her head on his shoulder.

"We didn't do so well, did we?" she asked.

"*I* didn't do so well," he said. "You're amazing."

She tipped her head to look up at him. "So what do we do now, cowboy?"

"I share. Something I probably should have done sooner."

She placed a hand on his chest. "Ty, you don't have to. I understand this has to be beyond difficult for you."

He shook his head. "It's time. Everybody in town knows the story, so I'm not used to telling it. I'm sure you've already figured out there are no secrets when you grow up in a small place like this. No need to explain. Guess I've gotten so used to that I've forgotten how."

He stood and walked to the fireplace. Opening the screen, he placed another log on top and watched as the flames leaped up to lick around the edges, consuming the bark. Blues and reds danced over the surface.

Then he dropped onto the hearth and, forearms resting on his thighs, faced her. "I'm not quite sure where to begin."

She said nothing, simply watched him with those big, gold-flecked brown eyes. How easy it would be to simply lose himself in them, put this off.

But he couldn't. He'd expected her to open up to him, to share secrets and concerns, but he was holding back, too.

"I can't actually remember the first time I saw Julia. She was simply always there. In all my memories. There were no secrets, no getting to know each other. It was comfortable. Not in an old slipper sort of way. More like a favorite book. You've already read it, you know what's coming, but you still can't wait to get there."

She nodded.

"The grief when I lost her was so devastating, I couldn't deal with it. I broke. I totally fell apart. I was worth less than nothing, yet I had three babies who needed me. The—and God, this is going to sound awful, but the saving grace for me, and ultimately for the boys, too, was that because they were preemies, they had to stay in the hospital awhile. That gave me time I desperately needed to get my feet under me. To bury their mama."

He fisted his hands in his lap. "My world was a dark place, Tink. A very, very dark place. And I honestly didn't know if I wanted to crawl out of that cavernous hole. I didn't know if it was worth it. And then the boys came home."

He glanced at her, tears swimming in his eyes. "I fell in love all over again. So I dragged myself out of that dark hole and worked to put together a life for us.

"It's been over four years. That's a place I never want to go again. A place I cannot open myself to. Do you understand? It has nothing to do with you." He thumped a fist on his chest. "It's me. My fears. I'm sorry."

She crossed to him, took hold of his fist, and uncurled his fingers, making *shush*ing sounds. "There's no need to be sorry."

"I can't block it out, Sophie. I can't pretend it never happened. It did, and it changed me. Julia is the boys' mother. She'll always be part of our lives, but I'm also beginning to understand it's time to start a new chapter. She'd kick my ass if she saw where I am right now. She wouldn't want this for me. But I'm afraid." He stared into her eyes. "That's a humbling thing for a man to have to admit."

"It shouldn't be. If a person has no fear, he has nothing to lose. Nothing he loves."

Sophie laced her fingers with his, and they sat quietly.

Finally, he said, "When I look at you, Tink, I get confused."

He kissed her gently. When he drew away, she snaked an arm around his neck and pulled him back. She kissed him and he fell into the need, the thrill.

He moved to the floor and tugged her down beside him. The firelight flickered over her, accentuating the amber in her eyes, turning her skin into molten gold.

"It's been a long, long time for me, sweetheart, so I've got an awfully short fuse."

"That's okay. We have all night for encores if the first movie's too short."

"Thank you." Gazing into her eyes, he said, "I'm not sure what I've done to deserve you."

His hand slid beneath her sweater. He had to see her. In one swift move, he pulled it up and over her head. He drew back to look at her, his breath catching. "You're beautiful."

He undid the snap and zipper on her jeans and slid them down her legs. Taking in the matching bra and panties, he grinned and traced the edges.

"Nice."

"Again, thank Maggie. They're from her store."

"I'll do that." Then his lips moved where his finger had been.

She groaned.

"Fair play," she insisted, unbuttoning his shirt and running a hand over his bare chest, along the six-pack abs. "Oh, cowboy, you're in some shape, aren't you?"

"I could say the same about you, sweetheart. And mine. All mine," he murmured into her hair. "God, you're so damn hot. I can't get enough of you."

When he saw the tattoo of Tinker Bell, complete with wings and magic wand, riding high on Sophie's left buttock, he laughed. "I should have known."

"I believe in fairies. I believe in magic."

"Part of what makes you who you are." He ran a finger over the tattoo. "I envy the tattoo artist who put this here."

She smiled, slow and sexy. "But he only got to see it once. I'll let you visit any time you want."

Her words pushed him over the edge.

He rolled her to her back, felt her curves against his hard body. Damp flesh against damp flesh. "I need you. Now."

As he entered her, he raised his head, their eyes meeting.

"I want to see you. Know I'm making love to Sophie London. You overwhelm me. I've dreamed about this."

"I'm so glad," she whispered, "because I'd sure hate to be the only one feeling so needy."

And then the intensity devoured him, and he was lost to her.

* * *

Sophie stretched her arms over her head. Sometime during the night, she and Ty had moved upstairs, showered, then tumbled into his bed. Together. Who'd have thought shower sex could be that incredible? The water sluicing over them, his hands slick with soap sending shock waves through her.

This was a first for her. She'd never, ever spent the entire night with a man. Never cuddled in her sleep. Never woke to find one still in her bed...or his bed, as the case might be.

And she hadn't meant to do it this time. As intimate as sex was, actually sleeping with someone had always felt bigger to her. More important.

But then, she and Ty hadn't had sex. They'd made love. There was a huge difference, and, holy fireflies, it scared her.

Careful not to wake him, she rolled her head on the pillow. Sleeping, he was relaxed. At peace. So much responsibility lay on those broad shoulders. But in sleep it all slid away.

Her mind drifted to last night, on the floor by the fireplace. He'd made it crystal clear he was making love to her, Sophie London, not Julia. She understood what a huge step that was for him. And for her.

When she looked at him again, he was awake and watching her. The corners of his lips curved in a sleepy smile.

"Good morning," he said. "Come here."

His arm snagged her around the waist. "Let's not get up just yet."

* * *

When they finally made it downstairs, Ty, dressed in nothing but unsnapped jeans, his feet bare, set to work making a pot of coffee. Sophie, dwarfed by one of his shirts, sat at the table, watching the play of muscles over his bare back. The man was unbelievably sexy.

She brought the collar of his shirt to her face, smelled him, and smiled. What a night they'd had. Her heart kicked up a notch, remembering what those hands now scooping coffee had done to her. What that beautiful mouth had done.

As the coffee dripped into the pot, he reached into the cupboard for a mug but turned at the rap on the front door.

"Oh, no." Eyes wide, Sophie jumped up from the chair.

"Relax, Tink. I'll see who it is."

Too late. He'd only taken a couple steps when they heard the charge of feet toward them. The boys were home.

Babs followed them into the kitchen. Her brows arched as she looked from Ty's half-dressed body to Sophie.

Sophie dropped back onto her chair, tucking her bare legs under it.

"I take it dinner went well?" Babs asked.

"Hard to talk with that tongue stuck in your cheek?" Ty handed her the first cup of coffee. "From the look on your face, I think you probably need this worse than Sophie or me."

He turned to the pot and poured a second cup for Sophie. "Here you go, Tink. Drink up."

Jesse sidled up to Sophie and laid his little hand on her arm. "Did you and Daddy have a sleepover, too?"

Her eyes flew to Ty's. He hid behind a mug of coffee. "Um, yes, we did. It was, uh, late when we finished eating, so—" Cripes, what was she supposed to say?

Jonah came to stand by her. He rested both his hands on her legs and looked into her face. "Sometimes when we have a bad dream, Daddy lets us sleep in his bed. Did he let you sleep in his bed?"

Babs spit coffee across the table. "Sorry," she choked out. "Ty, hand me a paper towel."

Sophie didn't need a mirror to know her face had turned as red as the ribbon on the Christmas wreath they'd hung yesterday on the front door.

"Anybody want French toast?" Ty tossed his sister-in-law a towel before moving to the fridge. He turned, a carton of eggs in hand.

"I do. I do." Josh danced around the kitchen. His brothers joined in.

"Nice save," Babs muttered.

"There you go. I always have been quick. Sophie, if you want to run upstairs and grab a shower, things should be pulled together here when you're done." He winked at her.

"Thank you. That's a really good idea." Her dignity in shreds, she rose and picked up her coffee mug. "Think I'll take this with me."

As she headed up the steps, she could only imagine the conversation Ty and Babs were about to have.

Chapter Twenty-Four

What had she done? Sophie's mind ping-ponged, back and forth, back and forth, her mood changing second to second. She'd sworn off the man; she'd *slept* with him. Holy raindrops and fairy whispers!

She swung the Chevy into Dottie's drive and simply sat there. The temperature had dropped dramatically, and Christmas music played over the radio.

December. She could hardly believe she'd been here almost a month.

Maggie and Annelise would be by in a little bit to pick her up. They wanted to hit the shops today, soak up some Christmas cheer, and indulge in a little retail therapy.

Before they got here, she needed a quick change of clothes. Needed to settle her mind.

Last night? Whew. How could it possibly get any better? Ty. Everything she could ever have imagined. Considerate.

Passionate. Tender. And that body. All those ripped muscles. A cowboy who rocked!

She liked him—a lot.

And she could name a thousand reasons why he was bad for her. No, not bad. Just wrong.

It had almost killed her to see Julia's picture beside Ty's bed last night. Did he talk to her once he had the boys safely tucked into bed and fast asleep? Did he ask her advice? Tell her how much he loved her? How much he missed her?

How did you compete with a dead wife?

The answer was simple. You didn't. You couldn't.

She'd been right the other night when she'd told him she needed to end their relationship. It was the safe thing, the smart thing to do. Still, she couldn't regret these past couple days with him and the Triple Threat. They'd been beyond wonderful, and she wouldn't wish away a single minute of them.

As for last night? She didn't regret that, either. She could and would regret there'd be no repeats, but not that it happened.

Argh. She needed to shake off this mood of hers because today? She and the girls were going shopping! And Maggie and Annelise deserved better than a pouty, pity-me tagalong.

Bracing herself, she opened the car door and stepped out into the cold.

Since she'd showered at Ty's while he and Babs had their little chat, all she needed now was some makeup and a fresh outfit. She'd slap on her happy face while she was at it.

Her credit card couldn't deal with too much more therapy, but there was still a little wiggle room on it. Besides, it would take a few weeks for the billing cycle to catch up to her. And wasn't that mature? Digging the key from her purse, she leaned her hip into the door and it swung open.

What the heck? Openmouthed, she stood in the doorway, chill air blowing into the tiny apartment. A huge grin split her face. How had Ty managed all this so quickly? It hadn't taken her that long to drive in from the ranch.

Her cowboy really was a romantic!

She forgot her decision to call it quits, pushed aside all the reasons she and Ty couldn't be, and simply enjoyed the moment. With a happy little sigh, she stepped in, closing the door behind her.

Flowers filled her apartment. Red roses in a crystal vase on the dining room table. Soft pink ones in a little teapot on the coffee table. Yellow ones spilled from another container on the counter.

She clapped a hand over her mouth and all but danced to the table. Putting her face in the largest bouquet, she breathed in its scent, then slid the accompanying card from its white envelope.

Her purse, along with the door key, clattered to the floor. The florist's card fluttered from suddenly nerveless fingers and landed facedown on the table.

Even behind her closed eyes, she saw the message.

Time to come home. Now. Nathan.

Her head swiveled, searching right, then left. She spun around to look behind her. Oh, God! Her gaze skittered across the room, darted toward the bedroom, the bath.

He was here!

* * *

Ty saddled Beau and rode away from the stable. He turned up the collar of his coat and settled his Stetson more firmly on his head. Damn. It was colder than he'd thought.

Still, he needed to check on the herd in the south pasture, be sure the trough hadn't frozen over. This weather was tough on cattle. Thank God it didn't hit very often.

As he rode, his mind drifted to Sophie. Sophie of the incredible brandy-colored eyes, the long lashes that feathered her cheek as she slept.

The woman made everything right. Made his world a far, far better place.

And he'd taken her to his room last night, to his bed—with Julia's picture sitting right there. Talk about rubbing Sophie's face in his past. He'd called himself every kind of fool. Still couldn't believe he'd botched things so badly.

The photo had been there so long, he rarely noticed it anymore. He'd told Sophie the truth about having put it there for the boys. Still...He couldn't blame her for her reaction. Hard to make love with a guy with the dead wife watching.

What a jumbled mess. Maybe Sophie London really *was* part fairy. She sure had worked her magic on him.

When the kids had come home earlier than expected this morning, despite his nonchalant handling of it, he'd been worried about what they'd think when they found her there.

He needn't have given it a second thought. They'd acted as though it was the most natural thing in the world and couldn't have been happier.

Ty's eyes swept the landscape as he rode, on the watch for cattle that might be in trouble. So far, so good.

When Jonah had asked if she'd slept in his bed, Ty'd thought Tink was going to have a coronary. Or maybe Babs.

Now there was the real threat. He'd asked his sister-in-law to stay quiet about him and Sophie, but that was like asking the first reporter at the scene not to tell anyone the *Titanic* had gone down. The chances of it actually happening? Realistically? Nil to none.

Of course, it probably didn't matter a whit, because the first person any of the triplets ran into would undoubtedly hear all about Sophie sleeping with Daddy. He turned his horse east and gave him his head.

For himself, he didn't care. Sophie was another matter entirely. He hadn't considered what this might do to her reputation, how she might feel about everyone knowing. Truth? He hadn't really thought any of it through. He'd just reacted. And that wasn't like him.

Sophie had pegged him on that. He wasn't a spur-of-the-moment person.

Ty swore under his breath. This shouldn't be so hard.

He hadn't so much as dated since Julia died. At some point in the future he figured it might be an issue, but by then, he'd assumed the boys would be older and he'd be able to explain—or wouldn't need to.

He rode along a stretch of fencing, checking it for breaks. In the distance he heard the lowing of cattle and set his horse to a gallop.

His mind kept pace, trying to come to terms with what had happened. Thing was, he flat-out hadn't seen any of this coming, but he probably should have. When Annie had said she'd chosen her cousin as maid of honor, he'd flash backed instantly, in living color, to the incredibly beautiful woman wearing Jonah's cherry soda on her lap. He'd wanted her from the moment he'd laid eyes on her.

Maybe he was over-worrying all this. Maybe the boys

had it right. This thing between him and Sophie was perfectly normal. Perfectly natural. Two unattached adults enjoying each other.

Yeah, and maybe, just maybe, he was setting them all up for heartbreak.

* * *

Panic swept through Sophie as she stood beside the table.

Dottie wasn't home. She'd left yesterday for her daughter's again, wanting to spend Christmas with the grandkids. Her son and his family would be there, too. All of which meant Sophie was alone here in this big house.

With Nathan?

She'd locked her door. She knew she had. Yet the flowers were here. Her gaze moved over the room, looking for anything else out of place. Anything else different.

Other than the flowers, she saw nothing.

Her brain kicked into gear, and common sense surfaced. A few roses didn't mean Nathan was actually here. In town. A semblance of relief washed over her. He was in Chicago at work—where he'd picked up his phone, called a florist, and had the flowers delivered.

But the door had been locked. Unless the florist was also a locksmith...Her gaze still traveling around the room, phone in one hand, she drew in a shaky breath and told herself to calm down. She'd overreacted. On alert, ready to run at the slightest sound, she picked up the card from the floor. On it was the logo and phone number for Heaven Scent, Maverick Junction's only flower shop. Cell in one hand ready to dial 911 if anyone popped out, Sophie stepped into her bedroom, peeked into the bath, then opened the closet. Even though she was alone, she felt silly. But she wasn't taking any chances.

No Nathan.

No cat, either.

"Lilybelle? Lilybelle? Come here, kitty. Please be here. Be okay."

A soft meow came from beneath the bed. When she lifted the dust ruffle, the cat slunk out. Nearly weeping with relief, Sophie scooped up the cat and buried her face in its soft fur.

Retracing her steps to the living room, she lowered Lilybelle to the couch, then sat down beside her. Tapping the flower shop's card on her thigh, she decided to give them a call.

Bitsy Devlin answered. Sophie had met the florist at Annelise and Cash's wedding.

"The flowers are absolutely beautiful, Bitsy. You do such great work. I, ah, wanted to ask about Nathan, the man who had them delivered. He didn't actually come into your store, did he?"

"Nope, he called in the order."

The tightness in Sophie's chest relaxed.

Bitsy chuckled. "Let me tell you, he was very specific about what he wanted. The order kind of surprised me, though."

"Why?" Sophie asked.

"Well, everybody knows you and Ty have a thing going."

Sophie rolled her eyes. There was that *thing* again. Did the whole town know she'd spent last night with him?

Deciding not to remark on Bitsy's comment, she said, "Do you know where he called from?"

"No, ma'am. Sure don't." She hesitated. "Does it matter?"

Sophie made a noncommittal sound. "Can I ask, Bitsy, how you got inside to deliver them?"

Again, Bitsy paused. "He said your door was unlocked and that we should just go on in. He insisted it would be okay."

A shiver ran down Sophie's spine.

"Sophie, is everything okay? Was it all right for us to do that?"

"Yes. Sure." She forced a smile into her voice. "Again, they're gorgeous, Bitsy. Thank you."

She hung up. Hands still shaking, she pulled a trash bag from the pantry and dumped every single flower in it, containers and all, before tying it tightly. She tossed the whole lot outside onto the landing. She'd throw it in Dottie's garbage can on her way out.

Had she locked her door? Doubt crept in. She couldn't be sure, had gotten careless since she'd been here in Maverick Junction. With Dottie gone, she could have sworn she'd locked up, but maybe she'd forgotten.

Still, how had Nathan known her door would be unlocked? The question nagged at her.

He didn't know. A good guess on his part. Small town. People left their doors unlocked. He'd played the percentages. Nathan Richards was good at that.

Well, she'd definitely lock up when she left with the girls today. And double check.

*   *   *

Sophie had no more than finished the last swipe of mascara when a horn tooted in the drive. One quick check in the mirror and she ran to the front window. Raising it, she waved down at Maggie and Annelise. "Be right there."

"If you have any Coke, bring me one," Maggie hollered back.

"Got it." Grabbing her purse and a soda from the fridge, she stopped to give Lilybelle a quick rub. "You be a good girl. I'm counting on you to stay safe, you hear?" She tipped up the cat's head and stared into her eyes. "I'm locking the door. If somebody does get in, though, you run and hide, understand?"

The cat meowed in response.

"Good girl."

Stepping onto the landing, she turned the key in the door, jiggled it once, then again for good measure. Soda tucked in her purse, she picked up the trash bag. At the bottom of the stairs, she lifted the lid on the garbage can and dumped Heaven Scent's entire delivery in it.

Good riddance to bad garbage.

Instead of heading toward Austin, Maggie drove south toward San Antonio. "We're not actually going into the city, though," she said.

Sophie pouted. "Why not? I've never been there."

"Tell Ty to take you." Seeing the instant look of regret on Sophie's face, Maggie said, "What's wrong, honey? Did you and Ty have a fight?"

"No." Sophie shook her head. "Just the opposite, actually."

"The opposite? Make love, not war?"

Sophie laughed.

Cranking the car's stereo system down a notch, Maggie slipped in a Christmas CD. "If that's the case, you really should be doing cartwheels today. I'm wondering why you aren't. You gonna share?"

"I will. A little later. A lot's tumbling around in my head right now."

"Are you okay?" Annelise asked from the back seat.

"I think so."

Annelise nodded, and Sophie breathed a sigh of relief, understanding both women would give her time. Would let her talk when she was ready rather than nagging her into it now while her head was a combat zone.

The sun shone brightly. The wide open Texas sky was bluebird blue and virtually cloudless. Patches of snow still clung to a few tufts of grass along the road's edge, but the roads themselves were clear and dry.

The cool, forty-degree temperature made it perfect for Christmas shopping. It gave the illusion of winter without a person suffering frostbite. And as much as she missed the hustle and bustle of Chicago, she didn't miss that frigid wind whipping off the lake.

"By the way, Maggie, Ty says thank you very much."

"For?"

"My little pink and black undies. He enjoyed them last night."

"Now you're bragging."

"Maybe. A little."

Maggie's eyes twinkled. "I think, then, a new item deserves top billing on our shopping list."

"Oh?"

"Another set of tear-them-off-me-please undergarments."

"I don't know." She stared at the passing scenery. "I'm not sure there'll be another night with him."

"Well, tell you what. Why don't we think of them as an emergency pair. A just-in-case pair. Like all good scouts, we're always prepared."

"You're bad."

"I know." Maggie whipped around a slow-moving car. "Isn't it fun?"

* * *

Sophie had to hand it to the woman. Maggie knew all the best shopping places. No big stores for her. They stopped in little, hidden-away shops. And in every one, the owners greeted Maggie by name. The girls drank eggnog, ate sugar cookies decorated in red and green, and sang along with holiday music in the stores.

And they found not one, but two absolutely perfect sets of undergarments. One was the same deep brown as her eyes. She'd never have considered that color but, after trying them on, she had to have them. The other set? Pale, pale blue. She fell in love with them. Even if she had to eat Ramen noodles for a month to cover their cost, she'd count them worth every penny.

Maybe. If she and Ty ever got together again. If he had the chance to slowly undo the bra, peel away the panties. The dressing room's temperature spiked ten degrees, and she smiled. Heat could be good. Real good.

The girls' stomachs finally cried foul, forcing them to find something other than cookies. Again, Maggie came through with flying colors. The little restaurant she pulled up to billed itself as a tea shop, but Maggie insisted they had the best salads and sandwiches in the state.

The outside looked like a little English cottage that had been plopped down in the heart of Texas. Two steps inside, Sophie stopped and grinned. "This is fantastic!"

"Isn't it, though?" Maggie asked. "I found it on one of my buying trips and fell in love."

The floors had been hand painted to mimic garden stones, complete with ivy trailing over the stones and up stenciled trellises. Flowers rioted over the walls. With brush, paint, and a whole lot of skill, the place had been transformed into an English garden. The artist in Sophie sighed. She wished she'd been the creator of this magic.

"The owner did all this." Maggie waved a hand at the artwork.

"I need to meet her."

"You will. She's also the cook."

The lunch rush ended, and Sophie and Gail Brisbane, the owner, had a great chat over tea and dessert. Gail, familiar with Sophie's work, couldn't believe she was here in her shop.

"What I do is nothing compared to this," Sophie said.

"And we have ourselves a mutual admiration society," Maggie drawled.

Everyone laughed, and they left with Sophie and Gail promising to stay in touch.

Outside again, Maggie headed the car toward the next shopping destination.

"So are you going to tell us, Sophie, or do I have to beat it out of you?" Annelise asked.

"Oooh." Maggie glanced at Annelise in the rearview mirror, one brow raised. "Now here're some interesting family dynamics. Who'd have thought a little rich girl could be a bully?"

"You don't know the half of it," Annelise said. "Spill, cuz."

"Okay." Sophie pulled at her seat belt, suddenly feeling hemmed in. She decided to tackle her problems one at a time and told them about the flowers first. About Nathan.

"Did you let Ty know?" Annelise asked.

She shook her head.

"Tell me you called the cops." Maggie shot her a sharp look. "Jimmy would have taken care of the problem."

"And tell them what? That a guy in Chicago sent me flowers, so I want them to fly up there and lock him up? Last time I checked, sending roses wasn't against the law."

"No, but he's stalking you," Maggie persisted.

"Not really."

Annelise shook her head. "You always did have your head in the clouds, Soph. You insist on looking at the silver lining and miss all the rust on the outside."

"That's not true. I realize I need to keep my eye on Nathan. I made absolutely certain I locked my door when I left this morning. But I'm trying to keep things in perspective."

She fiddled with her sunglasses. "And speaking of that." A big sigh escaped.

"Here it comes," Maggie said. "Ty."

"I spent yesterday with him and the boys, and we had an incredible time. We made a gingerbread house, then strung popcorn for the tree. Do you remember doing that, Annelise?"

"Every Christmas Eve. We still do."

"You're off-topic. We were talking about Ty," Maggie reminded her.

"Oh, boy, you're tough."

"I can be tougher—and will be if you don't spill."

"Geez, who'd have thought I was heading out this morning with a pair of thugs?"

Sunglasses pushed down her nose, Maggie cut a quick glance at Sophie and scowled.

"Okay, okay. So after we were done decorating, Babs stopped by and picked up the kids for an overnighter."

"Ahhh," Annelise murmured.

"There's no ahhh. She thought it would be nice if Ty and I had some time alone. Went out to dinner and talked—without the distraction of triplets."

"Smart lady." Maggie turned left onto a narrow two-lane road.

"We never made it to dinner."

"Really?" Maggie hesitated a second, glanced back at Annelise. "I'm not sure what you know about Ty's situation, but he hadn't so much as dated since Julia. Until Sophie. And now, what? Second, third date?"

"Wow, so this is pretty big," Annelise said.

"Maybe."

"Maybe?"

"I mean, yes, it is a big step for him." Sophie scooted in her seat so that she sat nearly sideways and could see both Maggie and Annelise. She grimaced. "I'm confused. I feel like one of those crazy women playing the daisy game. He loves me, he loves me not."

"Ty is a good man," Maggie said.

Annelise agreed. "You can fight it all you want, cuz, but it won't help. When it happens, it happens."

Dread rose in Sophie's throat. "This, all of this, isn't what I expected. It isn't what I wanted."

Annelise smiled at her. "Join the club."

"But you're happy."

"Yes, I am." Annelise reached over the seat and laid a hand on Sophie's shoulder. "I have to admit, though, that I wasn't thrilled, either, when I first realized I was falling for Cash. This is so removed from the life I knew."

She sat silently for a few seconds, then added, "The place grows on you. Mel at the newspaper, Sally at the café, Stella at Sadler's. They're great people."

"I know."

"The thing is, Sophie, this is my life now. Cash is my life. And I've never, ever been happier. Sometimes you have to let go of those preconceived ideas. Let yourself wander outside the box." Her smile grew. "It's incredible out here, out of that box's confines."

"Good advice, Annie." Maggie shook her head. "Sometimes we hold on to the past so tightly, we don't leave room for the future."

Eyes narrowed, Sophie studied her friend. Was Maggie talking about Sophie and Ty or herself and Brawley? She sure wished she knew what had happened there.

Right now, though, she'd follow Maggie's earlier advice and stay focused. She hesitated, wondering if she really wanted the answer to her next question. As much as she dreaded what she might hear, it had to be asked.

"All right. So, what's the story with Julia? I mean, there are times when Ty almost seems angry over her death. And I suppose that's natural when someone's taken from you way too soon. But this almost seems more than that, and he won't really talk about her. He opened up a little bit last night, but there's something I'm missing. Something he's still holding back. Something important."

Annelise shrugged. "I can't help you on that front. It all happened before I got here. I've noticed it, too, but nobody talks about it."

The two women looked at Maggie.

"Even in a small town, everyone has a few secrets." She shrugged. "It's not my story to tell, Sophie. You'll have to wait till he's ready."

"What if he's never ready?"

"Then I guess you'd have your answer to the other question. The how do you know? He has to be willing to share."

"That's what I was afraid of." Sophie rubbed her forehead. "Well, if he's putting up barriers, I have to, too. I can't...Oh,

God, I can't give my heart to him if he can't give his back."
Panicked, her eyes flew to Annelise's. "I've already given this
Texas cowboy my heart, haven't I?"

She laid her head back against the seat. "I'm doomed."

"Worse things could happen," Maggie said.

"Oh, yeah?"

"Yeah. He could hand that heart back to you all minced
up like chopped liver. But Ty? He won't do that."

"I'm not so sure. I know he's got the power to."

Maggie turned up the volume on her CD player.

The conversation was over. Had they cut too close to the
truth about Maggie and Brawley? She seemed to have everything so together. But beneath it all, did she hurt?

Love was a strange animal.

Chapter Twenty-Five

Dusk had draped its mantle over the earth by the time she and Maggie dropped Annelise off and pulled into Dottie's drive.

The house threw shadows into the yard and gave the colorful gardens an almost eerie edge. Glancing up at the landing, Sophie realized she hadn't turned on her porch light.

"Let me walk you in." Maggie reached for her door handle.

Sophie shook her head. "Don't be a ninny. I'm perfectly capable of getting myself safely inside."

"But with Dottie gone—"

"I'm fine. Believe it or not, I manage quite nicely alone in Chicago. Get going. You'll be late for that dinner with your folks if you don't."

Maggie checked the car's dashboard clock and frowned. "You sure?"

"Positive. Now that you're staying in Lone Tree with your grandpa, I doubt you see your mom and dad nearly as much as they'd like. Go. When I'm inside, safe and sound, I'll flick the porch light on and off. And I'll lock up right behind me."

She slid from the car, gathered her festive bags from the back seat, and held up a couple. "Good shopping trip."

"It was, wasn't it?"

"The best. Night."

"I'm waiting right here till I see that light flashing."

"Got you." She turned and headed toward the stairs. The soft glow of the night-light Dottie had left on in her kitchen shone through the window but did little to alleviate the darkness.

Despite her reassurances to Maggie, she suddenly felt uneasy. "Silly," she mumbled. Tonight was no different from any other night.

It was those damn flowers. The e-mails and phone calls. They'd planted crazy thoughts in her head and left her spooked. Exactly what Nathan had intended. Next time she saw him, she'd give him a good piece of her mind.

Anger seeped in to replace worry.

Cursing herself for forgetting to leave the porch light on that morning, she set her packages down on the landing and fished in her purse. She fumbled with her key ring and finally found the right one.

She unlocked the door, and it creaked open. Tomorrow, she promised, she'd oil the hinges. Dropping her bags on the kitchen counter, she flashed the porch light. On, off. Then she locked the kitchen door and watched through the window as Maggie backed out of the drive and headed to her folks'.

What a wonderful day!

A small sound behind her broke the silence. Her heart hammered so hard she thought it would explode. Then, relieved, she remembered she didn't live alone anymore. That would take some getting used to.

"Hey, Lilybelle." She half-turned toward the sound.

"That your cat's name?"

Nathan. Every ounce of blood drained from her body. Run! Run! her mind screamed.

Her feet refused to cooperate. It was as though she stood on flypaper, waiting to be gathered up and tossed away. The hair on her nape stood on end.

Her hand dove into her pocket for the phone she prayed was there rather than in her purse. She'd call for help. Ty, Annie, the police. Anyone!

Before she could pull it free, his hand clamped over her mouth. Her eyes flew wide as she found herself dragged back against him, clawing and kicking.

Reflected in the kitchen window over the sink, Nathan Richards glared at her.

Oh, God.

* * *

Restless, Ty considered calling Sophie. He missed her. Today was her day with the girls though, so he dialed Brawley instead.

"What are you doing?" he asked when Brawley answered.

"Not much. I've put in a long day here with Doc Gibson. Or rather *at* Doc Gibson's. He left early this afternoon. The man can't keep up with this practice, Ty."

"I know, and I don't have the foggiest idea what we'll do without him."

"You bored?"

"I am. The kids are sawing logs, and I've been around the TV dial ten times now."

"It's Sophie."

Ty grunted in response.

"You know it is."

Because they'd been friends forever, he said, "Yeah, guess so."

"I'm gonna stop at her place on my way home. I ordered an ID tag for her cat's collar. Thought I'd drop it off, surprise her. Anything you want me to tell her?"

"What? Like passing a note in seventh-grade study hall? Jeez, Brawley, I think we're past that, don't you?"

He could almost hear his friend thinking. Finally, he said, "Nope. Don't know that we are."

"Well, maybe you're not, but I sure as hell am."

"Okay, that's fine. I'll tell her you didn't want to say hey."

"Now you're being a jerk."

"Probably. Want to grab a beer at Bubba's and talk about it? You think Haley'll keep an eye on the kids?"

"I'm sure she will. I have a standing invitation for that. I'll give her a call and meet you at Bubba's in, what? Thirty, forty minutes?"

"Better make it closer to an hour. I need to clean up here, then make that stop at Sophie's. I'm gonna check Lilybelle's leg while I'm there."

Ty hung up, still on edge. His gut was telling him something was wrong.

* * *

Panic ripped through Sophie. What did Nathan want? Why was he hiding in her darkened apartment?

Then a wave of relief surged through her that Maggie hadn't come upstairs. Who knew what Nathan would have done? Although she couldn't believe he'd actually hurt her...or anyone for that matter. A harmless pest, right?

No, she couldn't buy that anymore.

He'd followed her clear to Texas. Broke into her apartment. He'd crossed a line. A huge one.

She nearly gagged when he started to drop wet kisses on the back of her neck, in her hair. She struggled against his hold, but one arm wrapped around her waist like a steel band while his other hand covered the lower half of her face.

This wasn't the Nathan she knew. This was a darker, dangerous Nathan. Would either of Dottie's elderly neighbors hear her if she screamed? Maybe. But then she'd put them at risk.

"I've missed you, Sophie. Why'd you stay away so long?"

She tried to talk, but his hand held fast.

"I don't want to hurt you. I love you."

Her heart thudded in her chest. This was like something out of a bad movie. But it was real. She smelled stale sweat. Felt his breath on her neck.

"You didn't take my phone calls. Didn't call to thank me for mailing your package." He chuckled. "I need to thank Dee again for that. I'd never have found you without her help. Damned uppity Madison wouldn't say boo."

His head swiveled right, then left. "Did you like my flowers? I don't see them."

Again, Sophie mumbled, praying he'd remove his hand.

Barely able to breathe, she struggled to remain conscious. Maybe if she quit fighting, he'd lower his guard.

Willing herself to go completely limp, she relaxed her muscles and went lax against him.

"There you go, Sophie. Knew you'd be glad to see me, but I scared you, didn't I? Wasn't me you were fighting. You thought some stranger had sneaked into your house. Made myself a copy of that spare key you hid under your planter."

His hold loosened slightly, and she drew in a little more air.

"Great place, by the way. Looks like you've managed to get some work done. I saw your flower drawings. The one you did of that little kid and the guy in the barn, too."

She'd put those in one of her dresser drawers. That meant he'd gone through her things. Her stomach rebelled, and she swallowed hard.

His hand slipped from her mouth to reach around to the front of her blouse. Slowly, he undid the first two buttons. He ran a finger along the opening, over the top of her breasts.

"What are you doing?" Her voice sounded small and breathless. Fearful.

"I want us to be together. You and me."

"There is no us, Nathan."

"Why do you have to do that, Sophie? Say things you don't mean."

"I do mean them."

"No, you don't, and I'm tired of waiting. Tired of your games. You've put me off long enough." His voice grew gruff. "No more." With one quick tug, he rent her blouse from top to bottom.

With a gasp, she tried to pull away, but he slammed his body into hers, knocking her into the edge of a cabinet. A jarring pain rocked through her cheek and had her seeing stars. She tasted blood and ran her tongue over her cut lip.

Damned if she'd cry or beg. Desperately creating and discarding ideas, Sophie stilled. Had she heard footsteps on the outside stairs?

Please let it be someone who can help me, she prayed. Not Ty, though. Oh, God, she didn't want him to see her like this. Didn't want him to walk in on this. And, yet, she wanted him desperately. Wanted his strong arms around her.

Nathan heard the footsteps, too, and jerked her deeper into the kitchen, out of sight of the door's window. "Who's that?"

"I have no idea."

"Don't give me that. Who is it?"

"I don't know, Nathan."

When he jerked her arm up behind her back, tears sprang to her eyes. "Get rid of whoever it is."

"Nathan," she whispered. "You said you loved me, yet you're hurting me. Why are you doing this?"

"I asked you to come home, Sophie. Nicely. You didn't listen."

"I still had things to take care of here."

"Yeah. Ty Rawlins. I heard about him over lunch. His sister-in-law was at the café when I was there, and she's not opposed to sharing secrets with her friends."

Her cheeks flared with heat. "I—"

A knock sounded at the door.

"Sophie?"

Brawley. Tears clogged her throat.

"Who the hell is that?" Nathan demanded.

"A friend."

He tugged her arm again, and she bit her lip to keep from

whimpering. "You seem to have lots of friends here. A lot of male ones."

"Let go of me."

Brawley knocked again. "Sophie, you home?"

"I need help!" she screamed. "Call the cops, Brawley."

Nathan clamped a hand over her mouth, and the cut on her lip stung.

"Sophie!" Brawley rattled the knob, then shoved at the door, but it refused to budge. Putting his shoulder to it, he rammed it. Nothing.

Sophie shuddered. The old thing was stronger than it looked. She tried twisting out of Nathan's grasp, tried kicking back at him, but she couldn't get free.

She gasped as Brawley slammed an elbow through one of the windowpanes. Knocking out the shards, he reached inside and turned the lock.

Nathan put her body squarely between himself and a meaner-than-spit Brawley.

"What the hell is going on here?"

"This isn't any of your business. This is between my girlfriend and me."

"Really?" The deep voice made Sophie want to cry. Ty stood in the doorway, broken glass crunching under his boots.

He stepped in, glanced at Brawley. "I decided to meet you here instead of Bubba's." Face hard, he studied her bruised cheek. Her cut lip. Nathan's pressure on her arm intensified, and she let out a small cry.

Ty's eyes blazed. "You're gonna want to let go of her."

"I don't think so."

Before Sophie could open her mouth, Ty had covered the distance between them.

The coward in Nathan surfaced. He released his grip on her and backed up several steps.

Ty reached for Sophie and thrust her behind him. "Get her out of here, Brawley."

She shook her head. "I'm not leaving."

Catching Nathan by the shirtfront, Ty jerked his feet off the floor till they were nose to nose. "You must be Nathan. Give me one good reason why I shouldn't beat you to a bloody pulp."

"Brawley, call the cops," Sophie pleaded.

Without even glancing at them, Ty ground out, "You do that, pal. In the meantime, this joker and I are gonna have ourselves a come-to-Jesus moment."

"I don't have to say anything to you."

"No, you don't." In one quick move, Ty dropped him, turned him around, and jerked his arm up. He leaned over Nathan's shoulder, his mouth close to Nathan's ear. "How's it feel, buddy boy? Huh?"

Clutching at the torn shreds of her top, Sophie listened as Brawley gave the dispatcher her address, all the while keeping her eyes on Ty. She'd never seen this side of him. Never seen anything like it before, period.

"Ty—"

"Stay out of this, Sophie." Applying a little more pressure, he said, "So you're the guy who's been bothering our Sophie. And now you've broken into her home. Hurt her."

"She's *my* Sophie."

"She's not your Sophie," Brawley said, tucking his phone in his pocket. "From the looks of things when I got here, she didn't appear any too happy to see you."

"I flew here from Chicago, Sophie, just for you," Nathan whined. "I sent you flowers. Notes."

"You're stalking me, and it stops now. You're breaking the law."

"Your lip is bleeding, sugar," Ty said. "And you've got one hell of a bruise on your cheek."

"She made me do that. She wouldn't listen to me."

Sophie held her breath. The look on Ty's face surely meant death for someone, and Nathan had to know it.

Just then the sound of a siren split the air. *Thank you, God.* But before Jimmy and his deputy could make it up the stairs, Ty drew back his fist and caught Nathan with a right hook to the jaw.

The man dropped like a baby grand piano from a fifth-story window.

Ty shook his hand and caught her gaze. "He was resisting me."

"I saw him," Brawley said. "And I'll testify in court."

Sophie's swollen lips turned up in a hint of a smile.

"Oh, Ty."

"I owed him one—if for nothing else than that look of fear he put in your eyes." Nudging Nathan with the toe of his boot, he said, "Thank God you decided to stop by here, Brawley. If he'd laid his hand on Sophie once more, he'd be drinking his meals through a straw for a long, long time."

The sheriff and his deputy came through the door, guns drawn. Taking in Brawley and Ty, Nathan unconscious at their feet, they both stopped.

"You okay?" Jimmy asked Sophie.

"I am now. Ty and Brawley—" Her composure slipped. Now that it was over, she started to tremble and sat down right there in the middle of the kitchen floor. While Derik Mullens cuffed a shaky, dazed Nathan and listened to his complaints of brutality, Jimmy led Sophie to a chair and took several pictures of her bruises, her torn blouse. Asked questions.

When she told him about the florist delivery, he glanced up from his notepad. "You still have those flowers or the card that came with them?"

"I threw them in the trash. Outside."

"Mind if we dig them out?"

"Not at all."

"Got any of his e-mails? They'd help prove a pattern."

"On my laptop."

Jimmy nodded. "In and of itself, neither of those would be enough. But you put them all together, along with what he did tonight, we should be able to keep him behind bars for a good while."

"If it goes to court, there are several people in Chicago who will be more than happy to testify." She told him about Kyle's tires, Nathan's visits to Madison and Dee.

"He has a key."

"For your apartment?"

She nodded. "Both here and in Chicago, apparently. He found the ones I hid and had copies made."

"We'll relieve him of those."

"You'll be sorry," Nathan warned as Derik walked him out the door. "You're mine, Sophie. Forever."

"And that will help," Jimmy said, even as she paled. "Come on into the station tomorrow to fill out the paperwork, okay?" He cast an eye at Ty and Brawley. "You two gonna be here for a bit?"

"Yes, sir," Ty answered.

"Good." Jimmy tipped his hat at Sophie. "Get something over this broken window."

"I'll take care of that," Brawley said. "Dottie's got all kinds of stuff in her shed, so I'm sure I can find something to nail over the opening."

He left, and the cruiser—with Nathan in it—pulled from the drive.

Ty dragged Sophie to him and buried his face in her hair. The rapid beat of his heart matched her own. "Oh, Sophie, he hurt you."

"I'm okay, Ty. I'm okay. You stopped him."

"If Brawley hadn't decided to come by with that tag—" He broke off.

"Why did *you* come?"

"I had a gut feeling something was wrong. Oh, God, Tink." He kissed the top of her head, her forehead, her unmarked cheek.

"I...I think..." Her tears started then in earnest. "If you hadn't—"

"Shhh, darlin', don't go there." He wrapped her in his arms and held her close while she cried.

The cat crawled out from behind a chair and wound herself between their legs, making little mewing noises as if she, too, understood and sympathized.

Ty picked Sophie up and carried her across the room. After settling her on the old couch, he covered her with an afghan.

When he stood, Sophie grabbed his sleeve. "Don't leave me."

"Hush, sugar. I'll be right back." He disappeared into her bedroom and came back with a T-shirt. Slipping it over her head, he slid off the torn top, and helped her thread her arms into the shirt.

Brawley quietly came through the door with a piece of

plywood. He nailed it in place and swept up the glass. "If you're okay here, I'm going to head home."

When Sophie made to get up, Ty held her in place. "We're good. I owe you. Big-time. Thanks, pal."

Sophie blinked back still more tears. "Brawley, thank you."

"Oh, God, Soph. I'm so sorry neither of us got here before the jerk hurt you." He strode across the room, gave her a hard hug, then left, closing the door gently behind him.

"Sophie, I—" Ty's gray eyes darkened to the color of a winter day just before a major storm. "Pack a bag. I'm taking you home with me tonight."

"Ty, I don't want to take this to your home. To your kids. If anything happened—"

"Nathan's in jail, Tink. None of it goes with you. There's no danger to the boys."

"Then why do I—"

"Because I want you with me. Because *I* need it."

She said nothing, just stared at him openmouthed.

"What? You have nothing to say all of a sudden?"

She shook her head.

Chapter Twenty-Six

I'm sleeping in the guest room." Sophie stood uneasily in the middle of Ty's living room, clutching her overnighter. Lilybelle meowed angrily inside the cat carrier.

The house was silent, the kids and Trouble fast asleep upstairs. Haley had said her good-byes and hightailed it for home the minute she'd spied the less-than-happy expressions on their faces.

Ty jammed both hands in his back pockets and bit back an oath. "You've been through a hell of a scare tonight, Tink. You don't have to pretend everything's fine."

"You're coddling me."

"What? Because I wouldn't let you drive yourself here?" She nodded.

"Look at your hands, Sophie. They're still shaking." She quickly tucked them behind her.

"You're a mess. It wouldn't have been safe. For you or anybody else out there on the road."

She opened her mouth, ready to argue again.

"Don't," he said. "It's done. Brawley drove your car here, although, right now, he's not the steadiest thing I've seen on two legs, either. But he's a damn sight better off than you."

Sophie scowled. "You shouldn't have called him back to do that. And now he's driven home in your truck and his is back at my place. Which means tomorrow you two have to waste time shuffling vehicles."

"No big deal. In the meantime, everybody's got a ride. The van's here if we need it...and you've got your own car. I get that you need some control. As far as I'm concerned, it's a win-win." He paused a heartbeat. "But sleeping in the other room is just plain stupid."

"Is it?"

"Yeah. You've already spent a night in my bed."

"The kids weren't here then."

Exasperated, he swiped a hand over his face. "Look, sweetheart, tonight's been hard on you. Hard on all of us. Hell, when I walked in and saw Nathan with his hands on you..."

He stopped. Closed his eyes. "I can't begin to imagine what you went through. The fear. Walking in. Having him there. I swear they'd better keep him locked up a long, long time 'cause if I ever run into him, I'm not quite sure what I might do."

Sophie took his hand, raised it to her lips, and kissed the back of it, the knuckles scraped where they'd met with Nathan's jaw. "You came. And I can't tell you how much that means to me."

"I didn't know, Tink. When I decided I needed to see you, to meet Brawley at your place instead of Bubba's, I didn't know. I aged ten years in the few minutes it took me to get Nathan away from you. I can never repay Brawley for tonight."

Their eyes met. "Sophie, you're killing me."

He leaned down and their lips touched, setting off a fire so hot she wondered they didn't both burn to a crisp.

"Does your lip hurt?"

"Not anymore."

He kissed her again, gently.

When she pulled away, she patted his cheek. "I'm still sleeping in the guest room. Lilybelle and me."

She opened the carrier, and the huffy cat walked out, all straight-legged and injured pride.

Ty thumped his head against the wall behind him. "You might look delicate, but you're one tough cookie."

"Thank you."

"I didn't mean that as a compliment."

"I know."

"Tink, I'd sleep a whole hell of a lot better with you beside me."

She mustered a weak smile. "Liar. Neither one of us would get any sleep."

His dimples winked. "You're probably right, although I want you to know I can control myself when necessary."

Her eyes held his.

He raised a hand in surrender. "Okay, the guest room it is—if you're sure that's what you really want."

"It's what I need, Ty."

"Fine." He kissed the top of her head and took her bag. "I'll be lying awake in my room if you change your mind."

* * *

When Ty's alarm went off, Sophie hopped from bed and opened her door, Lilybelle following. She'd tossed and turned till dawn peeped around the edge of the blinds in her room, then had dropped into a dreamless sleep. Now, she felt groggy and disoriented.

Jesse and Jonah burst from their bedroom with ear-splitting whoops. Josh followed slowly, dragging a ratty old blanket and looking on the verge of tears.

Spotting Sophie, all three rushed her. When they caught sight of the cat, their onslaught turned into a stampede.

Lilybelle turned and scurried across the hardwood, taking refuge beneath the bed.

"Whoa, boys. You'll knock Sophie down." Ty stepped into the hall, shirtless, his hair on end. He looked rumpled and absolutely gorgeous.

Their eyes met over the kids.

"Good morning," he said, voice husky from sleep.

"Good morning." She felt ridiculously shy, considering she'd shared a bed with him last time she'd spent the night. Somehow, though, this was different.

"Not quite what you're used to?" he asked.

"Not even close. I like to ease into my day."

"Not gonna happen here. We start the day with a vengeance. Zero to ninety in the space of a heartbeat."

Josh patted her leg to get her attention. "Is the kitty coming out?"

"Probably not right now," she answered. Trouble had wandered into the guest room, and Lilybelle was now howling and spitting from her hidey-hole. Sophie shooed the puppy out of the room.

"Can we stay home and play with Sophie today?" Jesse asked.

"Now there's an idea," Ty whispered as they followed the kids downstairs.

"Yeah, can we, Daddy?"

"No, Josh, you can't. Grandma and Grandpa will be here soon to pick you up for Sunday school."

He started to whine.

"Enough, bud. Sophie will be here when you get home."

"Her kitty, too?"

"Her kitty, too."

She shot Ty a warning glance. "Don't make promises you can't deliver."

"I'm not." He kept his voice low-pitched. "You're staying here till I'm sure you're safe."

"I never said I'd stay more than last night. Even that was under protest."

"No, guess you didn't, but it's the only plan that makes any sense. Don't go cutting off your nose to spite your face."

She decided not to answer him. Right now wasn't the time for this discussion. Not with the kids and their little ears.

Bumping and jostling each other, the boys descended on the kitchen and scooted up to the table. They rested heads on folded arms, watching her and their dad dance around each other.

On the surface the day seemed so ordinary. Yet as Sophie poured chocolate and marshmallow cereal into bowls and drowned it in milk, she wondered if anything would ever be the same.

When the food hit the table, the boys wolfed it down so fast, she asked, "You did feed them last night, didn't you?"

"Hell, yes. They'd eat a person out of house and home if you'd let them. And they're only four. I'm gonna have to work a second job to feed them in a few years."

Watching them tip the bowls to slurp up the last of the milk, she said, "I've got a feeling you might be right about that."

"Sophie?" Jonah chewed his last mouthful of cereal.

"Yes, honey?"

"Did you falled down? You got a boo-boo on your face."

"A boo-boo?"

He nodded.

She raised a hand to her bruised cheek, and Ty's eyes grew stormy. "I did fall, yes."

She hadn't given it a thought this morning, or she'd have covered it with makeup before letting the boys see her. She should have combed her hair, too. Threading splayed fingers through the tangled mess, she could only imagine what she looked like. Purple cheek, disheveled hair. A wonder the kids hadn't gone running when they saw her—away rather than toward her.

Ty, coffeepot in one hand, mug in the other, looked angry enough to kick that ass as he'd promised last night.

She met those dark gray eyes and silently begged him not to contradict her. How did you explain someone like Nathan to young innocents? That kind of ugliness could wait till they were older. Till they could understand people like Nathan made up only a small minority of mankind.

"That's why I brought her home with me last night, Jonah. She got hurt, so I thought we could keep her here with us for a few days till we make sure she's okay."

"Thanks, Daddy." Jonah scooted off his chair and wrapped his arms around her legs. "Daddy'll take care of you. When we fall down, he always makes it better."

"I know." Despite her resolve, Sophie's eyes misted. God, she'd miss these boys. "He's a good daddy, isn't he?"

"Uh-huh." Satisfied, Jonah went back to his cereal bowl,

obviously hoping it had been magically refilled in his absence.

"Thank you," she mouthed to Ty.

His only answer was cocked brows.

"Okay, guys. Upstairs. Teeth brushed, hair combed, clothes on. All of you." He herded them out of the kitchen, and they tore off to do his bidding, leaving a stunned Sophie in their wake.

"I have to supervise," he said, trailing behind them. "Shouldn't take long."

Ten minutes later, they all swarmed back into the kitchen where she was loading the dishwasher.

"You didn't have to do that," Ty said.

"If I'm staying here, I'm pulling my weight. I'm not an invalid."

"I didn't imply—"

"What's an inbalid, Daddy?" Josh tugged on Ty's jeans.

"Somebody who's sick," Ty answered.

"Sophie's an inbalid 'cause of her boo-boo, Daddy?"

Drying her hands on a dish towel, she crouched in front of Josh. "My boo-boo doesn't hurt anymore. I'm okay."

The little boy nodded, so solemn Sophie's breath caught in her throat.

Before she could say anything else, the horn tooted outside announcing his parents. Sophie swore a Cat. 5 hurricane had been unleashed inside the house. Last-minute scrambling unearthed Josh's missing sneaker and Jonah's hat.

Jesse tried one last maneuver. "My belly hurts." His bottom lip pouted.

"Uh-uh." Ty shook his head. "You pulled that last week with day care. The minute Haley's bumper disappeared from sight, you were fine. Not gonna work again."

"But, Daddy—"

"No but daddies." He bent to kiss the child, and Jesse threw his arms around his neck.

"Love you, Daddy."

"Love you, too, pal."

The scene repeated twice more before he finally scooted them out the door. Sophie stood in the window and watched as he patiently got them all situated and buckled in. Then he rested his hands on the open passenger-side window and said something to his parents. Ty's mom glanced toward the house, and Sophie knew he was talking to them about last night. Her own stomach churned.

A minute later, Ty backed away from the car. He stood at the end of the drive and waved them off before stomping his feet on the porch and heading inside.

"Do you think Jesse might really be sick?" she asked.

"Nope. And they need routine. We all do." He rubbed his chin. "I asked Mom if she and Dad would take the kids home with them today after the service."

"You told them what happened."

"I did."

She closed her eyes. "I'm so ashamed."

"Hey." Ty pulled her hand away and held it in his own. "You have nothing to be ashamed of."

"Things should never have reached that point."

"Not your fault, Sophie. You did nothing to encourage him."

"Still..."

"Still nothing. You're just going to piss me off again if you try to take the blame for what that jerk did."

"You're right." She blew out her breath. "Will your mom mind keeping the kids?"

"Are you kidding? She and Dad love having them. They go there most Sundays, anyway. This will give you a bit longer to get your feet back under you."

"Thanks."

He leaned toward her for a careful kiss. "And that's thanks enough. As much as I hate to leave you, Tink, I have work to do. Livestock likes to eat—even on Sundays. Will you be okay here alone, or should I call one of the other hands to cover for me?"

She laughed. "I'll be fine, and I have work to do, too. I brought my laptop along. Besides, Lilybelle and Trouble are here to guard me."

The cat had sneaked down the stairs the minute the kids stepped out the door. She and Trouble eyed each other uneasily from the length of the room.

"Go on," Sophie said. "Go be a cowboy. Do whatever it is cowboys do."

He caught her around the waist and pulled her close. "They like kissing their women, for starters. Sure was tough sleeping last night, knowing you were across the hall. The temptation nearly swallowed me whole."

He nipped at her bottom lip, and she opened her mouth to him.

"I won't stay here any other way. Not with three little boys in the house."

"I told you they sleep like—"

"I know." She tugged at the neck of the flannel shirt he'd thrown on, drew him close again, and kissed him as if it had to last her a lifetime. "Now go to work. I'll finish pulling the kitchen together."

"You sure?"

"Positive."

"If you need me, all you have to do is stick your head out the door and holler. I'll be within shouting distance all day."

"Ty—"

"And keep your phone with you. All the time."

"Yes, Daddy."

"You've got a smart mouth, Sophie London. I ought to take you over my knee."

For a split-second, her mind flashed to last night. Nathan's fingers biting cruelly into her arm, his hand over her mouth.

Then she refocused on the man in front of her. This was Ty. A man good to the bone who would never in a million years hurt her. On purpose. But he had the power to break her heart.

"Sophie?" Ty narrowed his eyes. "Where'd you go?"

She shook her head. "Woolgathering. Sorry."

He cleared his throat. "Guess you're entitled, all things considered. But it's important you listen to me about this. I couldn't stand it if anything happened to you."

Contrite, she apologized. "I'll behave. Promise."

Reaching for his coat, he said, "You know, there are no little ones here now. We've got some time to misbehave—in private." The heat of his gaze nearly branded her.

"Ty—"

He pushed his arms into his jacket. "Yeah, yeah, yeah. You need some time. I got that." One last, quick kiss and he headed out the door.

She took a deep breath. When Ty and the kids were here, the place was a beehive of activity. Now, all alone, the rooms with their functional and uncluttered décor actually set her mind free.

She lit the tree and enjoyed the play of lights off the

decorations they'd hung. Then, with Christmas music in the background and sunlight pouring through the windows, she settled in at the kitchen table, both Trouble and Lilybelle at her feet in an uneasy truce, and lost herself in her designs.

It surprised her she was able to focus after last night, but Ty's house exuded an air of serenity. She actually managed to lose herself in her work.

Sometime later, the front door opened, and for one awful second, she panicked. *Nathan.*

"Tink? It's me."

Her heart settled down to a near-manic pace.

"Hate to bother you, but my stomach's thinking somebody slit my throat. Time to grab some lunch. I considered eating with the guys, but, well, I wanted to check on you. Besides, you're a whole lot better looking than Cook."

She took a peek at the still-crooked wall clock. Ten after one. How had that happened?

"I'm in the kitchen," she called, saving her work as she did.

"Fixing food?"

She laughed. "Hardly. I totally lost track of time."

He'd left his boots on the porch and padded into the room in stocking feet. He smelled of the outside, of brisk, cold winds, and, not unpleasantly, of horses.

Leaning down, his mouth moved close to hers. "How 'bout an appetizer?"

When their lips touched, she reached up, put her hand at the back of his head, and pulled him closer. One kiss led to another and another.

"I need you," he whispered.

"Oh, Ty. Yes."

With a growl, he slid his arms behind her knees and picked her up. His lips never leaving hers, he carried her up the stairs and into his room. He laid her down on the bed, stretching out beside her.

Slowly, he undressed her, exploring, tasting, worshipping as he went until she was nearly delirious.

"Your turn," she said, working on his buttons.

When they came together, the world stood still. It was only the two of them. Nothing else. No one else.

"Oh, Sophie, the more I have, the more I want."

Pensive, she ran a fingertip over his shoulder blade. She'd fallen off the wagon. Again. Right now it was awfully hard to be sorry about it.

"Want to go for a double feature?"

Laughing, she shoved at him. "You need to get back to work, and so do I." She sent him a searching look. "Won't your guys be wondering why lunch took so long?"

"Nah. I told them I was famished." He kissed the tip of her nose. "For you."

"You did not."

Those dark gray eyes grew solemn. "No. But I am."

His kiss this time was passionate but without the heated rush. His hands moved over her. "I've never felt like this. Never."

Half an hour later, he rolled out of bed and offered her a hand. "How about I fix us sandwiches for lunch? Maybe a few chips? I might even have a couple of Dottie's cookies stashed away where the boys can't find them."

"Sounds good, but only if you let me help."

"Well, then, let's get going. Day's wasting, woman."

She slanted him a look. "Really? You didn't seem to be in much of a hurry a few minutes ago."

"Priorities tend to slide around. Gotta take care of first things first."

"Really?"

"Really." He laughed and took her hand. They walked downstairs to the kitchen. Together.

Chapter Twenty-Seven

When the kids tore through the door at four, Sophie closed her laptop. There'd be no more work today. She and Ty'd had a slight tussle about the kids before he'd gone back out that afternoon. He'd planned to have Haley watch them after his parents brought them home. That made absolutely no sense when she was right here.

She could handle three little kids. Couldn't she? Her pulse raced.

Ty's mom followed the boys in and helped with the un-bundling, then sent them to the mudroom with their outerwear. Sophie forced herself not to squirm as Mrs. Rawlins turned her attention on her, searched her face, took in the bruising.

"Are you okay, sweetie?"

"I am. Yes. Thanks to your son and Brawley."

"They're good boys, both of them. If you need anything, will you call me?"

"I will. Thank you."

Ty's mom wrapped her in a quick, hard hug, then stepped away, giving her grandsons the eye. "You boys behave yourselves."

"We will, Grandma," came a trio of voices.

And then Mrs. Rawlins was gone, and Sophie found herself alone with three energetic four-year-olds. *What had she gotten herself into?*

While they bounced on the sofa, the boys gave her a running commentary on the entire day's events before deciding it was snack time.

Wandering into the kitchen, she dug out mini-yogurts and poured three glasses of milk, then stood back and watched while they devoured both. Afterward, the four of them put together a haphazard meal. None of the boys seemed to be too picky. They finally settled on sloppy Joes and a bag of tater-tots she found in the freezer.

Sophie insisted on a salad to go with it, though, so the boys sat on high stools and watched her slice and chop. They did the tossing—which meant cleaning up the floor when they finished. Although, truthfully, Trouble took care of most of the spillage.

Lilybelle, who'd run upstairs to cower under the bed again when the boys came home, stayed there despite their attempts to draw her out. The pup somehow managed to be in ten places at once, always underfoot. Every time Sophie made to scold him, he'd look at her with those big sad eyes, and she'd cave.

When she saw him start to squat, though, she said, "Jesse, take Trouble outside. Quick."

"Come here, Trouble."

The dog darted out when Jesse opened the back door, averting another cleanup.

* * *

ingly, with Sophie's help, it did turn into fun. And if
s a bit picky and a tad too careful, well, he chalked it
er artistic bent.

en they finally tied the last bow, he studied the mound
beautifully wrapped packages.

ey look a whole lot better, don't they?"

n't get cocky," he warned.

me on. Admit it."

ay, they look better."

w much better?"

whole lot better." Reaching out, he snagged her
the waist. "I can think of one package I'd like to un-
ight now."

lly?" She grinned. "And which one would that be?"

uried his face in her neck. "The one I've got here in
s. Let's go to bed, darlin'."

kids—"

asleep."

* * *

itchen sink, Sophie stared out the window at the
ndscape. Not her norm, but not bad, either. Just dif-
ery different.

caved and stayed with Ty all night…and slept like
e stretched her arms above her head, arching her
e felt good. Better than good.

both the cat and pup at her heels, Sophie carried her
aptop into the living room, facing the stables.

te her better judgment, she'd let Ty talk her into

Not wanting to be left out on an opportunity for a good
romp, Josh hollered, "Wait for me."

"Me, too," Jonah yelled.

Catching the door before it closed, they followed their
brother and Trouble outside.

Slumped in a chair, surveying the damage they'd done
in such a short time, Sophie wholeheartedly applauded their
decision.

Ty walked in and found her there.

"Tough day at the office?" he drawled.

"You'd better believe it."

He pulled her up, drew her in, and kissed her.

"Mmm." She licked her lips. "I'm feeling much better already."

He nodded toward the backyard. "The hooligans out
there?"

"Every one of them. Two and four-legged. Except Lilybelle. She's still in cowering mode."

Ty was the glue that held everything together. Once he
came on scene, things evened out and some semblance of order returned.

Fed, played with, bathed, and pajamaed, the boys finally
slowed down enough for the Sandman to catch them. By
eight, they were down for the count.

And thank God for that, Sophie thought. These boys of
Ty's were a miracle—but an exhausting one. She smiled.

"What?" Ty knelt down to light the fire.

"I know I sound like a broken record, but I honestly don't
know how you manage all this. The house, the ranch, the boys."

"You kind of grow into it. And Haley helps. Besides riding herd on the boys once in a while, she comes in every
week and digs us out, changes the bed linens, and pops a

couple casseroles in the freezer. Mom and Babs take pity on us, too, and send over dishes occasionally."

He stood. "Want a glass of wine?"

"I thought you'd never ask."

"Sophie—" He threaded his fingers in her hair.

She gave her head an almost imperceptible shake. "Let's not discuss anything serious. Not right now." She shivered.

"Cold?"

"A little."

"Instead of running upstairs for that ugly Cubs sweatshirt, why don't you dig in the closet there by the door? Should be something you can slip into to keep warm."

"You don't really hate my sweatshirt."

"Oh, yeah, I do."

"Sheesh. Some people have no taste whatsoever." Sophie opened the closet and rummaged around for something that would work. Tucked back in the corner, half-hidden under a blanket, she spotted a pile of gifts. "What's all this?"

Ty moved behind her, two glasses of wine in his hands. "Santa's gifts for the kids. Guess I need to move them to a better hiding spot. One of the boys is bound to find them there."

Perplexed, she stared at them. "What did you do to them?"

"What do you mean? I wrapped them."

She laughed. "No. You did *not* wrap these, Ty. You stapled them into bags."

"Same thing. What's the difference?"

"What's the difference? Paper would be nice. Held together with tape, maybe? Some ribbon and bows." She held up a bag with Santa and Rudolph flying through the

night sky. "The boys expect beautiful gif[...]

"Jeez, Sophie. They know Santa and hi[...] their way out of a paper bag."

She raised her brows.

"They're happy with stapled gift bags. [...] Besides, it's a whole heck of a lot easier."

"Really?"

"Look, I can't wrap fancy little package[...]

"I can. Let me rewrap them."

"Tink, they're good. The kids will be [...] way they are. It'll only take them thirty [...] package to tear them to shreds anyway."

"I don't care. When they're under the [...] look nice."

"Oh, for—"

"No, let me do this for them. Please. [...] for some paper." Reaching for her purse[...] Sadler's still open, do you think?"

"Forget it." He handed her one of the [...] a hand, ticking off items. "First, you're n[...] in the dark. Second, there's no good rea[...] to be done. Third, if you insist, I've got [...] paper already. Mom keeps toting it in he[...] Every year when Christmas rolls around[...] door with a semi full of wrapping crap. [...] of it stored in bins."

"Good. Then let's get it out and do t[...] He grimaced.

"It'll be fun, Ty."

"Yeah, I bet. Can I opt for lighted m[...] instead?"

"Hah, hah."

staying here one more day. He'd left for the barn after the two of them had managed to hustle the boys out the door and off to their day care. Afterward, she'd finished up the breakfast dishes, then spent a couple hours fussing around with some of yesterday's designs, tweaking them, and changing font or color.

Now, tired and restless, she yawned and stretched again. Maybe she'd do a little extra Christmas decorating. It would be fun to surprise the kids. Ty's mother had called earlier to chat and had given her a few ideas. With a plan in mind, she headed upstairs.

She loved attics.

A door opened downstairs, and she looked out the small window, surprised to find the sun much lower in the sky.

"Tink, where are you?" Ty's voice floated up from the first floor.

"In the attic."

"In the attic? What are you doing up there?"

She heard him coming up the stairs to the second floor. When he stopped at the landing, she stuck her head out of the attic opening. He looked tired. Probably was. Neither of them had slept much last night.

Who knew bedtime could be so much fun? Warmth flooded her.

"I'm snooping. Your mom said you had lots more ornaments and decorations stored up here. So I thought I'd take a look. See if there was anything you might want to use. Come take a peek at what I found."

"Don't need to. I know what you found. Put them away."

"What?"

"I said put the box away, Sophie."

"But, Ty." She held up a hand-blown-glass ornament. "Isn't this absolutely incredible?"

"We're not using any of those. Come on downstairs, and I'll start dinner."

"You don't have to worry about dinner tonight. I have a casserole ready to stick in the oven." She took time to really study his face, but she couldn't quite make out what she was seeing there. "What's wrong?"

"Those are Julia's ornaments, Sophie. Leave them be."

She felt suddenly light-headed. "I see."

"No, you don't."

Carefully, she replaced the ornament and put the lid back on the box. Only then did she let her eyes meet his.

"Tell me about her, Ty."

"Sophie, this isn't the time."

"It doesn't ever seem to be, does it?"

"You really want to hear about Julia now. How she left me?"

"She didn't leave," Sophie said quietly. "She died. It wasn't her choice."

"Like hell it wasn't." His jaw muscles tightened. "She lied to me. To everyone. Made a decision that left me devastated. That destroyed her parents."

"I don't understand."

"Of course you don't. How could you?"

"So tell me."

Lips white, he shook his head. "Not now."

"You won't let me in, will you? You'll take me to bed, let me move into your home—" She didn't miss the panicked expression that flickered across his face. "Temporarily, Ty. And if you remember, I didn't want to come. But that's all beside the point. The real point is you won't share what's going on here." She tapped a finger on the side of her head. "Or here." She thumped a fist over her heart.

"Let it be, Sophie. I'm tired. It's been a long, hard day."

"You're angry, Ty. I catch flashes of it every now and then. It's eating you up. If you don't confront whatever it is, you won't ever move on."

"I have," he bit out.

She tipped her head, focused on him at the base of the folding attic stairs. "Have you lied to me before this?"

"Excuse me?" His voice had gone glacial.

"Ooh. There's that anger. At least it's real."

"What's that supposed to mean?"

"So much of your life is spent hiding behind an emotional wall." Kneeling, she rested her hands on her thighs. "You're lying—to me and to yourself. None of this is behind you. You won't let it be."

"You don't know what you're talking about."

"Fine." She wiped the dust off her hands onto the legs of her jeans and shoved the box beneath the shelving unit where she'd found it.

Sophie climbed down the narrow attic stairs and walked past him. He put out a hand and grabbed her arm. She shook it off.

"I'll see you downstairs," she said.

In the kitchen, she turned on the oven and slid in the casserole. Ty hadn't come down yet, and she found herself relieved. Back on the second floor, she heard his shower running. Sneaking into the guest room, she closed the door behind her, pulled her overnighter from the closet, and stuffed in the few clothes and toiletries she'd brought with her.

A tear dripped off her chin. Wanting nothing more now

than to get away before Haley dropped the boys off from preschool, before Ty came down, she hurried downstairs.

Time for her to leave. Past time. She'd stayed too long. Left them all vulnerable, herself included. This was exactly what she'd hoped to avoid.

She crept to the tree in the living room and stacked her presents for the boys under a back branch, glad she'd thought to bring them with her. She'd miss seeing their faces when they opened the gifts she'd chosen for them, but it couldn't be helped. She added the rag doll she'd bought for Trouble to chew on, then leaned Ty's gift against the wall.

She'd painted a small watercolor of him and the boys asleep on the couch, all tumbled together and rumpled. Trouble, also on the sofa, had a paw on Josh's arm. She'd matted and framed it.

Maybe they'd look at it and think of her every once in a while. Would Ty notice the tiny fairy she'd perched on Trouble's floppy ear? She sniffed and tried to hold back the tears, but they came in a blinding flood. Thank God her car was here. She put an unhappy Lilybelle in her carrier, picked up her bag and purse, and softly closed the door behind her. Hands shaking, it took several tries before she finally managed to get the key in the ignition.

On the way to her apartment, the cat howling nonstop, she called the airlines. Since tomorrow was Christmas Eve, things were pretty well booked up. However, a redeye, with one empty seat, left tonight for Chicago.

She and Lilybelle would be on it.

* * *

Ty dried off and grabbed clean jeans and a tee from the closet. Reluctantly, he climbed the attic stairs. Hunkered down on the dusty floor, he looked across the room. An old mirror leaned against the wall, and he didn't like what he saw reflected there.

Time for a good heart-to-heart with himself before he went down to Sophie. He'd denied her claims, but too much of what she'd said hit home.

He pulled out the box Sophie had been going through and removed the lid. One at a time, he took out the ornaments—and the memories.

The first was a green, hand-painted glass ball with a red-nosed reindeer sprawled on a rooftop. It had been his gift to Julia when she was thirteen. Every year after that, he'd given her an ornament. And Julia, being Julia, had kept every single one.

He couldn't bring himself to hang them on the tree without her, but he'd carefully packed them away. The boys might like them when they started their own families.

The instant Sophie had said she was snooping, dread filled him. He'd known what she'd unearthed. She'd opened that one box he'd avoided for over four years now. His very own Pandora's box.

She'd unwittingly unleashed its powers, and he'd handled it badly. Very badly. This wouldn't be an easy fix. No simple kiss and make up here. This called for some serious atonement. He'd hurt her, and flowers, even jewelry, wouldn't compensate for what he'd done. What he'd said...and hadn't said.

But, damn, when he'd seen her holding that star, he'd about lost it. These past years had been hell. And it was Julia's fault. Her decision, her deceit, had caused all this hurt and pain.

Yet that hadn't been the real root of his anger this time. He met his eyes in the mirror. It was way past time to come clean. Anger was easier to deal with than the real emotion bubbling inside him.

Fear rode him hard.

Big bad Ty Rawlins was scared to death. His wife and friend was gone. He'd loved Julia. They'd been together since grade school. And then she'd made a decision that ripped them apart forever.

The fear raging through him now didn't come from losing her, though. The worst had already happened there, and he'd somehow survived. This overwhelming fear rose from somewhere else. Some*one* else. Sophie London.

She wasn't Julia. No. Sophie was unique. She was a promise. She was new secrets to learn.

He loved her.

And it was time he told her so.

But when he went downstairs, the house was empty. The oven was on, and the scent of food cooking caused his stomach to rumble.

"Tink? Where are you?"

She didn't answer. After a quick search through the downstairs rooms, he headed to the second floor. Not there, either. When he walked into the guest room, his stomach hit the floor. Empty. Her bag was gone.

But the room smelled like her, that light, flowery scent he loved. He dropped down on the edge of the bed and covered his face with his hands.

He'd pissed her off, and she'd gone back to Dottie's. Well, she was safe, at least. Before he left the barn, he'd checked with Jimmy, and Nathan was still behind bars.

But Ty had been an ass and hurt her, probably nearly as

badly as Nathan had. At least emotionally. Sophie'd put herself out there. Had come home with him, shared his bed, and loved his kids.

And when she'd asked him to share? He'd treated her like a pariah.

Pulling his cell from his shirt pocket, he called Haley. "You about home?"

"Fifteen minutes away."

"I hate to ask, but could you keep an eye on the boys when you get here? Dinner's in the oven."

"Trouble with Sophie?"

He swallowed. "Yeah."

"You know what you have to do."

"Maybe."

"Maybe? Come on, Ty. You're the boss man. You're used to taking the lead and making things happen. What are you waiting for?"

"Haley—"

"You love her."

"That obvious?"

"Oh, yeah. So tell her."

He pinched the bridge of his nose. "You're right. I'm gonna do just that when I find her."

"Find her?"

"Long story. I may be a while."

"That's okay. Take as long as you need."

"You're a doll." He hung up and sprinted down the stairs.

But when he got to Sophie's, she didn't answer the door. He let himself in with the key he'd pocketed the night before last.

He knew the instant he stepped inside that she wasn't there. The place felt empty. Dead. He swore a blue streak as he rushed from room to room.

With a sinking feeling, he realized all her things were gone. She'd packed. She'd left Maverick Junction. Heading outside, he called Cash.

When his friend answered, Ty asked, "Is Sophie there with Annie?"

After a slight hesitation, Cash said, "No. She and Annie are on their way to the airport. I thought you knew."

"Shit."

"I take it you screwed up."

"You don't know the half of it. She's leaving out of Austin?"

"Yep." Cash rattled off Sophie's flight information. "Don't think you'll catch her, but good luck."

Ty tried both Sophie's and Annie's numbers, but both went directly to voice mail. He tossed his phone on the seat, threw the truck into gear, and peeled out of the drive headed for the airport. But with every passing minute, he grew sicker. Cash had been right. He wouldn't make it.

Heading through the terminal doors, he saw Annie coming toward him. Too late.

*　　*　　*

Ty walked Annie to her car, then strolled through the crowded lot to his own truck. He needed a few minutes to get his head together. Sitting in the airport parking lot, he watched the sliver of moon ride higher and higher in the sky.

Haley would stay till he got home, so the boys were covered. Another call to the sheriff's office confirmed that the county taxpayers were still footing Nathan's room and board.

Ty opened his glove box and dug through the mess.

Somewhere mixed with all this crap, he had Dee's phone number. He let out with a small whoop when he struck pay dirt.

Dialing the number, he rubbed his chest. He'd lost Julia. That had totally been out of his control. But this situation with Sophie wasn't. Time for him to make some decisions. She'd been right. He could live in the past or confront it and move on.

At some point, without even realizing it, he'd made up his mind. He was more than ready to step into the future. With Sophie.

If she'd still have him.

She didn't know he loved her. How could she? He'd barely admitted it to himself. If she didn't love *him*, well, he'd just have to change her mind.

Dee answered the phone, sounding more chipper than a person had a right to be at this time of the night.

Quickly Ty explained who he was.

"Yeah, Sophie's mentioned you."

"She has?"

"Uh-huh."

"Listen, Dee, she's on her way home."

"Tonight?"

"Right. And she's not too happy with me."

"Uh-oh," she said.

"Uh-oh is right. Will you keep an eye on her? Make sure she's okay?"

"Is Nathan going to be a problem?"

"No. He's here in Maverick Junction, but right now he's warming a bunk in our jail."

"He didn't hurt her, did he?"

"No, not really." Ty didn't figure it would serve any purpose to go into details. She'd undoubtedly see Nathan's handiwork in the morning.

"Boy, I goofed up, didn't I?" Dee cleared her throat. "I'm sorry Nathan found out where she was. If she'd told me what was going on, I'd never have given him that package with her address on it."

"You had no way of knowing," Ty said. "It's not your fault. Sophie doesn't share well."

The minute the words left his mouth, Ty wished them back. Sharing didn't seem to be high on either of their skill lists. He certainly hadn't been open with her. And that's exactly why he was here and she was on a Chicago-bound plane.

The dashboard clock read twelve thirty-eight. a.m. It was officially December twenty-fourth. Christmas Eve.

He started his truck, and strains of Elvis's "Blue Christmas" came over the radio.

Ty could have wept.

A second chance at love had been dangled in front of him. Yet when he'd decided to reach out and grab it, it had been yanked away.

Damn her. And damn Annie for bringing her into his life.

But most of all? Damn himself for being too dim-witted to see what was right in front of him. For being too obstinate to let go of what he'd had, to snatch up what he could have.

And wasn't that a kick in the pants?

Chapter Twenty-Eight

Shouts and running feet woke Ty from a long-in-the-coming sleep.

Christmas Eve had been a bust without Sophie, but he'd struggled through it. Even after the boys finally crashed, sleep eluded him. It had been a little after two the last time he'd checked his bedside alarm. His sheets were tangled from hours of restless tossing and turning.

Opening one eye, he groaned when he registered the pale pink, pre-dawn sky. More than anything, he wanted to throw a pillow over his head and go back to the dream he'd been having. But that wouldn't work.

Santa and his reindeer had landed on their roof last night, and the jolly old guy had, undoubtedly, let himself in by way of the fireplace chimney to deposit gifts under the tree.

The triplets rushed the bed and clambered up.

"Get up, Daddy. Hurry!"

"Yeah, come on."

"We didn't peek," Jonah said. "We came to get you first."

"Like you said," Jesse added.

Ty tossed the covers aside and stretched. Then, surprising the boys, he rolled and caught all three in his arms, pinning them to the bed and tickling each in turn.

As they hooted and hollered, he said, "Merry Christmas, guys!"

"Merry Christmas, Daddy," they echoed.

Trouble scrambled into the room and leaped onto the bed. When his rough pink tongue slurped the side of Ty's face, he pushed him away, wiping the back of his hand over his cheek. "Ugh. Off me, you mangy mutt."

"That's not a mangy mutt," Jesse said. "That's Trouble."

Ty made a show of squinting at the pup, now licking Josh. "You're right. It is." He sat, bringing the boys upright with him. "You munchkins ready to see what Santa brought?"

"Yeah." They tumbled off the bed and raced for the door, Josh bouncing off the jamb when the three of them didn't all fit at the same time.

Ty waited for the tears, but they didn't come. *Well, what do you know?*

He'd plugged the tree in before he'd headed upstairs to bed last night—rather this morning—right after he'd forced himself to eat the cookies and drink the milk the boys insisted on leaving for Santa. He grinned. Tough job, but somebody had to do it. He sure was glad they'd decided on Oreos.

Ty didn't consider himself a romantic, but the tree, the room, the pile of cheerfully wrapped presents, all looked magical in the early-morning light.

The boys stopped in their tracks at the base of the stairs. The expressions on their faces said it all. Oh, to be a four-year-old on Christmas morning again.

His thoughts turned to Sophie. She'd insisted the gifts themselves needed to be beautiful, and she'd been right. It did matter. And it mattered that his boys meant enough to her to take the time to help make this morning special. More than anything, he wanted her here beside him to share this moment.

In a flash, awe gave way to the need for gratification. The boys made a mad dash for the tree and tore into the treasure trove like a wrecking ball on an old house. The three made short work of the wrappings, their shouts and screams of joy escalating with each scrap that hit the floor.

Buried at the back of the tree, they discovered the gifts Sophie'd placed there before she'd left.

"She got something for all of us, Daddy."

"Yes, she did." A knot formed in his stomach.

They unwrapped her presents and hung the Santa Claus fish ornaments she'd given them on the tree. Jesse added the one that looked like Trouble, then Ty hung the Wurlitzer jukebox decorated with Christmas greenery she'd chosen for him, remembering how good she'd felt in his arms dancing to the one at Bubba's.

Josh turned to him, the small art kit from Sophie in hand. "Why didn't she stay, Daddy? Is she mad at us?"

The lump in Ty's throat made it damn hard to speak. He swallowed, trying to come up with an answer. "No, honey, she's not mad at you." *She's mad at me.* "She had work to do. It was time for her to go home."

"Is she gonna come back?" Jesse asked.

"I don't think so."

"She could live with us," Jonah, ever the compromiser, suggested.

"Yeah," Josh agreed. "We can take our toys out of the extra bedroom. We don't need a playroom, do we?" He looked at his brothers.

They shook their heads.

"Call her, Daddy," Jesse insisted, toying with the hem of his pajama top.

God, these kids were breaking his heart. "Honey, I can't do that."

"Why?" Josh's bottom trembled.

"Because," Ty said, lifting the boy off his feet, "it's Christmas. We've got places to go. Grandma and Grandpa Rawlins expect us for lunch. Then we have to head over to Gram and Papa Taylor's house."

"Will they have presents for us?" Jesse's eyes glinted.

"I bet they will."

"Daddy?" Jonah tugged at Ty's pant leg. "Aren't you going to open your present?" He pointed at the sole wrapped gift, which leaned against the wall.

Ty hesitated.

"You have to open it, Daddy," Jesse said. "We want to see. It's from Sophie."

"You think so?"

Josh sighed. "Yes, 'cause she wrapped hers in special paper." His tone implied he really shouldn't have to be telling his father this as he held a shred of his up to the present. "They match. So it has to be from Sophie."

"By gosh, you're right." He grinned. Somewhere she'd managed to find Christmas paper with a tiny Tinker Bell flying around a decorated tree.

How could she have left without saying good-bye? Without giving him a chance to beg her forgiveness.

Josh tugged on the other leg of his jeans. "Come on, Daddy. Hurry up. What's in it?"

"I don't know. Let's see." He ran a finger beneath the fold on the paper and peeled it back. His heart staggered.

She'd caught him and the boys fast asleep on the sofa. In an unguarded moment, all of them relaxed. Even Trouble was catching a few z's.

His family.

And then he spotted the tiny fairy curled up asleep on Trouble's ear. His heart did a fast handstand before slipping back into place. He wasn't sure his life ever would.

* * *

When he and the boys hit his parents' home, the place turned into a madhouse of noise and activity. The boys practically crawled under the tree, shaking gifts and trying to guess what was in them. Football blared over the living room TV, the volume way too loud in order to accommodate his father's hearing.

His dad raised the beer he held. "Merry Christmas, Ty." He turned to the boys. "Santa make it to you hoodlums?"

"Uh-huh," Jesse answered.

The other two joined in to tell him what Santa had brought, then Jesse and Josh turned their attention back to the new packages.

Jonah crawled out from under the huge blue spruce and headed to the train set up on a table in the corner. Ty grinned. Boy after his own heart. He and his dad had put that together every Christmas. This year had been no exception. Amazing the thing still ran. But things used to be made to last.

Ty placed the bags of gifts they'd brought under the tree. "Why don't you boys unload those?"

"Okay, Daddy."

His mother stuck her head around the kitchen doorway. "There you are. Merry Christmas, honey."

Ty wrapped her in a hug and kissed her cheek. "I smelled your prime rib halfway down the drive. I'm starving."

"It's almost ready to come out." She turned to her husband. "Wyatt, don't just sit there. Get the boy a drink."

"He's got two feet," Wyatt groused.

"I can get it, Mom." Ty homed in on the fridge.

"I'll take another while you're there," his dad called.

"Men," his mother grumbled under her breath.

"Ouch," Ty said. "I fall in that category, too."

"That's right. You do."

Puzzled, he turned to a plate on the counter, grabbed a handful of olives, and popped them into his mouth.

"What'd I do?"

"You have to ask?"

"Obviously." He flipped the tops off a couple longnecks.

"You were supposed to bring Sophie with you."

"How can I do that? She's in Chicago."

"Exactly." At the sink, his mother didn't even turn around. "You screwed up, son of mine."

"I—" Ty closed his mouth. What could he say? He *had* screwed up.

"Nothing to say for yourself?"

"Not at this moment." Beers in hand, he moved into the living room, far safer territory.

Fifteen minutes later, drying her hands on a tea towel, his mother walked into that neutral zone. "Wyatt, why don't you turn that off—or at least down enough that the rest of us can hear ourselves think?"

Reluctantly, he picked up the remote and muted the sound.

Hands on her still-trim hips, Sadie said, "So, what do you say, kids? Want to open those packages before we eat?"

Enthusiastic hoots and hollers answered her.

"You're a smart woman, Mom. This way, the kids might actually sit down and eat when it's time."

"Grandmas are wise women." She smiled. "Boys, why don't you play Santa and distribute the gifts?"

"Okay, Grandma."

Ty sat in a rocker by the tree and read the tags for the kids.

The noise level rose considerably as kids and adults alike tore wrappings and exclaimed over gifts. Ty leaned back in his chair and watched the boys, wearing their new Dallas Cowboy helmets, race cars over the floor, the furniture, and each other.

It was a good day. He had a tremendous family, and he should be happy. One key element was missing, though. And he didn't know what to do about it.

Didn't know there was anything he *could* do.

His mom put an end to his reverie. "Come lift the casseroles out of the oven, Ty."

Within ten minutes, hands were washed and everyone seated at the table. Heads bowed as his dad said grace. Food was passed, plates filled, and Christmas dinner got under way.

His mom had set up a card table for the boys. It kept them close and a part of things but gave the adults a chance to talk.

"You look like you could use some of this." His dad held out a bottle of wine.

"Could I ever. It's been a long day already."

Wyatt leaned over and put a hand on Ty's shoulder. "Son,

I know I've said this before, but it bears repeating. You're doing one hell of a job with these boys. Your mother and I are proud of you."

"Thanks, Dad." He helped himself to a tamale, a slice of prime rib, and some sweet potato casserole. After a couple bites, though, he pushed the food around his plate.

His mother added several spoons of cornbread dressing to his mix. "You're not eating. You need to go see her."

"What?"

"Sophie made you happy again. She made you whole. You can't let her walk away without pleading your case."

"Mom, we're not what she wants."

"Are you sure of that?"

He raised his eyes to hers. "I'm not sure of anything anymore."

"There's only way to find out, son," his dad added. "Talk to the girl."

"Yeah, Daddy. Talk to the girl," Jonah piped up. Then he turned in his chair to face his grandfather. "Who's the girl, Grandpa?"

The adults' eyes met, and they started to laugh. Jonah joined in.

"Sophie, honey," his mom told Jonah. "Your daddy's going to take a trip."

"Where?"

"To Chicago. He's going to go talk to Sophie."

"Yay." All three boys, milk ringing their mouths, clapped their hands.

"Can we go, too?" Jesse asked.

"No, you're coming to stay with Grandpa and me for a few days," Ty's mom said.

The boys bounced another round of cheers off the walls.

"Hey," Ty said. "Don't you think I should have some say in this? That maybe you should consult me first?"

His mother stared at a spot on the far wall as though giving his question some thought, then simply said, "No."

"Mom, I'm not doing this." He kept his voice low.

"Yes, you are. I'm not having you mope around here like some lovesick calf."

"I'm not. Besides, what if she says no? What if she really, truly doesn't want us? This." He waved a hand to indicate the room, his family.

"Then she's not who I think she is . . . and you're better off without her." His mother pushed back her chair. "Who wants some Texas pecan pie?"

*   *   *

Ty thought the day would never end. After they totally stuffed themselves, they hung around his folks' for a while. Josh fell asleep, but Jonah and Jesse didn't stop for a minute.

After Josh woke, they loaded their haul in the car along with more leftovers than they could possibly eat and made their pilgrimage to Julia's folks. Matt and Babs and their kids were already there. More gifts, more food, more holiday cheer.

He wanted to gag the next person who wished him a Merry Christmas, but the kids had an incredible day. On the way home, they chatted nonstop about all their new toys.

"Can we play with our helicopters when we get home, Daddy?" Josh asked.

Ty rubbed his tired eyes. "It's pretty close to bedtime, bud." Stars were springing to life in the sky, and a crescent moon shed its paltry light.

"Ten minutes, Daddy?"

"We'll see."

"That means no." Jesse pouted.

"No," Ty said, his patience wearing thin. "It means we'll see."

By the time he pulled up in front of the house, though, the kids, worn out from a huge day, were sound asleep. One by one, he carried them in and put them to bed.

Thank God! Sprawled on the sofa, Ty stared across the living room at the watercolor he'd set on the fireplace mantel. Even in the dim light of the Christmas tree, he could make out the images Sophie'd captured on canvas. She'd nailed him and the kids and had even caught Trouble in a rare moment of stillness.

But it was that damn blond-haired, sleeping fairy clinging to Trouble's ear with the I've-got-a-secret smile that drew his eye. She'd stolen his heart, then stowed it away on a plane headed for Chicago.

Lord, he missed her.

Closing his eyes, he tried to imagine what it would be like to never see her again, never kiss her again. A pretty dismal picture.

It had taken Annie leaving for Cash to realize how much he loved her. Ty wondered if he could be as dense as that lunkhead. He'd never thought so, but the proof to the contrary was right in front on him, wasn't it?

As much as he hated to admit it, his mother was right. Time to step up to the plate. Without giving himself any more time to think, he picked up the phone and called her. He'd take his mom and dad up on their offer.

* * *

Christmas night. A few stars winked in the sky, and the slice of moon played hide-and-seek with some rather sinister looking snow clouds. Curled up in the window seat, Sophie leaned back against her collection of silk cushions, resting her head against her hand. Lilybelle snuggled into the curve of her legs. The scrawny Charlie Brown Christmas tree Sophie had decorated reflected in the window, and Christmas music filled the silence.

Her door was locked up tight, a new dead bolt installed. Nathan had scared her. If he was, for whatever reason, released, the boys and Ty were far safer with her gone.

Ty'd refused to share and that had hurt, but, then, so had she. And her secret had put them all in danger. Far better for everyone with her here in Chicago. But the decision to leave had been the hardest of her life.

Choosing the brightest star, she wished with all her heart for Ty Rawlins's happiness. Wished things had worked out differently between them.

But they hadn't.

A cup of cocoa in her other hand, she stared down at the cold, deserted street. Everybody was home with family or sharing the holiday with friends. Yet here she was. Alone.

Her choice, she reminded herself. Dee had gone to her small hometown of Kane, Pennsylvania, to share the holiday with her parents. She'd invited Sophie to join her, but she'd bowed out. Her mom and dad had tried to talk her into flying to Boston to be with them. Again, she'd cried off, saying she was so behind in her work she couldn't afford the time away.

An out-and-out lie.

She'd never worked so well in her life as she had in Maverick Junction. There at Dottie's, her creative juices had flowed, and she'd tapped into them, finishing her spring line and getting a heck of a jump on summer.

But she *had* needed to stay home. Had needed this time alone to put her life in perspective. She'd failed miserably so far. The only thing she'd determined for sure? She'd fallen head over cowboy boots for Ty Rawlins.

All day long, she'd prayed he'd call, that he might miss her as much as she did him. She'd stuck to her phone like glue.

But he hadn't phoned.

He didn't care.

Even a pint of Ben & Jerry's couldn't cure this.

Chapter Twenty-Nine

The plane circled O'Hare. A storm had dumped nearly a foot of snow on Chicago in the early-morning hours, stacking up traffic. Because of the lake-effect snow and winds, Ty had been delayed nearly two hours leaving Austin. He closed the book he'd been pretending to read and stared at the door of the storage bin across from him.

Was he doing the right thing, or would this trip move to the top of his blunder list? He'd toyed with the idea of waiting till the first. A new year. A new beginning. Added to that, the extra couple days would give Sophie a little more time to miss him.

At least, in his perfect-world scenario she would. But, then, it had been a long time since he'd believed in a perfect world. He missed Tink more than he'd imagined possible, and a perverse side of him hoped she was feeling every bit as wretched as he was.

When it came right down to the nitty-gritty, he hadn't

been able to wait for New Year's Day. Once he'd made up his mind, three days was the best he could do. Scrambling to put together his plan, he'd leaned on a college friend for a favor. As the tires made contact with the tarmac, he sent another prayer Heavenward that Parker would come through.

That his plan would work.

Once they'd touched down and disembarked, people scrambled down the corridors, everyone in a hurry. Thank God he hadn't checked a bag. The noise and the crowds made him long for the solitude of his ranch. He didn't belong here.

Sophie did, though, and there was the rub. One of them, anyway. Could he convince her to give this up? He sure as hell hoped so.

Could he convince her to accept him and the boys? To take on the bunch of them? There was an even bigger challenge, one that had his nerves taut as strung fence wire.

Stepping outside to catch a taxi, the wind whipped at him and almost tore the door out of his hand. An ineffectual sun had made an appearance, but the cold chewed right through his clothes. He shivered and stomped his feet, zipped his jacket a little higher. That anybody would choose to live in the frigid North never failed to amaze him.

The fresh snow that blanketed the streets and sidewalks had already begun to morph into gray sludge from exhaust fumes and other pollutants. Christmas decorations clung to lampposts. Now, though, instead of reminding travelers that something joyful waited, they served as a reminder the holiday was behind them and it was back to the daily grind.

And weren't those happy thoughts?